Praise for #1 *New York Times* bestselling author

NORA ROBERTS

"You can't bottle wish fulfillment, but Nora Roberts certainly knows how to put it on the page."
—*New York Times*

"Roberts' bestselling novels are some of the best in the romance genre."
—*USA TODAY*

"When Roberts puts her expert fingers on the pulse of romance, legions of fans feel the heartbeat."
—*Publishers Weekly*

"You can always count on Nora Roberts to deliver outstanding, character-driven novels that are destined to be bestsellers."
—*RT Book Reviews*

"Roberts is indeed a word artist."
—*Los Angeles Daily News*

"America's favorite writer."
—*The New Yorker*

NORA ROBERTS

First Snow

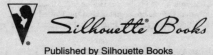
Silhouette Books

Published by Silhouette Books

America's Publisher of Contemporary Romance

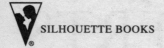 **SILHOUETTE BOOKS**

Recycling programs
for this product may
not exist in your area.

First Snow

ISBN-13: 978-1-335-01495-5

Copyright © 2018 by Harlequin Books S.A.

The publisher acknowledges the copyright holder
of the individual works as follows:

A Will and A Way
Copyright © 1986 by Nora Roberts

Local Hero
Copyright © 1987 by Nora Roberts

CONTENTS

A WILL AND A WAY

For my family members, who, fortunately, aren't as odd as the relatives in this book.

Chapter 1

One hundred fifty million dollars was nothing to sneeze at. No one in the vast, echoing library of Jolley's Folley would have dared. Except Pandora. She did so with more enthusiasm than delicacy into a tattered tissue. After blowing her nose, she sat back, wishing the antihistamine she had taken would live up to its promise of fast relief. She wished she'd never caught the wretched cold in the first place. More, she wished she were anywhere else in the world.

Surrounding her were dozens of books she'd read and hundreds more she'd never given a thought to, though she'd spent hours and hours in the library. The scent of the leather-bound volumes mixed with the lighter, homier scent of dust. Pandora preferred either to the strangling fragrance of lilies that filled three stocky vases.

In one corner of the room was a marble-and-ivory

chess set, where she'd lost a great many highly disputed matches. Uncle Jolley, bless his round, innocent face and pudgy fingers, had been a compulsive and skilled cheat. Pandora had never taken a loss in stride. Maybe that's why he'd so loved to beat her, by fair means or foul.

Through the three arching windows the light shone dull and a little gloomy. It suited her mood and, she thought, the proceedings. Uncle Jolley had loved to set scenes.

When she loved—and she felt this emotion for a select few who'd touched her life—she put everything she had into it. She'd been born with boundless energy. She'd developed iron-jawed stubbornness. She'd loved Uncle Jolley in her uninhibited, expansive fashion, acknowledging then accepting all of his oddities. He might have been ninety-three, but he'd never been dull or fussy.

A month before his death, they'd gone fishing—poaching actually—in the lake that was owned and stocked by his neighbor. When they'd caught more than they could eat, they'd sent a half-dozen trout back to the owner, cleaned and chilled.

She was going to miss Uncle Jolley with his round cherub's face, high, melodious voice and wicked humors. From his ten-foot, extravagantly framed portrait, he looked down at her with the same little smirk he'd worn whether he'd been making a million-dollar merger or handing an unsuspecting vice-president a drink in a dribble glass. She missed him already. No one else in her far-flung, contrasting family understood and accepted her with the same ease. It had been one more reason she'd adored him.

Miserable with grief, aggravated by a head cold, Pandora listened to Edmund Fitzhugh drone on, and on, with the preliminary technicalities of Uncle Jolley's will. Maximillian Jolley McVie had never been one for brevity. He'd always said if you were going to do something, do it until the steam ran out. His last will and testament bore his style.

Not bothering to hide her disinterest in the proceedings, Pandora took a comprehensive survey of the other occupants of the library.

To have called them mourners would have been just the sort of bad joke Jolley would have appreciated.

There was Jolley's only surviving son, Uncle Carlson, and his wife. What was her name? Lona—Mona? Did it matter? Pandora saw them sitting stiff backed and alert in matching shades of black. They made her think of crows on a telephone wire just waiting for something to fall at their feet.

Cousin Ginger—sweet and pretty and harmless, if rather vacuous. Her hair was Jean Harlow blond this month. Good old Cousin Biff was there in his black Brooks Brothers suit. He sat back, one leg crossed over the other as if he were watching a polo match. Pandora was certain he wasn't missing a word. His wife—was it Laurie?—had a prim, respectful look on her face. From experience, Pandora knew she wouldn't utter a word unless it were to echo Biff. Uncle Jolley had called her a silly, boring fool. Hating to be cynical, Pandora had to agree.

There was Uncle Monroe looking plump and successful and smoking a big cigar despite the fact that his sister, Patience, waved a little white handkerchief in front of her nose. Probably because of it, Pandora corrected. Uncle Monroe liked nothing better than to make his ineffectual sister uncomfortable.

Cousin Hank looked macho and muscular, but hardly more than his tough athletic wife, Meg. They'd hiked the Appalachian Trail on their honeymoon. Uncle Jolley had wondered if they stretched and limbered up before lovemaking.

The thought caused Pandora to giggle. She stifled it halfheartedly with the tissue just before her gaze wandered over to cousin Michael. Or was it second cousin Michael? She'd never been able to get the technical business straight. It seemed a bit foolish when you weren't talking blood relation anyway. His mother had been Uncle Jolley's niece by Jolley's son's second marriage. It was a complicated state of affairs, Pandora thought. But then Michael Donahue was a complicated man.

They'd never gotten along, though she knew Uncle Jolley had favored him. As far as Pandora was concerned, anyone who made his living writing a silly television series that kept people glued to a box rather than doing something worthwhile was a materialistic parasite. She had a momentary flash of pleasure as she remembered telling him just that.

Then, of course, there were the women. When a man dated centerfolds and showgirls it was obvious he wasn't interested in intellectual stimulation. Pandora smiled as she recalled stating her view quite clearly the last time Michael had visited Jolley's Folley. Uncle Jolley had nearly fallen off his chair laughing.

Then her smile faded. Uncle Jolley was gone. And if she was honest, which she was often, she'd admit that of all the people in the room at that moment, Michael

Donahue had cared for and enjoyed the old man more than anyone but herself.

You'd hardly know that to look at him now, she mused. He looked disinterested and slightly arrogant. She noticed the set, grim line around his lips. Pandora had always considered Donahue's mouth his best feature, though he rarely smiled at her unless it was to bare his teeth and snarl.

Uncle Jolley had liked his looks, and had told Pandora so in his early stages of matchmaking. A hobby she'd made sure he'd given up quickly. Well, he hadn't given it up precisely, but she'd ignored it all the same.

Being rather short and round himself, perhaps Jolley had appreciated Donahue's long lean frame, and the narrow intense face. Pandora might have liked it herself, except that Michael's eyes were often distant and detached.

At the moment he looked like one of the heroes in the action series he wrote—leaning negligently against the wall and looking just a bit out of place in the tidy suit and tie. His dark hair was casual and not altogether neat, as though he hadn't thought to comb it into place after riding with the top down. He looked bored and ready for action. Any action.

It was too bad, Pandora thought, that they didn't get along better. She'd have liked to have reminisced with someone about Uncle Jolley, someone who appreciated his whimsies as she had.

There was no use thinking along those lines. If they'd elected to sit together, they'd have been picking little pieces out of each other by now. Uncle Jolley, smirking down from his portrait, knew it very well.

With a half sigh she blew her nose again and tried

to listen to Fitzhugh. There was something about a bequest to whales. Or maybe it was whalers.

Another hour of this, Michael thought, and he'd be ready to chew raw meat. If he heard one more *whereas*… On a long breath, Michael drew himself in. He was here for the duration because he'd loved the crazy old man. If the last thing he could do for Jolley was to stand in a room with a group of human vultures and listen to long rambling legalese, then he'd do it. Once it was over, he'd pour himself a long shot of brandy and toast the old man in private. Jolley had had a fondness for brandy.

When Michael had been young and full of imagination and his parents hadn't understood, Uncle Jolley had listened to him ramble, encouraged him to dream. Invariably on a visit to the Folley, his uncle had demanded a story then had settled himself back, bright-eyed and eager, while Michael wove on. Michael hadn't forgotten.

When he'd received his first Emmy for *Logan's Run*, Michael had flown from L.A. to the Catskills and had given the statuette to his uncle. The Emmy was still in the old man's bedroom, even if the old man wasn't.

Michael listened to the dry impersonal attorney's voice and wished for a cigarette. He'd only given them up two days before. Two days, four hours and thirty-five minutes. He'd have welcomed the raw meat.

He felt stifled in the room with all these people. Every one of them had thought old Jolley was half-mad and a bit of a nuisance. The one-hundred-fifty-million-dollar estate was different. Stocks and bonds were extremely sane. Michael had seen several assessing glances roaming over the library furniture. Big, ornate Georgian might not suit some of the streamlined life-styles, but it would liquidate into very tidy cash. The old man, Michael knew, had loved every clunky chair and oversize table in the house.

He doubted if any of them had been to the big echoing house in the past ten years. Except for Pandora, he admitted grudgingly. She might be an annoyance, but she'd adored Jolley.

At the moment she looked miserable. Michael didn't believe he'd ever seen her look unhappy before— furious, disdainful, infuriated, but never unhappy. If he hadn't known better, he'd have gone to sit beside her, offer some comfort, hold her hand. She'd probably chomp it off at the wrist.

Still, her shockingly blue eyes were red and puffy. Almost as red as her hair, he mused, as his gaze skimmed over the wild curly mane that tumbled, with little attention to discipline or style, around her shoulders. She was so pale that the sprinkling of freckles over her nose stood out. Normally her ivory-toned skin had a hint of rose in it—health or temperament, he'd never been sure.

Sitting among her solemn, black-clad family, she stood out like a parrot among crows. She'd worn a vivid blue dress. Michael approved of it, though he'd never say so to Pandora. She didn't need black and crepe and lilies to mourn. That he understood, if he didn't understand her.

She annoyed him, periodically, with her views on his life-style and career. When they clashed, it didn't take long for him to hurl criticism back at her. After all, she was a bright, talented woman who was content to play around making outrageous jewelry for boutiques rather than taking advantage of her Master's degree in education.

She called him materialistic, he called her idealistic. She labeled him a chauvinist, he labeled her a pseudo-intellectual. Jolley had sat with his hands folded and chuckled every time they argued. Now that he was gone, Michael mused, there wouldn't be an opportunity for any more battles. Oddly enough, he found it another reason to miss his uncle.

The truth was, he'd never felt any strong family ties to anyone but Jolley. Michael didn't think of his parents very often. His father was somewhere in Europe with his fourth wife, and his mother had settled placidly into Palm Springs society with husband number three. They'd never understood their son who'd opted to work for a living in something as bourgeois as television.

But Jolley had understood and appreciated. More, much more important to Michael, he'd enjoyed Michael's work.

A grin spread over his face when he heard Fitzhugh drone out the bequest for whales. It was so typically Jolley. Several impatient relations hissed through their teeth. A hundred fifty thousand dollars had just spun out of their reach. Michael glanced up at the larger-than-life-size portrait of his uncle. You always said you'd have the last word, you old fool. The only trouble is you're not here to laugh about it.

"To my son, Carlson…" All the quiet muttering and whispers died as Fitzhugh cleared his throat. Without much interest Pandora watched her relatives come to attention. The charities and servants had their bequests. Now it was time for the big guns. Fitzhugh glanced up briefly before he continued. "Whose—aaah—

mediocrity was always a mystery to me, I leave my entire collection of magic tricks in hopes he can develop a sense of the ridiculous."

Pandora choked into her tissue and watched her uncle turn beet red. First point Uncle Jolley, she thought and prepared to enjoy herself. Maybe he'd left the whole business to the A.S.P.C.A.

"To my grandson, Bradley, and my granddaughter by marriage, Lorraine, I leave my very best wishes. They need nothing more."

Pandora swallowed and blinked back tears at the reference to her parents. She'd call them in Zanzibar that evening. They would appreciate the sentiment even as she did.

"To my nephew Monroe who has the first dollar he ever made, I leave the last dollar I made, frame included. To my niece, Patience, I leave my cottage in Key West without much hope she'll have the gumption to use it."

Monroe chomped on his cigar while Patience looked horrified.

"To my grand-nephew, Biff, I leave my collection of matches, with the hopes that he will, at last, set the world on fire. To my pretty grand-niece, Ginger, who likes equally pretty things, I leave the sterling silver mirror purported to have been owned by Marie Antoinette. To my grand-nephew, Hank, I leave the sum of 3528. Enough, I believe, for a lifetime supply of wheat germ."

The grumbles that had begun with the first bequest continued and grew. Anger hovered on the edge of outrage. Jolley would have liked nothing better. Pandora made the mistake of glancing over at Michael. He didn't seem so distant and detached now, but full of admiration. When their gazes met, the giggle she'd been holding back spilled out. It earned her several glares.

Carlson rose, giving new meaning to the phrase controlled outrage. "Mr. Fitzhugh, my father's will is nothing more than a mockery. It's quite obvious that he wasn't in his right mind when he made it, nor do I have any doubt that a court will overturn it."

"Mr. McVie." Again Fitzhugh cleared his throat. The sun began to push its way through the clouds but no one seemed to notice. "I understand perfectly your sentiments in this matter. However, my client was perfectly well and lucid when this will was drawn. He may have worded it against my advice, but it is legal and binding. You are, of course, free to consult with your own counsel. Meanwhile, there's more to be read."

"Hogwash." Monroe puffed on his cigar and glared at everyone. "Hogwash," he repeated while Patience patted his arm and chirped ineffectually.

"Uncle Jolley liked hogwash," Pandora said as she balled her tissue. She was ready to face them down, almost hoped she'd have to. It would take her mind off her grief. "If he wanted to leave his money to the Society for the Prevention of Stupidity, it was his right."

"Easily said, my dear." Biff polished his nails on his lapel. The gold band of his watch caught a bit of the sun and gleamed. "Perhaps the old lunatic left you a ball of twine so you can string more beads."

"You haven't got the matches yet, old boy." Michael spoke lazily from his corner, but every eye turned his way. "Careful what you light."

"Let him read, why don't you?" Ginger piped up,

quite pleased with her bequest. Marie Antoinette, she mused. Just imagine.

"The last two bequests are joint," Fitzhugh began before there could be another interruption. "And, a bit unorthodox."

"The entire document's unorthodox," Carlson tossed out, then harrumphed. Several heads nodded in agreement.

Pandora remembered why she always avoided family gatherings. They bored her to death. Quite deliberately, she waved a hand in front of her mouth and yawned. "Could we have the rest, Mr. Fitzhugh, before my family embarrasses themselves any further?"

She thought, but couldn't be sure, that she saw a quick light of approval in the fusty attorney's eyes. "Mr. McVie wrote this portion in his own words." He paused a moment, either for effect or courage. "To Pandora McVie and Michael Donahue," Fitzhugh read. "The two members of my family who have given me the most pleasure with their outlook on life, their enjoyment of an old man and old jokes, I leave the rest of my estate, in entirety, all accounts, all business interests, all stocks, bonds and trusts, all real and personal property, with all affection. Share and share alike."

Pandora didn't hear the half-dozen objections that sprang out. She rose, stunned and infuriated. "I can't take his money." Towering over the family who sat around her, she strode straight up to Fitzhugh. The lawyer, who'd anticipated attacks from other areas, braced for the unexpected. "I wouldn't know what to do with it. It'd just clutter up my life." She waved a hand at the papers on the desk as if they were a minor annoyance. "He should've asked me first."

"Miss McVie…"

Before the lawyer could speak again, she whirled on Michael. "You can have it all. You'd know what to do with it, after all. Buy a hotel in New York, a condo in L.A., a club in Chicago and a plane to fly you back and forth, I don't care."

Deadly calm, Michael slipped his hands in his pockets. "I appreciate the offer, cousin. Before you pull the trigger, why don't we wait until Mr. Fitzhugh finishes before you embarrass yourself any further?"

She stared at him a moment, nearly nose to nose with him in heels. Then, because she'd been taught to do so at an early age, she took a deep breath and waited for her temper to ebb. "I don't want his money."

"You've made your point." He lifted a brow in the cynical, half-amused way that always infuriated her. "You're fascinating the relatives by the little show you're putting on."

Nothing could have made her find control quicker. She angled her chin at him, hissed once, then subsided. "All right then." She turned and stood her ground. "I apologize for the interruption. Please finish reading, Mr. Fitzhugh."

The lawyer gave himself a moment by taking off his glasses and polishing them on a big white handkerchief. He'd known when Jolley had made the will the day would come when he'd be forced to face an enraged family. He'd argued with his client about it, cajoled, reasoned, pointed out the absurdities. Then he'd drawn up the will and closed the loopholes.

"I leave all of this," he continued, "the money, which is a small thing, the stocks and bonds, which are necessary but boring, the business interests, which are interesting weights around the neck. And my home and all in it, which is everything important to me, the memories made there, to Pandora and Michael because they understood and cared. I leave this to them, though it may annoy them, because there is no one else in my family I can leave what is important to me. What was mine is Pandora and Michael's now, because I know they'll keep me alive. I ask only one thing of each of them in return."

Michael's grip relaxed, and he nearly smiled again. "Here comes the kicker," he murmured.

"Beginning no more than a week after the reading of this document, Pandora and Michael will move into my home in the Catskills, known as Jolley's Folley. They will live there together for a period of six months, neither one spending more than two nights in succession under another roof. After this six-month period, the estate reverts to them, entirely and without encumbrance, share and share alike.

"If one does not agree with this provision, or breaks the terms of this provision within the six-month period, the estate, in its entirety, will be given over to all my surviving heirs and the Institute for the Study of Carnivorous Plants in joint shares.

"You have my blessing, children. Don't let an old, dead man down."

For a full thirty seconds there was silence. Taking advantage of it, Fitzhugh began straightening his papers.

"The old bastard," Michael murmured. Pandora would've taken offense if she hadn't agreed so completely. Because he judged the temperature in the room to be on the rise, Michael pulled Pandora out, down the hall and into one of the funny little parlors that could be found throughout the house. Just before he closed the door, the first explosion in the library erupted.

Pandora drew out a fresh tissue, sneezed into it, then plopped down on the arm of a chair. She was too flabbergasted and worn-out to be amused. "Well, what now?"

Michael reached for a cigarette before he remembered he'd quit. "Now we have to make a couple of decisions."

Pandora gave him one of the long lingering stares she'd learned made most men stutter. Michael merely sat across from her and stared back. "I meant what I said. I don't want his money. By the time it's divided up and the taxes dealt with, it's close to fifty million apiece. Fifty million," she repeated, rolling her eyes. "It's ridiculous."

"Jolley always thought so," Michael said, and watched the grief come and go in her eyes.

"He only had it to play with. The trouble was, every time he played, he made more." Unable to sit, Pandora paced to the window. "Michael, I'd suffocate with that much money."

"Cash isn't as heavy as you think."

With something close to a sneer, she turned and sat on the window ledge. "You don't object to fifty million or so after taxes I take it."

He'd have loved to have wiped that look off her face. "I haven't your fine disregard for money, Pandora, probably because I was raised with the illusion of it rather than the reality."

She shrugged, knowing his parents existed, and always had, mainly on credit and connections. "So, take it all then."

Michael picked up a little blue glass egg and tossed it from palm to palm. It was cool and smooth and worth several thousand. "That's not what Jolley wanted."

With a sniff, she snatched the egg from his hand. "He wanted us to get married and live happily ever after. I'd like to humor him...." She tossed the egg back again. "But I'm not that much of a martyr. Besides, aren't you engaged to some little blond dancer?"

He set the egg down before he could heave it at her. "For someone who turns their pampered nose up at television, you don't have the same intellectual snobbery about gossip rags."

"I *adore* gossip," Pandora said with such magnificent exaggeration Michael laughed.

"All right, Pandora, let's put down the swords a minute." He tucked his thumbs in his pockets and rocked back on his heels. Maybe they could, if they concentrated, talk civilly with each other for a few minutes. "I'm not engaged to anyone, but marriage wasn't a term of the will in any case. All we have to do is live together for six months under the same roof."

As she studied him a sense of disappointment ran through her. Perhaps they'd never gotten along, but she'd respected him if for nothing more than what she'd seen as his pure affection for Uncle Jolley. "So, you really want the money?"

He took two furious steps forward before he caught himself. Pandora never flinched. "Think whatever you like." He said it softly, as though it didn't matter. Oddly enough, it made her shudder. "You don't want the money, fine. Put that aside a moment. Are you going to stand by and watch this house go to the clan out there or a bunch of scientists studying Venus's-flytraps? Jolley loved this place and everything in it. I always thought you did, too."

"I do." The others would sell it, she admitted. There wasn't one person in the library who wouldn't put the house on the market and run with the cash. It would be lost to her. All the foolish, ostentatious rooms, the ridiculous archways. Jolley might be gone, but he'd left the house like a dangling carrot. And he still held the stick.

"He's trying to run our lives still."

Michael lifted a brow. "Surprised?"

With a half laugh, Pandora glanced over. "No."

Slowly she walked around the room while the sun shot through the diamond panes of glass and lit her hair. Michael watched her with a sense of detached admiration. She'd look magnificent on the screen. He'd always thought so. Her coloring, her posture. Her arrogance. The five or ten pounds the camera would add couldn't hurt that too angular, bean-pole body, either. And the fire-engine-red hair would make a statement on the screen while it was simply outrageous in reality. He'd often wondered why she didn't do something to tone it down.

At the moment he wasn't interested in any of that—just in what was in her brain. He didn't give a damn about the money, but he wasn't going to sit idly by and watch everything Jolley had had and built go to the vultures. If he had to play rough with Pandora, he would. He might even enjoy it.

Millions. Pandora cringed at the outrageousness of it. That much money could be nothing but a headache, she was certain. Stocks, bonds, accountants, trusts, tax shelters. She preferred a simpler kind of living. Though no one would call her apartment in Manhattan primitive.

She'd never had to worry about money and that was just the way she liked it. Above or below a certain income level, there were nothing but worries. But if you found a nice, comfortable plateau, you could just cruise. She'd nearly found it.

It was true enough that a share of this would help her tremendously professionally. With a buffer sturdy enough, she could have the artistic freedom she wanted and continue the life-style that now caused a bit of a strain on her bank account. Her work was artistic and critically acclaimed but reviews didn't pay the rent. Outside of Manhattan, her work was usually considered too unconventional. The fact that she often had to create more mainstream designs to keep her head above water grated constantly. With fifty or sixty thousand to back her, she could...

Furious with herself, she blocked it off. She was thinking like Michael, she decided. She'd rather die. He'd sold out, turned whatever talent he had to the main chance, just as he was ready to turn these circumstances to his own financial advantage. She would think of other areas. She would think first of Jolley.

As she saw it, the entire scheme was a maze of problems. How like her uncle. Now, like a chess match, she'd have to consider her moves.

She'd never lived with a man. Purposely. Pandora liked running by her own clock. It wasn't so much that she minded sharing *things*, she minded sharing space. If she agreed, that would be the first concession.

Then there was the fact that Michael was attractive,

attractive enough to be unsettling if he hadn't been so annoying. Annoying and easily annoyed, she recalled with a flash of amusement. She knew what buttons to push. Hadn't she always prided herself on the fact that she could handle him? It wasn't always easy; he was too sharp. But that made their altercations interesting. Still, they'd never been together for more than a week at a time.

But there was one clear, inarguable fact. She'd loved her uncle. How could she live with herself if she denied him a last wish? Or a last joke.

Six months. Stopping, she studied Michael as he studied her. Six months could be a very long time, especially when you weren't pleased with what you were doing. There was only one way to speed things up. She'd enjoy herself.

"Tell me, cousin, how can we live under the same roof for six months without coming to blows?"

"We can't."

He'd answered without a second's hesitation, so she laughed again. "I suppose I'd be bored if we did. I can tidy up loose ends and move in in three days. Four at the most."

"That's fine." When his shoulders relaxed, he realized he'd been tensed for her refusal. At the moment he didn't want to question why it mattered so much. Instead he held out a hand. "Deal."

Pandora inclined her head just before her palm met his. "Deal," she agreed, surprised that his hand was hard and a bit callused. She'd expected it to be rather soft and limp. After all, all he did was type. Perhaps the next six months would have some surprises.

"Shall we go tell the others?"

"They'll want to murder us."

Her smile came slowly, subtly shifting the angles of her face. It was, Michael thought, at once wicked and alluring. "I know. Try not to gloat."

When they stepped out, several griping relatives had spilled out into the hallway. They did what they did best together. They argued.

"You'd blow your share on barbells and carrot juice," Biff said spitefully to Hank. "At least I know what to do with money."

"Lose it on horses," Monroe said, and blew out a stream of choking cigar smoke. "Invest. Tax deferred."

"You could use yours to take a course in how to speak in complete sentences." Carlson stepped out of the smoke and straightened his tie. "I'm the old man's only living son. It's up to me to prove he was incompetent."

"Uncle Jolley had more competence than the lot of you put together." Feeling equal parts frustration and disgust, Pandora stepped forward. "He gave you each exactly what he wanted you to have."

Biff drew out a flat gold cigarette case as he glanced over at his cousin. "It appears our Pandora's changed her mind about the money. Well, you worked for it, didn't you, darling?"

Michael put his hand on Pandora's shoulder and squeezed lightly before she could spring. "You'd like to keep your profile, wouldn't you, cousin?"

"It appears writing for television's given you a taste for violence." Biff lit his cigarette and smiled. If he'd thought he could get in a blow below the belt... "I think I'll decline a brawl," he decided.

"Well, I think it's fair." Hank's wife came forward, stretching out her hand. She gave both Pandora and

Michael a hearty shake. "You should put a gym in this place. Build yourself up a little. Come on, Hank."

Silent, and his shoulders straining the material of his suit, Hank followed her out.

"Nothing but muscles between the head," Carlson mumbled. "Come, Mona." He strode ahead of his wife, pausing long enough to level a glare at Pandora and Michael. The inevitable line ran though Michael's mind before Carlson opened his mouth and echoed it. "You haven't heard the last of this."

Pandora gave him her sweetest smile. "Have a nice trip home, Uncle Carlson."

"Probate," Monroe said with a grunt, and waddled his way out behind them.

Patience fluttered her hands. "Key West, for heaven's sake. I've never been south of Palm Beach. My, oh my."

"Oh, Michael." Fluttering her lashes, Ginger placed a hand on his arm. "When do you think I might have my mirror?"

He glanced down into her perfectly lovely, heart-shaped face. Her eyes were as pure a blue as tropical waters. He thanked God Jolley hadn't asked that he spend six months with Cousin Ginger. "I'm sure Mr. Fitzhugh will have it shipped to you as soon as possible."

"Come along, Ginger, we'll give you a ride to the airport." Biff pulled Ginger's hand through his arm, patted it and smiled down at Pandora. "I'd be worried if I didn't know you better. You won't last six days with Michael much less six months. Beastly temper," he said confidentially to Michael. "The two of you'll murder each other before a week's out."

"Don't spend the old man's money yet," Michael warned. "We'll make the six months if for no other reason than to spite you." He smiled when he said it, a chummy, well-meaning smile that took the arrogance from Biff's face.

"We'll see who wins the game." Straight backed, Biff turned toward the door. His wife walked out behind him without having said a word since she'd walked in.

"Biff," Ginger began as they walked out. "What are you going to do with all those matches?"

"Burn his bridges, I hope," Pandora muttered. "Well, Michael, though I can't say there was a lot of love before, there's nearly none lost now."

"Are you worried about alienating them?"

With a shrug of her shoulders, she walked toward a bowl of roses, then gave him a considering look. "Well, I've never had any trouble alienating you. Why is that, do you suppose?"

"Jolley always said we were too much alike."

"Really?" Haughty, she lifted a brow. "I find myself disagreeing with him again. You and I, Michael Donahue, have almost nothing in common."

"If that's so we have six months to prove it." On impulse he moved closer and put a finger under her chin. "You know, darling, you might've been stuck with Biff."

"I'd've given the place to the plants first."

He grinned. "I'm flattered."

"Don't be." But she didn't move away from him. Not yet. It was an interesting feeling to be this close without snarling. "The only difference is you don't bore me."

"That's enough," he said with a hint of a smile. "I'm easily flattered." Intrigued, he flicked a finger down her cheek. It was still pale, but her eyes were direct and steady. "No, we won't bore each other, Pandora. In six months we might experience a lot of things, but boredom won't be one of them."

It might be an interesting feeling, she discovered, but it wasn't quite a safe one. It was best to remember that he didn't find her appealing as a woman but would, for the sake of his own ego, string her along if she permitted it. "I don't flatter easily. I haven't decided exactly what your reasons are for going through with this farce, but I'm doing it only for Uncle Jolley. I can set up my equipment here quite easily."

"And I can write here quite easily."

Pandora plucked a rose from the bowl. "If you can call those implausible scripts writing."

"The same way you call the bangles you string together art."

Color came back to her cheeks and that pleased him. "You wouldn't know art if it reached up and bit you on the nose. My jewelry expresses emotion."

His smile showed pleasant interest. "How much is lust going for these days?"

"I would have guessed you'd be very familiar with the cost." Pandora fumbled for a tissue, sneezed into it, then shut her bag with a click. "Most of the women you date have price tags."

It amused him, and it showed. "I thought we were talking about work."

"My profession is a time-honored one, while yours—yours stops for commercial breaks. And furthermore—"

"I beg your pardon."

Fitzhugh paused at the doorway of the library. He wanted nothing more than to be shed of the McVie clan and have a quiet, soothing drink. "Am I to assume that you've both decided to accept the terms of the will?"

Six months, she thought. It was going to be a long, long winter.

Six months, he thought. He was going to have the first daffodil he found in April bronzed.

"You can start counting the days at the end of the week," he told Fitzhugh. "Agreed, cousin?"

Pandora set her chin. "Agreed."

Chapter 2

It was a pleasant trip from Manhattan along the Hudson River toward the Catskills. Pandora had always enjoyed it. The drive gave her time to clear her mind and relax. But then, she'd always taken it at her own whim, her own pace, her own convenience. Pandora made it a habit to do everything just that way. This time, however, there was more involved than her own wants and wishes. Uncle Jolley had boxed her in.

He'd known she'd have to go along with the terms of the will. Not for the money. He'd been too smart to think she could be lured into such a ridiculous scheme with money. But the house, her ties to it, her need for the continuity of family. That's what he'd hooked her with.

Now she had to leave Manhattan behind for six months. Oh, she'd run into the city for a few hours here and there, but it was hardly the same as living in the center of things. She'd always liked that—being in the center, surrounded by movement, being able to watch and become involved whenever she liked. Just as she'd always liked long weekends in the solitude of Jolley's Folley.

She'd been raised that way, to enjoy and make the most of whatever environment she was in. Her parents were gypsies. Wealth had meant they'd traveled first class instead of in covered wagons. If there'd been campfires, there had also been a servant to gather kindling, but the spirit was the same.

Before she'd been fifteen, Pandora had been to more than thirty countries. She'd eaten sushi in Tokyo, roamed the moors in Cornwall, bargained in Turkish markets. A succession of tutors had traveled with them so that by her calculations, she'd spent just under two years in a classroom environment before college.

The exotic, vagabond childhood had given her a taste for variety—in people, in foods, in styles. And oddly enough the exposure to widely diverse cultures and mores had formed in her an unshakable desire for a home and a sense of belonging.

Though her parents liked to meander through countries, recording everything with pen and film, Pandora had missed a central point. Where was home? This year in Mexico, next year in Athens. Her parents made a name for themselves with their books and articles on the unusual, but Pandora wanted roots. She'd discovered she'd have to find them for herself.

She'd chosen New York, and in her way, Uncle Jolley.

Now, because her uncle and his home had become her central point, she was agreeing to spend six months living with a man she could hardly tolerate so that she could inherit a fortune she didn't want or need. Life, she'd discovered long ago, never moved in straight lines.

Jolley McVie's ultimate joke, she thought as she turned up the long drive toward his Folley. Well, he could throw them together, but he couldn't make them stick.

Still, she'd have felt better if she'd been sure of Michael. Was it the lure of the millions of dollars, or an affection for an old man that would bring him to the Catskills? She knew his *Logan's Run* was in its very successful fourth year, and that he'd had other lucrative ventures in television. But money was a seduction itself. After all, her Uncle Carlson had more than he could ever spend, yet he was already taking the steps for a probate of the will.

That didn't worry her. Uncle Jolley had believed in hiring the best. If Fitzhugh had drawn up the will, it was air-tight. What worried her was Michael Donahue.

Because of the trap she'd fallen into, she'd found herself thinking of him a great deal too much over the past couple of days. Ally or enemy, she wasn't sure. Either way, she was going to have to live with him. Or around him. She hoped the house was big enough.

By the time she arrived, she was worn-out from the drive and the lingering head cold. Though her equipment and supplies had been shipped the day before, she still had three cases in the car. Deciding to take one at a time, Pandora popped the trunk, then simply looked at Jolley's Folley.

He'd built it when he'd been forty, so the house was already over a half century old. It went in all directions at once, as if he'd never been able to decide where he wanted to start and where he wanted to finish. The truth about Jolley, she admitted, was that he'd never wanted to finish. The project, the game, the puzzle, was always more interesting to him before the last pieces were in place.

Without the wings, it might have been a rather somber and sedate late-nineteenth-century mansion. With them, it was a mass of walls and corners, heights and widths. There was no symmetry, yet to Pandora it had always seemed as sturdy as the rock it had been built on.

Some of the windows were long, some were wide, some of them were leaded and some sheer. Jolley had made up his mind then changed it again as he'd gone along.

The stone had come from one of his quarries, the wood from one of his lumberyards. When he'd decided to build a house, he'd started his own construction firm. McVie Construction, Incorporated was one of the five biggest companies in the country.

It struck her suddenly that she owned half of Jolley's share in the company and her mind spun at how many others. She had interests in baby oil, steel mills, rocket engines and cake mix. Pandora lifted the case and set her teeth. What on earth had she let herself in for?

From the upstairs window, Michael watched her. The jacket she wore was big and baggy with three vivid colors, blue, yellow and pink, patched in. The wind caught at her slacks and rippled them from thigh to ankle. She wasn't looking teary-eyed and pale this time, but grim and resigned. So much the better. He'd been tempted to comfort her during their uncle's funeral. Only the knowledge that too much sympathy for a woman like Pandora was fatal had prevented him.

He'd known her since childhood and had consid-

ered her a spoiled brat from the word go. Though she'd
often been off for months at a time on one of her parents' journalistic safaris, they'd seen enough of each
other to feed a mutual dislike. Only the fact that she
had cared for Jolley had given Michael some tolerance
for her. And the fact, he was forced to admit, that she
had more honesty and humanity in her than any of their
other relations.

There had been a time, he recalled, a brief time, during late adolescence that he'd felt a certain…stirring
for her. A purely shallow and physical teenage hunger,
Michael assured himself. She'd always had an intriguing face; it could be unrelentingly plain one moment
and striking the next, and when she'd hit her teens…
well, that had been a natural enough reaction. And it
had passed without incident. He now preferred a woman
with more subtlety, more gloss and femininity—and
shorter fangs.

Whatever he preferred, Michael left the arranging
of his own office to wander downstairs.

"Charles, did my shipment come?" Pandora pulled
off her leather driving gloves and dropped them on a
little round table in the hall. Since Charles was there,
the ancient butler who had served her uncle since before she was born, she felt a certain pleasure in coming.

"Everything arrived this morning, miss." The old
man would have taken her suitcase if she hadn't waved
him away.

"No, don't fuss with that. Where did you have them
put everything?"

"In the garden shed in the east yard, as you instructed."

She gave him a smile and a peck on the cheek, both
of which pleased him. His square bulldog's face grew

slightly pink. "I knew I could count on you. I didn't tell you before how happy I was that you and Sweeney are staying. The place wouldn't be the same without you serving tea and Sweeney baking cakes."

Charles managed to pull his back a bit straighter. "We wouldn't think about going anywhere else, miss. The master would have wanted us to stay."

But made it possible for them to go, Pandora mused. Leaving each of them three thousand dollars for every year of service. Charles had been with Jolley since the house was built, and Sweeney had come some ten years later. The bequest would have been more than enough for each to retire on. Pandora smiled. Some weren't made for retirement.

"Charles, I'd love some tea," she began, knowing if she didn't distract him, he'd insist on carrying her bags up the long staircase.

"In the drawing room, miss?"

"Perfect. And if Sweeney has any of those little cakes…"

"She's been baking all morning." With only the slightest of creaks, he made his way toward the kitchen.

Pandora thought of rich icing loaded with sugar. "I wonder how much weight a person can gain in six months."

"A steady diet of Sweeney's cakes wouldn't hurt you," Michael said from above her head. "Men are generally more attracted to flesh than bone."

Pandora spun around, then found herself in the awkward position of having to arch her neck back to see Michael at the top of the stairs. "I don't center my life around attracting men."

"I'd be the last one to argue with that."

He looked quite comfortable, she thought, feeling the first stirrings of resentment. And negligently, arrogantly attractive. From several feet above her head, he leaned against a post and looked down on her as though he was the master. She'd soon put an end to that. Uncle Jolley's will had been very clear. Share and share alike.

"Since you're already here and settled in, you can come help me with the rest of my bags."

He didn't budge. "I always thought the one point we were in perfect agreement on was feminism."

Pandora paused at the door to toss a look over her shoulder. "Social and political views aside, if you don't help me up with them before Charles comes back, he'll insist on doing it himself. He's too old to do it and too proud to be told he can't." She walked back out and wasn't surprised when she heard his footsteps on the gravel behind her.

She took a deep breath of crisp autumn air. All in all, it was a lovely day. "Drive up early?"

"Actually, I drove up late last night."

Pandora turned at the open trunk of her car. "So eager to start the game, Michael?"

If he hadn't been determined to start off peacefully, he'd have found fault with the tone of her voice, with the look in her eyes. Instead he let it pass. "I wanted to get my office set up today. I was just finishing it when you drove in."

"Work, work, work," she said with a long sigh. "You must put in slavish hours to come up with an hour of chase scenes and steam a week."

Peace wasn't all that important. As she reached for a suitcase, he closed a hand over her wrist. Later he'd think about how slim it was, how soft. Now he could only think how much he wished she were a man. Then he could've belted her. "The amount of work I do and what I produce is of absolutely no concern to you."

It occurred to Pandora, oddly, she thought, just how much she enjoyed seeing him on the edge of temper. All of her other relatives were so bland, so outwardly civilized. Michael had always been a contrast, and therefore of more interest. Smiling, she allowed her wrist to stay limp.

"Did I indicate that it was? Nothing, I promise you, could be further from the truth. Shall we get these in and have that tea? It's a bit chilly."

He'd always admired, grudgingly, how smoothly she could slip into the lady-of-the-manor routine. As a writer who wrote for actors and for viewers, he appreciated natural talent. He also knew how to set a scene to his best advantage. "Tea's a perfect idea." He hauled one case out and left the second for her. "We'll establish some guidelines."

"Will we?" Pandora pulled out the case, then let the trunk shut quietly. Without another word, she started back toward the house, holding the front door open for him, then breezing by the suitcase she'd left in the main hall. Because she knew Michael was fond of Charles, she hadn't a doubt he'd pick it up and follow.

The room she always took was on the second floor in the east wing. Jolley had let her decorate it herself, and she'd chosen white on white with a few startling splashes of color. Chartreuse and blazing blue in throw pillows, a long horizontal oil painting, jarring in its colors of sunset, a crimson waist-high urn stuffed with ostrich plumes.

Pandora set her case by the bed, noted with satisfaction that a fire had been laid in the small marble fireplace, then tossed her jacket over a chair.

"I always feel like I'm walking into *Better Homes*," he commented as he let her cases drop.

Pandora glanced down at them briefly, then at him. "I'm sure you're more at home in your own room. It's more—*Field and Stream*. I expect tea's ready."

He gave her a long, steady survey. Her jacket had concealed the trim cashmere sweater tucked into the narrow waist of her slacks. It reminded Michael quite forcibly just what had begun to attract him all those teenage years ago. For the second time he found himself wishing she were a man.

Though they walked abreast down the stairs, they didn't speak. In the drawing room, amid the Mideast opulence Jolley had chosen there, Charles was setting up the tea service.

"Oh, you lit the fire. How lovely." Pandora walked over and began warming her hands. She wanted a moment, just a moment, because for an instant in her room she thought she'd seen something in Michael's eyes. And she thought she'd felt the same something in response. "I'll pour, Charles. I'm sure Michael and I won't need another thing until dinner."

Casually she glanced around the room, at the flowing drapes, the curvy brocade sofas, the plump pillows and brass urns. "You know, this has always been one of my favorite rooms." Going to the tea set, she began to fill cups. "I was only twelve when we visited Turkey, but this room always makes me remember it vividly. Right down to the smells in the markets. Sugar?"

"No." He took the cup from her, plopped a generous slice of cake on a dish, then chose a seat. He preferred the little parlor next door with its tidy English country air. This was the beginning, he thought, with the old butler and plump cook as witnesses. Six months from today, they'd all sign a document swearing that the terms of the will had been adhered to and that would be that. It was the time in between that concerned him.

"Rule number one," Michael began without preamble. "We're both in the east wing because it makes it easier for Charles and Sweeney. But—" he paused, hoping to emphasize his point "—both of us will, at all times, respect the other's area."

"By all means." Pandora crossed her legs and sipped her tea.

"Again, because of the staff, it seems fair that we eat at the same time. Therefore, in the interest of survival, we'll keep the conversations away from professional matters."

Pandora smiled at him and nibbled on cake. "Oh yes, let's do keep things personal."

"You're a nasty little package—"

"See, we're off to a perfect start. Rule number two. Neither of us, no matter how bored or restless, will disturb the other during his or her set working hours. I generally work between ten and one, then again between three and six."

"Rule number three. If one of us is entertaining, the other will make him or herself scarce."

Pandora's eyes narrowed, only for a moment. "Oh, and I so wanted to meet your dancer. Rule number four. The first floor is neutral ground and to be shared equally unless specific prior arrangements are made and agreed upon." She tapped her finger against the arm of the chair. "If we both play fair, we should manage."

"I don't have any trouble playing fair. As I recall, you're the one who cheats."

Her voice became very cool, her tone very rounded. "I don't know what you're talking about."

"Canasta, poker, gin."

"That's absurd and you have absolutely no proof." Rising, she helped herself to another cup of tea. "Besides, cards are entirely different." Warmed by the fire, soothed by the tea, she smiled at him. As Michael recalled, that particular smile was lethal. And stunning. "Are you still holding a grudge over that five hundred I won from you?"

"I wouldn't if you'd won it fairly."

"I won it," she countered. "That's what counts. If I cheated and you didn't catch me, then it follows that I cheated well enough for it to be legal."

"You always had a crooked sense of logic." He rose as well and came close. She had to admire the way he moved. It wasn't quite a swagger because he didn't put the effort into it. But it was very close. "If we play again, whatever we play, you won't cheat me."

Confident, she smiled at him. "Michael, we've known each other too long for you to intimidate me." She reached a hand up to pat his cheek and found her wrist captured a second time. And a second time she saw and felt that same dangerous something she'd experienced upstairs.

There was no Uncle Jolley as a buffer between them now. Perhaps they'd both just begun to realize it. Whatever was between them that made them snarl and snap would have a long, cold winter to surface.

Perhaps neither one of them wanted to face it, but both were too stubborn to back down.

"Perhaps we're just beginning to know each other," Michael murmured.

She believed it. And didn't like it. He wasn't a posturing fool like Biff nor a harmless hulk like Hank. He might be a cousin by marriage only, but the blood between them had always run hot. There was violence in him. It showed sometimes in a look in his eyes, in the way he held himself. As though he wouldn't ward off a blow but counter it. Pandora recognized it because there was violence in her, as well. Perhaps that was why she always felt compelled to shoot darts at him, just to see how many he could boomerang back at her.

They stood as they were a moment, gauging each other, reassessing. The wise thing to do was for each to acknowledge a hit and step aside. Pandora threw up her chin. Michael set for the volley. "We'll go to the mat another time, Michael. At the moment, I'm a bit tired from the drive. If you'll excuse me?"

"Rule number five," he said without releasing her. "If one of us takes potshots at the other, they'll damn well pay the consequences." When he freed her arm, he went back for his cup. "See you at dinner, cousin."

Pandora awoke just past dawn fully awake, rested and bursting with energy. Whether it had been the air in the mountains or the six hours of deep sleep, she was ready and eager to work. Breakfast could wait, she decided as she showered and dressed. She was going out to the garden shed, organizing her equipment and diving in.

The house was perfectly quiet and still dim as she made her way downstairs. The servants would sleep another hour or two, she thought as she stuck her head in the pantry and chose a muffin. As she recalled, Michael might sleep until noon.

They had made it through dinner without incident. Perhaps they'd been polite to each other because of Charles and Sweeney or perhaps because both of them had been too tired to snipe. Pandora wasn't sure herself.

They'd dined under the cheerful lights of the big chandelier and had talked, when they'd talked, about the weather and the food.

By nine they'd gone their separate ways. Pandora to read until her eyes closed and Michael to work. Or so he'd said.

Outside the air was chill enough to cause Pandora's skin to prickle. She hunched up the collar of her jacket and started across the lawn. It crunched underfoot with the early thin frost. She liked it—the absolute solitude, the lightness of the air, the incredible smell of mountain and river.

In Tibet she'd once come close to frostbite because she hadn't been able to resist the snow and the swoop of rock. She didn't find this slice of the Catskills any less fascinating. The winter was best, she'd always thought, when the snow skimmed the top of your boots and your voice came out in puffs of smoke.

Winter in the mountains was a time for the basics. Heat, food, work. There were times Pandora wanted only the basics. There were times in New York she'd argue for hours over unions, politics, civil rights because the fact was, she loved an argument. She wanted the stimulation of an opposing view over broad issues or niggling ones. She wanted the challenge, the heat and the exercise for her brain. But...

There were times she wanted nothing more than a

quiet sunrise over frost-crisped ground and the promise of a warm drink by a hot fire. And there were times, though she'd rarely admit it even to herself, that she wanted a shoulder to lay her head against and a hand to hold. She'd been raised to see independence as a duty, not a choice. Her parents had the most balanced of relationships, equal to equal. Pandora saw them as something rare in a world where the scales tipped this way or that too often. At age eighteen, Pandora had decided she'd never settle for less than a full partnership. At age twenty, she decided marriage wasn't for her. Instead she put all her passion, her energy and imagination into her work.

Straight-line dedication had paid off. She was successful, even prominent, and creatively she was fulfilled. It was more than many people ever achieved.

Now she pulled open the door of the utility shed. It was a big square building, as wide as the average barn, with hardwood floors and paneled walls. Uncle Jolley hadn't believed in the primitive. Hitting the switch, she flooded the building with light.

As per her instructions, the crates and boxes she'd shipped had been stacked along one wall. The shelves where Uncle Jolley had kept his gardening tools during his brief, torrid gardening stage had been packed away. The plumbing was good, with a full-size stainless-steel sink and a small but more than adequate bath with shower enclosed in the rear. She counted five workbenches. The light and ventilation were excellent.

It wouldn't take her long, Pandora figured, to turn the shed into an organized, productive workroom.

It took three hours.

Along one shelf were boxes of beads in various

sizes—jet, amethyst, gold, polished wood, coral, ivory. She had trays of stones, precious and semiprecious, square cut, brilliants, teardrops and chips. In New York, they were kept in a safe. Here, she never considered it. She had gold, silver, bronze, copper. There were solid and hollow drills, hammers, tongs, pliers, nippers, files and clamps. One might have thought she did carpentry. Then there were scribes and drawplates, bottles of chemicals, and miles of string and fiber cord.

The money she'd invested in these materials had cost her every penny of an inheritance from her grandmother, and a good chunk of savings she'd earned as an apprentice. It had been worth it. Pandora picked up a file and tapped it against her palm. Well worth it.

She could forge gold and silver, cast alloys and string impossibly complex designs with the use of a few beads or shells. Metals could be worked into thin, threadlike strands or built into big bold chunks. Pandora could do as she chose, with tools that had hardly changed from those used by artists two centuries earlier.

It was and always had been both the sense of continuity and the endless variety that appealed to her. She never made two identical pieces. That, to her, would have been manufacturing rather than creating. At times, her pieces were elegantly simple, classic in design. Those pieces sold well and allowed her a bit of artistic freedom. At other times, they were bold and brash and exaggerated. Mood guided Pandora, not trends. Rarely, very rarely, she would agree to create a piece along specified lines. If the lines, or the client, interested her.

She turned down a president because she'd found his ideas too pedestrian but had made a ring at a new father's request because his idea had been unique. Pandora had been told that the new mother had never taken the braided gold links off. Three links, one for each of the triplets she'd given birth to.

At the moment, Pandora had just completed drafting the design for a three-tiered necklace commissioned to her by the husband of a popular singer. Emerald. That was her name and the only requirement given to Pandora. The man wanted lots of them. And he'd pay, Pandora mused, for the dozen she'd chosen just before leaving New York. They were square, three karats apiece and of the sharp, sharp green that emeralds are valued for.

This was, she knew, her big chance, professionally and, most importantly, artistically. If the necklace was a success, there'd not only be reviews for her scrapbook, but acceptance. She'd be freer to do more of what she wanted without compromise.

The trick would be to fashion the chain so that it held like steel and looked like a cobweb. The stones would hang from each tier as if they'd dripped there.

For the next two hours, she worked in gold.

Between the two heaters at each end of the shed and the flame from her tools, the air became sultry. Sweat rolled down under her sweater, but she didn't mind. In fact, she barely noticed as the gold became pliable. Again and again, she drew the wire through the drawplate, smoothing out the kinks and subtly, slowly, changing the shape and size. When the wire looked like angel hair she began working it with her fingers, twisting and braiding until she matched the design in her head and on her drawing paper.

It would be simple—elegantly, richly simple. The

emeralds would bring their own flash when she attached them.

Time passed. After careful, meticulous use of drawplate, flame and her own hands, the first thin, gold tier formed.

She'd just begun to stretch out the muscles in her back when the door of the shed opened and cool air poured in. Her face glowing with sweat and concentration, she glared at Michael.

"Just what the hell do you think you're doing?"

"Following orders." He had his hands stuffed in his jacket pockets for warmth, but hadn't buttoned the front. Nor, she noticed, had he bothered to shave. "This place smells like an oven."

"I'm working." She lifted the hem of the big apron she wore and wiped at her brow. It was being interrupted that annoyed her, Pandora told herself. Not the fact that he'd walked in on her when she looked like a steelworker. "Remember rule number three?"

"Tell that to Sweeney." Leaving the door ajar, he wandered in. "She said it was bad enough that you skipped breakfast, but you're not getting away with missing lunch." Curious, he poked his finger into a tray that held brilliant colored stones. "I have orders to bring you back."

"I'm not ready."

He picked up a tiny sapphire and held it to the light. "I had to stop her from tramping out here herself. If I go back alone, she's going to come for you. Her arthritis is acting up again."

Pandora swore under her breath. "Put that down," she ordered, then yanked the apron off.

"Some of this stuff looks real," he commented.

Though he put the sapphire back, he picked up a round, winking diamond.

"Some of this stuff is real." Pandora crouched to turn the first heater down.

The diamond was in his hand as he scowled down at her head. "Why in hell do you have it sitting out like candy? It should be locked up."

Pandora adjusted the second heater. "Why?"

"Don't be any more foolish than necessary. Someone could steal it."

"Someone?" Straightening, Pandora smiled at him. "There aren't many someones around. I don't think Charles and Sweeney are a problem, but maybe I should worry about you."

He cursed her and dropped the diamond back. "They're your little bag of tricks, cousin, but if I had several thousand dollars sitting around that could slip into a pocket, I'd be more careful."

Though under most circumstances she fully agreed, Pandora merely picked up her jacket. After all, they weren't in Manhattan but miles away from anyone or anything. If she locked everything up, she'd just have to unlock it again every time she wanted to work. "Just one of the differences between you and me, Michael. I suppose it's because you write about so many dirty deeds."

"I also write about human nature." He picked up the sketch of the emerald necklace she had drawn. It had the sense of scale that would have pleased an architect and the flair and flow that would appeal to an artist. "If you're so into making bangles and baubles, why aren't you wearing any?"

"They get in the way when I'm working. If you write

about human nature, how come the bad guy gets caught every week?"

"Because I'm writing for people, and people need heroes."

Pandora opened her mouth to argue, then found she agreed with the essence of the statement. "Hmm," was all she said as she turned out the lights and went out ahead of him.

"At least lock the door," Michael told her.

"I haven't a key."

"Then we'll get one."

"*We* don't need one."

He shut the door with a snap. "*You* do."

Pandora only shrugged as she started across the lawn. "Michael, have I mentioned that you've been more crabby than usual?"

He pulled a piece of hard candy out of his pocket and popped it into his mouth. "Quit smoking."

The candy was lemon. She caught just a whiff. "So I noticed. How long?"

He scowled at some leaves that skimmed across the lawn. They were brown and dry and seemed to have a life of their own. "Couple weeks. I'm going crazy."

She laughed sympathetically before she tucked her arm into his. "You'll live, darling. The first month's the toughest."

Now he scowled at her. "How would you know? You never smoked."

"The first month of anything's the toughest. You just have to keep your mind occupied. Exercise. We'll jog after lunch."

"We?"

"And we can play canasta after dinner."

He gave a quick snort but brushed the hair back from her cheek. "You'll cheat."

"See, your mind's already occupied." With a laugh, she turned her face up to his. He looked a bit surly, but on him, oddly, it was attractive. Placid, good-natured good looks had always bored her. "It won't hurt you to give up one of your vices, Michael. You have so many."

"I like my vices," he grumbled, then turned his head to look down at her. She was giving him her easy, friendly smile, one she sent his way rarely. It always made him forget just how much trouble she caused him. It made him forget he wasn't attracted to dramatically bohemian women with wild red hair and sharp bones. "A woman who looks like you should have several of her own."

Her mouth was solemn, her eyes wicked. "I'm much too busy. Vices take up a great deal of time."

"When Pandora opened the box, vices popped out."

She stopped at the back stoop. "Among other miseries. I suppose that's why I'm careful about opening boxes."

Michael ran a finger down her cheek. It was the sort of gesture he realized could easily become a habit. She was right, his mind was occupied. "You have to lift off the lid sooner or later."

She didn't move back, though she'd felt the little tingle of tension, of attraction, of need. Pandora didn't believe in moving back, but in plowing through. "Some things are better off locked up."

He nodded. He didn't want to release what was in their private box any more than she did. "Some locks aren't as strong as they need to be."

They were standing close, the wind whistling lightly

between them. Pandora felt the sun on her back and the chill on her face. If she took a step nearer, there'd be heat. That she'd never doubted and had always avoided. He'd use whatever was available to him, she reminded herself. At the moment, it just happened to be her. She let her breath come calmly and easily before she reached for the doorknob.

"We'd better not keep Sweeney waiting."

Chapter 3

The streets are almost deserted. A car turns a corner and disappears. It's drizzling. Neon flashes off puddles. It's garish rather than festive. There's a gray, miserable feel to this part of the city. Alleyways, cheap clubs, dented cars. The small, neatly dressed blonde walks quickly. She's nervous, out of her element, but not lost. Close-up on the envelope in her hands. It's damp from the rain. Her fingers open and close on it. Tires squeal offscreen and she jolts. The blue lights of the club blink off and on in her face as she stands outside. Hesitates. Shifts the envelope from hand to hand. She goes in. Slow pan of the street. Three shots and freeze.

Three knocks sounded at the door of Michael's office. Before he could answer, Pandora swirled in. "Happy anniversary, darling."

Michael looked up from his computer. He'd been up

most of the night working the story line out in his mind. It was nine in the morning, and he'd only had one cup of coffee to prime him for the day. Coffee and cigarettes together were too precious a memory. The scene that had just jelled in his mind dissolved.

"What the hell are you talking about?" He reached his hand into a bowl of peanuts and discovered he'd already eaten all but two.

"Two full weeks without any broken bones." Pandora swooped over to him, clucked her tongue at the disorder, then chose the arm of a chair. It was virtually the only free space. She brushed at the dust on the edge of the table beside her and left a smear. "And they said it wouldn't last."

She looked fresh with her wild mane of red pulled back from her face, comfortable in sweater and slacks that were too big for her. Michael felt like he'd just crawled out of a cave. His sweatshirt had ripped at the shoulder seam two years before, but he still favored it. A few weeks before, he'd helped paint a friend's apartment. The paint smears on his jeans showed her preference for baby pink. His eyes felt as though he'd slept facedown in the sand.

Pandora smiled at him like some bright, enthusiastic kindergarten teacher. She had a fresh, clean, almost woodsy scent. "We have a rule about respecting the other's work space," he reminded her.

"Oh, don't be cranky." It was said with the same positive smile. "Besides, you never gave me any schedule. From what I've noticed in the past couple of weeks, this is early for you."

"I'm just starting the treatment for a new episode."

"Really?" Pandora walked over and leaned over his

shoulder. "Hmm," she said, though she wondered who had shot whom. "Well, I don't suppose that'll take long."

"Why don't you go play with your beads?"

"Now you're being rude when I came up here to invite you to go with me into town." After brushing off the sleeve of her sweater, she sat on the edge of the desk. She didn't know exactly why she was so determined to be friendly. Maybe it was because the emerald necklace was nearly finished and was exceeding even her standards. Maybe it was because in the past two weeks she'd found a certain enjoyment in Michael's company. Mild enjoyment, Pandora reminded herself. Nothing to shout about.

Suspicious, Michael narrowed his eyes. "What for?"

"I'm going in for some supplies Sweeney needs." She found the turtle shell that was his lampshade intriguing, and ran her fingers over it. "I thought you might like to get out for a while."

He would. It had been two weeks since he'd seen anything but the house and grounds. He glanced back at the page on his computer. "How long will you be?"

"Oh, two, three hours I suppose." She moved her shoulders. "It's an hour's round trip to begin with."

He was tempted. Free time and a change of scene. But the half-blank page remained on his computer. "Can't. I have to get this fleshed out."

"All right." Pandora rose from the desk a bit surprised by the degree of disappointment she felt. Silly, she thought. She loved to drive alone with the radio blaring. "Don't strain your fingers."

He started to growl something at her back, then because his bowl of nuts was empty, thought better of it.

"Pandora, how about picking me up a couple pounds of pistachios?"

As she stopped at the door, she lifted a brow. "Pistachios?"

"Real ones. No red dye." He ran a hand over the bristle on his chin and wished for a pack of cigarettes. One cigarette. One long deep drag.

She glanced at the empty bowl and nearly smiled. The way he was nibbling, he'd lose that lean, rangy look quickly. "I suppose I could."

"And a copy of the *New York Times*."

Her brow rose. "Would you like to make me a list?"

"Be a sport, will you? Next time Sweeney needs supplies, I'll go in."

She thought about it a moment. "Very well then, nuts and news."

"And some pencils," he called out.

She slammed the door smartly.

Nearly two hours passed before Michael decided he deserved another cup of coffee. The story line was bumping along just as he'd planned, full of twists and turns. The fans of *Logan's Run* expected the gritty with occasional bursts of color and magic. That's just the way it was panning out.

Critics of the medium aside, Michael enjoyed writing for the small screen. He liked knowing his stories would reach literally millions of people every week and that for an hour, they could involve themselves with the character he had created.

The truth was, Michael liked Logan—the reluctant but steady heroism, the humor and the flaws. He'd made Logan human and fallible and reluctant because Michael had always imagined the best heroes were just that.

The ratings and the mail proved he was on target. His writing for Logan had won him critical acclaim and awards, just as the one-act play he'd written had won him critical acclaim and awards. But the play had reached a few thousand at best, the bulk of whom had been New Yorkers. *Logan's Run* reached the family of four in Des Moines, the steelworkers in Chicago and the college crowd in Boston. Every week.

He didn't see television as the vast wasteland but as the magic box. Michael figured everyone was entitled to a bit of magic.

Michael switched off the laptop so that the screen died. For a moment he sat in silence. He'd known he could work at the Folley. He'd done so before, but never long-term. What he hadn't known was that he'd work so well, so quickly or be so content. The truth was, he'd never expected to get along half so well with Pandora. Not that it was any picnic, Michael mused, absently running the stub of a pencil between his fingers.

They fought, certainly, but at least they weren't taking chunks out of each other. Or not very big ones. All in all he enjoyed the evenings when they played cards if for no other reason than the challenge of trying to catch her cheating. So far he hadn't.

Also true was the odd attraction he felt for her. That hadn't been in the script. So far he'd been able to ignore, control or smother it. But there were times... There were times, Michael thought as he rose and stretched, when he'd like to close her smart-tongued mouth in a more satisfactory way. Just to see what it'd be like, he told himself. Curiosity about people was part of his makeup. He'd be interested to see how Pandora would react if he hauled her against him and kissed her until she went limp.

He let out a quick laugh as he wandered to the window. Limp? Pandora? Women like her never went soft. He might satisfy his curiosity, but he'd get a fist in the gut for his trouble. Even that might be worth it....

She wasn't unmoved. He'd been sure of that since the first day they'd walked back together from her workshop. He'd seen it in her face, heard it, however briefly in her voice. They'd both been circling around it for two weeks. Or twenty years, Michael speculated.

He'd never felt about another woman exactly the way he felt about Pandora McVie. Uncomfortable, challenged, infuriated. The truth was that he was almost always at ease around women. He liked them—their femininity, their peculiar strengths and weaknesses, their style. Perhaps that was the reason for his success in relationships, though he'd carefully kept them short-term.

If he romanced a woman, it was because he was interested in her, not simply in the end result. True enough he was interested in Pandora, but he'd never considered romancing her. It surprised him that he'd caught himself once or twice considering seducing her.

Seducing, of course, was an entirely different matter than romancing. But all in all, he didn't know if attempting a casual seduction of Pandora would be worth the risk.

If he offered her a candlelight dinner or a walk in the moonlight—or a mad night of passion—she'd come back with a sarcastic remark. Which would, inevitably, trigger some caustic rebuttal from him. The merry-go-round would begin again.

In any case, it wasn't romance he wanted with Pandora. It was simply curiosity. In certain instances, it was best to remember what had happened to the intrepid cat. But as he thought of her, his gaze was drawn toward her workshop.

They weren't so very different really, Michael mused. Pandora could insist from dawn to dusk that they had nothing in common, but Jolley had been closer to the mark. They were both quick-tempered, opinionated and passionately protective of their professions. He closed himself up for hours at a time with a laptop. She closed herself up with tools and torches. The end result of both of their work was entertainment. And after all, that was...

His thoughts broke off as he saw the shed door open. Odd, he hadn't thought she was back yet. His rooms were on the opposite end of the house from the garage, so he wouldn't have heard her car, but he thought she'd drop off what she'd picked up for him.

He started to shrug and turn away when he saw the figure emerge from the shed. It was bundled deep in a coat and hat, but he knew immediately it wasn't Pandora. She moved fluidly, unselfconsciously. This person walked with speed and wariness. Wariness, he thought again, that was evident in the way the head swiveled back and forth before the door was closed again. Without stopping to think, Michael dashed out of the room and down the stairs.

He nearly rammed into Charles at the bottom. "Pandora back?" he demanded.

"No, sir." Relieved that he hadn't been plowed down, Charles rested a hand on the rail. "She said she might stay in town and do some shopping. We shouldn't worry if—"

But Michael was already halfway down the hall.

With a sigh for the agility he hadn't had in thirty years, Charles creaked his way into the drawing room to lay a fire.

The wind hit Michael the moment he stepped outside, reminding him he hadn't stopped for a coat. As he began to race toward the shed, his face chilled and his muscles warmed. There was no one in sight on the grounds. Not surprising, he mused as he slowed his pace just a bit. The woods were close at the edge, and there were a half a dozen easy paths through them.

Some kid poking around? he wondered. Pandora would be lucky if he hadn't pocketed half her pretty stones. It would serve her right.

But he changed his mind the minute he stood in the doorway of her workshop.

Boxes were turned over so that gems and stones and beads were scattered everywhere. Balls of string and twine had been unraveled and twisted and knotted from wall to wall. He had to push some out of his way to step inside. What was usually almost pristine in its order was utter chaos. Gold and silver wire had been bent and snapped, tools lay where they'd been carelessly tossed to the floor.

Michael bent down and picked up an emerald. It glinted sharp and green in his palm. If it had been a thief, he decided, it had been a clumsy and shortsighted one.

"Oh, God!" Pandora dropped her purse with a thud and stared.

When Michael turned, he saw her standing in the doorway, ice pale and rigid. He swore, wishing he'd had a moment to prepare her. "Take it easy," he began as he reached for her arm.

She shoved him aside forcibly and fought her way into the shed. Beads rolled and bounced at her feet. For a moment there was pure shock, disbelief. Then came a white wall of fury. "How could you?" When she turned back to him she was no longer pale. Her color was vivid, her eyes as sharp as the emerald he still held.

Because he was off guard, she nearly landed the first blow. The air whistled by his face as her fist passed. He caught her arms before she tried again. "Just a minute," he began, but she threw herself bodily into him and knocked them both against the wall. Whatever had been left on the shelves shuddered or fell off. It took several moments, and a few bruises on both ends, before he managed to pin her arms back and hold her still.

"Stop it." He pressed her back until she glared up at him, dry-eyed and furious. "You've a right to be upset, but putting a hole in me won't accomplish anything."

"I knew you could be low," she said between her teeth. "But I'd never have believed you could do something so filthy."

"Believe whatever the hell you want," he began, but he felt her body shudder as she fought for control. "Pandora," and his voice softened. "I didn't do this. Look at me," he demanded with a little shake. "Why would I?"

Because she wanted to cry, her voice, her eyes were hard. "You tell me."

Patience wasn't one of his strong points, but he tried again. "Pandora, listen to me. Try for common sense a minute and just listen. I got here a few minutes before you. I saw someone coming out of the shed from my window and came down. When I got here, this is what I found."

She was going to disgrace herself. She felt the tears backing up and hated them. It was better to hate him. "Let go of me."

Perhaps he could handle her anger better than her despair. Cautiously Michael released her arms and stepped back. "It hasn't been more than ten minutes since I saw someone coming out of here. I figured they cut through the woods."

She tried to think, tried to clear the fury out of her head. "You can go," she said with deadly calm. "I have to clean up and take inventory."

Something hot backed up in his throat at the casual dismissal. Remembering his own reaction when he'd opened the shed door, he swallowed it. "I'll call the police if you like, but I don't know if anything was stolen." He opened his palm and showed her the emerald. "I can't imagine any thief leaving stones like this behind."

Pandora snatched it out of his hand. When her fingers closed over it, she felt the slight prick of the hoop she'd fastened onto it only the day before. The emerald seemed to grow out of the braided wire.

Her heart was thudding against her ribs as she walked to her worktable. There was what was left of the necklace she'd been fashioning for two weeks. The deceptively delicate tiers were in pieces, the emeralds that had hung gracefully from them, scattered. Her own nippers had been used to destroy it. She gathered up the pieces in her hands and fought back the urge to scream.

"It was this, wasn't it?" Michael picked up the sketch from the floor. It was stunning on paper—at once fanciful and bold. He supposed what she had drawn had some claim to art. He imagined how he'd feel if someone took scissors to one of his scripts. "You'd nearly finished."

Pandora dropped the pieces back on the table. "Leave me alone." She crouched and began to gather up stones and beads.

"Pandora." When she ignored him, Michael grabbed her by the shoulders and shook. "Dammit, Pandora, I want to help."

She sent him a long, cold look. "You've done enough, Michael. Now leave me alone."

"All right, fine." He released her and stormed out. Anger and frustration carried him halfway across the lawn. Michael stopped, swore and wished bitterly for a cigarette. She had no right to accuse him. Worse, she had no right to make him feel responsible. The guilt he was experiencing was nearly as strong as it would have been if he'd actually vandalized her shop. Hands in his pockets, he stood staring back at the shed and cursing her.

She really thought he'd done that to her. That he was capable of such meaningless, bitter destruction. He'd tried to talk to her, soothe her. Every offer of help had been thrown back at him. Just like her, he thought with his teeth gritted. She deserved to be left alone.

He nearly started back to the house again when he remembered just how shocked and ill she'd looked in the doorway of the shed. Calling himself a fool, he went back.

When he opened the door of the shed again, the chaos was just as it had been. Sitting in the middle of it on the floor by her workbench was Pandora. She was weeping quietly.

He felt the initial male panic at being confronted with feminine tears and surprise that they came from Pandora who never shed them. Yet he felt sympathy for someone who'd been dealt a bull's-eye blow. Without saying a word, he went to her and slipped his arms around her.

She stiffened, but he'd expected it. "I told you to go away."

"Yeah. Why should I listen to you?" He stroked her hair.

She wanted to crawl into his lap and weep for hours. "I don't want you here."

"I know. Just pretend I'm someone else." He drew her against his chest.

"I'm only crying because I'm angry." With a sniff, she turned her face into his shirt.

"Sure." He kissed the top of her head. "Go ahead and be angry for a while. I'm used to it."

She told herself it was because she was weakened by shock and grief, but she relaxed against him. The tears came in floods. When she cried, she cried wholeheartedly. When she was finished, she was done.

Tears dry, she sat cushioned against him. Secure. She wouldn't question it now. Along with the anger came a sense of shame she was unaccustomed to. She'd been filthy to him. But he'd come back and held her. Who'd have expected him to be patient, or caring? Or strong enough to make her accept both. Pandora let out a long breath and kept her eyes shut for just a moment. He smelled of soap and nothing else.

"I'm sorry, Michael."

She was soft. Hadn't he just told himself she wouldn't be? He let his cheek brush against her hair. "Okay."

"No, I mean it." When she turned her head her lips skimmed across his cheek. It surprised them both. That kind of contact was for friends—or lovers. "I couldn't think after I walked in here. I—" She broke off a moment, fascinated by his eyes. Wasn't it strange how small the world could become if you looked into someone's eyes? Why hadn't she ever noticed that before? "I need to sort all this out."

"Yeah." He ran a fingertip down her cheek. She was soft. Softer than he'd let himself believe. "We both do."

It was so easy to settle herself in the crook of his arm. "I can't think."

"No?" Her lips were only an inch from his—too close to ignore, too far to taste. "Let's both not think for a minute."

When he touched his mouth to hers, she didn't draw away but accepted, experimented with the same sense of curiosity that moved through him. It wasn't an explosion or a shock, but a test for both of them. One they'd both known would come sooner or later.

She tasted warm, and her sweetness had a bite. He'd known her so long, shouldn't he have known that? Her body felt primed to move, to act, to race. Soft, yes, she was soft, but not pliant. Perhaps he'd have found pliancy too easy. When he slipped his tongue into her mouth hers met it teasingly, playfully. His stomach knotted. She made him want more, much more of that unapologetically earthy scent, the taut body. His fingers tangled in her hair and tightened.

He was as mysterious and bold as she'd always thought he would be. His hands were firm, his mouth giving. Sometimes she'd wondered what it would be like to meet him on these terms. But she'd always closed her mind before any of the answers could slip through. Michael Donahue was dangerous simply because he was Michael Donahue. By turns he'd attracted and alienated her since they'd been children. It was more than any other man had been able to do for more than a week.

Now, as her mouth explored his, she began to understand why. He was different, for her. She didn't feel altogether safe in his arms, and not completely in control. Pandora had always made certain she was both those things when it came to a man. The scrape of his unshaved cheek didn't annoy her as she'd thought it would. It aroused. The discomfort of the hard floor seemed suitable, as was the quick rush of cold air through the still-open door.

She felt quietly and completely at home. Then the quick nip of his teeth against her lip made her feel as though she'd just stepped on uncharted land. New territory was what she'd been raised on, and yet, in all her experience, she'd never explored anything so unique, so exotic or so comfortable.

She wanted to go on and knew she had to stop.

Together they drew away.

"Well." She scrambled for composure as she folded her hands in her lap. Be casual, she ordered herself while her pulse thudded at her wrists. Be careless. She couldn't afford to say anything that might make him laugh at her. "That's been coming for a while, I suppose."

He felt as though he'd just slid down a roller coaster without a cart. "I suppose." He studied her a moment, curious and a bit unnerved. When he saw her fingers twist together he felt a small sense of satisfaction. "It wasn't altogether what I'd expected."

"Things rarely are." Too many surprises for one day, Pandora decided, and rose unsteadily to her feet. She made the mistake of looking around and nearly sunk to the floor again.

"Pandora—"

"No, don't worry." She shook her head as he rose. "I'm not going to fall apart again." Concentrating on breathing evenly, she took one long look at her workshop. "It looks like you were right about the locks. I suppose I should be grateful you haven't said I told you so."

"Maybe I would if it applied." Michael picked up the emeralds scattered on her table. "I'm no expert, cousin, but I'd say these are worth a few thousand."

"So?" She frowned as her train of thought began to march with his. "No thief would've left them behind." Reaching down, she picked up a handful of stones. Among them were two top-grade diamonds. "Or these."

As was his habit, he began to put the steps together in a sort of mental scenario. Action and reaction, motive and result. "I'd wager once you've inventoried, you won't be missing anything. Whoever did this didn't want to risk more than breaking and entering and vandalism."

With a huff, she sat down on her table. "You think it was one of the family."

"'They said it wouldn't last,'" he quoted, and stuck his hands in his pockets. "You may've had something there, Pandora. Something neither of us considered when we were setting out the guidelines. None of them believed we'd be able to get through six months together. The fact is, we've gotten through the first two weeks without a hitch. It could make one of them nervous enough to want to throw in a complication. What was your first reaction when you saw all this?"

She dragged her hand through her hair. "That you'd done it for spite. Exactly what our kith and kin would expect me to think. Dammit, I hate to be predictable."

"You outsmarted them once your mind cleared."

She sent him a quick look, not certain if she should thank him or apologize again. It was best to do neither. "Biff," Pandora decided with relish. "This sort of low-minded trick would be just up his alley."

"I'd only vote for Biff if you find a few rocks missing." Michael rocked back on his heels. "He'd never be able to resist picking up a few glitters that could be liquidated into nice clean cash."

"True enough." Uncle Carlson—no, it seemed a bit crude for his style. Ginger would've been too fascinated with the sparkles to have done any more than fondle. Pulling a hand through her hair, she tried to picture one of her bland, civilized relations wielding a pair of nippers. "Well, I don't suppose it matters a great deal which one of them did it. They've put me two weeks behind on my commission." Again she picked up pieces of thin gold. "It'll never be quite the same," she murmured. "Nothing is when it's done over."

"Sometimes it's better."

With a shake of her head, she walked over to a heater. If he gave her any more sympathy now, she wouldn't be able to trust herself. "One way or the other I've got to get started. Tell Sweeney I won't make it in for lunch."

"I'll help you clean this up."

"No." She turned back when he started to frown. "No, really, Michael, I appreciate it. I need to be busy. And alone."

He didn't like it, but understood. "All right. I'll see you at dinner."

"Michael…" He paused at the doorway and looked back. Amid the confusion she looked strong and vivid. He nearly closed the door and went back to her. "Maybe Uncle Jolley was right."

"About what?"

"You may have one or two redeeming qualities."

He smiled at her then, quick and dashing. "Uncle Jolley was always right, cousin. That's why he's still pulling the strings."

Pandora waited until the door shut again. Pulling the strings he was, she mused. "But you're not playing matchmaker with my life," she mumbled. "I'm staying free, single and unattached. Just get that through your head."

She wasn't superstitious, but Pandora almost thought she heard her uncle's high, cackling laugh. She rolled up her sleeves and got to work.

Chapter 4

Because after a long, tedious inventory Pandora discovered nothing missing, she vetoed Michael's notion of calling in the police. If something had been stolen, she'd have seen the call as a logical step. As it was, she decided the police would poke and prod around and lecture on the lack of locks. If the vandal had been one of the family—and she had to agree with Michael's conclusion there—a noisy, official investigation would give the break-in too much importance and undoubtedly too much publicity.

Yes, the press would have a field day. Pandora had already imagined the headlines. "Family vs. family in the battle of eccentric's will." There was, under her independent and straightforward nature, a prim part of her that felt family business was private business.

If one or more of the members of the family were

keeping an eye on Jolley's Folley and the goings-on there, Pandora wanted them to think that she'd brushed off the vandalism as petty and foolish. As a matter of pride, she didn't want anyone to believe she'd been dealt a stunning blow. As a matter of practicality, she didn't want anyone to know that she had her eyes open. She was determined to find out who had broken into her shop and how they'd managed to pick such a perfect time for it.

Michael hadn't insisted on calling the police because his thoughts had run along the same lines as Pandora's. He'd managed, through a lot of maneuvering and silence, to keep his career totally separate from his family. In his business, he was known as Michael Donahue, award-winning writer, not Michael Donahue, relative of Jolley McVie, multimillionaire. He wanted to keep it that way.

Stubbornly, each had refused to tell the other of their reasons or their plans for some personal detective work. It wasn't so much a matter of trust, but more the fact that neither of them felt the other could do the job competently. So instead, they kept the conversation light through one of Sweeney's four-star meals and let the vandalism rest. More important, they carefully avoided any reference that might trigger some remark about what had happened on a more personal level in Pandora's workshop.

After two glasses of wine and a generous portion of chicken fricassee, Pandora felt more optimistic. It would have been much worse if any of her stock or tools had been taken. That would have meant a trip into Manhattan and days, perhaps weeks of delay. As it was, the worst crime that she could see was the fact that she'd been spied on. Surely that was the only explanation for the break-in coinciding so perfectly with her trip to town. And that would be her first order of business.

"I wonder," Pandora began, probing lightly, "if the Saundersons are in residence for the winter."

"The neighbors with the pond." Michael had thought of the Saunderson place himself. There were certain points on that property where, with a good set of binoculars, someone could watch the Folley easily. "They spend a lot of time in Europe, don't they?"

"Hmm." Pandora toyed with her chicken. "He's in hotels, you know. They tend to pop off here or there for weeks at a time."

"Do they ever rent the place out?"

"Oh, not that I know of. I'm under the impression that they leave a skeleton staff there even when they fly off. Now that I think of it, they were home a few months ago." The memory made her smile. "Uncle Jolley and I went fishing and Saunderson nearly caught us. If we hadn't scrambled back to the cabin—" She broke off as the thought formed.

"Cabin." Michael picked up where she'd left off. "That old two-room wreck Jolley was going to use as a hunting lodge during his eat-off-the-land stage? I'd forgotten all about it."

Pandora shrugged as though it meant nothing while her mind raced ahead. "He ended up eating more beans than game. In any case, we caught a bundle of trout, ate like pigs and sent the rest along to Saunderson. He never sent a thank-you note."

"Poor manners."

"Well, I've heard his grandmother was a barmaid in Chelsea. More wine?"

"No, thanks." He thought it best to keep a clear head if he was going to carry out the plans that were just beginning to form. "Help yourself."

Pandora set the bottle down and sent him a sweet smile. "No, I'm fine. Just a bit tired really."

"You're entitled." It would clear his path beautifully if he could ship her off to bed early. "What you need is a good night's sleep."

"I'm sure you're right." Both of them were too involved with their own moves to notice how excruciatingly polite the conversation had become. "I'll just skip coffee tonight and go have a bath." She feigned a little yawn. "What about you? Planning to work late?"

"No—no, I think I'll get a fresh start in the morning."

"Well then." Pandora rose, still smiling. She'd give it an hour, she calculated, then she'd be out and gone. "I'm going up. Good night, Michael."

"Good night." Once the light in her room was off, he decided, he'd be on his way.

Pandora sat in her darkened room for exactly fifteen minutes and just listened. All she had to do was get outside without being spotted. The rest would be easy. Opening her door a crack, she held her breath, waited and listened a little longer. Not a sound. It was now or never, she decided and bundled into her coat. Into the deep pockets, she shoved a flashlight, two books of matches and a small can of hair spray. As good as mace, Pandora figured, if you ran into something unfriendly. She crept out into the hall and started slowly down the stairs, her back to the wall.

An adventure, she thought, feeling the familiar pulse

of excitement and anxiety. She hadn't had one since Uncle Jolley died. As she let herself out one of the side doors, she thought how much he'd have enjoyed this one. The moon was only a sliver, but the sky was full of stars. The few clouds that spread over them were hardly more than transparent wisps. And the air—she took a deep breath—was cool and crisp as an apple. With a quick glance over her shoulder at Michael's window, she started toward the woods.

The starlight couldn't help her there. Though the trees were bare, the branches were thick enough to block out big chunks of sky. She dug out her flashlight and, turning it side to side, found the edges of the path. She didn't hurry. If she rushed, the adventure would be over too soon. She walked slowly, listened and imagined.

There were sounds—the breeze blew through pine needles and scattered the dry leaves. Now and again there was a skuttle in the woods to the right or left. A fox, a raccoon, a bear not quite settled down to hibernate? Pandora liked not being quite certain. If you walked through the woods alone, in the dark, and didn't have some sense of wonder, it was hardly worth the trip.

She liked the smells—pine, earth, the hint of frost that would settle on the ground before morning. She liked the sense of being alone, and more, of having something up ahead that warranted her attention.

The path forked, and she swung to the left. The cabin wasn't much farther. She stopped once, certain she'd heard something move up ahead that was too big to be considered a fox. For a moment she had a few uncomfortable thoughts about bears and bobcats. It was one thing to speculate and another to have to deal with them. Then there was nothing. Shaking her head, Pandora went on.

What would she do if she got to the cabin, and it wasn't dusty and deserted? What would she do if she actually found one of her dear, devoted relatives had set up housekeeping? Uncle Carlson reading the *Wall Street Journal* by the fire? Aunt Patience fussing around the rocky wooden table with a dust cloth? The thought was almost laughable. Almost, until Pandora remembered her workshop.

Drawing her brows together, she walked forward. If someone was there, they were going to answer to her. In moments, the shadow of the cabin loomed up before her. It looked as it was supposed to look, desolate, deserted, eerie. She kept her flashlight low as she crept toward the porch, then nearly let out a scream when her own weight caused the narrow wooden stair to creak. She held a hand to her heart until it no longer felt as though it would break her ribs. Then slowly, quietly, stealthily, she reached for the doorknob and twisted it.

The door moaned itself open. Wincing at the sound, Pandora counted off ten seconds before she took the next step. With a quick sweep of her light, she stepped in.

When the arm came around her neck, she dropped the flashlight with a clatter. It rolled over the floor, sending an erratic beam over the log walls and brick fireplace. Even as she drew the breath to scream, she reached in her pocket for the hair spray. After she was whirled around, she found herself face-to-face with Michael. His fist was poised inches from her face, her can inches from his. Both of them stood just as they were.

"Dammit!" Michael dropped his arm. "What are you doing here?"

"What are you doing here?" she tossed back. "And what do you mean by grabbing me that way? You may've broken my flashlight."

"I almost broke your nose."

Pandora shook back her hair and walked over to retrieve her light. She didn't want him to see her hands tremble. "Well, I certainly think you should find out who someone is before you throw a headlock on them."

"You followed me."

She sent him a cool, amused look. It helped to be able to do so when her stomach was still quaking. "Don't flatter yourself. I simply wanted to see if something was going on out here, and I didn't want you to interfere."

"Interfere." He shone his own light directly in her face so that she had to throw up a hand in defense. "And what the hell were you going to do if something was going on? Overpower them?"

She thought of how easily he'd taken her by surprise. It only made her lift her chin higher. "I can take care of myself."

"Sure." He glanced down at the can she still held. "What have you got there?"

Having forgotten it, Pandora looked down herself, then had to stifle a chuckle. Oh, how Uncle Jolley would've appreciated the absurdity. "Hair spray," she said very precisely. "Right between the eyes."

He swore, then laughed. He couldn't have written a scene so implausible. "I guess I should be glad you didn't get a shot off at me."

"I look before I pounce." Pandora dropped the can

back into her pocket. "Well, since we're here, we might as well look around."

"I was doing just that when I heard your catlike approach." She wrinkled her nose at him, but he ignored her. "It looks like someone's been making themselves at home." To prove his point, Michael shone his light at the fireplace. Half-burnt logs still smoldered.

"Well, well." With her own light, Pandora began to walk around the cabin. The last time she'd been there, the chair with the broken rung had been by the window. Jolley had sat there himself, keeping a lookout for Saunderson while she'd opened a tin of sardines to ward off starvation. Now the chair was pulled up near the fire. "A vagrant, perhaps."

Watching her, Michael nodded. "Perhaps."

"But not likely. Suppose they'll be back?"

"Hard to say." The casual glance showed nothing out of place. The cabin was neat and tidy. Too tidy. The floor and table surfaces should have had a film of dust. Everything had been wiped clean. "It could be they've done all the damage they intend to do."

Disgruntled, Pandora plopped down on the bunk and dropped her chin in her hands. "I'd hoped to catch them."

"And what? Zap them with environmentally safe hair spray?"

She glared up at him. "I suppose you had a better plan."

"I think I might've made them a bit more uncomfortable."

"Black eyes and broken noses." She made an impatient sound. "Really, Michael, you should try to get your mind out of your fists."

"I suppose you just wanted to talk reasonably with whichever member of our cozy family played search and destroy with your workshop."

She started to snap, caught herself, then smiled. It was the slow, wicked smile Michael could never help admiring. "No," she admitted. "Reason wasn't high on my list. Still, it appears we've both missed our chance for brute force. Well, you write the detective stories—so to speak—shouldn't we look for clues?"

His lips curved in something close to a sneer. "I didn't think to bring my magnifying glass."

"You can almost be amusing when you put your mind to it." Rising, Pandora began to shine her light here and there. "They might've dropped something."

"A name tag?"

"Something," she muttered, and dropped to her knees to look under the bunk. "Aha!" Hunkering down, she grabbed at something.

"What is it?" Michael was beside her before she'd straightened up.

"A shoe." Feeling foolish and sentimental, she held it in both hands. "It's nothing. It was Uncle Jolley's."

Because she looked lost, and more vulnerable than he'd expected, Michael offered the only comfort he knew. "I miss him, too."

She sat a moment, the worn sneaker in her lap. "You know, sometimes it's as though I can almost feel him. As though he's around the next corner, in the next room, waiting to pop up and laugh at the incredible joke he's played."

With a quick laugh, Michael rubbed a hand over her back. "I know what you mean."

Pandora looked at him, steady, measuring. "Maybe

you do," she murmured. Briskly she set the sneaker on the bunk and rose. "I'll have a look in the cupboards."

"Let me know if you find any cookies." He met the look she tossed over her shoulder with a shrug. "In the early stages of nonsmoking, you need a lot of oral satisfaction."

"You ought to try chewing gum." Pandora opened a cupboard and shone her light over jars and cans. There was peanut butter, chunky, and caviar, Russian. Two of Jolley's favorite snacks. She passed over taco sauce and jumbo fruit cocktail, remembering that her ninety-three-year-old uncle had had the appetite of a teenager. Then reaching in, she plucked out a can and held it up.

"Aha!"

"Again?"

"Tuna fish," Pandora announced waving the can at Michael. "It's a can of tuna."

"Right you are. Any mayo to go with it?"

"Don't be dense, Michael. Uncle Jolley hated tuna."

Michael started to say something sarcastic, then stopped. "He did, didn't he?" he said slowly. "And he never kept anything around he didn't like."

"Exactly."

"Congratulations, Sherlock. Now which of the suspects has an affection for canned fish?"

"You're just jealous because I found a clue and you didn't."

"It's only a clue," Michael pointed out, a little annoyed at being outdone by an amateur, "if you can do something with it."

He'd never give her credit, she thought, for anything, not her craft, her intelligence and never her womanhood. There was an edge to her voice when she spoke again. "If you're so pessimistic, why did you come out here?"

"I was hoping to find someone." Restless, Michael moved his light from wall to wall. "As it is all we've done is prove someone was here and gone."

Pandora dropped the can of tuna in disgust. "A waste of time."

"You shouldn't've followed me out."

"I didn't follow you out." She shone her light back at him. He looked too male, too dangerous in the shadows. She wished, only briefly, that she had the spectacular build and stunning style that would bring him whimpering to his knees. Their breath came in clouds and merged together. "For all I know, you followed me."

"Oh, I see. That's why I was here first."

"Beside the point. If you'd planned to come out here tonight, why didn't you tell me?"

He came closer. But if he came too close to her, he discovered, he began to feel something, something like an itch along the skin. Try to scratch it, he reminded himself, and she'd rub you raw in seconds. "For the same reason you didn't tell me. I don't trust you, cousin. You don't trust me."

"At least we can agree on something." She started to brush by him and found her arm captured. In one icy movement, she tilted her head down to look at his hand, then up to look at his face. "That's a habit you should try to break, Michael."

"They say when you break one habit, you pick up another."

The ice in Pandora's voice never changed, but her blood was warming. "Do they?"

"You're easier to touch than I'd once thought, Pandora."

"Don't be too sure, Michael." She took a step back, not in retreat, she told herself. It was a purely offensive move. Still, he moved with her.

"Some women have trouble dealing with physical attraction."

The temper that flared in her eyes appealed to him as much as the passion he'd seen there briefly that afternoon. "Your ego's showing again. This dominant routine might work very well with your centerfolds, but—"

"You've always had an odd fascination with my sex life." Michael grinned at her, pleased to see frustration flit over her face.

"The same kind of educated fascination one has with the sex lives of lower mammals." It infuriated her that her heart was racing. And not from anger. She was too honest to pretend it was anger. She'd come looking for an adventure, and she'd found one. "It's getting late," she said, using the tone of a parochial schoolteacher to a disruptive student. "You'll have to excuse me."

"I've never asked about your sex life." When she took another step away, he boxed her neatly into a corner. Pandora's hand slipped into her pocket and rested on the can of hair spray. "Let me guess. You prefer a man with a string of initials after his name who philosophizes about sex more than he acts on it."

"Why, you pompous, arrogant—"

Michael shut her mouth the way he'd once fantasized. With his own.

The kiss was no test this time, but torrid, hot, edging toward desperate. Whatever she might feel, she'd dissect later. Now she'd accept the experience. His mouth was warm, firm, and he used it with the same cocky male confidence that would have infuriated her at any other time. Now she met it with her own.

He was strong, insistent. For the first time Pandora felt herself body to body with a man who wouldn't treat her delicately. He demanded, expected and gave a completely uninhibited physicality. Pandora didn't have to think her way through the kiss. She didn't have to think at all.

He'd expected her to rear back and take a swing at him. Her instant and full response left him reeling. Later Michael would recall that nothing as basic and simple as a kiss had made his head spin for years.

She packed a punch, but she did it with soft lips. If she knew just how quickly she'd knocked him out, would she gloat? He wouldn't think of it now. He wouldn't think of anything now. Without a moment's hesitation, he buried his consciousness in her and let the senses rule.

The cabin was cold and dark without even a single stream of moonlight for romance. It smelled of dying smoke and settling dust. The wind had kicked up enough to moan grumpily at the windows. Neither of them noticed. Even when they broke apart, neither of them noticed.

He wasn't steady. That was something else he'd think about later. At least he had the satisfaction of seeing she wasn't steady, either. She looked as he felt, stunned, off balance and unable to set for the next blow. Needing some equilibrium, he grinned at her.

"You were saying?"

She wanted to slug him. She wanted to kiss him again until he didn't have the strength to grin. He'd expect her to fall at his feet as other women probably did. He'd expect her to sigh and smile and surrender so he'd have one more victory. Instead she snapped, "Idiot."

"I love it when you're succinct."

"Rule number six," Pandora stated, aiming a killing look. "No physical contact."

"No physical contact," Michael agreed as she stomped toward the doorway, "unless both parties enjoy it."

She slammed the door and left him grinning.

When two people are totally involved in their own projects, they can live under the same roof for days at a time and rarely see each other. Especially if the roof is enormous and the people very stubborn. Pandora and Michael brushed together at meals and otherwise left each other alone. This wasn't out of any sense of politeness or consideration. It was simply because each of them was too busy to heckle the other.

Separately, however, each felt a smug satisfaction when the first month passed. One down, five to go.

When they were into their second month, Michael drove into New York for a day to handle a problem with a script that had to be dealt with personally. He left, cross as a bear and muttering about imbeciles. Pandora prepared to enjoy herself tremendously in his absence. She wouldn't have to keep up her guard or share the Folley for hours. She could do anything she wanted without worrying about anyone coming to look over her shoulder or make a caustic remark. It would be wonderful.

She ended up picking at her dinner, then watching for his car through the heavy brocade drapes. Not because she missed *him*, she assured herself. It was just that she'd become used to having someone in the house.

Wasn't that one of the reasons she'd never lived with anyone before? She wanted to avoid any sense of dependence. And dependence, she decided, was natural when you shared the same space—even when it was with a two-legged snake.

So she waited, and she watched. Long after Charles and Sweeney had gone to bed, she continued to wait and watch. She wasn't concerned, and certainly not lonely. Only restless. She told herself she didn't go to bed herself because she wasn't tired. Wandering the first floor, she walked into Jolley's den. Game room would have been a more appropriate name. The decor was a cross between video arcade and disco lounge with its state-of-the-art components and low, curved-back sofas.

She turned on the huge, fifty-four-inch television, then left it on the first show that appeared. She wasn't going to *watch* it. She just wanted the company.

There were two pinball tables where she passed nearly an hour trying to beat the high scores Jolley had left behind. Another legacy. Then there was an arcade-size video game that simulated an attack on the planet Zarbo. Under her haphazard defense system, the planet blew up three times before she moved on. There was computerized chess, but she thought her mind too sluggish to take it on. In the end she stretched out on the six-foot sofa in front of the television. Just to rest, not to watch.

Within moments, she was hooked on the late-night syndication of a cop show. Squealing tires and blasting bullets. Head pillowed on her arms, one leg thrown over the top of the sofa, she relaxed and let herself be entertained.

When Michael came to the doorway, she didn't notice him. He'd had a grueling day and had hit some nasty traffic on the drive back. The fact was he'd considered staying in the city overnight—the sensible thing to do. He'd found himself making a dozen weak excuses why he had to go back instead of accepting the invitation of the assistant producer—a tidily built brunette with big brown eyes.

He'd intended to crawl upstairs, fall into his bed and sleep until noon, but he'd seen the lights and heard the racket. Now, here was Pandora, self-proclaimed critic of the small screen, sprawled on a sofa watching reruns at one in the morning. She looked suspiciously as though she were enjoying herself.

Not a bad show, Michael mused, recognizing the series. In fact, he'd written a couple of scripts for it in his early days. The central character had a sly sort of wit and a fumbling manner that caused the perpetrator to spill out enough information for an arrest by the end of the show.

Michael watched Pandora as she shifted comfortably on the couch. He waited until the commercial break. "Well, how the mighty have fallen."

She nearly did, rolling quickly to look back toward the doorway. She sat up, scowled and searched her mind for a plausible excuse. "I couldn't sleep," she told him, which was true enough. She wouldn't add it was because he hadn't been home. "I suppose television is made for the insomniac. Valium for the mind."

He was tired, bone tired, but he realized how glad he was she'd had a comeback. He came over, plopped down beside her and propped his feet on a coffee table made out of a fat log. "Who done it?" he asked, and sighed. It was good to be home.

"The greedy business partner." She was too pleased to have him back to be embarrassed. "There's really very little challenge in figuring out the answers."

"This show wasn't based on the premise of figuring out who did the crime, but in how the hero maneuvers them into betraying themselves."

She pretended she wasn't interested, but shifted so that she could still see the screen. "So, how did things go in New York?"

"They went." Michael pried off one shoe with the toe of the other. "After several hours of hair tearing and blame casting, the script's intact."

He looked tired. Really tired, she realized, and unbent enough to take off his other shoe. He merely let out a quick grunt of appreciation. "I don't understand why people would get all worked up about one silly hour a week."

He opened one eye to stare at her. "It's the American way."

"What's there to get so excited about? You have a crime, the good guys chase the bad guys and catch them before the final credits. Seems simple enough."

"I can't thank you enough for clearing that up. I'll point it out at the next production meeting."

"Really, Michael, it seems to me things should run fairly smoothly, especially since you've been on the air with this thing for years."

"Know anything about ego and paranoia?"

She smiled a little. "I've heard of them."

"Well, multiply that with artistic temperament, the

ratings race and an escalating budget. Don't forget to drop in a good dose of network executives. Things haven't run smoothly for four years. If *Logan* goes another four, it still won't run smoothly. That's show biz."

Pandora moved her shoulders. "It seems a foolish way to make a living."

"Ain't it just," Michael agreed, and fell sound asleep.

She let him doze for the next twenty minutes while she watched the sly, fumbling cop tighten the ropes on the greedy business partner. Satisfied that justice had been done, Pandora rose to switch off the set and dim the lights.

She could leave him here, she considered as she watched Michael sleep. He looked comfortable enough at the moment. She thought about it as she walked over to brush his hair from his forehead. But he'd probably wake up with a stiff neck and a nasty disposition. Better get him upstairs into bed, she decided, and shook his shoulder.

"Michael."

"Mmm?"

"Let's go to bed."

"Thought you'd never ask," he mumbled, and reached halfheartedly for her.

Amused, she shook him harder. "Never let your reach exceed your grasp. Come on, cousin, I'll help you upstairs."

"The director's a posturing idiot," he grumbled as she dragged him to his feet.

"I'm sure he is. Now, see if you can put one foot in front of the other. That's the way. Here we go." With an arm around his waist, she began to lead him from the room.

"He kept screwing around with my script."

"Of all the nerve. Here come the steps."

"Said he wanted more emotional impact in the second act. Bleaches his hair," Michael muttered as she half pulled him up the steps. "Lot he knows about emotional impact."

"Obviously a mental midget." Breathlessly she steered him toward his room. He was heavier than he looked. "Here we are now, home again." With a little strategy and a final burst of will, she shoved him onto the bed. "There now, isn't that cozy?" Leaving him fully dressed, she spread an afghan over him.

"Aren't you going to take my pants off?"

She patted his head. "Not a chance."

"Spoilsport."

"If I helped you undress this late at night, I'd probably have nightmares."

"You know you're crazy about me." The bed felt like heaven. He could've burrowed in it for a week.

"You're getting delirious, Michael. I'll have Charles bring you some warm tea and honey in the morning."

"Not if you want to live." He roused himself to open his eyes and smile at her. "Why don't you crawl in beside me? With a little encouragement, I could show you the time of your life."

Pandora leaned closer, closer, until her mouth was inches from his. Their breath mixed quickly, intimately. She hovered there a moment while her hair fell forward and brushed his cheek. "In a pig's eye," she whispered.

Michael shrugged, yawned and rolled over. "'Kay."

In the dark, Pandora stood for a moment with her

hands on her hips. At least he could've acted insulted. Chin up, she walked out—making sure she slammed the door at her back.

Chapter 5

Tier by painstaking tier, Pandora had completed the emerald necklace. When it was finished, she was pleased to judge it perfect. This judgment pleased her particularly because she was her own toughest critic. Pandora didn't feel emotionally attached or creatively satisfied by every piece she made. With the necklace, she felt both. She examined it under a magnifying glass, held it up in harsh light, went over the filigree inch by inch and found no flaws. Out of her own imagination she'd conceived it, then with her own skill created it. With a kind of regret, she boxed the necklace in a bed of cotton. It wasn't hers any longer.

With the necklace done, she looked around her workshop without inspiration. She'd put so much into that one piece, all her concentration, her emotion, her skill. She hadn't made a single plan for the next project. Restless, wanting to work, she picked up her pad and began to sketch.

Earrings perhaps, she mused. Something bold and chunky and ornate. She wanted a change after the fine, elegant work she'd devoted so much time to. Circles and triangles, she thought. Something geometric and blatantly modern. Nothing romantic like the necklace.

Romantic, she mused, and sketched strong, definite lines. She'd been working with a romantic piece; perhaps that's why she'd nearly made a fool of herself with Michael. Her emotions were involved with her work, and her work had been light and feminine and romantic. It made sense, she decided, satisfied. Now, she'd work with something strong and brash and arrogant. That should solve the problem.

There shouldn't be a problem in the first place. Teeth gritted, she flipped a page and started over. Her feelings for Michael had always been very definite. Intolerance. If you were intolerant of someone, it went against the grain to be attracted to him.

It wasn't real attraction in any case. It was more some sort of twisted...curiosity. Yes, curiosity. The word satisfied her completely. She'd been curious, naturally enough, to touch on the sexuality of a man she'd known since childhood. Curious, again naturally, to find out what it was about Michael Donahue that attracted all those poster girls. She'd found out.

So he had a way of making a woman feel utterly a woman, utterly involved, utterly willing. It wasn't something that had happened to her before nor something she'd looked for. As Pandora saw it, it was a kind of skill. She decided he'd certainly honed it as meticulously as any craftsman. Though she found it difficult to fault him for that, *she* wasn't about to fall in with the horde. If he knew, if he even suspected, that she'd had the same reaction to him that she imagined dozens of other women had, he'd gloat for a month. If he guessed that from time to time she'd wished—just for a moment—that he'd think of her the way he thought of those dozens of other women, he'd gloat for twice as long. She wouldn't give him the pleasure.

Individuality was part of her makeup. She didn't want to be one of his women, even if she could. Now that her curiosity had been satisfied, they'd get through the next five months without any more...complications.

Just because she'd found him marginally acceptable as a human being, almost tolerable as a companion wouldn't get in the way. It would, if anything, make the winter pass a bit easier.

And when she caught herself putting the finishing touches on a sketch of Michael's face, she was appalled. The lines were true enough, though rough. She'd had no trouble capturing the arrogance around the eyes or the sensitivity around the mouth. Odd, she realized; she'd sketched him to look intelligent. She ripped the sheet from her pad, crumpled it up in a ball and tossed it into the trash. Her mind had wandered, that was all. Pandora picked up her pencil again, put it down, then dug the sketch out again. Art was art, after all, she told herself as she smoothed out Michael's face.

He wasn't having a great deal of success with his own work. Michael sat at his desk and typed like a maniac for five minutes. Then he stared into space for fifteen. It wasn't like him. When he worked, he worked steadily, competently, smoothly until the scene was set.

Leaning back in his chair, he picked up a pencil and ran his fingers from end to end. Whatever the statistics said, he should never have given up smoking. That's what had him so edgy. Restless, he pushed away from the desk and wandered over to the window. He stared down at Pandora's workshop. It looked cheerful under a light layer of snow that was hardly more than a dusting. The windows were blank.

That's what had him so edgy.

She wasn't what he'd expected. She was softer, sweeter. Warmer. She was fun to talk to, whether she was arguing and snipping and keeping you on the edge of temper, or whether she was being easy and companionable. There wasn't an overflow of small talk with Pandora. There weren't any trite conversations. She kept your mind working, even if it was in defense of her next barb.

It wasn't easy to admit that he actually enjoyed her company. But the weeks they'd been together at the Folley had gone quickly. No, it wasn't easy to admit he liked being with her, but he'd turned down an interesting invitation from his assistant producer because...

Because, Michael admitted on a long breath, he hadn't wanted to spend the night with one woman when he'd known his thoughts would have been on another.

Just how was he going to handle this unwanted and unexpected attraction to a woman who'd rather put on the gloves and go a few rounds than walk in the moonlight?

Romantic women had always appealed to him because he was, unashamedly, a romantic himself. He enjoyed candlelight, quiet music, long, lonely walks. Michael courted women in old-fashioned ways because he felt comfortable with old-fashioned ways. It didn't interfere with the fact that he was, and had been since college, a staunch feminist. Romance and sociopolitical views were worlds apart. He had no trouble balancing equal pay for equal work against offering a woman a carriage ride through the park.

And he knew if he sent Pandora a dozen white roses, she'd complain about the thorns.

He wanted her. Michael was too much a creature of the senses to pretend otherwise. When he wanted something, he worked toward it in one of two ways. First, he planned out the best approach, then took the steps one at a time, maneuvering subtly. If that didn't work, he tossed out subtlety and went after it with both hands. He'd had just as much success the first way as the second.

As he saw it, Pandora wouldn't respond to patience and posies. She wouldn't go for being swept off her feet, either. With Pandora, he might just have to toss his two usual approaches and come up with a whole new third.

An interesting challenge, Michael decided with a slow smile. He liked nothing better than arranging and rearranging plot lines and shifting angles. And hadn't he always thought Pandora would make a fascinating character? So, he'd work it like a screenplay.

Hero and heroine living as housemates, he began. Attracted to each other but reluctant. Hero is intelligent, charming. Has tremendous willpower. Hadn't he given up smoking—five weeks, three days and fourteen hours ago? Heroine is stubborn and opinionated, often mistakes arrogance for independence. Hero gradually cracks through her brittle shield to their mutual satisfaction.

Michael leaned back in his chair and grinned. He might just make it a play. A great deal of the action would be ad-lib, of course, but he had the general theme. Satisfied, and looking forward to the opening scene, Michael went back to work with a vengeance.

Two hours breezed by with Michael working steadily. He answered the knock at his door with a grunt.

"I beg your pardon, Mr. Donahue." Charles, slightly out of breath from the climb up the stairs, stood in the doorway.

Michael gave another grunt and finished typing the paragraph. "Yes, Charles?"

"Message for you, sir."

"Message?" Scowling, he swiveled around in the chair. If there was a problem in New York—as there was at least once a week—the phone was the quickest way to solve it. "Thanks." He took the message, but only flapped it against his palm. "Pandora still out in her shop?"

"Yes, sir." Grateful for the chance to rest, Charles expanded a bit. "Sweeney is a bit upset that Miss McVie missed lunch. She intends to serve dinner in an hour. I hope that suits your schedule."

Michael knew better than to make waves where Sweeney was concerned. "I'll be down."

"Thank you, sir, and if I may say, I enjoy your television show tremendously. This week's episode was particularly exciting."

"I appreciate that, Charles."

"It was Mr. McVie's habit to watch it every week in my company. He never missed an episode."

"There probably wouldn't have been a *Logan's Run* without Jolley," Michael mused. "I miss him."

"We all do. The house seems so quiet. But I—" Charles reddened a bit at the thought of overstepping his bounds.

"Go ahead, Charles."

"I'd like you to know that both Sweeney and I are pleased to remain in your service, yours and Miss McVie's. We were glad when Mr. McVie left you the house. The others..." He straightened his back and plunged on. "They wouldn't have been suitable, sir. Sweeney and I had both discussed resigning if Mr. McVie had chosen to leave the Folley to one of his other heirs." Charles folded his bony hands. "Will there be anything else before dinner, sir?"

"No, Charles. Thank you."

Message in hand, Michael leaned back as Charles went out. The old butler had known him since childhood. Michael could remember distinctly when Charles had stopped calling him Master Donahue. He'd been sixteen and visiting the Folley during the summer months. Charles had called him Mr. Donahue and Michael had felt as though he'd just stepped from childhood, over adolescence and into adulthood.

Strange how much of his life had been involved with the Folley and the people who were a part of it. Charles had served him his first whisky—with dignity if not approval on his eighteenth birthday. Years before that, Sweeney had given him his first ear boxing. His parents had never bothered to swat him and his tutors wouldn't have dared. Michael still remembered that after the sting had eased, he'd felt like part of a family.

Pandora had been both bane and fantasy during his adolescence. Apparently that hadn't changed as much as Michael had thought. And Jolley. Jolley had been father, grandfather, friend, son and brother.

Jolley had been Jolley, and Michael had spoken no less than the truth when he'd told Charles he missed the old man. In some part of himself, he always would. Thinking of other things, Michael tore open the message.

Your mother is gravely ill. The doctors are not hopeful. Make arrangements to fly to Palm Springs immediately. L. J. KEYSER.

Michael stared at the message for nearly a minute. It wasn't possible; his mother was never ill. She considered it something of a social flaw. He felt a moment's disbelief, a moment's shock. He was reaching for the phone before either had worn off.

When Pandora walked by his room fifteen minutes later, she saw him tossing clothes into a bag. She lifted a brow, leaned against the jamb and cleared her throat. "Going somewhere?"

"Palm Springs." He tossed in his shaving kit.

"Really?" Now she folded her arms. "Looking for a sunnier climate?"

"It's my mother. Her husband sent me a message."

Instantly she dropped her cool, sarcastic pose and came into the room. "Is she ill?"

"The message didn't say much, but it doesn't sound good."

"Oh, Michael, I'm sorry. Can I do anything? Call the airport?"

"I've already done it. I've got a flight in a couple of

hours. They're routing me through half a dozen cities, but it was the best I could do."

Feeling helpless, she watched him zip up his bag. "I'll drive you to the airport if you like."

"No, thanks anyway." He dragged a hand through his hair as he turned to face her. The concern was there, though he realized she'd only met his mother once, ten, perhaps fifteen years before. The concern was for him and unexpectedly solid. "Pandora, it's going to take me half the night to get to the coast. And then I don't know——" He broke off, not able to imagine his mother seriously ill. "I might not be able to make it back in time—not in forty-eight hours."

She shook her head. "I don't want you to think about it. I'll call Fitzhugh and explain. Maybe he'll be able to do something. After all, it's an emergency. If he can't, he can't."

He was taking a step that could pull millions of dollars out from under her. Millions of dollars and the home she loved. Torn, Michael went to her and rested his hands on her shoulders. She was so slender. He'd forgotten just how fragile a strong woman could be. "I'm sorry, Pandora. If there was any other way..."

"Michael, I told you I didn't want the money. I meant it."

He studied her a moment. Yes, the strength was there, the stubbornness and the basic goodness he often overlooked. "I believe you did," he murmured.

"As for the rest, well, we'll see. Now go ahead before you miss your plane." She waited until he'd grabbed his bag then walked with him to the hall. "Call me if you get the chance and let me know how your mother is."

He nodded, started for the stairs, then stopped. Setting his bag down, he came back and pulled her against him. The kiss was hard and long, with hints of a fire barely banked. He drew her away just as abruptly. "See you."

"Yeah." Pandora swallowed. "See you."

She stood where she was until she heard the front door slam.

She had a long time to think about the kiss, through a solitary dinner, during the hours when she tried to read by the cheery fire in the parlor. It seemed to Pandora that there'd been more passion concentrated in that brief contact than she'd experienced in any of her carefully structured relationships. Was it because she'd always been able to restrict passion to her temper, or her work?

It might have been because she'd been sympathetic, and Michael had been distraught. Emotions had a way of feeding emotions. But for the second time she found herself alone in the house, and to her astonishment, lonely. It was foolish because the fire was bright, the book entertaining and the brandy she sipped warming.

But lonely she was. After little more than a month, she'd come to depend on Michael's company. Even to look forward to it, as strange as that may have been. She liked sitting across from him at meals, arguing with him. She especially liked watching the way he fought, exploding when she poked pins in his work. Perverse? she wondered with a sigh. Perhaps she was, but life was so boring without a bit of friction. No one seemed to provide it more satisfactorily than Michael Donahue.

She wondered when she'd see him again. And she wondered if now they'd have to forgo spending the winter together. If the terms of the will were broken, there would be no reason for them to stay on together. In fact, they'd have no right to stay at the Folley at all. They'd both go back to New York where, due to separate lifestyles, they never saw one another. Not until now, when it was a possibility, did Pandora fully realize how much she didn't want it to happen.

She didn't want to lose the Folley. There were so many memories, so many important ones. Wouldn't they begin to fade if she couldn't walk into a room and bring them back? She didn't want to lose Michael. His companionship, she amended quickly. It was more satisfying than she'd imagined to have someone near who could meet you head to head. If she lost that daily challenge, life would be terribly flat. Since it was Michael who was adding that certain spark to the days, it was only natural to want him around. Wasn't it?

With a sigh, Pandora shut the book and decided an early night would be more productive than idle speculation. Just as she reached over to shut out the lamp, it went out on its own. She was left with the glow of the fire.

Odd, she thought and reached for the switch. After turning it back and forth, she rose, blaming a defective bulb. But when she walked into the hall she found it in darkness. The light she'd left burning was out, along with the one always left on at the top of the stairs. Again Pandora reached for a switch and again she found it useless.

Power failure, she decided but found herself hesitating in the dark. There was no storm. Electricity at the Folley went out regularly during snow and thunderstorms, but the back-up generator took over within minutes. Pandora waited, but the house remained dark.

It occurred to her as she stood there hoping for the best, that she'd never really considered how dark dark could be. She was already making her way back into the parlor for a candle when the rest occurred to her. The house was heated with electricity, as well. If she didn't see about the power soon, the house was going to be very cold as well as very dark before too long. With two people in their seventies in the house, she couldn't let it go.

Annoyed, she found three candles in a silver holder and lit them. It wasn't any use disturbing Charles's sleep and dragging him down to the basement. It was probably only a faulty fuse or two. Holding the candles ahead of her, Pandora wound her way through the curving halls to the cellar door.

She wasn't bothered about going down into the cellar in the dark. So she told herself as she stood with her hand on the knob. It was, after all, just another room. And one, if memory served, which was full of the remains of several of Uncle Jolley's rejected hobbies. The fuse box was down there. She'd seen it when she'd helped her uncle cart down several boxes of photographic equipment after he'd decided to give up the idea of becoming a portrait photographer. She'd go down, check for faulty fuses and replace them. After the lights and heat were taken care of, she'd have a hot bath and go to bed.

But she drew in a deep breath before she opened the door.

The stairs creaked. It was to be expected. And they were steep and narrow as stairs were in any self-respecting cellar. The light from her candles set the shadows dancing over the crates and boxes her uncle had stored there. She'd have to see if she could talk

Michael into helping her sort through them. On some bright afternoon. She was humming nervously to herself before she reached the bottom stair.

Pandora held the candles high and scanned the floor as far as the light circled. She knew mice had an affection for dark, dank cellars and she had no affection for them. When nothing rushed across the floor, she skirted around two six-foot crates and headed for the fuse box. There was the motorized exercise bike that Uncle Jolley had decided took the fun out of staying fit. There was a floor-to-ceiling shelf of old bottles. He'd once been fascinated by a ten-dollar bottle cutter. And there, she saw with a sigh of relief, was the fuse box. Setting the candles on a stack of boxes, she opened the big metal door and stared inside. There wasn't a single fuse in place.

"What the hell's this?" she muttered. Then as she shifted to look closer, her foot sent something rattling over the concrete floor. Jolting, she stifled a scream and the urge to run. Holding her breath, she waited in the silence. When she thought she could manage it, she picked up the candles again and crouched. Scattered at her feet were a dozen fuses. She picked one up and let it lie in her palm. The cellar might have its quota of mice, but they weren't handy enough to empty a fuse box.

She felt a little shudder, which she ignored as she began to gather up the fuses. Tricks, she told herself. Just silly tricks. Annoying, but not as destructive as the one played in her workshop. It wasn't even a very clever trick, she decided, as it was as simple to put fuses back as it had been to take them out.

Working quickly, and trying not to look over her shoulder, Pandora put the fuses back in place. Whoever had managed to get into the basement and play games had wasted her time, nothing more.

Finished, she went over to the stairs, and though she hated herself, ran up them. But her sigh of relief was premature. The door she'd carefully left open was closed tightly. For a few moments she simply refused to believe it. She twisted the knob, pushed, shoved and twisted again. Then she forgot everything but the fear of being closed in a dark place. Pandora beat on the door, shouted, pleaded, then collapsed half sobbing on the top step. No one would hear her. Charles and Sweeney were on the other side of the house.

For five minutes she gave in to fear and self-pity. She was alone, all alone, locked in a dark cellar where no one would hear her until morning. It was already cold and getting colder. By morning…her candles would go out by then, and she'd have no light at all. That was the worst, the very worst, to have no light.

Light, she thought, and called herself an idiot as she wiped away tears. Hadn't she just fixed the lights? Scrambling up, Pandora hit the switch at the top of the stairs. Nothing happened. Holding back a scream, she held the candles up. The socket over the stairs was empty.

So, they'd thought to take out the bulbs. It had been a clever trick after all. She swallowed fresh panic and tried to think. They wanted her to be incoherent, and she refused to give them the satisfaction. When she found out which one of her loving family was playing nasty games…

That was for later, Pandora told herself. Now she was going to find a way out. She was shivering, but she told herself it was anger. There were times it paid to lie to yourself. Holding the candles aloft, she forced herself to go down the steps again when cowering at the top seemed so much easier.

The cellar was twice the size of her apartment in New York, open and barnlike without any of the ornate decorating Uncle Jolley had been prone to. It was just dark and slightly damp with concrete floors and stone walls that echoed. She wouldn't think about spiders or things that scurried into corners right now. Slowly, trying to keep calm, she searched for an exit.

There were no doors, but then she was standing several feet underground. Like a tomb. That particular thought didn't soothe her nerves so she concentrated on other things. She'd only been down in the cellar a handful of times and hadn't given a great deal of thought to the setup. Now she had to think about it—and pretend her palms weren't clammy.

She eased by a pile of boxes as high as her shoulders, then let out a scream when she ran into a maze of cobwebs. More disgusted than frightened, she brushed and dragged at them. It didn't sit well with her to make a fool out of herself, even if no one was around to see it. Someone was going to pay, she told herself as she fought her way clear.

Then she saw the window, four feet above her head and tiny. Though it was hardly the size of a transom, Pandora nearly collapsed in relief. After setting the candles on a shelf, she began dragging boxes over. Her muscles strained and her back protested, but she hauled and stacked against the wall. The first splinter had her swearing. After the third, she stopped counting. Out of breath, streaming with sweat, she leaned against her makeshift ladder. Now all she had to do was climb it.

With the candles in one hand, she used the other to haul herself up. The light shivered and swayed. The boxes groaned and teetered a bit. The thought passed through her mind that if she fell, she could lie there on the frigid concrete with broken bones until morning. She pulled herself high and refused to think at all.

When she reached the window, she found the little latch rusted and stubborn. Swearing, praying, she balanced the candles on the box under her and used both hands. She felt the latch give, then stick again. If she'd only thought to find a tool before she'd climbed up. She considered climbing back down and finding one, then made the mistake of looking behind her. The stack of boxes looked even more rickety from up there.

Turning back to the window, she tugged with all the strength she had. The latch gave with a grind of metal against metal, the boxes swayed from the movement. She saw her candles start to tip and grabbed for them. Out of reach, they slid from the box and clattered to the concrete, their tiny flames extinguished as they hit the ground. She almost followed them, but managed to fight for balance. Pandora found herself perched nine feet off the floor in pitch-darkness.

She wouldn't fall, she promised herself as she gripped the little window ledge with both hands. Using her touch to guide her, she pulled the window out and open, then began to ease herself through. The first blast of cold air made her almost giddy. After she'd pushed her shoulders through she gave herself a moment to breathe and adjust to the lesser dark of starlight. From somewhere to the west, she heard a hardy night bird call twice and fall silent. She'd never heard anything more beautiful.

Grabbing the base of a rhododendron, she pulled

herself through to the waist. When she heard the crash of boxes behind her, she laid her cheek against the cold grass. Inch by inch, she wiggled her way out, ignoring the occasional rip and scratch. At last, she was flat on her back, looking up at the stars. Cold, bruised and exhausted, she lay there, just breathing. When she was able, Pandora dragged herself up and walked around to the east terrace doors.

She wanted revenge, but first, she wanted a bath.

After three layovers and two plane changes, Michael arrived in Palm Springs. Nothing, as far as he could see, had changed. He never came to the exclusive little community but that he came reluctantly. Now, thinking of his mother lying ill, he was swamped with guilt.

He rarely saw her. True, she was no more interested in seeing him than he was her. Yet, she was still his mother. They had been on a different wavelength since the day he'd been born, but she'd taken care of him. At least, she'd hired people to take care of him. Affection, Michael realized, didn't have to enter into a child's feelings for his parent. The bond was there whether or not understanding followed it.

With no more than a flight bag, he bypassed the crowd at baggage claim and hailed a cab. After giving his mother's address, he sat back and checked his watch, subtracting time zones. Even with the hours he'd gained, it was probably past visiting hours. He'd get around that, but first he had to know what hospital his mother was in. If he'd been thinking straight, he would have called ahead and checked.

If his mother's husband wasn't in, one of the servants could tell him. It might not be as bad as the message made it sound. After all, his mother was still young. Then it struck Michael that he didn't have the vaguest idea how old his mother was. He doubted his father knew, and certainly not her current husband. At another time, it might have struck him as funny.

Impatient, he watched as the cab glided by the gates and pillars of the elite. His career had caused him to stay in California for extended lengths of time, but he preferred L.A. to Palm Springs. There, at least, was some action, some movement, some edge. But he liked New York best of all; the pace matched his own and the streets were tougher.

He thought of Pandora. Both of them lived in New York, but they never saw each other unless it was miles north of the city at the Folley. The city could swallow you. Or hide you. It was another aspect Michael appreciated.

Didn't he often use it to hide—from his stifling upbringing, from his recurring lack of faith in the human race? It was at the Folley that he felt the easiest, but it was in New York that he felt the safest. He could be anonymous there if he chose to be. There were times he wanted nothing more. He wrote about heroes and justice, sometimes rough but always human. He wrote, in his own fashion, about basic values and simple rights.

He'd been raised with the illusions and hypocrisy of wealth and with values that were just as unstable. He'd broken away from that, started on his own. New York had helped make it possible because in the city backgrounds were easily erased. So easily erased, Michael mused, that he rarely thought of his.

The cab cruised up the long semicircle of macadam, under the swaying palms, toward the towering white house where his mother had chosen to live. Michael remembered there was a lily pond in the back with goldfish the size of groupers. His mother refused to call them carp.

"Wait," he told the driver, then dashed up two levels of stairs to the door. The butler who answered was new. It was his mother's habit to change the staff regularly, before, as she put it, they got too familiar. "I'm Michael Donahue, Mrs. Keyser's son."

The butler glanced over his shoulder at the waiting cab, then back at Michael's disheveled sweater and un- shaven face. "Good evening, sir. Are you expected?"

"Where's my mother? I want to go to the hospital directly."

"Your mother isn't in this evening, Mr. Donahue. If you'll wait, I'll see if Mr. Keyser's available."

Intolerant, as always, of cardboard manners, he stepped inside. "I know she's not in. I want to go see her tonight. What's the name of the hospital?"

The butler gave a polite nod. "What hospital, Mr. Donahue?"

"Jackson, where did that cab come from?" Wrapped in a deep-rose smoking jacket, Lawrence Keyser strolled downstairs. He had a thick cigar between the fingers of one hand and a snifter of brandy in the other.

"Well, Lawrence," Michael began over a wave of fury. "You look comfortable. Where's my mother?"

"Well, well, it's—ah, it's Matthew."

"It's Michael."

"Michael, of course. Jackson, pay off Mr. ah, Mr. Donavan's cab."

"No, thanks, Jackson." Michael held up a hand. An- other time, he'd have been amused at his stepfather's groping for his name. "I'll use it to get to the hospital. Wouldn't want to put you out."

"No trouble at all, not at all." Big, round and only partially balding, Keyser gave Michael a friendly grin. "Veronica will be pleased to see you, though we didn't know you were coming. How long are you in town?"

"As long as I'm needed. I left the minute I got the message. You didn't mention the name of the hospital. Since you're home and relaxing," he said with only the slightest trace of venom, "should I assume that my mother's condition's improved?"

"Condition?" Keyser gave a jovial laugh. "Well now, I don't know how she'd take to that term, but you can ask her yourself."

"I intend to. Where is she?"

"Playing bridge at the Bradleys'. She'll be coming along in about an hour. How about a brandy?"

"Playing bridge!" Michael stepped forward and grabbed his surprised stepfather by the lapels. "What the hell do you mean she's playing bridge?"

"Can't stomach the game myself," Keyser began warily. "But Veronica's fond of it."

It came to Michael, clear as a bell. "You didn't send me a message about Mother?"

"A message?" Keyser patted Michael's arm, and hoped Jackson stayed close. "No need to send you a message about a bridge game, boy."

"Mother's not ill?"

"Strong as a horse, though I wouldn't let her hear me say so just that way."

Michael swore and whirled around. "Someone's going to pay," he muttered.

"Where are you going?"

"Back to New York," Michael tossed over his shoulder as he ran down the steps.

Relieved, Keyser opted against the usual protests about his departure. "Is there a message for your mother?"

"Yeah." Michael stopped with a hand on the door of the cab. "Yeah, tell her I'm glad she's well. And I hope she wins—in spades." Michael slammed the door shut behind him.

Keyser waited until the cab shot out of sight. "Odd boy," Keyser grumbled to his butler. "Writes for television."

Chapter 6

Pandora, sleeping soundly, was awakened at seven in the morning when Michael dropped on her bed. The mattress bounced. He snuggled his head into the pillow beside her and shut his eyes.

"Sonofabitch," he grumbled.

Pandora sat up, remembered she was naked and grabbed for the sheets. "Michael! You're supposed to be in California. What are you doing in my bed?"

"Getting horizontal for the first time in twenty-four hours."

"Well, do that in your own bed," she ordered, then saw the lines of strain and fatigue. "Your mother." Pandora grabbed for his hand. "Oh, Michael, is your mother—"

"Playing bridge." He rubbed his free hand over his face. Even to him it felt rough and seedy. "I bounced across country, once in a tuna can with propellers, to find out she was sipping sherry and trumping her partner's ace."

"She's better then?"

"She was always better. The message was a hoax." He yawned, stretched and settled. "God, what a night."

"You mean..." Pandora tugged on the sheets and glowered. "Well, the rats."

"Yeah. I plotted out several forms of revenge when I was laid over in Cleveland. Maybe our friend who stomped through your workshop figured it was my turn. Now we each owe them one."

"I owe 'em two." Pandora leaned back against the headboard with the sheets tucked under her arms. Her hair fell luxuriously over her naked shoulders. "Last night while you were off on your wild-goose chase, I was locked in the cellar."

Michael's attention shot away from the thin sheet that barely covered her. "Locked in? How?"

Crossing one ankle over the other, Pandora told him what happened from the time the lights went out.

"Climbed up on boxes? To that little window? It's nearly ten feet."

"Yes, I believe I noticed that at the time."

Michael scowled at her. The anger he'd felt at being treated to a sleepless night doubled. He could picture her groping her way around in the dank cellar all too well. Worse, he could see her very clearly climbing on shaky boxes and crates. "You could've broken your neck."

"I didn't. What I did do was rip my favorite pair of slacks, scratch both knees and bruise my shoulder."

Michael managed to hold back his fury. He'd let it go, he promised himself, when the time was right. "It could've been worse," he said lightly, and thought of what he'd do to whoever had locked her in.

"It was worse," Pandora tossed back, insulted. "While you were sipping Scotch at thirty thousand feet, I was locked in a cold, damp cellar with mice and spiders."

"We might reconsider calling the police."

"And do what with them? We can't prove anything. We don't even know whom we can't prove anything against."

"New rule," Michael decided. "We stick together. Neither of us leaves the house overnight without the other. At least until we find out which of our devoted relations is playing games."

Pandora started to protest, then remembered how frightened she'd been, and before the cellar, before the fear, how lonely. "Agreed. Now…" With one hand hanging onto the sheet, she shifted toward him. "I vote for Uncle Carlson on this one. After all, he knows the house better than any of the others. He lived here."

"It's as good a guess as any. But it's only a guess." Michael stared up at the ceiling. "I want to know. Biff stayed here for six weeks one summer when we were kids."

"That's right." Pandora frowned at the ceiling herself. The mirror across the room reflected them lying companionably, hip to hip. "I'd forgotten about that. He hated it."

"He's never had a sense of humor."

"True enough. As I recall he certainly didn't like you."

"Probably because I gave him a black eye."

Pandora's brow lifted. "You would." Then, because

the image of Biff with a shiner wasn't so unappealing, she added: "Why did you? You never said."

"Remember the frogs in your dresser?"

Pandora sniffed and smoothed at the sheets. "I certainly do. It was quite immature of you."

"Not me. Biff."

"Biff?" Astonished, she turned toward him again. "You mean that little creep put the frogs in my underwear?" The next thought came, surprisingly pleasing. "And you punched him for it?"

"It wasn't hard."

"Why didn't you deny it when I accused you?"

"It was more satisfying to punch Biff. In any case, he knows the house well enough. And I imagine if we checked up, we'd find most of our happy clan has stayed here, at least for a few days at a time. Finding a fuse box in the cellar doesn't take a lot of cunning. Think it through, Pandora. There are six of them, seven with the charity added on. Split a hundred fifty million seven ways and you end up with plenty of motive. Every one of them has a reason for wanting us to break the terms of the will. None of them, as far as I'm concerned, is above adding a little pressure to help us along."

"Another reason the money never appealed to me," she mused. "They haven't done anything but vandalize and annoy, but, dammit, Michael, I want to pay them back."

"The ultimate payback comes in just under five months." Without thinking about it, Michael put his arm around her shoulders. Without thinking about it, Pandora settled against him. A light fragrance clung to her skin. "Can't you see Carlson's face when the will holds up and he gets nothing but a magic wand and a trick hat?"

His shoulder felt more solid than she'd imagined. "And Biff with three cartons of matchbooks." Comfortable, she chuckled. "Uncle Jolley's still having the last laugh."

"We'll have it with him in a few months."

"It's a date. And you've got your shoes on my sheets."

"Sorry." With two economical movements, he pried them off.

"That's not exactly what I meant. Don't you want to wander off to your own room now?"

"Not particularly. Your bed's nicer than mine. Do you always sleep naked?"

"No."

"My luck must be turning then." He shifted to press his lips to a bruise on her shoulder. "Hurt?"

She shrugged and prayed it came off as negligent. "A little."

"Poor little Pandora. And to think I always thought you were tough-skinned."

"I am—"

"Soft," he interrupted, and skimmed his fingers down her arm. "Very soft. Any more bruises?" He brushed his lips over the curve of her neck. They both felt her quick, involuntary shudder.

"Not so you'd notice."

"I'm very observant." He rolled, smoothly, so that his body pressed more intimately into hers as he looked down on her. He was tired. Yes, he was tired and more than a little punchy with jet lag, but he hadn't forgotten he wanted her. Even if he had, the way her body yielded, the way her face looked rosy and soft with sleep, would've jogged his memory. "Why don't I look for myself?" He ran his fingers down to where the sheet lay, neat, prim and arousing, at her breast.

She sucked in her breath, incredibly moved by his lightest touch. She couldn't let it show...could she? She couldn't reach out for something that was only an illusion. He wasn't stable. He wasn't real. He was with her now because she was here and no one else was. Why was it becoming so hard to remember that?

His face was close, filling her vision. She saw the little things she'd tried not to notice over the years. The way a thin ring of gray outlined his irises, the straight, almost aristocratic line of his nose that had remained miraculously unbroken through countless fistfights. The soft, sculpted, somehow poetic shape of his mouth. A mouth, she remembered, that was hot and strong and inventive when pressed against hers.

"Michael..." The fact that she hesitated, then fumbled before she reached down to take his hand both pleased and unnerved him. She wasn't as cool and self-contained as she'd always appeared. And because she wasn't, he could slip his way under her skin. But he might not slip out again so easily.

Be practical, she told herself. Be realistic. "Michael, we have almost five months more to get through."

"Good point." He needed the warmth. He needed the woman. Maybe it was time to risk the consequences. He lowered his head and nibbled at her mouth. "Why waste it?"

She let herself enjoy him. For just a moment, she promised herself. For only a moment. He was warm and his hands were easy. The night had been long and cold and frightening. No matter how much she hated to admit it, she'd needed him. Now, with the sun pouring through the tiny square panes in the windows, falling bright and hard on the bed, she had him. Close, secure, comforting.

Her lips opened against his.

He'd had no plan when he'd come into her room. He'd simply been drawn to her; he'd wanted to lie beside her and talk to her. Passion hadn't guided him. Desire hadn't pushed him. There'd only been the basic need to be home, to be home with her. When she'd snuggled against him, hair tousled, eyes heavy, it had been so natural that the longing had snuck up on him. He wanted nothing more than to stay where he was, wrapped around her, slowly heating.

And for her, passion didn't bubble wildly, but easily, like a brew that had been left to simmer through the day while spices were added. One sample, then another, and the taste changed, enriched, deepened. With Michael, there the flavors were only hinted at, an aroma to draw in and savor. She could have gone on, and on, hour after hour, until what they made between them was perfected. She wanted to give in to the need, the beginnings of greed. If she did, everything would change. It was a change she couldn't predict, couldn't see clearly, could only anticipate. So she resisted him and herself and what could happen between them.

"Michael…" But she let her fingers linger in his hair for just a minute more. "This isn't smart."

He kissed her eyes closed. It was something no one had done before. "It's the smartest thing either of us has done in years."

She wanted to agree, felt herself on the edge of agreeing. "Michael, things are complicated enough. If we were lovers and things went wrong, how could we manage to go on here together? We've made a commitment to Uncle Jolley."

"The will doesn't have a damn thing to do with you and me in this bed."

How could she have forgotten just how intense he could look when he was bent on something? How was it she'd never noticed how attractive it made him? She'd have to make a stand now or go under. "The will has everything to do with you and me in this house. If we go to bed together and our relationship changes, then we'll have to deal with all the problems and complications that go with it."

"Name some."

"Don't be amusing, Michael."

"Giving you a laugh wasn't my intention." He liked the way she looked against the pillow—hair spread out like wildfire, cheeks a bit flushed, her mouth on the edge of forming a pout. Strange he'd never pictured her this way before. It didn't take any thought to know he'd picture her like this again and again. "I want you, Pandora. There's nothing amusing about it."

No, that wasn't something she could laugh or shrug off, not when the words brushed over her skin and made her muscles limp. He didn't mean it. He couldn't mean it. But she wanted to believe it. If she couldn't laugh it off, she had to throw up a guard and block it. "Becoming lovers is something that takes a lot of thought. If we're going to discuss it—"

"I don't want to discuss it." He pressed his lips against hers until he felt her body soften. "We're not making a corporate merger, Pandora, we're making love."

"That's just it." She fought back an avalanche of longing. Be practical. It was her cardinal rule. "We're business partners. Worse, we're family business partners, at least for the next few months. If we change that now it could—"

"If," he interrupted. "It could. Do you always need guarantees?"

Her brows drew together as annoyance competed with desire. "It's a matter of common sense to look at all the angles."

"I suppose you have any prospective lover fill out an application form."

Her voice chilled. It was, in a distorted way, close to the truth. "Don't be crude, Michael."

Pushed to the limit, he glared down at her. "I'd rather be crude than have your brand of common sense."

"You've never had any brand of common sense," she tossed back. "Why else would every busty little blonde you've winked at be public knowledge? You don't even have the decency to be discreet."

"So that's it." Shifting, Michael drew her into a sitting position. There was no soft yielding now. She faced him with fire in her eyes. "Don't forget the brunettes and the redheads."

She hadn't. She promised herself she wouldn't. "I don't want to discuss it."

"You brought it up, and we'll finish it. I've gone to bed with women. So put me in irons. I've even enjoyed it."

She tossed her hair behind her shoulder. "I'm sure you have."

"And I haven't had a debate with every one of them

beforehand. Some women prefer romance and mutual enjoyment."

"Romance?" Her brows shot up under her tousled hair. "I've always had another word for it."

"You wouldn't recognize romance if it dropped on your head. Do you consider it discreet to take lovers and pretend you don't? To pledge undying fidelity to one person while you're looking for another? What you want to call discretion, I call hypocrisy. I'm not ashamed of any of the women I've known, in bed or out."

"I'm not interested in what you are or aren't ashamed of. I'm not going to be your next mutual enjoyment. Keep your passion for your dancers and starlets and chorus girls."

"You're as big a snob as the rest of them."

That hit home and had her shoulders stiffening. "That's not true. I've simply no intention of joining a crowd."

"You flatter me, cousin."

"There's another word for that, too."

"Think about this." He gave her a shake, harder than he'd intended. "I've never made love with a woman I didn't care for and respect." Before he cut loose and did more than shake her, he got up and walked to the door while she sat in the middle of the bed clutching sheets and looking furious.

"It appears you give respect easily."

He turned back to study her. "No," he said slowly. "But I don't make people jump through hoops for it."

A cold war might not be as stimulating as an active battle, but with the right participants, it could be equally destructive. For days Pandora and Michael circled around each other. If one made a sarcastic comment, the other reached into the stockpile and used equal sarcasm. Neither drew out the red flag for full-scale attack, instead they picked and prodded at each other while the servants rolled their eyes and waited for bloodshed.

"Foolishness," Sweeney declared as she rolled out the crust for two apple pies. "Plain foolishness." She was a sturdy, red-faced woman, as round as Charles was thin. In her pragmatic, no-nonsense way, she'd married and buried two husbands, then made her way in the world by cooking for others. Her kitchen was always neat and tidy, all the while smelling of the sinfully rich food she prepared. "Spoiled children," she told Charles. "That's what they are. Spoiled children need the back of the hand."

"They've over four months to go." Charles sat gloomily at the kitchen table, hunched over a cup of tea. "They'll never make it."

"Hah!" Sweeney slammed the rolling pin onto a fresh ball of dough. "They'll make it. Too stubborn not to. But it's not enough."

"The master wanted them to have the house. As long as they do, we won't lose it."

"What'll we be doing in this big empty house when both of them go back to the city? How often will either of them be visiting with the master gone?" Sweeney turned the crust into a pan and trimmed it expertly. "The master wanted them to have the house, true enough. And he wanted them to have each other. The house needs a family. It's up to us to see it gets one."

"You didn't hear them over breakfast." Charles

sipped his tea and watched Sweeney pour a moist apple mixture into the crust.

"That has nothing to do with it. *I've* seen the way they look at each other when they think the other one's not noticing. All they need's a push."

With quick, economic movements, she filled the second crust. "We're going to give 'em one."

Charles stretched out his legs. "We're too old to push young people."

Sweeney gave a quick grunt as she turned. Her hands were thick, and she set them on her hips. "Being old's the whole trick. You've been feeling poorly lately."

"No, to tell you the truth, I've been feeling much better this week."

"You've been feeling poorly," Sweeney repeated, scowling at him. "Now here's our Pandora coming in for lunch. Just follow my lead. Look a little peaked."

Snow had come during the night, big fat flakes that piled on the ground and hung in the pines. As she walked, Pandora kicked it up, pleased with herself. Her work couldn't have been going better. The earrings she'd finally fashioned had been unique, so unique, she'd designed a necklace to complement them. It was chunky and oversize with geometric shapes of copper and gold. Not every woman could wear it, but the one who could wouldn't go unnoticed.

It was, to Pandora, a statement of the strong, disciplined woman. She was just as pleased with the shoulder-brushing earrings she was making with jet and silver beads. They had been painstakingly strung together and when finished would be elegantly flirtatious. Another aspect of woman. If her pace kept steady, she'd have a solid inventory to ship off to the boutique she supplied. In time for the Christmas rush, she reminded herself smugly.

When she opened the kitchen door, she was ravenously hungry and in the best of moods.

"…if you're feeling better in a day or two," Sweeney said briskly, then turned as if surprised to see Pandora inside. "Oh, time must've got away from me. Lunch already and I'm just finishing up the pies."

"Apple pies?" Grinning, Pandora moved closer. But Sweeney saw with satisfaction that Pandora was already studying Charles. "Any filling left?" she began, and started to dip her fingers into the bowl. Sweeney smacked them smartly.

"You've been working with those hands. Wash them up in the sink, and you'll have your lunch as soon as I can manage it."

Obediently, Pandora turned on a rush of water. Under the noise, she murmured to Sweeney. "Is Charles not feeling well?"

"Bursitis is acting up. Cold weather's a problem. Just being old's a problem in itself." She pushed a hand at the small of her back as though she had a pain. "Guess we're both slowing down a bit. Aches and pains," Sweeney sighed and cast a sidelong look at Pandora. "Just part of being old."

"Nonsense." Concerned, Pandora scrubbed her hands harder. She told herself she should have been keeping a closer eye on Charles. "You just try to do too much."

"With the holidays coming…" Sweeney trailed off and made a business out of arranging a top crust. "Well, decorating the house is a lot of work, but it's its own reward. Charles and I'll deal with the boxes in the attic this afternoon."

"Don't be silly." Pandora shut off the water and reached for a towel. "I'll bring the decorations down."

"No, now, missy, there're too many boxes and most of them are too heavy for a little girl like you. That's for us to see to. Isn't that right, Charles?"

Thinking of climbing the attic stairs a half-dozen times, Charles started to sigh. A look from Sweeney stopped him. "Don't worry, Miss McVie, Sweeney and I will see to it."

"You certainly will not." Pandora hung the towel back on the hook. "Michael and I will bring everything down this afternoon, and that's that. Now I'll go tell him to come to lunch."

Sweeney waited until the door swung shut behind Pandora before she grinned.

Upstairs, Pandora knocked twice on Michael's office door, then walked in. He kept on typing. Putting her pride on hold, Pandora walked over to his desk and folded her arms. "I need to talk to you."

"Come back later. I'm busy."

Abuse rose up in her throat. Remembering Sweeney's tired voice, she swallowed it. "It's important." She ground her teeth on the word, but said it. "Please."

Surprised, Michael stopped typing in midword. "What? Has one of the family been playing games again?"

"No, it's not that. Michael, we have to decorate the house for Christmas."

He stared at her a moment, swore and turned back to his machine. "I've got a twelve-year-old boy kidnapped and being held for a million-dollar ransom. That's important."

"Michael, will you put away fantasyland for a moment? This is real."

"So's this. Just ask my producer."

"Michael!" Before he could stop her, Pandora grabbed the laptop. He was halfway out of his chair to retaliate. "It's Sweeney and Charles."

It stopped him, though he snatched the computer back from her. "What about them?"

"Charles's bursitis is acting up again, and I'm sure Sweeney's not feeling well. She sounded, well, old."

"She is old." But Michael tossed the paper on the desk. "Think we should call in a doctor?"

"No, they'd be furious." She swung around his desk, trying to pretend she wasn't reading part of his script. "I'd rather just keep an eye on them for a few days and make sure they don't overdo. That's where the Christmas decorations come in."

"I figured you'd get to them. Look, if you want to deck the halls, go ahead. I haven't got time to fool with it today."

"Neither do I." She folded her arms in a manner that amused him. "Sweeney and Charles have it in their heads that it has to be done. Unless we want them dragging up and down the attic stairs, we have to take care of it."

"Christmas is three weeks away."

"I know the date." Frustrated, she strode to the window then back. "They're old and they're set on it. You know Uncle Jolley would've had them up the day after Thanksgiving. It's traditional."

"All right, all right." Trapped, Michael rose. "Let's get started."

"Right after lunch." Satisfied she'd gotten her way, Pandora swept out.

Forty-five minutes later, she and Michael were pushing open the attic door. The attic was, in Jolley's tradition, big enough to house a family of five. "Oh, I'd forgotten what a marvelous place this is." Forgetting herself, Pandora grabbed Michael's hand and pulled him in. "Look at this table, isn't it horrible?"

It was. Old and ornate with curlicues and cupids, it had been shoved into a corner to hold other paraphernalia Jolley had discarded. "And the bird cage out of Popsicle sticks. Uncle Jolley said it took him six months to finish it, then he didn't have the heart to put a bird inside."

"Lucky for the bird," Michael muttered, but found himself, as always, drawn to the dusty charm of the place. "Spats," he said, and lifted a pair from a box. "Can't you see him in them?"

"And this hat." Pandora found a huge circular straw hat with a garden of flowers along the brim. "Aunt Katie's. I've always wished I'd met her. My father said she was just as much fun as Uncle Jolley."

Michael watched Pandora tip the brim over her eyes. "If that was her hat, I believe it. How about this?" He found a black derby and tilted it rakishly.

"It's you," Pandora told him with her first easy laugh in days. "All you need's a high white collar and a walking stick. Look." She pulled him in front of a tall cheval mirror that needed resilvering. Together, they studied themselves.

"An elegant pair," Michael decided, though his sweater bagged over his hips, and she already had dust on her nose. "All you need is one of those slim little skirts that sweep the floor and a lace blouse with padded shoulders."

"And a cameo on a ribbon," she added as she tried to visualize herself. "No, I probably would've worn bloomers and picketed for women's rights."

"The hat still suits you." He turned to adjust it just a bit. "Especially with your hair long and loose. I've always liked it long, though you looked appealingly lost and big-eyed when you had it all chopped short."

"I was fifteen."

"And you'd just come back from the Canary Islands with the longest, brownest legs I'd ever seen in my life. I nearly ate my saucer when you walked into the parlor."

"You were in college and had some cheerleader hanging on your arm."

Michael grinned. "You had better legs."

Pandora pretended little interest. She remembered the visit perfectly, but was surprised, and pleased, that he did. "I'm surprised you noticed or remembered."

"I told you I was observant."

She acknowledged the thrust with a slight nod. There were times when it was best to pad quietly over dangerous ground. "We'd better start digging out the decorations. Sweeney said the boxes were back along the left and clearly marked." Without waiting for agreement, she turned and began to look. "Oh good grief." She stopped again when she saw the stacks of boxes, twenty, perhaps twenty-five of them. Michael stood at her shoulder and stuck his hands in his pockets.

"Think we can hire some teamsters?"

Pandora blew out a breath. "Roll up your sleeves."

On some trips, they could pile two or three boxes apiece and maneuver downstairs. On others, it took both of them to haul one. Somewhere along the way they'd stopped arguing. It was just too much effort.

Grimy and sweaty, they dropped the last boxes in the parlor. Ignoring the dust on her slacks, Pandora collapsed in the nearest chair. "Won't it be great fun hauling them all up again after New Year's?"

"Couldn't we've settled on a plastic Santa?"

"It'll be worth it." Drumming up the energy, she knelt on the floor and opened the first box. "Let's get started."

Once they did, they went at it with a vengeance. Boxes were opened, garland strewed and bulbs tested. They squabbled good-naturedly about what looked best where and the proper way to drape lights at the windows. When the parlor, the main hall and the staircase were finished, Pandora stood at the front door and took a long look.

The garland was white and silver, twisting and twining down the banister. There were bright red bells, lush green ribbon and tiny lights just waiting for evening.

"It looks good," she decided. "Really good. Of course, Sweeney and Charles will want to decorate the servants' quarters and that entire box goes into the dining room, but it's a wonderful start."

"Start?" Michael sat on the stairs. "We're not entering a contest, cousin."

"These things have to be done right. I wonder if my parents will make it home for Christmas. Well..." She brushed that off. They always considered wherever they were home. "I'd say we're ready for the tree. Let's go find one."

"You want to drive into town now?"

"Of course not." Pandora was already pulling coats

out of the hall closet. "We'll go right out in the woods and dig one up."

"We?"

"Certainly. I hate it when people cut trees down and then toss them aside after the new year. The woods are loaded with nice little pines. We'll dig one up, then re-plant it after the holidays."

"How handy are you with a shovel?"

"Don't be a spoilsport." Pandora tossed his coat to him, then pulled on her own. "Besides, it'll be nice to spend some time outside after being in that stuffy attic. We can have some hot buttered rum when we're finished."

"Heavy on the rum."

They stopped at the toolshed for a shovel. Michael picked two and handed one to Pandora. She took it without a blink, then together they walked through the ankle-high snow to the woods. The air had a bite and the scent of pine was somehow stronger in the snow.

"I love it when it's like this." Pandora balanced the shovel on her shoulder and plowed through the woods. "It's so quiet, so—separated. You know, sometimes I think I'd rather live here and visit the city than the other way around."

He'd had the same thought, but was surprised to hear it from her. "I always thought you liked the bright lights and confusion."

"I do. But I like this, too. How about this one?" She paused in front of a spruce. "No, the trunk's too crooked." She walked on. "Besides, I wonder if it wouldn't be more exciting to go into the city for a week now and again and know you had someplace like this to come back to. I seem to work better here. Here's one."

"Too tall. We're better off digging up a young one. Wouldn't it put a crimp in your social life?"

"What?" She studied the tree in question and was forced to agree with him. "Oh. My social life isn't a priority, my work is. In any case, I could entertain here."

He had a picture of her spending long, cozy weekends with flamboyant, artsy types who read Keats aloud. "You don't have to come all the way to the Catskills to play house."

Pandora merely lifted a brow. "No, I don't. This one looks good." She stopped again and took a long study of a four-and-a-half-foot spruce. Behind her, Michael worked hard to keep his mouth shut. "It's just the right size for the parlor."

"Fine." Michael stuck his shovel into the ground. "Put your back into it."

As he bent over to dig, Pandora scooped up a shovelful of snow and tossed it into his face. "Oh, sorry." She smiled and batted her eyes. "Looks like my aim's off." Digging with more effort, she began to hum.

He let it go, probably because he appreciated the move and wished he'd thought of it himself. Within fifteen minutes, they had the hole dug.

"There now." Only a little out of breath, Pandora leaned on her shovel. "The satisfaction of a job well done."

"We only have to carry it back to the house, set it up and…damn, we need something to wrap the roots and dirt in. There was burlap in the shed."

They eyed each other blandly.

"All right," he said after a moment. "I'll go get it, then you have to sweep up the needles and dirt we trail on the floor."

"Deal."

Content, Pandora turned away to watch a cardinal when a snowball slapped into the back of her head. "Sorry." Michael gave her a companionable smile. "Aim must be off." He whistled as he walked back to the shed.

Pandora waited until he was out of sight, then smiling smugly, knelt down to ball snow. By the time he got back, she calculated, she could have an arsenal at hand. He wouldn't have a chance. She took her time, forming and smoothing each ball into a sophisticated weapon. Secure in her advantage, she nearly fell on her face when she heard a sound behind her. She had the ball in her hand and was already set to throw as she whirled. No one was there. Narrowing her eyes, she waited. Hadn't she seen a movement back in the trees? It would be just like him to skirt around and try to sneak up on her. She saw the cardinal fly up again as if startled and heard the quiet plop of snow hitting snow as it was shaken from branches.

"All right, Michael, don't be a coward." She picked up a ball in her left hand, prepared to bombard.

"Guarding your flank?" Michael asked so that this time when she whirled back around, she slid onto her bottom. He grinned at her and dropped the burlap sack in her lap.

"But weren't you…" She trailed off and looked behind her again. How could he be here if he was there? "Did you circle around?"

"No, but from the looks of that mound of balls, I should've. Want to play war?"

"It's just a defense system," she began, then looked over her shoulder again. "I thought I heard you. I would've sworn there was someone just beyond the trees there."

"I went straight to the shed and back." He looked beyond her. "You saw something out there?"

"Michael, if you're playing tricks—"

"No." He cut her off and reached down to pull her to her feet. "No tricks. Let's have a look."

She moved her shoulders but didn't remove her hand from his as they walked deeper into the trees. "Maybe I was a bit jumpy."

"Or expecting me to be sneaky?"

"That, too. It was probably just a rabbit."

"A rabbit with big feet," he murmured as he looked down at the tracks. They were clear enough in the snow, tracks leading to and away from the spot ten yards behind where they'd dug up the tree. "Rabbits don't wear boots."

"So, we still have company. I was beginning to think they'd given the whole business up." She kept her voice light, but felt the uneasiness of anyone who'd been watched. "Maybe it's time we talked to Fitzhugh, Michael."

"Maybe, in the meantime—" The sound of an engine cut him off. He was off in a sprint with Pandora at his heels. After a five-minute dash, they came, clammy and out of breath, to what was hardly more than a logging trail. Tire tracks had churned up the snow and blackened it. "A Jeep, I'd guess." Swearing, Michael stuck his hands in his pockets. If he'd started out right away, he might have caught someone or at least have caught a glimpse of someone.

Pandora let out an annoyed breath. Racing after

someone was one thing, being outmaneuvered another. "Whoever it is is only wasting his time."

"I don't like being spied on." He wanted physical contact. Longed for it. Frustrated, he stared at the tracks that led back to the main road. "I'm not playing cat and mouse for the next four months."

"What are we going to do?"

His smile spread as he looked at the tracks. "We'll spread the word through Fitzhugh that we've been bothered by trespassers. Being as there's any number of valuables on the premises, we've decided to haul out one of Jolley's old .30-.30's."

"Michael! They may be a nuisance, but they're still family." Unsure, she studied him. "You wouldn't really shoot at anyone."

"I'd rather shoot at family than strangers," he countered, then shrugged. "They're also fond of their own skin. I can't think of one of them who wouldn't hesitate to play around if they thought they might be picking buckshot out of embarrassing places."

"I don't like it. Guns, even the threat of guns, are trouble."

"Got a better idea?"

"Let's buy a dog. A really big, mean dog."

"Great, then we can let him loose and have him sink his teeth into one of our favorite relatives. They'd like that a lot better than buckshot."

"He doesn't have to be that mean."

"We'll compromise and do both."

"Michael—"

"Let's call Fitzhugh."

"And take his advice?" Pandora demanded.

"Sure...if I like it."

Pandora started to object, then laughed. It was all as silly as a plot of one of his shows. "Sounds reasonable," she decided, then tucked her arm through his. "Let's get the tree inside first."

Chapter 7

"I know it's Christmas Eve, Darla." Michael picked up his coffee cup, found it empty and lifted the pot from his hot plate. Dregs. He bit off a sigh. The trouble with the Folley was that you had to hike a half a mile to the kitchen whenever the pot ran dry. "I know it'll be a great party, but I can't get away."

That wasn't precisely true, Michael mused as he listened to Darla's rambles about a celebration in Manhattan. *Everyone*, according to her estimate, was going to be there. That meant a loud, elbow-to-elbow party with plenty of booze. He could have taken a day and driven into the city to raise a glass or two with friends. He was well ahead of schedule. So far ahead, he could have taken off a week and not felt the strain. The precise truth was, he didn't want to get away.

"I appreciate that...you'll just have to tell everyone

Merry Christmas for me. No, I like living in the country, Darla. Weird? Yeah, maybe." He had to laugh. Darla was a top-notch dancer and a barrel of laughs, but she didn't believe life went on outside of the island of Manhattan. "New Year's if I can manage it. Okay, babe. Yeah, yeah, *ciao*."

More than a little relieved, Michael hung up. Darla was a lot of fun, but he wasn't used to being clung to by a woman, especially one he'd only dated casually. The truth was, she was just as attracted to the influence he had with certain casting agents as she was interested in him. He didn't hold it against her. She had ambition and talent, a combination that could work in the tough-edged business of entertaining if a dash of luck was added. After the holidays he'd make a few calls and see what he could do.

From the doorway, Pandora watched as Michael ran a hand along the back of his neck. Darla, she repeated silently. She imagined the women his taste leaned toward had names like Darla, or Robin and Candy. Sleek, smooth, sophisticated and preferably empty-headed.

"Popularity's such a strain, isn't it, darling?"

Michael turned in his chair to give her a long, narrowed look. "Eavesdropping's so rude, isn't it, darling?"

She shrugged but didn't come in. "If you'd wanted privacy, you should've closed your door."

"Around here you have to nail it shut for privacy."

One brow raised, head slightly inclined, Pandora looked as aloof as royalty. "Your phone conversations have absolutely no interest for me. I only came up as a favor to Charles. You've a package downstairs."

"Thanks." He didn't bother to hide amusement at her tone. If he knew Pandora, and he did, she'd listened to every word. "I thought these were your sacred working hours."

"Some of us schedule our work well enough that we can take some time off during the holidays. No, no, let's not bicker," she decided abruptly before he could retaliate. "It is nearly Christmas after all, and we've had three weeks of peace from our familial practical jokers. Truce," Pandora offered with a smile Michael wasn't sure he should trust. "Or a moratorium if you prefer."

"Why?"

"Let's just say I'm a sucker for holly and ivy. Besides, I'm relieved we didn't have to buy a big drooling dog or a supply of buckshot."

"For now." Not completely satisfied, Michael tipped back in his chair. "Fitzhugh's notion of notifying the local police of trespassers and spreading the rumor of an official investigation might be working temporarily. Or maybe our friends and family are just taking a holiday break themselves. Either way I'm not ready to relax."

"You'd rather break someone's nose than solve things peaceably," Pandora began, then waved a hand. "Never mind. I, for one, am going to enjoy the holidays and not give any of our dear family a thought." She paused a moment, toying with her braided chain of gold and amethyst. "I suppose Darla was disappointed."

Michael watched the way the stones caught the thin winter light and made sparks from it. "She'll pull through."

Pandora twisted the chain one way, twisted it back, then let it go. It was the sort of nervous gesture Michael hadn't expected from her. "Michael, you know you don't have to stay. I really will be fine if you want to run into New York for the holiday."

"Rule number six," he reminded her. "We stick together, and you've turned down a half-dozen invitations for the holidays yourself."

"My choice." She reached for the chain again, then dropped her hands. "I don't want you to feel obligated—"

"My choice," he interrupted. "Or have you suddenly decided I'm chivalrous and unselfish?"

"Certainly not," she tossed back, but smiled. "I prefer thinking you're just too lazy to make the trip."

He shook his head, but his lips curved in response. "I'm sure you would."

She hesitated in the doorway until he lifted a brow in question. "Michael, would you become totally obnoxious if I told you I'm glad you're staying?"

He studied her as she stood, looking slim and neat in the doorway, her hair a riotous contrast to the trim sweater and stovepipe pants. "I might."

"Then I won't tell you." Without another word, she slipped out of the doorway and disappeared.

Contrary woman, Michael thought. He was close to being crazy about her. And crazy was the perfect word. She baited him or, he admitted, he baited her at every possible opportunity. He could imagine no two people less inclined to peaceful coexistence, much less harmony. And yet…and yet he was close to being crazy about her. Knowing better than to try to go back to work, he rose and followed her downstairs.

He found her in the parlor, rearranging packages under the tree. "How many have you shaken?"

"All of them," she said easily. But she didn't turn because he might have seen how pleased she was he'd come downstairs with her. "I don't want to show any preference. Thing is," she added, poking at an elegantly wrapped box, "I seem to have missed my present from you."

Michael gave her a bland smile. "Who says I got you anything?"

"You would have been terribly rude and insensitive otherwise."

"Yep. In any case, you seem to've done well enough." He crouched down to study the stacks of boxes under the tree. "Who's Boris?" Idly he picked up a small silver box with flowing white ribbon.

"A Russian cellist who defected. He admires my... gold links."

"I bet. And Roger?"

"Roger Madison."

His mouth dropped open, but only for a moment. "The Yankee shortstop who batted .304 last year?"

"That's right. You may've noticed the silver band he wears on his right wrist. I made that for him last March. He seems to think it straightened out his bat or something." She lifted the blue-and-gold box and shook it gently. "He tends to be very generous."

"I see." Michael took a comprehensive study of the boxes. "There don't seem to be a great many packages here for you from women."

"Really?" Pandora took a scan herself. "It appears you make up for that with your pile. Chi-Chi?" she asked as she picked up a box with a big pink bow.

"She's a marine biologist," Michael said with his tongue in his cheek.

"Fascinating. And I imagine Magda's a librarian."

"Corporate attorney," he said blandly.

"Hmm. Well, whoever sent this one's obviously shy."

She picked up a magnum of champagne with a glittering red ribbon. The tag read "Happy Holidays, Michael," and nothing more.

Michael scanned the label with approval. "Some people don't want to advertise their generosity."

"How about you?" She tilted her head. "After all, it is a magnum. Are you going to share?"

"With whom?"

"I should've known you'd be greedy." She picked up a box with her name on it. "Just for that I'm eating this entire box of imported chocolates myself."

Michael eyed the box. "How do you know they're chocolates?"

She only smiled. "Henri always gives me chocolate."

"Imported?"

"Swiss."

Michael put out a hand. "Share and share alike."

Pandora accepted it. "I'll chill the wine."

Hours later when there was starlight on the snow and a fire in the hearth, Pandora lit the tree. Like Michael, she didn't miss any of the crowded, frenzied parties in the city. She was where she wanted to be. It had taken Pandora only a matter of weeks to discover she wasn't as attached to the rush of the city as she'd once thought. The Folley was home. Hadn't it always been? No, she no longer thought of going back to Manhattan in the spring. But what would it be like to live in the Folley alone?

Michael wouldn't stay. True, he'd own half of the Folley in a few months, but his life—including his active social life—was in the city. He wouldn't stay, she thought again, and found herself annoyed with her own sense of regret. Why should he stay? she asked herself as she wandered over to poke at the already crackling fire. How could he stay? They couldn't go on living together indefinitely. Sooner or later she'd have to approach him about her decision to remain there. To do so, she'd have to explain herself. It wouldn't be easy.

Still, she was grateful to Jolley for doing something she'd once resented. Boxing her in. She may have been forced into dealing with Michael on a day-to-day level, but in the few months she'd done so, her life had had more energy and interest than in the many months before. It was that, Pandora told herself, that she hated to give up.

She'd dealt with her attraction to him semisuccessfully. The fact was, he was no more her type than she was his. She jammed hard at a log. From all the many reports, Michael preferred a more flamboyant, exotic sort of woman. Actresses, dancers, models. And he preferred them in droves. She, on the other hand, looked for more intellectual men. The men she spent time with could discuss obscure French novelists and appreciate small, esoteric plays. Most of them wouldn't have known if *Logan's Run* was a television show or a restaurant in SoHo.

The fact that she had a sort of primitive desire for Michael was only a tempest in a teapot. Pandora smiled as she replaced the poker. She couldn't deny she enjoyed a tempest now and again.

When a small one erupted behind her, Pandora turned in disbelief. A little white dog with oversize feet scrambled into the room, slid on the Aubusson carpet and rammed smartly into a table. Barking madly, it rolled over twice, righted itself, then dashed at Pandora to leap halfheartedly and loll its tongue. Entertained,

Pandora crouched down and was rewarded when the puppy sprang onto her lap and licked her face.

"Where'd you come from?" Laughing, and defending herself as best she could, Pandora found the card attached to the red bow around the puppy's neck. It read:

My name is Bruno. I'm a mean, ugly dog looking for a lady to defend.

"Bruno, huh?" Laughing again, Pandora stroked his unfortunately long ears. "How mean are you?" she asked as he contented himself with licking her chin.

"He especially likes to attack discontented relatives," Michael announced as he wheeled in a tray carrying an ice bucket and champagne. "He's been trained to go after anyone wearing a Brooks Brothers suit."

"We might add Italian loafers."

"That's next."

Moved, incredibly moved, she concentrated on the puppy. She hadn't the least idea how to thank Michael without making a fool of herself. "He isn't really ugly," she murmured.

"They promised me he would be."

"They?" She buried her face in the puppy's fur a moment. "Where did you get him?"

"Pound." Watching her, Michael ripped the foil from the champagne. "When we went into town for supplies last week and I deserted you in the supermarket."

"And I thought you'd gone off somewhere to buy pornographic magazines."

"My reputation precedes me," he said half to himself. "In any case, I went to the pound and walked through the kennels. Bruno bit another dog on the—on a sensitive area in order to get to the bars first. Then he grinned at me with absolutely no dignity. I knew he was the one."

The cork came out with a bang and champagne sprayed up and dripped onto the floor. Bruno scrambled out of Pandora's lap and greedily licked it up. "Perhaps his manners are lacking a bit," Pandora observed. "But his taste is first class." She rose, but waited until Michael had poured two glasses. "It was a lovely thing to do, dammit."

He grinned and handed her a glass. "You're welcome."

"It's easier for me when you're rude and intolerable."

"I do the best I can." He touched his glass to hers.

"When you're sweet, it's harder for me to stop myself from doing something foolish."

He started to lift his glass, then stopped. "Such as?"

"Such as." Pandora set down her champagne, then took Michael's and set it on the table as well. Watching him, only him, she put her arms around his neck. Very slowly—unwise acts done slowly often take on a wisdom of their own—she touched her mouth to his.

It was, as she'd known it would be, warm and waiting. His hands came to her shoulders, holding her without pressure. Perhaps they'd both come to understand that pressure would never hold her. When she softened, when she gave, she gave through her own volition, not through seduction, not through demand. So it was Pandora who moved closer, Pandora who pressed body to body, offering hints of intimacy with no submission.

It wasn't submission he wanted. It wasn't submission he looked for, though it was often given to him. He didn't look for matching strength, but strength that meshed. In Pandora, where he'd never thought to search for it, he found it. Her scent twisted around him, heightening emotions her taste had just begun to stir. Under his hands, her body was firm with the underlying softness women could exploit or be exploited by. He thought she'd do neither, but would simply be. By being alone, she drew him in.

She didn't resist his touch, not when his hands slipped down to her hips or skimmed up again. It seemed he'd done so before, though only in dreams she'd refused to acknowledge. If this was the time for acceptance, she'd accept. If this was the time for pleasure, she'd take it. If she found both with him, she wouldn't refuse. Even questions could come later. Maybe tonight was a night without questions.

She drew back, but only to smile at him. "You know, I don't think of you as a cousin when I'm kissing you."

"Really?" He nipped at her lips. She had an incredibly alluring mouth—full and pouty. "What do you think of me as?"

She cocked a brow. His arms surrounded her, but didn't imprison. Pandora knew she'd have to analyze the difference later. "I haven't figured that out yet."

"Then maybe we should keep working it out." He started to pull her back, but she resisted.

"Since you've broken tradition to give me my Christmas present a few hours early, I'll do the same." Going to the tree, Pandora reached down and found the square, flat box. "Happy Christmas, Michael."

He sat down on the arm of a chair to open it while Pandora picked up her glass of champagne. She sipped, watching a bit nervously for his reaction. It was only a token after all, she told herself, as she played with the stem of her glass. When he ripped off the paper then said nothing, she shrugged. "It's not as inventive as a guard dog."

Michael stared down at the pencil sketch of their uncle without any idea what to say. The frame she'd made herself, he knew. It was silver and busily ornate in a style Jolley would have appreciated. But it was the sketch that held him silent. She'd drawn Jolley as Michael remembered him best, standing, a bit bent forward from the waist as though he were ready to pop off on a new tangent. What thin hair he'd had left was mussed. His cheeks were stretched out in a big, wide-open grin. It had been drawn with love, talent and humor, three qualities Jolley had possessed and admired. When Michael looked up, Pandora was still twisting the stem of the glass in her hands.

Why, she's nervous, he realized. He'd never expected her to be anything but arrogantly confident about her work. About herself. The secrets he was uncovering were just as unnerving to him as they were to her. A man tended to get pulled into a woman who had soft spots in unexpected places. If he was pulled in, how would he work his way out again? But she was waiting, twisting the stem of her glass in her hand.

"Pandora. No one's ever given me anything that's meant more."

The line between her brows smoothed out as her smile bloomed. The ridiculous sense of pleasure was difficult to mask. "Really?"

He held a hand out to her. "Really." He glanced down at the sketch again and smiled. "It looks just like him."

"It looks like I remember him." She let her fingers link with Michael's. Pandora could tell herself it was

Jolley who drew them together, and nothing else. She could nearly believe it. "I thought you might remember him that way, too. The frame's a bit gaudy."

"And suitable." He studied it with more care. The silver shone dully, set off with the deep curls and lines she'd etched. It could, he realized, be put in an antique shop and pass for an heirloom. "I didn't know you did this sort of thing."

"Now and again. The boutique carries a few of them."

"Doesn't fit in the same category as bangles and beads," he mused.

"Doesn't it?" Her chin tilted. "I thought about making you a big gold collar with rhinestones just to annoy you."

"It would have."

"Maybe next year then. Or perhaps I'll make one for Bruno." She glanced around. "Where'd he go?"

"He's probably behind the tree gnawing on presents. During his brief stay in the garage, he ate a pair of golf shoes."

"We'll put a stop to that," Pandora declared, and went to find him.

"You know, Pandora, I'd no idea you could draw like this." Michael settled against the back of the chair to study the sketch again. "Why aren't you painting?"

"Why aren't you writing the Great American Novel?"

"Because I enjoy what I'm doing."

"Exactly." Finding no sign of the puppy around the tree, Pandora began to search under the furniture. "Though certainly a number of painters have toyed with jewelry design successfully enough—Dali for one—I feel... Michael!"

He set his untouched champagne back down and hurried over to where she knelt by a divan. "What is it?" he demanded, then saw for himself. Eyes closed, breathing fast and heavy, the puppy lay half under the divan. Even as Pandora reached for him, Bruno whimpered and struggled to stand.

"Oh, Michael, he's sick. We should get him to a vet."

"It'll be midnight before we get to town. We won't find a vet at midnight on Christmas Eve." Gently Michael laid a hand on Bruno's belly and heard him moan. "Maybe I can get someone on the phone."

"Do you think it's something he ate?"

"Sweeney's been supervising his feeding like a new mother." On cue Bruno struggled and shuddered and relieved himself of what offended his stomach. Exhausted from the effort, he lay back and dozed fitfully. "Something he drank," Michael murmured.

Pampering and soothing, Pandora stroked the dog. "That little bit of champagne shouldn't have made him ill." Because the dog was already resting easier, she relaxed a bit. "Charles isn't going to be pleased Bruno cast up his accounts on the carpet. Maybe I should—" She broke off as Michael grabbed her arm.

"How much champagne did you drink?"

"Only a sip. Why—" She broke off again to stare. "The champagne. You think something's wrong with it?"

"I think I'm an idiot for not suspecting an anonymous present." He grabbed her by the chin. "Only a sip. You're sure? How do you feel?"

Her skin had gone cold, but she answered calmly enough. "I'm fine. Look at my glass, it's still full." She turned her head to look at it herself. "You—you think it was poisoned?"

"We'll find out."

Logic seeped through, making her shake her head. "But, Michael, the wine was corked. How could it have been tampered with?"

"The first season on *Logan* I used a device like this." He thought back, remembering how he'd tested the theory by adding food coloring to a bottle of Dom Perignon. "The killer poisoned champagne by shooting cyanide through the cork with a hypodermic."

"Fiction," Pandora claimed, and fought a shiver. "That's just fiction."

"Until we find out differently, we're going to treat it as fact. The rest of the bottle's going into New York to Sanfield Labs for testing."

Shaky, Pandora swallowed. "For testing," she said on an unsteady breath. "All right, I suppose we'll both be easier when we're sure. Do you know someone who works there?"

"We own Sanfield." He looked down at the sleeping puppy. "Or we will own it in a matter of months. That's just one of the reasons someone might've sent us some doctored champagne."

"Michael, if it was poisoned..." She tried to imagine it and found it nearly impossible. "If it was poisoned," she repeated, "this wouldn't just be a game anymore."

He thought of what might have happened if they hadn't been distracted from the wine. "No, it wouldn't be a game."

"It doesn't make any sense." Uneasy and fighting to calm herself, Pandora rose. "Vandalism I can see, petty annoyances I can understand, but I just can't attribute something like this to one of the family. We're probably overreacting. Bruno's had too much excitement. He could very well have picked up something in the pound."

"I had him sent to the vet for his shots before he was delivered here yesterday." Michael's voice was calm, but his eyes were hot. "He was healthy, Pandora, until he lapped up some spilled champagne."

One look at him told her rationalizing was useless. "All right. The wine should be tested in any case so we can stop speculating. We can't do anything about it until day after tomorrow. In the meantime, I don't want to dwell on it."

"Pulling the blinds down, Pandora?"

"No." She picked up Bruno, who whimpered and burrowed into her breast. "But until it's proven, I don't want to consider that a member of my family tried to kill me. I'll fix him something warm to drink, then I'm going to take him upstairs. I'll keep an eye on him tonight."

"All right." Fighting a combination of frustration and fury, Michael stood by the fire.

Long after midnight when he couldn't sleep, couldn't work, Michael looked in on her. She'd left a light burning low across the room so that the white spreads and covers took on a rosy hue. Outside snow was falling again in big, festive flakes. Michael could see her, curled in the wide bed, the blankets up to her chin. The fire was nearly out. On the rug in front of it, the puppy snored. She'd put a mohair throw over him and had set a shallow bowl filled with what looked like tea nearby. Michael crouched beside the dog.

"Poor fella," he murmured. As he stroked, Bruno stirred, whimpered, then settled again.

"I think he's better."

Glancing over, Michael saw the light reflected in Pandora's eyes. Her hair was tousled, her skin pale and soft. Her shoulders, gently sloped, rose just above the covers pooled around her. She looked beautiful, desirable, arousing. He told himself he was mad. Pandora didn't fit into his carefully detailed notion of beauty. Michael looked back at the dog.

"Just needs to sleep it off. You could use another log on this fire." Needing to keep busy, Michael dug in the woodbox, then added a log to the coals.

"Thanks. Can't sleep?"

"No."

"Me, either." They sat in silence a moment, Pandora in the big bed, Michael on the hearth rug. The fire crackled greedily at the fresh log and flickered light and shadow. At length, she drew her knees up to her chest. "Michael, I'm frightened."

It wasn't an easy admission. He knew it cost her to tell him. He stirred at the fire a moment, then spoke lightly as he replaced the screen. "We can leave. We can drive into New York tomorrow and stay there. Forget this whole business and enjoy the holidays."

She didn't speak for a minute, but she watched him carefully. His face was turned away toward the fire so that she had to judge his feelings by the way he held himself. "Is that what you want to do?"

He thought of Jolley, then he thought of Pandora. Every muscle in his body tightened. "Sure." He tossed it off like a shrug. "I've got to think about myself." He said it as if to remind himself it had once been true.

"For someone who earns his living by making up stories, you're a lousy liar." She waited until he turned to face her. "You don't want to go back. What you want is to gather all our relatives together and beat them up."

"Can you see me pounding Aunt Patience?"

"With a few exceptions," Pandora temporized. "But the last thing you want is to give up."

"All right, that's me." He rose and, hands in pockets, paced back and forth in front of the fire. He could smell the woodsmoke mixed with some light scent from one of the bottles on Pandora's dresser. "What about you? You didn't want to hassle with this whole business from the beginning. I talked you into it. I feel responsible."

For the first time in hours she felt her humor return. "I hate to dent your ego, Michael, but you didn't talk me into anything. No one does. And I'm completely responsible for myself. I don't want to quit," she added before he could speak. "I said I didn't want the money, and that was true. I also said I didn't need it, and that's not precisely true. Over and above that, there's pride. I'm frightened, yes, but I don't want to quit. Oh, stop pacing around and come sit down." The order was cross and impatient, nearly making him smile. He came over and sat on the bed.

"Better?"

She gave him a long, steady look that had the hint of a smile fading. "Yes. Michael, I've been lying here for hours thinking this thing through. I've realized a few things. You called me a snob once, and perhaps you were right in a way. I've never thought much about money. Never allowed myself to. When Uncle Jolley cut everyone out, I thought of it as a cross between a joke and a slap on the wrist. I figured they'd grumble and complain certainly, but that was all." She lifted her hand palm up. "It was only money, and every one of them has their own."

"Ever heard of greed or the lust for power?"

"That's just it, I didn't think. How much do I know about any of those people? They bore or annoy me from time to time, but I've never thought about them as individuals." Now she ran the hand through her hair so that the blankets fell to her waist. "Ginger must be about the same age as I am, and I can't think of two things we have in common. I'd probably pass Biff's wife on the street without recognizing her."

"I have a hard time remembering her name," Michael put in, and earned a sigh from Pandora.

"That's my point. We don't really know them. The family, in a group, is a kind of parlor joke. Separately, who are they and what are they capable of? I've just begun to consider it. It's not a joke, Michael."

"No, it's not."

"I want to fight back, but I don't know how."

"The surest way is by staying. And maybe," he added, and took her hand. It was cool and soft. "Add a little psychological warfare."

"Such as?"

"What if we sent each one of our relatives a nice bottle of champagne?"

Her smile came slowly. "A magnum."

"Naturally. It'd be interesting to see what sort of reaction we get."

"It would be a nasty gesture, wouldn't it?"

"Uh-hmm."

"Maybe I haven't given your creative brain enough

credit." She fell silent as he wound her hair around his finger. "I suppose we should get some sleep."

"I suppose." But his fingers skimmed down her shoulders.

"I'm not very tired."

"We could play canasta."

"We could." But she made no move to stop him when he nudged the thin straps of her chemise from her shoulders. "There's always cribbage."

"That, too."

"Or…" It was her decision, they both understood that. "We might finish playing out the hand we started downstairs earlier."

He lifted her hand and pressed his lips to the palm. "Always best to finish what you start before going on. As I recall, we were…here." He lowered his mouth to hers. Slowly, on a sigh, she wound her arms around his neck.

"That seems about right."

Holding fast, they sunk into the bed together.

Perhaps it was because they knew each other well. Perhaps it was because they'd already waited a lifetime, but each moved slowly. Desire, for the moment, was comfortable, easy to satisfy with a touch, a taste. Passion curled inside him then unwound with a sigh. There was inch after inch of her to explore with his fingertips, with his lips. He'd waited too long, wanted too long, to miss any part of what they could give to each other.

She was more generous than he'd imagined, less inhibited, more open. She didn't ask to be coaxed, she didn't pretend to need persuasion. She ran her hands over him with equal curiosity. Her mouth took from him and gave again. When his lips parted from hers, her eyes were on him, clouded with desire, dark with amusement of a shared joke. They were together, Michael thought as he buried his face in her hair. About to become lovers. The joke was on both of them.

Her hands were steady when she pulled his sweatshirt over his head, steady still as she ran them over his chest. Her pulse wasn't. She'd avoided this, refused this. Now she was accepting it though she knew there would be consequences she couldn't anticipate.

The fire crackled steadily. The soft light glowed. Consequences were for more practical times.

Her skin slid over his with each movement. Each movement enticed. With his heartbeat beginning to hammer in his head, he journeyed lower. With open-mouthed kisses he learned her body in a way he'd only been able to imagine. Her scent was everywhere, subtle at the curve of her waist, stronger at the gentle underside of her breasts. He drew it in and let it swim in his head.

He felt the instant her lazy enjoyment darkened with power. When her breath caught on a moan, he took her deeper. They reached a point where he no longer knew what they did to each other, only that strength met need and need became desperation.

His skin was damp. She tasted the moistness of it and craved more. So this was passion. This was the trembling, churning hunger men and women longed for. She'd never wanted it. That's what she told herself as her body shuddered. Pleasure and pain mixed, needs and fears tangled. Her mind was as swamped with sensations as her flesh—heat and light, ecstasy and terror. The vulnerability overwhelmed her though her body arched taut and her hands clung. No one had ever brushed back her defenses so effortlessly and taken. Taken and taken.

Breathless and desperate, she dragged his mouth back to hers. They rolled over the bed, rough, racing. Neither had had enough. While she tugged and pulled at his jeans, Michael drove her higher. He'd wanted the madness, for himself and for her. Now he felt the wild strength pouring out of her. No thought here, no logic. He rolled on top of her again, reveling in her frantic breathing.

She curled around him, legs and arms. When he plunged into her, they watched the astonishment on each other's faces. Not like this—it had never been like this. They'd come home. But home, each discovered, wasn't always a peaceful place.

There was silence, stunned, awkward silence. They lay tangled in the covers as the log Michael had set to fire broke apart and showered sparks against the screen. They knew each other well, too well to speak of what had happened just yet. So they lay in silence as their skin cooled and their pulses leveled. Michael shifted to pull the spread up over them both.

"Merry Christmas," he murmured.

With a sound that was both sigh and laugh, Pandora settled beside him.

Chapter 8

They left the Folley in the hard morning light the day after Christmas. Sun glared off snow, melting it at the edges and forming icicles down branches and eaves. It was a postcard with biting wind.

After a short tussle they'd agreed that Pandora would drive into the city and Michael would drive back. He pushed his seat back to the limit and managed to stretch out his legs. She maneuvered carefully down the slushy mountain road that led from the Folley. They didn't speak until she'd reached clear highway.

"What if they don't let us in?"

"Why shouldn't they?" Preferring driving to sitting, Michael shifted in his seat. For the first time he was impatient with the miles of road between the Folley and New York.

"Isn't that like counting your chickens?" Pandora

turned the heat down a notch and loosened the buttons of her coat. "We don't own the place yet."

"Just a technicality."

"Always cocky."

"You always look at the negative angles."

"Someone has to."

"Look…" He started to toss back something critical, then noticed how tightly she gripped the wheel. All nerves, he mused. Though the scenery was a print by Currier and Ives, it wasn't entirely possible to pretend they were off on a holiday jaunt. He was running on nerves himself, and they didn't all have to do with doctored champagne. How would he have guessed he'd wake up beside her in the cool light of dawn and feel so involved? So responsible. So hungry.

He took a deep breath and watched the scenery for another moment. "Look," he began again in a lighter tone. "We may not own the lab or anything else at the moment, but we're still Jolley's family. Why should a lab technician refuse to do a little analysis?"

"I suppose we'll find out when we get there." She drove another ten miles in silence. "Michael, what difference is an analysis going to make?"

"I have this odd sort of curiosity. I like to know if someone's tried to poison me."

"So we'll know if, and we'll know why. We still won't know who."

"That's the next step." He glanced over. "We can invite them all to the Folley for New Year's and take turns grilling them."

"Now you're making fun of me."

"No, actually, I'd thought of it. I just figure the time's not quite right." He waited a few minutes. In thin leather gloves, her fingers curled and uncurled on the wheel. "Pandora, why don't you tell me what's really bothering you?"

"Nothing is." Everything was. She hadn't been able to think straight for twenty-four hours.

"Nothing?"

"Nothing other than wondering if someone wants to kill me." She tossed it off arrogantly. "Isn't that enough?"

He heard the edge under the sarcasm. "Is that why you hid in your room all day yesterday?"

"I wasn't hiding." She had enough pride to sound brittle. "I was tending to Bruno. And I was tired."

"You hardly ate any of that enormous goose Sweeney slaved over."

"I'm not terribly fond of goose."

"I've had Christmas dinner with you before," he corrected. "You eat like a horse."

"How gallant of you to point it out." For no particular reason, she switched lanes, pumped the gas and passed another car. "Let's just say I wasn't in the mood."

"How did you manage to talk yourself into disliking what happened between us so quickly?" It hurt. He felt the hurt, but it didn't mean he had to let it show. His voice, as hers had been, was cool and hard.

"I haven't. That's absurd." Dislike? She hadn't been able to think of anything else, feel anything else. It scared her to death. "We slept together." She managed to toss it off with a shrug. "I suppose we both knew we would sooner or later."

He'd told himself precisely the same thing. He'd lost count of the number of times. He'd yet to figure out when he'd stopped believing. For himself. "And that's it?"

The question was deadly calm, but she was too pre-occupied with her own nerves to notice. "What else?" She had to stop dwelling on a moment of impulse. Didn't she? She couldn't go on letting her common sense be overrun by an attraction that would lead no-where. Could she? "Michael, there's no use blowing what happened out of proportion."

"Just what is that proportion?"

The car felt stuffy and close. Pandora switched off the heat and concentrated on the road. "We're two adults," she began, but had to swallow twice.

"And?"

"Dammit, Michael, I don't have to spell it out."

"Yes, you do."

"We're two adults," she said again, but with temper replacing nerves. "We have normal adult needs. We slept together and satisfied them."

"How practical."

"I am practical." Abruptly, and very badly, she wanted to weep. "Much too practical to weave fanta-sies about a man who likes his women in six packs. Too practical," she went on, voice rising, "to picture myself emotionally involved with a man I spent one night with. And too practical to romanticize what was no more than an exchange of normal and basic lust."

"Pull over."

"I will not."

"Pull over to the shoulder, Pandora, or I'll do it for you."

She gritted her teeth and debated calling his bluff. There was just enough traffic on the road to force her hand. With only a slight squeal of tires, Pandora pulled off to the side of the road. Michael turned off the key then grabbed her by the lapels and pulled her half into his seat. Before she could struggle away, he closed his mouth over hers.

Heat, anger, passion. They seemed to twist together into one emotion. He held her there as cars whizzed by, shaking the windows. She infuriated him, she aroused him, she hurt him. In Michael's opinion, it was too much for one man to take from one woman. As abruptly as he'd grabbed her, he released her.

"Make something practical out of that," he challenged.

Breathless, Pandora struggled back into her own seat. In a furious gesture, she turned the key, gunning the motor. "Idiot."

"Yeah." He sat back as she pulled back onto the highway. "We finally agree on something."

It was a long ride into the city. Longer still when you sat in a car in tense silence. Once they entered Manhattan, Pandora was forced to follow Michael's directions to the lab.

"How do you know where it is?" she demanded after they left the car in a parking garage. The sidewalk was mobbed with people hurrying to exchange what had been brightly boxed and wrapped the day before. As they walked, Pandora held her coat closed against the wind.

"I looked the address up in Jolley's files yesterday." Michael walked the half block hatless, his coat flapping open, clutching the box with the champagne under one arm. He wasn't immune to the cold but found it a relief after the hot tension of the drive. With a brisk gesture to Pandora, he pushed through revolving doors and entered the lobby of a steel-and-glass building. "He owned the whole place."

Pandora looked across the marble floor. It sloped upward and widened into a crowded, bustling area with men and women carrying briefcases. "This whole place?"

"All seventy-two floors."

It hit her again just how complicated the estate was. How many companies operated in the building? How many people worked there? How could she possibly crowd her life with this kind of responsibility? If she could get her hands on Uncle Jolley—Pandora broke off, almost amused. How he must be enjoying this, she thought.

"What am I supposed to do with seventy-two floors in midtown?"

"There are plenty of people to do it for you." Michael gave their names to the guard at the elevators. With no delay, they were riding to the fortieth floor.

"So there are people to do it for us. Who keeps track of them?"

"Accountants, lawyers, managers. It's a matter of hiring people to look after people you hire."

"That certainly clears that up."

"If you're worried, think about Jolley. Having a fortune didn't seem to keep him from enjoying himself. For the most part, he looked at the whole business as a kind of hobby."

Pandora watched the numbers above the door. "A hobby."

"Everyone should have a hobby."

"Tennis is a hobby," she muttered.

"The trick is to keep the ball moving. Jolley tossed it in our court, Pandora."

She folded her arms. "I'm not ready to be grateful for that."

"Look at it this way then." He put a hand on her shoulder and squeezed lightly. "You don't have to know how to build a car to own one. You just have to drive steady and follow the signs. If Jolley didn't think we could follow the signs, he wouldn't have given us the keys."

It helped to look at it that way. Still it was odd to consider she was riding on an elevator she would own when the six months were up. "Do we know whom to go to?" Pandora glanced at the box Michael held, which contained the bottle of champagne.

"A man named Silas Lockworth seems to be in charge."

"You did your homework."

"Let's hope it pays off."

When the elevator stopped, they walked into the reception area for Sanfield Laboratories. The carpet was pale rose, the walls lacquered in cream. Two huge split-leaf philodendrons flanked the wide glass doors that slid open at their approach. A woman behind a gleaming desk folded her hands and smiled.

"Good morning. May I help you?"

Michael glanced at the computer terminal resting on an extension of her desk. Top of the line. "We'd like to see Mr. Lockworth."

"Mr. Lockworth's in a meeting. If I could have your names, perhaps his assistant can help you."

"I'm Michael Donahue. This is Pandora McVie."

"McVie?"

Pandora saw the receptionist's eyebrows rise. "Yes, Maximillian McVie was our uncle."

Already polite and efficient, the receptionist became gracious. "I'm sure Mr. Lockworth would have greeted you himself if we'd known you were coming. Please have a seat. I'll ring through."

It took under five minutes.

The man who strode out into reception didn't look like Pandora's conception of a technician or scientist. He was six-three, lean as a gymnast with blond hair brushed back from a tanned, lantern-jawed face. He looked, Pandora thought, more like a man who'd be at home on the range than in a lab with test tubes.

"Ms. McVie." He walked with an easy rolling gait, hand outstretched. "Mr. Donahue. I'm Silas Lockworth. Your uncle was a good friend."

"Thank you." Michael accepted the handshake. "I apologize for dropping in unannounced."

"No need for that." Lockworth's smile seemed to mean it. "We never knew when Jolley was going to drop in on us. Let's go back to my office."

He led them down the corridor. Lockworth's office was the next surprise. It was plush enough, with curvy chairs and clever lithographs, to make you think of a corporate executive. The desk was piled high with enough files and papers to make you think of a harried clerk. It carried the scent from the dozens of leather-bound books on a floor-to-ceiling shelf. Built into one wall was a round aquarium teeming with exotic fish.

"Would you like coffee? I can guarantee it's hot and strong."

"No." Pandora was already twisting her gloves in her

hands. "Thank you. We don't want to take too much of your time."

"It's my pleasure," Lockworth assured her. "Jolley certainly spoke often of both of you," Lockworth went on as he gestured to chairs. "There was never a doubt you were his favorites."

"And he was ours," Pandora returned.

"Still you didn't come to pass the time." Lockworth leaned back on his desk. "What can I do for you?"

"We have something we'd like analyzed," Michael began. "Quickly and quietly."

"I see." Silas stopped there, brow raised. Lockworth was a man who picked up impressions of people right away. In Pandora he saw nerves under a sheen of politeness. In Michael he saw violence, not so much buried as thinly coated. He thought he detected a bond between them though they hadn't so much as looked at each other since entering the room.

Lockworth could have refused. His staff was slimmed down during the holidays, and work was backlogged. He was under no obligation to either of them yet. But he never forgot his obligation to Jolley McVie. "We'll try to accommodate you."

In silence, Michael opened the box and drew out the bottle of champagne. "We need a report on the contents of this bottle. A confidential report. Today."

Lockworth took it and examined the label. His lips curved slightly. "Seventy-two. A good year. Were you thinking of starting a vineyard?"

"We need to know what's in there other than champagne."

Rather than showing surprise, Lockworth leaned back on the desk again. "You've reason to think there is?"

Michael met the look. "We wouldn't be here otherwise."

Lockworth only inclined his head. "All right. I'll run it through the lab myself."

With a quick scowl for Michael's manners, Pandora rose and offered her hand. "We appreciate the trouble, Mr. Lockworth. I'm sure you have a great many other things to do, but the results are important to Michael and me."

"No problem." He decided he'd find out why it was important after he'd analyzed the wine. "There's a coffee shop for the staff. I'll show you where it is. You can wait for me there."

"There was absolutely no reason to be rude." Pandora settled herself at a table and looked at a surprisingly varied menu.

"I wasn't rude."

"Of course you were. Mr. Lockworth was going out of his way to be friendly, and you had a chip on your shoulder. I think I'm going to have the shrimp salad."

"I don't have a chip on my shoulder. I was being cautious. Or maybe you think we should spill everything to a total stranger."

Pandora folded her hands and smiled at the waitress. "I'd like the shrimp salad and coffee."

"Two coffees," Michael muttered. "And the turkey platter."

"I've no intention of spilling, as you put it, everything to a total stranger." Pandora picked up her napkin. "However, if we weren't going to trust Lockworth, we'd have been better off to buy a chemistry set and try to handle it ourselves."

"Drink your coffee," Michael muttered, and picked up his own the moment the waitress served it.

Pandora frowned as she added cream. "How long do you think it'll take?"

"I don't know. I'm not a scientist."

"He didn't look like one, either, did he?"

"Bronc rider." Michael sipped his black coffee and found it as strong as Lockworth had promised.

"What?"

"Looks like a bronc rider. I wonder if Carlson or any of the others have any interest in this building."

Pandora set her coffee down before she tasted it. "I hadn't thought of that."

"As I remember, Jolley turned over Tristar Corporation to Monroe about twenty-five years ago. I remember my parents talking about it."

"Tristar. Which one is that?"

"Plastics. I know he gave little pieces of the pie out here and there. He told me once he wanted to give all his relatives a chance before he crossed them off the list."

After a moment's thought, she shrugged and picked up her coffee again. "Well, if he did give a few shares of Sanfield to one of them, what difference does it make?"

"I don't know how much we should trust Lockworth."

"You'd have felt better if he'd been bald and short with Coke-bottle glasses and a faint German accent."

"Maybe."

"See?" Pandora smiled. "You're just jealous because he has great shoulders." She fluttered her lashes. "Here's your turkey."

They ate slowly, drank more coffee, then passed more time with pie. After an hour and a half, both of them were restless and edgy. When Lockworth came in, Pandora forgot to be nervous about the results.

"Thank God, here he comes."

After maneuvering around chairs and employees on lunch break, Lockworth set a computer printout on the table and handed the box back to Michael. "I thought you'd want a copy." He took a seat and signaled for coffee. "Though it's technical."

Pandora frowned down at the long, chemical terms printed out on the paper. It meant little more than nothing to her, but she doubted trichloroethanol or any of the other multisyllabic words belonged in French champagne. "What does it mean?"

"I wondered that myself." Lockworth reached in his pocket and drew out a pack of cigarettes. Michael looked at it for a moment with longing. "I wondered why anyone would put rose dust in vintage champagne."

"Rose dust?" Michael repeated. "Pesticide. So it was poisoned."

"Technically, yes. Though there wasn't enough in the wine to do any more than make you miserably ill for a day or two. I take it neither one of you had any?"

"No." Pandora looked up from the report. "My puppy did," she explained. "When we opened the bottle, some spilled and he lapped it up. Before we'd gotten around to drinking it, he was ill."

"Luckily for you, though I find it curious that you'd jumped to the conclusion that the champagne had been poisoned because a puppy was sick."

"Luckily for us, we did." Michael folded the report and slipped it into his pocket.

"You'll have to pardon my cousin," Pandora said. "He has no manners. We appreciate you taking time out to do this for us, Mr. Lockworth. I'm afraid it isn't possible to fully explain ourselves at this point, but I can tell you that we had good reason to suspect the wine."

Lockworth nodded. As a scientist he knew how to theorize. "If you find you need a more comprehensive report, let me know. Jolley was an important person in my life. We'll call it a favor to him."

As he rose, Michael stood with him. "I'll apologize for myself this time." He held out a hand.

"I'd be a bit edgy myself if someone gave me pesticide disguised as Moët et Chandon. Let me know if I can do anything else."

"Well," Pandora began when they were alone. "What next?"

"A little trip to the liquor store. We've some presents to buy."

They sent, first-class, a bottle of the same to each of Jolley's erstwhile heirs. Michael signed the cards simply, "One good turn deserves another." After it was done and they walked outside in the frigid wind, Pandora huffed and pulled on her gloves.

"An expensive gesture."

"Look at it as an investment," Michael suggested.

It wasn't the money, she thought, but the sudden futility she felt. "What good will it do really?"

"Several bottles'll be wondered over, then appreciated. But one," Michael said with relish. "One makes a statement, even a threat."

"An empty threat," Pandora returned. "It's not as if we'll be there when everyone gets one to gauge reactions."

"You're thinking like an amateur."

Michael was halfway across the street when Pandora grabbed his arm. "Just what does that mean?"

"When an amateur plays a practical joke, he thinks he has to be in on the kill."

Ignoring the people who brushed by them, Pandora held her ground. "Since when is pesticide poisoning a practical joke?"

"Revenge follows the same principle."

"Oh, I see. And you're an expert."

The light changed. Cars started for them, horns blaring. Gritting his teeth, Michael grabbed her arm and pulled her to the curb. "Maybe I am. It's enough for me to know someone's going to look at the bottle and be very nervous. Someone's going to look at it and know we intend to give as good as we get. Your trouble is you don't like to let your emotions loose long enough to appreciate revenge."

"Leave my emotions alone."

"That's the plan," he said evenly, and started walking again.

In three strides she'd caught up with him. Her face was pink from the wind, the anger in her voice came out in thin wisps. "You're not annoyed with Lockworth or about the champagne or over differing views on revenge. You're mad because I defined our relationship in practical terms."

He stared at her as her phrasing worked on both his temper and his humor. "Okay," he declared, turning to walk on. Patience straining, he turned back when Pandora grabbed his arm. "You want to hash this out right here?"

"I won't let you make me feel inadequate just because I broke things off before you had a chance to."

"Before I had a chance to?" He took her by the coat. With the added height from the heels on her boots, she looked straight into his eyes. Another time, another place, he might have considered her magnificent. "I barely had the chance to recover from what happened before you were shoving me out. I wanted you. Dammit, I still want you. God knows why."

"Well, I want you, too, and I don't like it, either."

"Looks like that puts us in the same fix, doesn't it?"

"So what're we going to do about it?"

He looked at her and saw the anger. But he looked closely enough to see confusion, as well. One of them had to make the first move. He decided it was going to be him. Taking her hand, he dragged her across the street.

"Where are we going?"

"The Plaza."

"The Plaza Hotel? Why?"

"We're going to get a room, put the chain on the door and make love for the next twenty-four hours. After that, we'll decide how we want to handle it."

There were times, Pandora decided, when it was best to go along for the ride. "We don't have any luggage."

"Yeah. My reputation's about to be shattered."

She made a sound that might have been a laugh. When they walked into the elegant lobby, the heat warmed her skin and stirred up her nerves. It was all impulse, she told herself. She knew better than to make any important decision on impulse. He could change everything. That was something she hadn't wanted to admit but had known for years. When she started to draw away, his hand locked on her arm.

"Coward," he murmured. He couldn't have said

anything more perfectly designed to make her march forward.

"Good afternoon." Michael smiled at the desk clerk. Pandora wondered briefly if the smile would have been so charming if the clerk had been a man. "Checking in."

"You have a reservation?"

"Donahue. Michael Donahue."

The clerk punched some buttons and stared at her computer screen. "I'm afraid I don't show anything under Donahue for the twenty-sixth."

"Katie," Michael said on a breath of impatience. He sent Pandora a long suffering look. "I should never have trusted her to handle this."

Catching the drift, Pandora patted his hand. "You're going to have to let her go, Michael. I know she's worked for your family for forty years, but when a person gets into their seventies…" She trailed off and let Michael take the ball.

"We'll decide when we get home." He turned back to the desk clerk. "Apparently there's been a mix-up between my secretary and the hotel. We'll only be in town overnight. Is anything available?"

The clerk went back to her buttons. Most people in her experience raised the roof when there was a mix-up in reservations. Michael's quiet request touched her sympathies. "You understand there's a problem because of the holiday." She punched more buttons, wanting to help. "We do have a suite available."

"Fine." Michael took the registration form and filled it out. With the key in his hand, he sent the clerk another smile. "I appreciate the trouble." Noting the bellhop hovering at his elbow, he handed him a bill. "We'll handle it, thanks."

The clerk looked at the twenty in his palm and the lack of luggage. "Yes, sir!"

"He thinks we're having an illicit affair," Pandora murmured as they stepped onto the elevator.

"We are." Before the doors had closed again, Michael grabbed her to him and locked her in a kiss that lasted twelve floors. "We don't know each other," he told her as they stepped into the hallway. "We've just met. We don't have mutual childhood memories or share the same family." He put the key in the lock. "We don't give a damn what the other does for a living nor do we have any long-standing opinions about each other."

"Is that supposed to simplify things?"

Michael drew her inside. "Let's find out."

He didn't give her a chance to wonder, a chance to debate. The moment the door was shut behind them, he had her in his arms. He took questions away. He took choice away. For once, she wanted him to. In a fury of passions, of hungers, of cravings, they came together. Each fought to draw more, still more out of the other, to touch faster, to possess more quickly. They forgot what they knew, what they thought and reveled in what they felt.

Coats, still chill from the wind, were pushed to the floor. Sweaters and shirts followed. Hardly more than a foot inside the door, they slid to the carpet.

"Damn winter," Michael muttered as he fought with her boots.

Laughing, Pandora struggled with his, then moaned when he pressed his lips to her breast.

It was a race, part warring, part loving. Neither gave the other respite. When their clothes were shed, they sprinted ahead, hands reaching, lips arousing. There was none of the dreamy déjà vu they'd experienced the first time. This was new. The fingers tracing her skin had never been felt before. The lips, hot and searing, had never been tasted. Fresh, erotically fresh, their mouths met and clung.

Her heart had never beat so fast. She was sure of it. Her body had never ached and pulsed so desperately. She'd never wanted it to. Now she wanted more, everything. Him. She rolled so that she could press quick, hungry kisses over his face, his neck, his chest. Everywhere.

His mind was teeming with her, with every part of her that he could touch or taste or smell. She was wild in a way he'd never imagined. She was demanding in a way any man would desire. His body seemed to fascinate her, every curve, every angle. She exploited it until he was half mad, then he groped for her.

She'd never known a man could give so much. Racked with sensations, she arched under him. Hot and ready, she offered. But he was far from through. The taste of her thighs was subtle, luring him toward the heat. He found her, drove her and kept her helplessly trapped in passion. Helplessly. The sensation shivered over her. She'd never known what it had meant to be truly vulnerable to another. He could have taken anything from her then, asked anything and she couldn't have refused. But he didn't ask, he gave.

She crested wave after wave. Between heights and depths she pinwheeled, delighting in the spin. On the rug with the afternoon light streaming through the windows, she was locked in blinding darkness without any wish to see. *Make me feel,* her mind seemed to shout. More. Again. Still.

And he was inside her, joined, melded. She found there was more. Impossibly more.

They stayed where they were, sprawled on scattered clothes. Gradually Pandora found her mind swimming back to reality. She could see the pastel walls, the sunlight. She could smell the body heat that was a mix of hers and his. She could feel Michael's hair brushing over her cheek, the beat of his heart, still fast, against her breast.

It happened so fast, she thought. Or had it taken hours? All she was certain of was that she'd never experienced anything like it. Never permitted herself to, she amended. Strange things could happen to a woman who lifted the lid from her passion. Other things could sneak in before the top closed again. Things like affection, understanding. Even love.

She caught herself stroking Michael's hair and let her hand fall to the carpet. She couldn't let love in, not even briefly. Love took as well as gave. That she'd always known. And it didn't always give and take in equal shares. Michael wasn't a man a woman could love practically, and certainly not wisely. That she understood. He wouldn't follow the rules.

She'd be his lover, but she wouldn't love him. Though there would be no pretending they could live with each other for the next three months platonically, she wouldn't risk her heart. For an instant Pandora thought she felt it break, just a little. Foolishness, she told herself. Her heart was strong and unimpaired. What she and Michael had together was a very basic, very uncomplicated arrangement. Arrangement, she thought, sounded so much more practical than romance.

But her sigh was quiet, and a little wistful.

"Figure it all out?" He shifted a little as he spoke, just enough so that he could brush his lips down her throat.

"What do you mean?"

"Have you figured out the guidelines for our relationship?" Lifting his head, he looked down at her. He wasn't smiling, but Pandora thought he was amused.

"I don't know what you're talking about."

"I can almost hear the wheels turning. Pandora, I can see just what's going on in your head."

Annoyed that he probably could, she lifted a brow. "I thought we'd just met."

"I'm psychic. You're thinking...." He trailed off to nibble at her lips. "That there should be a way to keep our...relationship on a practical level. You're wondering how you'll keep an emotional distance when we're sleeping together. You've decided that there'll be absolutely no romantic overtones to any arrangement between us."

"All right." He made her feel foolish. Then he ran a hand over her hip and made her tremble. "Since you're so smart, you'll see that I've only been using common sense."

"I like it better when your skin gets hot, and you haven't any sense at all. But—" he kissed her before she could answer "—we can't stay in bed all the time. I don't believe in practical affairs, Pandora. I don't believe in emotional distance between lovers."

"You've had a great deal of experience there."

"That's right." He sat up, drawing her with him. "And I'll tell you this. You can wall up your emotions all you want. You can call whatever we have here by any practical term you can dream up. You can turn up your nose at candlelight dinners and quiet music. It's not going to make any difference." He gathered her hair in his hand and pulled her head back. "I'm going to get to you, cousin. I'm going to get to you until you can't think of anything, anyone but me. If you wake up in the middle of the night and I'm not there, you'll wish I were. And when I touch you, any time I touch you, you're going to want me."

She had to fight the shudder. She knew, as well as she'd ever known anything, that he was right. And she knew, perhaps they both did, that she'd fight it right down to the end. "You're arrogant, egocentric and simpleminded."

"True enough. And you're stubborn, willful and perverse. The only thing we can be sure of at this point is that one of us is going to win."

Sitting on the pile of discarded clothes, they studied each other. "Another game?" Pandora murmured.

"Maybe. Maybe it's the only game." With that, he stood and lifted her into his arms.

"Michael, I don't need to be carried."

"Yes, you do."

He walked across the suite toward the bedroom. Pandora started to struggle, then subsided. Maybe just this once, she decided, and relaxed in his arms.

Chapter 9

January was a month of freezing wind, pelting snow and gray skies. Each day was as bitterly cold as the last, with tomorrow waiting frigidly in the wings. It was a month of frozen pipes, burst pipes, overworked furnaces and stalled engines. Pandora loved it. The frost built up on the windows of her shop, and the inside temperature always remained cool even with the heaters turned up. She worked until her fingers were numb and enjoyed every moment.

Throughout the month, the road to the Folley was often inaccessible. Pandora didn't mind not being able to get out. It meant no one could get in. The pantry and freezer were stocked, and there was over a cord of wood stacked beside the kitchen door. The way she looked at it, they had everything they needed. The days were short and productive, the nights long and relaxing. Since the incident of the champagne, it had been a quiet, uneventful winter.

Uneventful, Pandora mused, wasn't precisely the right term. With quick, careful strokes, she filed the edges of a thick copper bracelet. It certainly wasn't as though nothing had happened. There'd been no trouble from outside sources, but... Trouble, as she'd always known, was definitely one of Michael Donahue's greatest talents.

Just what was he trying to pull by leaving a bunch of violets on her pillow? She was certain a magic wand would have been needed to produce the little purple flowers in January. When she'd questioned him about them, he'd simply smiled and told her violets didn't have thorns. What kind of an answer was that? Pandora wondered, and examined the clasp of the bracelet through a magnifying glass. She was satisfied with the way she'd designed it to blend with the design.

Then, there'd been the time she'd come out of the bath to find the bedroom lit with a dozen candles. When she'd asked if there'd been a power failure, Michael had just laughed and pulled her into bed.

He did things like reaching for her hand at dinner and whispering in her ear just before dawn. Once he'd joined her in the shower uninvited and silenced her protests by washing every inch of her body himself. She'd been right. Michael Donahue didn't follow the rules. He'd been right. He was getting to her.

Pandora removed the bracelet from the vise, then absently began to polish it. She'd made a half a dozen others in the last two weeks. Big chunky bracelets, some had gaudy stones, some had ornate engraving. They suited her mood—daring, opinionated and a bit silly.

She'd learned to trust her instincts, and her instincts told her they'd sell faster than she could possibly make them—and be copied just as quickly.

She didn't mind the imitations. After all, there was only one of each type that was truly a Pandora McVie. Copies would be recognized as copies because they lacked that something special, that individuality of the genuine.

Pleased, she turned the bracelet over in her hand. No one would mistake any of her work for an imitation. She might often use glass instead of precious or semi-precious stones because glass expressed her mood at the time. But each piece she created carried her mark, her opinion and her honesty. She never gave a thought to the price of a piece when she crafted it or its market value. She created what she needed to create first, then after it was done, her practical side calculated the profit margin. Her art varied from piece to piece, but it never lied.

Looking down at the bracelet, Pandora sighed. No, her art never lied, but did she? Could she be certain her emotions were as genuine as the jewelry she made? A feeling could be imitated. An emotion could be fraudulent. How many times in the past few weeks had she pretended? Not pretended to feel, Pandora thought, but pretended not to feel. She was a woman who'd always prided herself on her honesty. Truth and independence went hand in hand with Pandora's set of values. But she'd lied—over and over again—to herself, the worst form of deception.

It was time to stop, Pandora told herself. Time to face the truth of her feelings if only in the privacy of her own heart and mind.

How long had she been in love with Michael? She had to stand and move around the shop as the question formed in her mind. Weeks? Months? Years? It wasn't something she could answer because she would never be sure. But she was certain of the emotion. She loved. Pandora understood it because she loved only a few people, and when she did, she loved boundlessly. Perhaps that was the biggest problem. Wasn't it a sort of suicide to love Michael boundlessly?

Better to face it, she told herself. No problem resolved itself without being faced first and examined second. However much a fool it made her, she loved Michael. Pandora rubbed at the steam on the windows and looked out at the snow. Strange, she'd really believed once she accepted it she'd feel better. She didn't.

What options did she have? She could tell him. And have him gloat, Pandora thought with a scowl. He would, too, before he trotted off to his next conquest. *She* certainly wasn't fool enough to think he'd be interested in a long-term relationship. Of course, she wasn't interested in one either, Pandora told herself as she began to noisily pack her tools.

Another option was to cut and run. What the relatives hadn't been able to accomplish with their malice and mischief, her own heart would succeed in doing. She could get in the car, drive to the airport and fly to anywhere. Escape was the honest word. Then, she'd not only be a coward, she'd be a traitor. No, she wouldn't let Uncle Jolley down; she wouldn't run. That left her, as Pandora saw it, with one option.

She'd go on as she was. She'd stay with Michael, sleep with Michael, share with Michael—share with him everything but what was in her heart. She'd take the two months they had left together and prepare herself to walk away with no regrets.

He'd gotten to her, Pandora admitted. Gotten to her in places no other man had touched. She loved him for it. She hated him for it. With her mood as turbulent as her thoughts, she locked the shop and stomped across the lawn.

"Here she comes now." With a new plan ready to spring, Sweeney turned away from the kitchen window and signaled to Charles.

"It's never going to work."

"Of course it is. We're going to push those children together for their own good. Any two people who spat as much as they do should be married."

"We're interfering where it's not our place."

"What malarkey!" Sweeney took her seat at the kitchen table. "Whose place is it to interfere if not ours, I'd like to know? Who'll be knocking around this big empty house if they go back to the city if not us? Now pick up that cloth and fan me. Stoop over a bit and look feeble."

"I am feeble," Charles muttered, but picked up the cloth.

When Pandora walked into the kitchen she saw Sweeney sprawled back in a chair, eyes closed, with Charles standing over her waving a dishcloth at her face.

"God, what's wrong? Charles, did she faint?" Before he could answer, Pandora had dashed across the room. "Call Michael," she ordered. "Call Michael quickly." She brushed Charles away and crouched. "Sweeney, it's Pandora. Are you in pain?"

Barely suppressing a sigh of satisfaction, Sweeney let her eyes flutter open and hoped she looked pale. "Oh, missy, don't you worry now. Just one of my spells is all. Now and then my heart starts to flutter so that I feel it's coming right out of my head."

"I'm going to call the doctor." Pandora had taken only one step when her hand was caught in a surprisingly strong grip.

"No need for that." Sweeney made her voice thin and weary. "Saw him just a few months past and he told me I'd have to expect one of these now and again."

"I don't believe that," Pandora said fiercely. "You're just plain working too hard, and it's going to stop."

A little trickle of guilt worked its way in as Sweeney saw the concern. "Now, now, don't fret."

"What is it?" Michael swung through the kitchen door. "Sweeney?" He knelt down beside her and took her other hand.

"Now look at all this commotion." Mentally she leaped up and kicked her heels. "It's nothing but one of my little spells. The doctor said I'd have to watch for them. Just a nuisance, that's all." She looked hard at Charles when he came in. Eventually she looked hard enough so that he remembered his cue.

"And you know what he said."

"Now, Charles—"

"You're to have two or three days of bed rest."

Pleased that he'd remembered his lines, Sweeney pretended to huff. "Pack of nonsense. I'll be right as rain in a few minutes. I've dinner to cook."

"You won't be cooking anything." In a way Sweeney considered properly masterful, Michael picked her up. "Into bed with you."

"Just who'll take care of things?" Sweeney demanded. "I'll not have Charles spreading his germs around my kitchen."

Michael was nearly out of the room with Sweeney before Charles remembered the next step. He coughed into his hand, looked apologetic and coughed again.

"Listen to that!" Pleased, Sweeney let her head rest against Michael's shoulder. "I won't go to bed and let him infect my kitchen."

"How long have you had that cough?" Pandora demanded. When Charles began to mutter, she stood up. "That's enough. Both of you into bed. Michael and I will take care of everything." Taking Charles's arm, she began to lead him into the servants' wing. "Into bed and no nonsense. I'll make both of you some tea. Michael, see that Charles gets settled, I'll look after Sweeney."

Within a half hour, Sweeney had them both where she wanted them. Together.

"Well, they're all settled in and there's no fever." Satisfied, Pandora poured herself a cup of tea. "I suppose all they need is a few days' rest and some pampering. Tea?"

He made a face at the idea and switched on the coffee. "Since the days of house calls are over, I'd think they'd be better off here in bed than being dragged into town. We can take turns keeping an eye on them."

"Mmm-hmm." Pandora opened the refrigerator and studied. "What about meals? Can you cook?"

"Sure." Michael rattled cups in the cupboard. "Badly, but I can cook. Meat loaf's my specialty." When this was met with no enthusiasm, he turned his head. "Do you?"

"Cook?" Pandora lifted a plastic lid hopefully. "I can broil a steak and scramble eggs. Anything else is chancy."

"Life's nothing without a risk." Michael joined her in her rummage through the refrigerator. "Here's almost half an apple cobbler."

"That's hardly a meal."

"It'll do for me." He took it out and went for a spoon. Pandora watched as he sat down at the table and dug in. "Want some?"

She started to refuse on principle, then decided not to cut off her nose. Going to the cupboard, she found a bowl. "What about the bedridden?" she asked as she scooped out cobbler.

"Soup," Michael said between bites. "Nothing better than hot soup. Though I'd let them rest awhile first."

With a nod of agreement, she sat across from him. "Michael…" She trailed off as she played with her cobbler. The steam from her tea rose up between them. She'd been thinking about how to broach the subject for days. It seemed the time had come. "I've been thinking. In two months, the will should be final. When Fitzhugh wrote us last week, he said Uncle Carlson's lawyers were advising him to drop the probate."

"So?"

"The house, along with everything else, will be half yours, half mine."

"That's right."

She took a bite of cobbler, then set down her spoon. "What're you smiling at?"

"You're nice to look at. I find it relaxing to sit here alone in the kitchen, in the quiet, and look at you."

It was that sort of thing, just that sort of thing, that left her light-headed and foolish. She stared at him a moment, then dropped her gaze to her bowl. "I wish you wouldn't say things like that."

"No, you don't. So you've been thinking," he prompted.

"Yes." She gave herself a moment, carefully spooning out another bite of cobbler. "We'll have the house between us, but we won't be living here together any longer. Sweeney and Charles will be here alone. I've worried about that for a while. Now, after this, I'm more concerned than ever. They can't stay here alone."

"No, I think you're right. Ideas?"

"I mentioned before that I was considering moving here on a semipermanent basis." She found she had no appetite after all and switched back to her tea. "I think I'm going to make it permanent all around."

He heard a trace of nervousness in her voice. "Because of Charles and Sweeney?"

"Only partly." She drank more tea, set the cup down and toyed with her cobbler again. She wasn't accustomed to discussing her decisions with anyone. Though she found it difficult, Pandora had already resolved that she had an obligation to do so. More, she'd realized she needed to talk to him, to be, as she couldn't be on other levels, honest. "I always felt the Folley was home, but I didn't realize just how much of a home. I need it, for myself. You see, I never had one." She lifted her gaze and met his. "Only here."

To say her words surprised him was to say too little. All his life he'd seen her as the pampered pet, the golden girl with every advantage. "But your parents—"

"Are wonderful," Pandora said quickly. "I adore them. There's nothing about them I'd change. But…" How could she explain? How could she not? "We never had a kitchen like this—a place you could come back to day after day and know it'd be the same. Even if you changed the wallpaper and the paint, it would be the same. It sounds silly." She shifted restlessly. "You wouldn't understand."

"Maybe I would." He caught her hand before she could rise. "Maybe I'd like to."

"I want a home," she said simply. "The Folley's been that to me. I want to stay here after the term's up."

He kept her hand in his, palm to palm. "Why are you telling me this, Pandora?"

Reasons. Too many reasons. She chose the only one she could give him safely. "In two months, the house belongs to you as much as to me. According to the terms of the will—"

He swore and released her hand. Rising, he stuck his hands in his back pockets and strode to the window. He'd thought for a moment, just for a moment, she'd been ready to give him more. By God, he'd waited long enough for only a few drops more. There'd been something in her voice, something soft and giving. Perhaps he'd just imagined it because he'd wanted to hear it. Terms of the will, he thought. It was so like her to see nothing else.

"What do you want, my permission?"

Disturbed, Pandora stayed at the table. "I suppose I wanted you to understand and agree."

"Fine."

"You needn't be so curt about it. After all, you haven't any plans to use the house on a regular basis."

"I haven't made any plans," he murmured. "Perhaps it's time I did."

"I didn't mean to annoy you."

He turned slowly, then just as slowly smiled. "No, I'm sure you didn't. There's never any doubt when you annoy me intentionally."

There was something wrong here, something she couldn't quite pinpoint. So she groped. "Would you mind so much if I were to live here?"

It surprised him when she rose to come to him, offering a hand. She didn't make such gestures often or casually. "No, why should it?"

"It would be half yours."

"We could draw a line down the middle."

"That might be awkward. I could buy you out."

"No."

He said it so fiercely, her brows shot up. "It was only an offer."

"Forget it." He turned to look for soup.

Pandora stood back a moment, watching his back, the tension in the muscles. "Michael…" With a sigh, she wrapped her arms around his waist. She felt him stiffen, but didn't realize it was from surprise. "I seem to be saying all the wrong things. Maybe I have an easier time when we snap at each other than when I try to be considerate."

"Maybe we both do." He turned to frame her face with his hands. For a moment they looked like friends, like lovers. "Pandora…." Could he tell her he found it impossible to think about leaving her or her leaving him? Would she understand if he told her he wanted to go on living with her, being with her? How could she possibly take in the fact that he'd been in love with her for years when he was just becoming able to accept it himself? Instead he kissed her forehead. "Let's make soup."

They couldn't work together without friction, but they discovered over the next few days that they could work together. They cooked meals, washed up, dusted furniture while the servants stayed in bed or sat, bundled up, on sofas drinking tea. True, there were times when Sweeney itched to get up and be about her business, or when Charles suffered pangs of conscience, but they were convinced they were doing their duty. Both servants felt justified when they heard laughter drift through the house.

Michael wasn't sure there had been another time in his life when he'd been so content. He was, in essence, playing house, something he'd never had the time or inclination for. He would write for hours, closed off in his office, wrapped up in plots and characters and what-ifs. Then he could break away and reality was the scent of cooking or furniture polish. He had a home, a woman, and was determined to keep them.

Late in the afternoon, he always laid a fire in the parlor. After dinner they had coffee there, sometimes quietly, sometimes during a hard-fought game of rummy. It seemed ordinary, Michael admitted. It was ordinary, unless you added Pandora. He was just setting fire to the kindling when Bruno raced into the room and upset a table. Knickknacks went flying.

"We're going to have to send you to charm school," Michael declared as he rose to deal with the rubble. Though it had been just over a month, Bruno had nearly doubled in size already. He was, without a doubt, going to grow into his paws. After righting the table, he saw the dog wiggling its way under a sofa. "What've you got there?"

Besides being large, Bruno had already earned a reputation as a clever thief. Just the day before, they'd lost a slab of pork chops. "All right, you devil, if that's tonight's chicken, you're going into solitary confinement in the garage." Getting down on all fours, Michael looked under the couch. It wasn't chicken the dog was gnawing noisily on, but Michael's shoe.

"Damn!" Michael made a grab but the dog backed out of reach and kept on chewing. "That shoe's worth five times what you are, you overgrown mutt. Give it here." Flattening, Michael scooted halfway under the sofa. Bruno merely dragged the shoe away again, enjoying the game.

"Oh, how sweet." Pandora walked into the parlor and eyed Michael from the waist down. He did, she decided, indeed have some redeeming qualities. "Are you playing with the dog, Michael, or dusting under the sofa?"

"I'm going to make a rug out of him."

"Dear, dear, we sound a little cross this evening. Bruno, here baby." Carrying the shoe like a trophy, Bruno squirmed out from under the couch and pranced over to her. "Is this what you were after?" Pandora held up the shoe while petting Bruno with her other hand. "How clever of you to teach Bruno to fetch."

Michael pulled himself up, then yanked the shoe out of her hand. It was unfortunately wet and covered with teeth marks. "That's the second shoe he's ruined. And he didn't even have the courtesy to take both from one pair."

She looked down at what had been creamy Italian leather. "You never wear anything but tennis shoes or boots anyway."

Michael slapped the shoe against his palm. Bruno, tongue lolling, grinned up at him. "Obedience school."

"Oh, Michael, we can't send our child away." She patted his cheek. "It's just a phase."

"This phase has cost me two pairs of shoes, my dinner and we never did find that sweater he dragged off."

"You shouldn't drop your clothes on the floor," Pandora said easily. "And that sweater was already ratty. I'm sure Bruno thought it was a rag."

"He never chews up anything of yours."

Pandora smiled. "No, he doesn't, does he?"

Michael gave her a long look. "Just what're you so happy about?"

"I had a phone call this afternoon."

Michael saw the excitement in her eyes and decided the issue of the shoe could wait. "And?"

"From Jacob Morison."

"The producer?"

"*The* producer," Pandora repeated. She'd promised herself she wouldn't overreact, but the excitement threatened to burst inside her. "He's going to be filming a new movie. Jessica Wainwright's starring."

Jessica Wainwright, Michael mused. Grande dame of the theater and the screen. Eccentric and brilliant, her career had spanned two generations. "She's retired. Wainwright hasn't made a film in five years."

"She's making this one. Billy Mitchell's directing."

Michael tilted his head in consideration as he studied Pandora's face. It made him think of the cat and the canary. "Sounds like they're pulling out all the stops."

"She plays a half-mad reclusive countess who's dragged back to reality by a visit from her granddaughter. Cass Barkley's on the point of signing for the part of the granddaughter."

"Oscar material. Now, are you going to tell me why Morison called you?"

"Wainwright's an admirer of my work. She wants

me to design all her jewelry for the movie. All!" After an attempt to sound businesslike, Pandora laughed and did a quick spin. "Morison said the only way he could talk her out of retirement was to promise her the best. She wants me."

Michael grabbed her close and spun her around. Bruno raced around the room barking and shaking tables. "We'll celebrate," he decided. "Champagne with our fried chicken."

Pandora held on tight. "I feel like an idiot."

"Why?"

"I've always thought I was, well, beyond star adoration. I'm a professional." Bubbling with excitement, she clung to Michael. "While I was talking to Morison I told myself it was a great career opportunity, a wonderful chance to express myself in a large way. Then I hung up and all I could think was Jessica Wainwright! A Morison production! I felt as silly as any bubble-headed fan."

"Proves you're not half the snob you think you are." Michael cut off her retort with a kiss. "I'm proud of you," he murmured.

That threw her off. All of her pleasure in the assignment was dwarfed by that one sentence. No one but Jolley had ever been proud of her. Her parents loved her, patted her head and told her to do what she wanted. Pride was a valued addition to affection. "Really?"

Surprised, Michael drew her back and kissed her again. "Of course I am."

"But you've never thought much of my work."

"No, that's not true. I've never understood why people feel the need to deck themselves out in bangles, or why you seemed content to design on such a small scale.

But as far as your work goes I'm not blind, Pandora. Some of it's beautiful, some of it's extraordinary and some of it's incomprehensible. But it's all imaginative and expertly crafted."

"Well." She let out a long breath. "This is a red-letter day. I always thought you felt I was playing with beads because I didn't want to face a real job. You even said so once."

He grinned. "Only because it made you furious. You're spectacular to look at when you're furious."

She thought about it a moment, then let out a sigh. "I suppose this is the best time to tell you."

He tensed, but forced his voice to come calmly. "To tell me what?"

"I watch the Emmy Awards every time you're nominated."

Tension flowed out in a laugh. There'd been guilt in every syllable. "What?"

"Every time," Pandora repeated, amazed that her cheeks were warm. "It made me feel good to watch you win. And…" She paused to clear her throat. "I've watched a few episodes of *Logan's Run*."

Michael wondered if she realized she sounded as though she was confessing a major social flaw. "Why?"

"Uncle Jolley was always going on about it; I'd even hear it discussed at parties. So I thought I'd see for myself. Naturally, it was just a matter of intellectual curiosity."

"Naturally. And?"

She moved her shoulders. "Of its kind—"

He stopped that line of response by twisting her ear. "Some people only tell the truth under duress."

"All right." Half laughing, she reached to free herself. "It's good!" she shouted when he held on. "I liked it."

"Why?"

"Michael, that hurts!"

"We have ways of making you talk."

"I liked it because the characters are genuine, the plots are intelligent. And—" she had to swallow hard on this one "—it has style."

When he let go of her ear to kiss her soundly, she gave him a halfhearted shove. "If you repeat that to anyone, I'll deny it."

"It'll be our little secret." He kissed her again, not so playfully.

Pandora was almost becoming used to the sensation of having her muscles loosen and feeling as if her bones were dissolving. She moved closer, delighting in the feeling of having her body mold against his. When his heart thudded, she felt the pulse inside herself. When his tiny moan escaped, she tasted it on her tongue. When the need leaped forward, she saw it in his eyes.

She pressed her mouth to his again and let her own hunger rule. There would be consequences. Hadn't she already accepted it? There would be pain. She was already braced for it. She couldn't stop what would happen in the weeks ahead, but she could direct what would happen tonight and perhaps tomorrow. It had to be enough. Everything she felt, wanted, feared, went into the kiss.

It left him reeling. She was often passionate, wildly so. She was often demanding, erotically so. But he'd never felt such pure emotion from her. There was a softness under the strength, a request under the urgency. He drew her closer, more gently than was his habit, and let her take what she wanted.

Her head tilted back, inviting, luring. His grip tightened. His fingers wound into her hair and were lost in the richness of it. He felt the need catapult through his body so that he was tense against her sudden, unexpected yielding. She never submitted, and until that moment he hadn't known how stirring it could be to have her do so. Without a thought to time and place, they lowered to the sofa.

Because she was pliant, he was tender. Because he was gentle, she was patient. In a way they'd never experienced, they made love without rush, without fire, without the whirlwind. Thoroughly, they gave to each other. A touch, a taste, a murmured request, a whispered answer. The fire sizzled gently behind them as night fell outside the windows. Fingers brushed, lips skimmed so that they learned the power of quiet arousal. Though they'd been lovers for weeks, they brought love to passion for the first time.

The room was quiet, the light dim. If she'd never looked for romance, it found her there, wrapped easily in Michael's arms. Closer they came, but comfortably. Deeper they dived, but lazily. As they came together, Pandora felt her firm line of independence crack to let him in. But the weakness she'd expected didn't follow. Only contentment.

It was contentment that followed her into that quick and final burst of pleasure.

They were still wrapped together, half dozing, when the phone rang. With a murmur of complaint, Michael reached over his head to the table and lifted the receiver.

"Hello."

"Michael Donahue, please."

"Yeah, this is Michael."

"Michael, it's Penny."

He rubbed a hand over his eyes as he tried to put a face with the name. Penny—the little blonde in the apartment next to his. Wanted to be a model. He remembered vaguely leaving her the number of the Folley in case something important was delivered to his apartment. "Hi." He watched Pandora's eyes flutter open.

"Michael, I hate to do this, but I had to call. I've already phoned the police. They're on their way."

"Police?" He struggled into a half-sitting position. "What's going on?"

"You've been robbed."

"What?" He sat bolt upright, nearly dumping Pandora on the floor. "When?"

"I'm not sure. I got home a few minutes ago and noticed your door wasn't closed all the way. I thought maybe you'd come back so I knocked. Anyway, I pushed the door open a bit. The place was turned upside down. I came right over here and called the cops. They asked me to contact you and told me not to go back over."

"Thanks." Dozens of questions ran through his mind but there was no one to answer them. "Look, I'll try to come in tonight."

"Okay. Hey, Michael, I'm really sorry."

"Yeah. I'll see you."

"Michael?" Pandora grabbed his hand as soon as he hung up the receiver.

"Somebody broke into my apartment."

"Oh no." She'd known the peace couldn't last. "Do you think it was—"

"I don't know." He dragged a hand through his hair.

"Maybe. Or maybe it was someone who noticed no one had been home for a while."

She felt the anger in him but knew she couldn't soothe it. "You've got to go."

Nodding, he took her hand. "Come with me."

"Michael, one of us has to be here with Sweeney and Charles."

"I'm not leaving you alone."

"You have to go," she repeated. "If it was one of the family, maybe you can find something to prove it. In any case, you have to see to this. I'll be fine."

"Just like the last time I was away."

Pandora lifted a brow. "I'm not incompetent, Michael."

"But you'll be alone."

"I have Bruno. Don't give me that look," she ordered. "He may not be ferocious, but he certainly knows how to bark. I'll lock every door and window."

He shook his head. "Not good enough."

"All right, we'll call the local police. They have Fitzhugh's report about trespassers. We'll explain that I'm going to be alone for the night and ask them to keep an eye on the place."

"Better." But he rose to pace. "If this is a setup…"

"Then we're prepared for it this time."

Michael hesitated, thought it through, then nodded. "I'll call the police."

Chapter 10

The moment Michael left, Pandora turned the heavy bolt on the main door. Though it had taken them the better part of an hour, she was grateful he'd insisted on checking all the doors and windows with her. The house, with Pandora safely in it, was locked up tight.

It was entirely too quiet.

In defense, Pandora went to the kitchen and began rattling pots and pans. She had to be alone, but she didn't have to be idle. She wanted to be with Michael, to stand by him when he faced the break-in of his apartment. Was it as frustrating for him to go on alone, she wondered, as it was for her to stay behind? It couldn't be helped. There were two old people in the house who couldn't be left. And they needed to eat.

The chicken was to have been a joint effort and a respite from the haphazard meals they'd managed to date. Michael had claimed to know at least the basics of deep frying. While he'd volunteered to deal with the chicken, she'd been assigned to try her hand at mashing potatoes. She'd thought competition if nothing else would have improved the end result.

Pandora resigned herself to a solo and decided the effort of cooking would keep her mind off fresh trouble. Needing company, she switched on the tuner on the kitchen wall unit and fiddled with the dial until she found a country-music station. Dolly Parton bubbled out brightly. Satisfied, she pulled one of Sweeney's cookbooks from the shelf and began to search the index. Fried chicken went on picnics, she mused. How much trouble could it be?

She had two counters crowded and splattered, and flour up to her wrists when the phone rang. Using a dishcloth, Pandora plucked the receiver from the kitchen extension. Her foot was tapping to a catchy rendition of "On the Road Again."

"Hello."

"Pandora McVie?"

Her mind on more immediate matters, Pandora stretched the cord to the counter and picked up a drumstick. "Yes."

"Listen carefully."

"Can you speak up?" Tongue caught between her teeth, Pandora dipped the drumstick in her flour mixture. "I can't hear you very well."

"I have to warn you and there's not much time. You're in danger. You're not safe in that house, not alone."

The cookbook slid to the floor and landed on her foot. "What? Who is this?"

"Just listen. You're alone because it was arranged. Someone's going to try to break in tonight."

"Someone?" She shifted the phone and listened hard. It wasn't malice she detected, but nervousness. Whoever was on the other end was as shaky as she was. She was certain—almost certain—it was a man's voice. "If you're trying to frighten me—"

"I'm trying to warn you. When I found out…" Already low and indistinct, the voice became hesitant. "You shouldn't have sent the champagne. I don't like what's going on, but it won't stop. No one was going to be hurt, do you understand? But I'm afraid of what might happen next."

Pandora felt fear curl in her stomach. Outside the kitchen windows it was dark, pitch-dark. She was alone in the house with two old, sick servants. "If you're afraid, tell me who you are. Help me stop what's going on."

"I'm already risking everything by warning you. You don't understand. Get out, just get out of the house."

It was a ploy, she told herself. A ploy to make her leave. Pandora straightened her shoulders, but her gaze shifted from blank window to blank window. "I'm not going anywhere. If you want to help, tell me who I should be afraid of."

"Just get out," the voice repeated before the line went dead.

Pandora stood holding the silent receiver. The oil in the fryer had begun to sizzle, competing with the radio. Watching the windows, listening, she hung up the phone. It was a trick, she told herself. It was only a trick to get her out of the house in hopes she'd be frightened enough to stay out. She wouldn't be shooed away by a quivering voice on the telephone.

Besides, Michael had already called the police. They knew she was alone in the house. At the first sign of trouble, she only had to pick up the phone.

Her hands weren't completely steady, but she went back to cooking with a vengeance. She slipped coated chicken into the fryer, tested the potatoes she had cooking, then decided a little glass of wine while she worked was an excellent idea. She was pouring it when Bruno raced into the room to run around her feet.

"Bruno." Pandora crouched and gathered the dog close. He felt warm, solid. "I'm glad you're here," she murmured. But for a moment, she allowed herself to wish desperately for Michael.

Bruno licked her face, made a couple of clumsy leaps toward the counter, then dashed to the door. Jumping up against it, he began to bark.

"Now?" Pandora demanded. "I don't suppose you could wait until morning."

Bruno raced back to Pandora, circled her then raced back to the door. When he'd gone through the routine three times, she relented. The phone call had been no more than a trick, a clumsy one at that. Besides, she told herself as she turned the lock, it wouldn't hurt to open the door and take a good look outside.

The moment she opened it, Bruno jumped out and tumbled into the snow. He began to sniff busily while Pandora stood shivering in the opening and straining her eyes against the dark. Music and the smells of cooking poured out behind her.

There was nothing. She hugged herself against the cold and decided she hadn't expected to see anything.

The snow was settled, the stars bright and the woods quiet. It was as it should have been; a very ordinary evening in the country. She took a deep breath of winter air and started to call the dog back. They saw the movement at the edge of the woods at the same time.

Just a shadow, it seemed to separate slowly from a tree and take on its own shape. A human shape. Before Pandora could react, Bruno began to bark and plow through the snow.

"No, Bruno! Come back." Without giving herself a chance to think, Pandora grabbed the old pea coat that hung beside the door and threw it on. As an afterthought, she reached for a cast-iron skillet before bolting through the door after her dog. "Bruno!"

He was already at the edge of the woods and hot on the trail. Picking up confidence as she went, Pandora raced in pursuit. Whoever had been watching the house had run at the sight of the clumsy, overgrown puppy. She'd found she was susceptible to fear, but she refused to be frightened by a coward. With as much enthusiasm as Bruno, Pandora sprinted into the woods. Out of breath and feeling indestructible, she paused long enough to look around and listen. For a moment there was nothing, then off to the right, she heard barking and thrashing.

"Get 'em, Bruno!" she shouted, and headed toward the chaos. Excited by the chase, she called encouragement to the dog, changing direction when she heard his answering bark. As she ran, snow dropped from the branches to slide cold and wet down the back of her neck. The barking grew wilder, and in her rush, Pandora fell headlong over a downed tree. Spitting out

snow and swearing, she struggled to her knees. Bruno
bounded out of the woods and sent her sprawling again.

"Not me." Flat on her back, Pandora shoved at the
dog. "Dammit, Bruno, if you don't—" She broke off
when the dog stiffened and began to growl. Sprawled
on the snow, Pandora looked up and saw the shadow
move through the trees. She forgot she was too proud
to fear a coward.

Though her hands were numb from cold, she gripped
the handle of the skillet and, standing, inched her way
along toward the nearest tree. Struggling to keep her
breathing quiet, she braced herself for attack and defense. Relative or stranger, she'd hold her own. But her
knees were shaking. Bruno tensed and hurled himself
forward. The moment he did, Pandora lifted the skillet
high and prepared to swing.

"What the hell's going on?"

"Michael!" The skillet landed in the snow with a plop
as she followed Bruno's lead and hurled herself forward.
Giddy with relief, she plastered kisses over Michael's
face. "Oh, Michael, I'm so glad it's you."

"Yeah. You sure looked pleased when you were hefting that skillet. Run out of hair spray?"

"It was handy." Abruptly she drew back and glared
at him. "Dammit, Michael, you scared me to death.
You're supposed to be halfway to New York, not skulking around the woods."

"And you're supposed to be locked in the house."

"I would've been if you hadn't been skulking in the
woods. Why?"

In an offhanded gesture, he brushed snow from her
face. "I got ten miles away, and I couldn't get rid of this

bad feeling. It was too pat. I decided to stop at a gas station and phone my neighbor."

"But your apartment."

"I talked to the police, gave them a list of my valuables. We'll both run into New York in a day or two." Snow was scattered through her hair and matted to her coat. He thought of what might have happened and resisted the urge to shake her. "I couldn't leave you alone."

"I'm going to start believing you're chivalrous after all." She kissed him. "That explains why you're not in New York, but what were you doing in the woods?"

"Just a hunch." He bent to retrieve the frying pan. A good whack with that, he discovered, and he'd have been down for the count.

"The next time you have a hunch, don't stand at the edge of the woods and stare at the house."

"I wasn't." Michael took her arm and headed back toward the house. He wanted her inside again, behind locked doors.

"I saw you."

"I don't know who you saw." Disgusted, Michael looked back at the dog. "But if you hadn't let the dog out we'd both know. I decided to check around outside before coming in, and I saw footprints. I followed them around, then cut into the woods." He glanced over his shoulder, still tight with tension. "I was just coming up behind whoever made them when Bruno tried his attack. I started chasing." He swore and slapped a palm against the skillet. "I was gaining when this hound ran between my legs and sent me face first into the snow. About that time, you started yelling at the dog. Whoever I was chasing had enough time to disappear."

Pandora swore and kicked at the snow. "If you'd let

me know what was going on, we could've worked together."

"I didn't know what was going on until it was already happening. In any case, the deal was you'd stay inside with the doors locked."

"The dog had to go out," Pandora muttered. "And I had this phone call." She looked back over her shoulder and sighed. "Someone called to warn me."

"Who?"

"I don't know. I thought it was a man's voice, but—I'm just not sure."

Michael's hand tightened on her arm. "Did he threaten you?"

"No, no it wasn't like a threat. Whoever it was certainly seemed to know what's been going on and isn't happy about it. That much was clear. He—she said someone was going to try to break into the Folley, and I should get out."

"And, of course, you handled that by running into the woods with a skillet. Pandora." This time he did shake her. "Why didn't you call the police?"

"Because I thought it was another trick and it made me mad." She sent Michael a stubborn look. "Yes, it frightened me at first, then it just plain made me mad. I don't like intimidation. When I looked out and saw someone near the woods, I only wanted to fight back."

"Admirable," he said but took her shoulders. "Stupid."

"You were doing the same thing."

"It's not the same thing. You've got brains, you've got style. I'll even give you guts. But, cousin, you're not a heavyweight. What if you'd caught up with whoever was out there and they wanted to play rough?"

"I can play rough, too," Pandora muttered.

"Fine." With a quick move, he hooked a foot behind hers and sent her bottom first into the snow. She didn't have the opportunity to complain before he was standing over her, gesturing with the skillet. Bruno decided it was a game and leaped on top of her. "I might've come back tomorrow and found you half-buried in the snow." Before she could speak, he hauled her to her feet again. "I'm not risking that."

"You caught me off balance," she began.

"Shut up." He had her by the shoulders again, and this time his grip wasn't gentle. "You're too important, Pandora, I'm through taking chances. We're going inside and calling the cops. We're going to tell them everything."

"What can they do?"

"We'll find out."

She let out a long breath, then leaned against him. The chase might have been exciting, but her knees had yet to stop shaking. "Okay, maybe you're right. We're no farther along now than when we started."

"Calling the police isn't giving up, it's just changing the odds. I might not have come back here tonight, Pandora. The dog may not have frightened anyone off. You'd have been alone." He took both her hands, pressing them to his lips and warming them. "I'm not going to let anything happen to you."

Confused by the sense of pleasure his words gave her, she tried to draw her hands away. "I can take care of myself, Michael."

He smiled but didn't let go. "Maybe. But you're not going to have the chance to find out. Let's go home. I'm hungry."

"Typical," she began, needing to lighten the mood. "You'd think of your stomach—oh my God, the chicken!" Breaking away, Pandora loped toward the house.

"I'm not that hungry." Michael sprinted after her. The relief came again when he scooped her up into his arms. When he'd heard her shout in the woods, had realized she was outside and vulnerable, his blood had simply stopped flowing. "In fact," he said as he scooped her up, "I can think of more pressing matters than eating."

"Michael." She struggled, but laughed. "If you don't put me down, there won't be a kitchen to eat in."

"We'll eat somewhere else."

"I left the pan on. There's probably nothing left of the chicken but charred bones."

"There's always soup." With that, he pushed open the kitchen door.

Rather than a smoky, splattered mess, they found a platter piled high with crisp, brown chicken. Sweeney had wiped up the spills, and had the pans soaking in the sink.

"Sweeney." From her perch in Michael's arms, Pandora surveyed the room. "What are you doing out of bed?"

"My job," she said briskly, but gave them a quick sidelong look. As far as she was concerned, her plans were working perfectly. She imagined Pandora and Michael had decided to take a little air while dinner was cooking, and, as young people would, had forgotten the time.

"You're supposed to be in bed," Pandora reminded her.

"Posh. I've been in bed long enough." And the days

of little or no activity had nearly bored her to tears. It was worth it, however, to see Pandora snug in Michael's arms. "Feeling fit as a fiddle now, I promise you. Wash up for dinner."

Michael and Pandora each took separate and careful studies. Sweeney's cheeks were pink and round, her eyes bright. She bustled from counter to counter in her old businesslike fashion. "We still want you to take it easy," Michael decided. "No heavy work."

"That's right. Michael and I'll take care of the washing up." She saw him scowl, just a little, and patted his shoulder. "We like to do it."

At Michael and Pandora's insistence, all four ate in the kitchen. Charles, sitting next to Sweeney, was left uncertain how much he should cough and settled on a middle road, clearing his throat every so often. In an unspoken agreement, Pandora and Michael decided to keep the matter of trespassers to themselves. Both of them felt the announcement that someone was watching the house would be too upsetting for the two old people while they were recuperating.

On the surface, dinner was an easy meal, but Pandora kept wondering how soon they could nudge the servants along to bed and contact the police. More than once, Pandora caught Sweeney looking from her to Michael with a smug smile. Sweet old lady, Pandora mused, innocently believing the cook to be pleased to have her kitchen back. It made Pandora only more determined to protect her and Charles from any unpleasantness. She concentrated on cleaning up and packing them off to bed, and it was nearly nine before she was able to meet Michael in the parlor.

"Settled?"

She heard the familiar restlessness in his voice and merely nodded, pouring a brandy. "It's a bit like cajoling children, but I managed to find a Cary Grant movie that interested them." She sipped the brandy, waiting for her muscles to relax with it. "I'd rather be watching it myself."

"Another time." Michael took a sip from her snifter. "I've called the police. They'll be here shortly."

She took the glass back. "It still bothers me to take the business to outsiders. After all, anything beyond simple trespass is speculation."

"We'll let the police speculate."

She managed to smile. "Your Logan always handles things on his own."

"Someone told me once that that was just fiction." He poured himself a brandy and toasted her. "I discovered I don't like having you in the middle of a story line."

The brandy and firelight gave the evening an illusion of normalcy. Pandora took his statement with a shrug. "You seem to have developed a protect-the-woman syndrome, Michael. It's not like you."

"Maybe not." He tossed back a gulp. "It's different when it's my woman."

She turned, brow lifted. It was ridiculous to feel pleasure at such a foolish and possessive term. "Yours?"

"Mine." He cupped the back of her neck with his hand. "Got a problem with that?"

Her heart beat steadily in her throat until she managed to swallow. Maybe he meant it—now. In a few months when he was back moving in his own world, with his own people, she'd be no more than his somewhat annoying cousin. But for now, just for now, maybe he meant it. "I'm not sure."

"Give it some thought," he advised before he lowered his mouth to hers. "We'll come back to it."

He left her flustered and went to answer the door.

When he returned, Pandora was sitting calmly enough in a high-backed chair near the fire. "Lieutenant Randall, Pandora McVie."

"How d'you do?" The lieutenant pulled off a wool muffler and stuck it in his coat pocket. He looked, Pandora thought, like someone's grandfather. Comfy, round and balding. "Miserable night," he announced, and situated himself near the fire.

"Would you like some coffee, Lieutenant?"

Randall gave Pandora a grateful look. "Love it."

"Please, have a seat. I'll be back in a minute."

She took her time heating coffee and arranging cups and saucers on a tray. Not putting off, Pandora insisted, just preparing. She'd never had occasion to talk to a policeman on any subject more complex than a parking ticket. She'd come out on the short end on that one. Now, she was about to discuss her family and her relationship with Michael.

Her relationship with Michael, she thought again as she fussed with the sugar bowl. That's what really had her hiding in the kitchen. She hadn't yet been able to dull the feeling that had raced through her when he'd called her his woman. Adolescent, Pandora told herself. It was absolutely absurd to feel giddy and self-satisfied and unnerved because a man had looked at her with passion in his eyes.

But they'd been Michael's eyes.

She found linen napkins and folded them into triangles. She didn't want to be anyone's woman but her own. It had been the strain and excitement of the evening that had made her react like a sixteen-year-old being offered a school ring. She was an adult; she was self-sustaining. She was in love. Talk yourself out of that one, Pandora challenged herself. Taking a long breath, she hefted the tray and went back to the parlor.

"Gentlemen." Pandora set the tray on a low table and stuck on a smile. "Cream and sugar, Lieutenant?"

"Thanks. A healthy dose of both." He set a dog-eared notepad on his knee when Pandora handed him a cup. "Mr. Donahue's been filling me in. Seems you've had a few annoyances."

She smiled at the term. Like his looks, his voice was comfortable. "A few."

"I'm not going to lecture." But he gave them both a stern look. "Still, you should've notified the police after the first incident. Vandalism's a crime."

"We'd hoped by ignoring it, it would discourage repetition." Pandora lifted her cup. "We were wrong."

"I'll need to take the champagne with me." Again, he sent them a look of disapproval. "Even though you've had it analyzed, we'll want to run it through our own lab."

"I'll get it for you." Michael rose and left them alone.

"Miss McVie, from what your cousin tells me, the terms of Mr. McVie's will were a bit unconventional."

"A bit."

"He also tells me he talked you into agreeing to them."

"That's Michael's fantasy, Lieutenant." She sipped her coffee. "I'm doing exactly what I chose to do."

Randall nodded and noted. "You agree with Mr. Donahue's idea that these incidents are connected and one of your relatives is responsible."

"I can't think of any reason to disagree."

"Do you have any reason to suspect one more than another?"

Pandora thought it through as she'd thought it through before. "No. You see, we're not at all a close family. The truth is I don't know any of them very well."

"Except Mr. Donahue."

"That's right. Michael and I often visited our uncle, and we ran into each other here at the Folley." Whether we wanted to or not, she added to herself in her own private joke. "None of the others came by very often."

"The champagne, Lieutenant." Michael brought in the box. "And the report from Sanfield Laboratories."

Randall skimmed the printout, then tucked the sheet into the box. "Your uncle's attorney…" He referred quickly to his notes. "Fitzhugh reported trespassing several weeks ago. We've had a squad car cruise the area, but at this point you might agree to having a man patrol the grounds once a day."

"I'd prefer it," Michael told him.

"I'll contact Fitzhugh." Seeing his cup was empty, Pandora took it and filled it again. "I'll also need a list of the relatives named in the will."

Pandora frowned over her rim. Between her and Michael, they tried to fill in the lieutenant, as best as they could. When they had finished, Pandora sent Randall an apologetic look. "I told you we aren't close."

"I'll get the lawyer to fill in the details." Randall rose and tried not to think about the cold drive back to town. "We'll keep the inquiries as quiet as possible. If anything else happens, call me. One of my men will be around to look things over."

"Thank you, Lieutenant." Michael helped the pudgy man on with his coat.

Randall took another look around the room. "Ever think of installing a security system?"

"No."

"Think again," he advised, and made his way out.

"We've just been scolded," Pandora murmured.

Michael wondered if *Logan's Run* had room for a cranky, well-padded cop. "Seems that way."

"You know, Michael, I have two schools of thought on bringing in the police."

"Which are?"

"It's either going to calm things down or stir things up."

"You pay your money and take your choice."

She gave him a knowing look. "You're counting on the second."

"I came close tonight." He bypassed the coffee and poured another brandy. "I nearly had my hands on something. Someone." When he looked at her, the faint amusement in his eyes had faded. The recklessness was back. "I like my fights in the open, face-to-face."

"It's better if we look at it as a chess game rather than a boxing match." She came close to wrap her arms around him and press her cheek to his shoulder. It was the kind of gesture he didn't think he'd ever get used to from her. As he rested his head on her hair, he realized that the fact that he wouldn't only added to the sweetness of the feeling. When had he stopped remembering that she didn't fit into his long-established picture of the ideal woman? Her hair was too red, her body too thin, her tongue too sharp. Michael nuzzled against her and found they fit very well.

"I've never had the patience for chess."

"Then we'll just leave it to the police." She held him tighter. The need to protect rose as sharply as the desire to be protected. "I've been thinking about what might have happened out there tonight. I don't want you hurt, Michael."

With two fingers under her chin, he lifted it. "Why not?"

"Because…" She looked into his eyes and felt her heart melt. But she wouldn't be a fool; she wouldn't risk her pride. "Because then I'd have to do the dishes by myself."

He smiled. No, he didn't have a great deal of patience, but he could call on it when circumstances warranted. He brushed a kiss on either side of her mouth. Sooner or later, he'd have more out of her. Then he'd just have to decide what to do with it. "Any other reason?"

Absorbing the sensations, Pandora searched her mind for another easy answer. "If you were hurt, you couldn't work. I'd have to live with your foul temper."

"I thought you were already living with it."

"I've seen it fouler."

He kissed her eyes closed in his slow, sensuous way. "Try one more time."

"I care." She opened her eyes, and her look was tense and defiant. "Got a problem with that?"

"No." His kiss wasn't gentle this time, it wasn't patient. He had her caught close and reeling within moments. If there was tension in her still, he couldn't feel it. "The only problem's been dragging it out of you."

"You're family after all—"

With a laugh, he nipped the lobe of her ear. "Don't try to back out."

Indignant, she stiffened. "I never back out."

"Unless you can rationalize it. Just remember this." He had her molded against him again. "The family connection's distant." Their lips met, urgently, then parted. "This connection isn't."

"I don't know what you want from me," she whispered.

"You're usually so quick."

"Don't joke, Michael."

"It's no joke." He drew her away, holding her by the shoulders. Briefly, firmly, he ran his hands down to her elbows, then back. "No, I'm not going to spell it out for you, Pandora. I'm not going to make it easy on you. You have to be willing to admit we both want the same thing. And you will."

"Arrogant," she warned.

"Confident," he corrected. He had to be, or he'd be on his knees begging. There'd come a time, he'd promised himself, when she'd drop the last of her restrictions. "I want you."

A tremor skipped up her spine. "I know."

"Yeah." He linked his fingers with hers. "I think you do."

Chapter 11

Winter raged its way through February. There came a point when Pandora had to shovel her way from the house to her workshop. She found herself grateful for the physical labor. Winter was a long quiet time that provided too many hours to think.

In using this time, Pandora came to several uncomfortable realizations. Her life, as she'd known it, as she'd guided it, would never be the same. As far as her art was concerned, she felt the months of concentrated effort with dashes of excitement had only improved her crafting. In truth, she often used her jewelry to take her mind off what was happening to and around her. When that didn't work, she used what was happening to and around her in her work.

The sudden blunt understanding that her health, even her life, had been endangered made her take a step away from her usual practical outlook. It caused her to appreciate little things she'd always taken for granted. Waking up in a warm bed, watching snow fall while a fire crackled beside her. She'd learned that every second in life was vital.

Already she was considering taking a day to drive back to New York and pack what was important to her. More than packing, it would be a time of decision making. What she kept, what she didn't, would in some ways reflect the changes she'd accepted in herself.

Both the lease on her apartment and the lease on the shop over the boutique were coming up for renewal. She'd let them lapse. Rather than living alone, she'd have the company and the responsibility of her uncle's old servants. Though she'd once been determined to be responsible only to herself and her art, Pandora made the choice without a qualm. Though she had lived in the city, in the rush, in the crowds, she'd isolated herself. No more.

Through it all wove Michael.

In a few short weeks, what they had now would be over. The long winter they'd shared would be something to think of during other winters. As she prepared for a new and different life, Pandora promised herself she'd have no regrets. But she couldn't stop herself from having wishes. Things were already changing.

The police had come, and with their arrival had been more questions. Everything in her shop had to be locked up tightly after dark, and there were no more solitary walks in the woods after a snowfall. It had become a nightly ritual to go through the Folley and check doors and windows that had once been casually ignored. Often when she walked back to the house from her shop, she'd see Michael watching from the window of his room. It should have given her a warm, comfortable feeling, but she knew he was waiting for something else to happen. She knew, as she knew him, that he wanted it. Inactivity was sitting uneasily on him.

Since they'd driven into New York to deal with the break-in at his apartment, he'd been distant, with a restlessness roiling underneath. Though they both understood the wisdom of having the grounds patrolled, she thought they felt intruded upon.

They had no sense of satisfaction from the police investigation. Each one of their relatives had alibis for one or more of the incidents. So far the investigation seemed to have twin results. Since the police had been called in, nothing else had happened. There'd been no anonymous phone calls, no shadows in the woods, no bogus messages. It had, as Pandora had also predicted, stirred things up. She'd dealt with an irate phone call from Carlson who insisted they were using the investigation in an attempt to undermine his case against the will.

On the heels of that had come a disjointed letter from Ginger who'd had the idea that the Folley was haunted. Michael had had a two-minute phone conversation with Morgan who'd muttered about private family business, overreacting and hogwash. Biff, in his usual style, had sent a short message:

Cops and robbers? Looks like you two are playing games with each other.

From Hank they heard nothing.
The police lab had confirmed the private analysis of

the champagne; Randall was plodding through the investigation in his precise, quiet way. Michael and Pandora were exactly where they'd been weeks before: waiting.

He didn't know how she could stand it. As Michael made his way down the narrow path Pandora had shoveled, he wondered how she could remain so calm when he was ready to chew glass. It had only taken him a few days of hanging in limbo to realize it was worse when nothing happened. Waiting for someone else to make the next move was the most racking kind of torture. Until he was sure Pandora was safe, he couldn't relax. Until he had his hands around someone's throat, he wouldn't be satisfied. He was caught in a trap of inactivity that was slowly driving him mad. Pausing just outside her shop, he glanced around.

The house looked big and foolish with icicles hanging and dripping from eaves, gutters and shutters. It belonged in a book, he thought, some moody, misty gothic. A fairy tale—the grim sort. Perhaps one day he'd weave a story around it himself, but for now, it was just home.

With his hands in his pockets he watched smoke puff out of chimneys. Foolish it might be, but he'd always loved it. The longer he lived in it, the surer he was that he was meant to. He was far from certain how Pandora would take his decision to remain after the term was over.

His last script for the season was done. It was the only episode to be filmed before the show wrapped until fall. He could, as he often did, take a few weeks in the early spring and find a hot, noisy beach. He could fish, relax and enjoy watching women in undersize bikinis. Michael knew he wasn't going anywhere.

For the past few days, he'd been toying with a screenplay for a feature film. He'd given it some thought before, but somehow something had always interfered. He could write it here, he knew. He could perfect it here with Pandora wielding her art nearby, criticizing his work so that he was only more determined to make it better. But he was waiting. Waiting for something else to happen, waiting to find who it was who'd used fear and intimidation to try to drive them out. And most of all, he was waiting for Pandora. Until she gave him her complete trust, willingly, until she gave him her heart unrestrictedly, he had to go on waiting.

His hands curled into fists and released. He wanted action.

He tried the door and satisfied himself that she'd kept her word and locked it from the inside. "Pandora?" He knocked with the side of his fist. She opened the door with a drill in her hand. After giving her flushed face and tousled hair a quick look, Michael lifted his hands, palms out. "I'm unarmed."

"And I'm busy." But her lips curved. There was a light of pleasure in her eyes. He found it easy to notice such small things.

"I know, I've invaded scheduled working hours, but I have a valid excuse."

"You're letting in the cold," she complained. Once, she might have shut the door in his face without a second thought. This time she shut it behind him.

"Not a hell of a lot warmer in here."

"It's fine when I'm working. Which I am."

"Blame Sweeney. She's sending me in for supplies, and she insisted I take you." He sent Pandora a bland look. "'That girl holes herself up in that shed too much. Needs some sun.'"

"I get plenty of sun," Pandora countered. Still, the idea of a drive into town appealed. It wouldn't hurt to talk to the jeweler in the little shopping center. She was beginning to think her work should spread out a bit, beyond the big cities. "I suppose we should humor her, but I want to finish up here first."

"I'm in no hurry."

"Good. Half an hour then." She went to exchange the drill for a jeweler's torch. Because she didn't hear the door open or shut, she turned and saw Michael examining her rolling mill. "Michael," she said with more than a trace of exasperation.

"Go ahead, take your time."

"Don't you have anything to do?"

"Not a thing," he said cheerfully.

"Not one car chase to write?"

"No. Besides, I've never seen you work."

"Audiences make me cranky."

"Broaden your horizons, love. Pretend I'm an apprentice."

"I'm not sure they can get that broad."

Undaunted, he pointed to her worktable. "What is that thing?"

"This thing," she began tightly, "is a pendant. A waterfall effect made with brass wire and some scraps of silver I had left over from a bracelet."

"No waste," he murmured. "Practical as ever. So what's the next step?"

With a long breath, she decided it would be simpler to play along than to throw him out. "I've just finished adjusting the curves of the wires. I've used different thicknesses and lengths to give it a free-flowing effect. The silver scraps I've cut and filed into elongated teardrops. Now I solder them onto the ends of the wires."

She applied the flux, shifting a bit so that he could watch. After she'd put a square of solder beside each wire, she used the torch to apply heat until the solder melted. Patient, competent, she repeated the procedure until all twelve teardrops were attached.

"Looks easy enough," he mused.

"A child of five could do it."

He heard the sarcasm and laughed as he took her hands. "You want flattery? A few minutes ago I saw a pile of metal. Now I see an intriguing ornament. Ornate and exotic."

"It's supposed to be exotic," Pandora replied. "Jessica Wainwright will wear it in the film. It's to have been a gift from an old lover. The countess claims he was a Turkish prince."

Michael studied the necklace again. "Very appropriate."

"It'll droop down from brass and silver wires twisted together. The lowest teardrop should hang nearly to her waist." Pleased, but knowing better than to touch the metal before the solder cooled, Pandora held up her sketch. "Ms. Wainwright was very specific. She wants nothing ordinary, nothing even classic. Everything she wears should add to the character's mystique."

She set the sketch down and tidied her tools. She'd solder on the hoop and fashion the neck wire when they returned from town. Then if there was time, she'd begin the next project. The gold-plated peacock pin with its three-inch filigree tail would take her the better part of two weeks.

"This thing has potential as a murder weapon," Michael mused, picking up a burnisher to examine the curved, steel tip.

"I beg your pardon?"

He liked the way she said it, so that even with her back turned she was looking down her nose. "For a story line."

"Leave my tools out of your stories." Pandora took the burnisher from him and packed it away. "Going to buy me lunch in town?" She stripped off her apron then grabbed her coat.

"I was going to ask you the same thing."

"I asked first." She locked the shop and welcomed the cold. "The snow's beginning to melt."

"In a few weeks, the five dozen bulbs Jolley planted during his gardening stage will be starting to bloom."

"Daffodils," she murmured. It didn't seem possible when you felt the air, saw the mounds of snow, but spring was closing in. "The winter hasn't seemed so long."

"No, it hasn't." He slipped an arm around her shoulders. "I never expected six months to go so quickly. I figured one of us would've attempted murder by this time."

With a laugh, Pandora matched her step to his. "We've still got a month to go."

"Now we have to behave ourselves," he reminded her. "Lieutenant Randall has his eye on us."

"I guess we blew our chance." She turned to wind her arms around his neck. "There have been times I've wanted to hit you with a blunt instrument."

"Feeling's mutual," he told her as he lowered his mouth. Her lips were cool and curved.

At the side window, Sweeney drew back the drape. "Look at this!" Cackling, she gestured to Charles. "I told you it would work. In a few more weeks, I'll be putting bells on a wedding cake."

As Charles joined Sweeney at the window, Pandora scooped a hand into the snow and tossed it in Michael's face. "Don't count your chickens," he muttered.

In a desperate move to avoid retaliation, Pandora raced to the garage. She ducked seconds before snow splattered against the door. "Your aim's still off, cousin." Hefting the door, she sprinted inside and jumped into his car. Smug, she settled into the seat. He wouldn't, she was sure, mar his spotless interior with a snowball. Michael opened the door, slid in beside her and dumped snow over her head. She was still squealing when he turned the key.

"I'm better at close range."

Pandora sputtered as she wiped at the snow. Because she'd appreciated the move, it was difficult to sound indignant. "One would have thought that a man who drives an ostentatious car would be more particular with it."

"It's only ostentatious if you buy it for status purposes."

"And, of course, you didn't."

"I bought it because it gets terrific gas mileage." When she snorted, he turned to grin at her. "And because it looks great wrapped around redheads."

"And blondes and brunettes."

"Redheads," he corrected, twining her hair around his finger. "I've developed a preference."

It shouldn't have made her smile, but it did. She was still smiling when they started down the long, curvy road. "We can't complain about the road crews," she said idly. "Except for those two weeks last month, the roads've been fairly clear." She glanced toward the mounds of snow the plows had pushed to the side of the road.

"Too bad they won't do the driveway."

"You know you loved riding that little tractor. Uncle Jolley always said it made him feel tough and macho."

"So much so he'd race it like a madman over the yard."

As they came to a curve, Michael eased on the brake and downshifted. Pandora leaned forward and fiddled with the stereo. "Most people have equipment like this in their den."

"I don't have a den."

"You don't have a stereo to put in one, either," she remembered. "Or a television."

He shrugged, but mentally listed what he'd lost from his apartment. "Insurance'll cover it."

"The police are handling that as though it were a normal break-in." She switched channels. "It might've been."

"Or it might've been a smoke screen. I wish we—" He broke off as they approached another curve. He'd pressed the brake again, but this time, the pedal had gone uselessly to the floor.

"Michael, if you're trying to impress me with your skill as a driver, it's not working." Instinctively Pandora grabbed the door handle as the car careered down the curve.

Whipping the steering wheel with one hand, Michael yanked on the emergency brake. The car continued to barrel down. He gripped the wheel in both hands and fought the next curve. "No brakes." As he told her, Michael glanced down to see the speedometer hover at seventy.

Pandora's knuckles turned white on the handle. "We won't make it to the bottom without them."

He never considered lying. "No." Tires squealed as he rounded the next curve. Gravel spit under the wheels as the car went wide. There was the scrape and scream of metal as the fender kissed the guardrail.

She looked at the winding road spinning in front of her. Her vision blurred then cleared. The sign before the S-turn cautioned for a safe speed of thirty. Michael took it at seventy-five. Pandora shut her eyes. When she opened them and saw the snowbank dead ahead, she screamed. With seconds to spare, Michael yanked the car around. Snow flew skyward as the car skidded along the bank.

Eyes intense, Michael stared at the road ahead and struggled to anticipate each curve. Sweat beaded on his forehead. He knew the road, that's what terrified him. In less than three miles, the already sharp incline steepened. At high speed, the car would ram straight through the guardrail and crash on the cliffs below. The game Jolley had begun would end violently.

Michael tasted his own fear, then swallowed it. "There's only one chance; we've got to turn off on the lane leading into the old inn. It's coming up after that curve." He couldn't take his eyes from the road to look at her. His fingers dug into the wheel. "Hang on."

She was going to die. Her mind was numb from the thought of it. She heard the tires scream as Michael dragged at the wheel. The car tilted, nearly going over. She saw trees rush by as the car slid on the slippery edge of the lane. Almost, for an instant, the rubber seemed to grip the gravel beneath. But the turn was too sharp, the speed too fast. Out of control, the car spiraled toward the trees.

"I love you," she whispered, and grabbed for him before the world went black.

He came to slowly. He hurt, and for a time didn't understand why. There was noise. Eventually he turned his head toward it. When he opened his eyes, Michael saw a boy with wide eyes and black hair gawking through the window.

"Mister, hey, mister. You okay?"

Dazed, Michael pushed open the door. "Get help," he managed, fighting against blacking out again. He took deep gulps of air to clear his head as the boy dashed off through the woods. "Pandora." Fear broke through the fog. In seconds, he was leaning over her.

His fingers shook as he reached for the pulse of her neck, but he found it. Blood from a cut on her forehead ran down her face and onto his hands. With his fingers pressed against the wound, he fumbled in the glove compartment for the first-aid kit. He'd stopped the bleeding and was checking her for broken bones when she moaned. He had to stop himself from dragging her against him and holding on.

"Take it easy," he murmured when she began to stir. "Don't move around." When she opened her eyes, he saw they were glazed and unfocused. "You're all right." Gently he cupped her face in his hands and continued to reassure her. Her eyes focused gradually. As they did, she reached for his hand.

"The brakes...."

"Yeah." He rested his cheek against hers a moment. "It was a hell of a trip, but it looks like we made it."

Confused, she looked around. The car was stopped, leaning drunkenly against a tree. It had been the deep, slushy snow that had slowed them down enough to prevent the crash from being fatal. "We—you're all right?" The tears started when she reached out and took his face in her hands as he had with hers. "You're all right."

"Terrific." His wrist throbbed like a jackhammer and his head ached unbelievably, but he was alive. When she started to move, he held her still. "No, don't move around. I don't know how badly you're hurt. There was a kid. He's gone for help."

"It's just my head." She started to take his hand, and saw the blood. "Oh God, you're bleeding. Where?" Before she could begin her frantic search, he gripped her hands together.

"It's not me. It's you. Your head's cut. You probably have a concussion."

Shaky, she lifted her hand and touched the bandage. The wound beneath it hurt, but she drew on that. If she hurt, she was alive. "I thought I was dead." She closed her eyes but tears slipped through the lashes. "I thought we were both dead."

"We're both fine." They heard the siren wail up the mountain road. He was silent until she opened her eyes again. "You know what happened?"

Her head ached badly, but it was clear. "Attempted murder."

He nodded, not turning when the ambulance pulled into the slushy lane. "I'm through waiting, Pandora. I'm through waiting all around."

* * *

Lieutenant Randall found Michael in the emergency-room lounge. He unwrapped his muffler, unbuttoned his coat and sat down on the hard wooden bench. "Looks like you've had some trouble."

"Big time."

Randall nodded toward the Ace bandage on Michael's wrist. "Bad?"

"Just a sprain. Few cuts and bruises and a hell of a headache. Last time I saw it, my car looked something like an accordion."

"We're taking it in. Anything we should look for?"

"Brake lines. It seemed I didn't have any when I started the trip down the mountain."

"When's the last time you used your car?" Randall had his notepad in hand.

"Ten days, two weeks." Wearily, Michael rubbed a temple. "I drove into New York to talk to police about the robbery in my apartment."

"Where do you keep your car?"

"In the garage."

"Locked?"

"The garage?" Michael kept his eye on the hallway where Pandora had been wheeled away. "No. My uncle had installed one of those remote control devices a few years back. Never worked unless you turned on the television. Anyway, he took it out again and never replaced the lock. Pandora's car's in there," he remembered suddenly. "If—"

"We'll check it out," Randall said easily. "Miss McVie was with you?"

"Yeah, she's with a doctor." For the first time in weeks, Michael found himself craving a cigarette. "Her head was cut." He looked down at his hands and remembered her blood on them. "I'm going to find out who did this, Lieutenant, and then I'm going to—"

"Don't say anything to me I might have to use later," Randall warned. There were some people who threatened as a means to let off steam or relieve tension. Randall didn't think Michael Donahue was one of them. "Let me do my job, Mr. Donahue."

Michael gave him a long, steady look. "Someone's been playing games, deadly ones, with someone very important to me. If you were in my place, would you twiddle your thumbs and wait?"

Randall smiled, just a little. "You know, Donahue, I never miss your show. Great entertainment. Some of this business sounds just like one of your shows."

"Like one of my shows," Michael repeated slowly.

"Problem is, things don't work the same way out here in the world as they do on television. But it sure is a pleasure to watch. Here comes your lady."

Michael sprang up and headed for her.

"I'm fine," she told him before he could ask.

"Not entirely." Behind her a young, white-coated doctor stood impatiently. "Miss McVie has a concussion."

"He put a few stitches in my head and wants to hold me prisoner." She gave the doctor a sweet smile and linked arms with Michael. "Let's go home."

"Just a minute." Keeping her beside him, Michael turned to the doctor. "You want her in the hospital?"

"Michael—"

"Shut up."

"Anyone suffering from a concussion should be routinely checked. Miss McVie would be wise to remain overnight with professional care."

"I'm not staying in the hospital because I have a bump on the head. Good afternoon, Lieutenant."

"Miss McVie."

Lifting her chin, she looked back at the doctor. "Now, Doctor…"

"Barnhouse."

"Dr. Barnhouse," she began. "I will take your advice to a point. I'll rest, avoid stress. At the first sign of nausea or dizziness, I'll be on your doorstep. I can assure you, now that you've convinced Michael I'm an invalid, I'll be properly smothered and hovered over. You'll have to be satisfied with that."

Far from satisfied, the doctor directed himself to Michael. "I can't force her to stay, of course."

Michael lifted a brow. "If you think I can, you've got a lot to learn about women."

Resigned, Barnhouse turned back to Pandora. "I want to see you in a week, sooner if any of the symptoms we discussed show up. You're to rest for twenty-four hours. That means horizontally."

"Yes, Doctor." She offered a hand, which he took grudgingly. "You were very gentle. Thank you."

His lips twitched. "A week," he repeated and strode back down the hall.

"If I didn't know better," Michael mused, "I'd say he wanted to keep you here just to look at you."

"Of course. I look stunning with blood running down my face and a hole in my head."

"I thought so." He kissed her cheek, but used the gesture to get a closer look at her wound. The stitches were small and neat, disappearing into her hairline. After counting six of them, his determination iced. "Come on, we'll go home so I can start pampering you."

"I'll take you myself." Randall gestured toward the door. "I might as well look around a bit while I'm there."

Sweeney clucked like a mother hen and had Pandora bundled into bed five minutes after she'd walked in the door. If she'd had the strength, Pandora would have argued for form's sake. Instead she let herself be tucked under a comforter, fed soup and sweet tea, and fussed over. Though the doctor had assured her it was perfectly safe to sleep, she thought of the old wives' tale and struggled to stay awake. Armed with a sketch pad and pencil, she whiled away the time designing. But when she began to tire of that, she began to think.

Murder. It would have been nothing less than murder. Murder for gain, she mused, an impossible thing for her to understand. She'd told herself before that her life was threatened, but somehow it had seemed remote. She had only to touch her own forehead now to prove just how direct it had become.

An uncle, a cousin, an aunt? Which one wanted Jolley's fortune so badly to murder for it? Not for the first time, Pandora wished she knew them better, understood them better. She realized she'd simply followed Jolley's lead and dismissed them as boring.

And that was true enough, Pandora assured herself. She'd been to a party or two with all of them. Monroe would huff, Biff would preen, Ginger would prattle, and so on. But boring or not, one of them had slipped over the line of civilized behavior. And they were willing to step over her to do it. Slowly, from memory, she began to sketch each of her relatives. Perhaps that way, she'd see something that was buried in her subconscious.

When Michael came in, she had sketches lined in rows over her spread. "Quite a rogues' gallery."

He'd come straight from the garage, where he and Randall had found the still-wet brake fluid on the concrete. Not all of it, Michael mused. Whoever had tampered with the brakes had left enough fluid in so that the car would react normally for the first few miles. And then, nothing. Michael had already concluded that the police would find a hole in the lines. Just as they'd find one in the lines of Pandora's, to match the dark puddle beneath her car. It had been every bit as lethal as his.

He wasn't ready to tell Pandora that whoever had tried to kill them had been as close as the garage a day, perhaps two, before. Instead he looked at her sketches.

"What do you see?" she demanded.

"That you have tremendous talent and should give serious thought to painting."

"I mean in their faces." Impatient with herself, she drew her legs up cross-legged. "There's just nothing there. No spark, no streak of anything that tells me this one's capable of killing."

"Anyone's capable of killing. Oh yes," Michael added when she opened her mouth to disagree. "Anyone. It's simply that the motive has to fit the personality, the circumstances, the need. When a person's threatened, he kills. For some it's only when their lives or the lives of someone they love are threatened."

"That's entirely different."

"No." He sat on the bed. "It's a matter of different degrees. Some people kill because their home is threatened, their possessions. Some kill because a desire is threatened. Wealth, power, those are very strong desires.

"So a very ordinary, even conventional person might kill to achieve that desire."

He gestured to her sketches. "One of them tried. Aunt Patience with her round little face and myopic eyes."

"You can't seriously believe—"

"She's devoted to Morgan, obsessively so. She's never married. Why? Because she's always taken care of him."

He picked up the next sketch. "Or there's Morgan himself, stout, blunt, hard-nosed. He thought Jolley was mad and a nuisance."

"They all did."

"Exactly. Carlson, straitlaced, humorless, and Jolley's only surviving son."

"He tried contesting the will."

"Going the conventional route. Still, he knew his father was shrewd, perhaps better than anyone. Who's to say he wouldn't cover his bases in a more direct way? Biff…" He had a laugh as he looked at the sketch. Pandora had drawn him precisely as he was. Self-absorbed.

"I can't see him getting his hands dirty."

"For a slice of a hundred fifty million? I can. Pretty little Ginger. One wonders if she can possibly be as sweet and spacey as she appears. And Hank." Pandora had drawn him with his arm muscle flexed. "Would he settle for a couple of thousand when he could have millions?"

"I don't know—that's just the point." Pandora shuffled the sketches. "Even when I have them all lined up in front of me, I don't know."

"Lined up," Michael murmured. "Maybe that is the answer. I think it's time we had a nice, family party."

"Party? You don't mean actually invite them all here."

"It's perfect."

"They won't come."

"Oh yes, they will." He was already thinking ahead. "You can bank on it. A little hint that things aren't going well around here, and they'll jump at the chance to give us an extra push. You see the doctor in a week. If he gives you a clean bill of health, we're going to start a little game of our own."

"What game?"

"In a week," he repeated, and took her face in his hands. It was narrow, dominated by the mop of hair and sharp eyes. Not beautiful, but special. It had taken him a long time to admit it. "A bit pale."

"I'm always pale with a concussion. Are you going to pamper me?"

"At least." But his smile faded as he gathered her close. "Oh God, I thought I'd lost you."

The trace of desperation in his voice urged her to soothe. "We'd both have been lost if you hadn't handled the car so well." She snuggled into his shoulder. It was real and solid, like the one she'd sometimes imagined leaning on. It wouldn't hurt, just this once, to pretend it would always be there. "I never thought we'd walk away from that one."

"But we did." He drew back to look at her. She looked tired and drawn, but he knew her will was as strong as ever. "And now we're going to talk about what you said to me right before we crashed."

"Wasn't I screaming?"

"No."

"If I criticized your driving, I apologize."

He tightened his grip on her chin. "You told me you loved me." He watched her mouth fall open in genuine surprise. Some men might have been insulted. Michael could bless his sense of humor. "It could technically be called a deathbed confession."

Had she? She could only remember reaching for him in those last seconds, knowing they were about to die together. "I was hysterical," she began, and tried to draw back.

"It didn't sound like raving to me."

"Michael, you heard Dr. Barnhouse. I'm not supposed to have any stress. If you want to be helpful, see about some more tea."

"I've something better for relaxing the muscles and soothing the nerves." He laid her back against the pillows, sliding down with her. Sweetly, tenderly, he ran his lips down the lines of her cheekbones. "I want to hear you tell me again, here."

"Michael—"

"No, lie back." And his hands, gentle and calm, stilled her. "I need to touch you, just touch you. There's plenty of time for the rest."

He was so kind, so patient. More than once she'd wondered how such a restive, volatile man could have such comforting hands. Taking off only his shoes, he slipped into bed with her. He held her in the crook of his arm and stroked until he felt her sigh of relief. "I'm going to take care of you," he murmured. "When you're well, we'll take care of each other."

"I'll be fine tomorrow." But her voice was thick and sleepy.

"Sure you will." He'd keep her in bed another twenty-four hours if he had to chain her. "You haven't told me again. Are you in love with me, Pandora?"

She was so tired, so drained. It seemed she'd reached a point where she could fight nothing. "What if I am?" She managed to tilt her head back to stare at him. His fingers rubbed gently at her temple, easing even the dull echo of pain. "People fall in and out of love all the time."

"People." He lowered his head so that he could just skim her lips with his. "Not Pandora. It infuriates you, doesn't it?"

She wanted to glare but closed her eyes instead. "Yes. I'm doing my best to reverse the situation."

He snuggled down beside her, content for now. She loved him. He still had time to make her like the idea. "Let me know how it works out," he said, and lulled her to sleep.

Chapter 12

Michael studied the dark stains on the garage floor with a kind of grim fascination. Draining the brake fluid from an intended victim's car was a hackneyed device, one expected from time to time on any self-respecting action-adventure show. Viewers and readers alike developed a certain fondness for old, reliable angles in the same way they appreciated the new and different. Though it took on a different picture when it became personal, the car careering out of control down a steep mountain road was as old as the Model T.

He'd used it himself, just as he'd used the anonymous gift of champagne. And the bogus-message routine, he mused as an idea began to stir. Just last season one of *Logan's* heroines of the week had been locked in a cellar—left in the dark after going to investigate a window slamming in the wind. It too was a classic.

Each and every one of the ploys used against himself
and Pandora could have been lifted from one of his own
plots. Randall had pointed it out, though he'd been joking. It didn't seem very funny.

Michael cursed himself, knowing he should have
seen the pattern before. Perhaps he hadn't simply because it had been a pattern, a trite one by Hollywood
standards. Whether it was accidental or planned, Michael decided he wasn't about to be outplotted. He'd
make his next move taking a page from the classic mystery novels. Going into the house, Michael went to the
phone and began to structure his scene.

He was just completing his last call when Pandora
came down the hall toward him. "Michael, you've got
to do something about Sweeney."

Michael leaned back against the newel post and studied her. She looked wonderful—rested, healthy and annoyed. "Isn't it time for your afternoon nap?"

"That's just what I'm talking about." The annoyance
deepened between her brows and pleased him. "I don't
need an afternoon nap. It's been over a week since the
accident." She pulled a leather thong out of her hair and
began to run it through her fingers. "I've seen the doctor, and he said I was fine."

"I thought it was more something along the lines of
you having a head like a rock."

She narrowed her eyes. "He was annoyed because I
healed perfectly without him. The point is, I am healed,
but if Sweeney keeps nagging and hovering, I'll have
a relapse." It came out as a declaration as she stood
straight in front of him, chin lifted, looking as though
she'd never been ill a day in her life.

"What would you like me to do?"

"She'll listen to you. For some reason she has the idea that you're infallible. Mr. Donahue this, Mr. Donahue that." She slapped the leather against her palm. "For the past week all I've heard is how charming, handsome and strong you are. It's a wonder I recovered at all."

His lips twitched, but he understood Sweeney's flattery could undo any progress he'd made. "The woman's perceptive. However…" He stopped Pandora's retort by holding up a hand. "Because I'd never refuse you anything—" when she snorted he ignored it "—and because she's been driving me crazy fussing over my wrist, I'm going to take care of it."

Pandora tilted her head. "How?"

"Sweeney's going to be too busy over the next few days to fuss over us. She'll have the dinner party to fuss over."

"What dinner party?"

"The dinner party we're going to give next week for all our relatives."

She glanced at the phone, remembering he'd been using it when she'd come down the hall. "What have you been up to?"

"Just setting the scene, cousin." He rocked back on his heels, already imagining. "I think we'll have Sweeney dig out the best china, though I doubt we'll have time to use it."

"Michael." She didn't want to seem a coward, but the accident had taught her something about caution and self-preservation. "We won't just be inviting relatives. One of them tried to kill us."

"And failed." He took her chin in his hand. "Don't you think he'll try again, Pandora, and again? The police can't patrol the grounds indefinitely. And," he added with his fingers tightening, "I'm not willing to let bygones be bygones." His gaze skimmed up to where her hair just covered the scar on her forehead. The doctor had said it would fade, but Michael's memory of it never would. "We're going to settle this, my way."

"I don't like it."

"Pandora." He gave her a charming smile and pinched her cheek. "Trust me."

The fact that she did only made her more nervous. With a sigh, she took his hand. "Let's tell Sweeney to kill the fatted calf."

Right down to the moment the first car arrived, Pandora was certain no one would come. She'd sat through a discussion of Michael's plan, argued, disagreed, admired and ultimately she'd given up. Theatrics, she'd decided. But there was enough Jolley in her to look forward to the show, especially when she was one of the leads. And she had, as they said in the business, her part cold.

She'd dressed for the role in a slim, strapless black dress. For flair, she'd added a sterling silver necklace she'd fashioned in an exaggerated star burst. Matching earrings dripped nearly to her chin. If Michael wanted drama, who was she to argue? As the night of the dinner party had grown closer, her nerves had steeled into determination.

When he saw her at the top of the stairs, he was speechless. Had he really convinced himself all these years she had no real beauty? At the moment, poised, defiant and enjoying herself, she made every other woman he'd known look like a shadow. And if he told her so, she wouldn't believe it for a moment. Instead he merely nodded and rocked back on his heels.

"Perfect," he told her as she walked down the main stairs. Standing at the base in a dark suit, Michael looked invincible, and ruthless. "The sophisticated heroine." He took her hand. "Cool and sexy. Hitchcock would've made you a star."

"Don't forget what happened to Janet Leigh."

He laughed and sent one of her earrings spinning. "Nervous?"

"Not as much as I'd thought I'd be. If this doesn't work—"

"Then we're no worse off than we are now. You know what to do."

"We've rehearsed it a half-dozen times. I still have the bruises."

He leaned closer to kiss both bare shoulders. "I always thought you'd be a natural. When this is over, we have a scene of our own to finish. No, don't pull back," he warned as she attempted to. "It's too late to pull back." They stood close, nearly mouth to mouth. "It's been too late all along."

Nerves she'd managed to quell came racing back, but they had nothing to do with plots or plans. "You're being dramatic."

With a nod, he tangled his fingers in her hair. "My sense of drama, your streak of practicality. An interesting combination."

"An uneasy one."

"If life's too easy you sleep through it," Michael decided. "It sounds like the first of our guests are arriving," he murmured as they heard the sound of a car. He kissed her briefly. "Break a leg."

She wrinkled her nose at his back. "That's what I'm afraid of."

Within a half hour, everyone who had been at the reading of the will, except Fitzhugh, was again in the library. No one seemed any more relaxed than they'd been almost six months before. Jolley beamed down on them from the oil painting. From time to time Pandora glanced up at it almost expecting him to wink. To give everyone what they'd come for, Pandora and Michael kept arguing about whatever came to mind. Time for the game to begin, she decided.

Carlson stood with his wife near a bookshelf. He looked cross and impatient and glowered when Pandora approached.

"Uncle Carlson, I'm so glad you could make it. We don't see nearly enough of each other."

"Don't soft-soap me." He swirled his scotch but didn't drink. "If you've got the idea you can talk me out of contesting this absurd will, you're mistaken."

"I wouldn't dream of it. Fitzhugh tells me you don't have a chance." She smiled beautifully. "But I have to agree the will's absurd, especially after being forced to live in the same house with Michael all these months." She ran a finger down one of the long, flattened prongs of her necklace. "I'll tell you, Uncle Carlson, there have been times I've seriously considered throwing in the towel. He's done everything possible to make the six months unbearable. Once he pretended his mother was ill, and he had to go to California. Next thing I knew I was locked in the basement. Childish games," she muttered sending Michael a look of utter dislike. Out of the corner of her eye, she saw Carlson take a quick, nervous drink. "Well, the sentence is nearly up." She turned back with a fresh smile. "I'm so glad we could have this little celebration. Michael's finally going to open a bottle of champagne he's been hoarding since Christmas."

Pandora watched Carlson's wife drop her glass on the Turkish carpet. "Dear me," Pandora said softly. "We'll have to get something to mop that up. Freshen your drink?"

"No, she's fine." Carlson took his wife by the elbow. "Excuse me."

As they moved away, Pandora felt a quick thrill of excitement. So, it had been Carlson.

"I quit smoking about six months ago," Michael told Hank and his wife, earning healthy approval.

"You'll never regret it," Hank stated in his slow, deliberate way. "You're responsible for your own body."

"I've been giving that a lot of thought lately," Michael said dryly. "But living with Pandora the past few months hasn't made it easy. She's made this past winter miserable. She had someone send me a fake message so I'd go flying off to California thinking my mother was ill." He glanced over his shoulder and scowled at Pandora's back.

"If you've gotten through six months without smoking…" Meg began, guiding the conversation back to Michael's health.

"It's a miracle I have living with that woman. But it's almost over." He grinned at Hank. "We're having champagne instead of carrot juice for dinner. I've been saving this bottle since Christmas for just the right occasion."

He saw Hank's fingers whiten around his glass of Perrier and Meg's color drain. "We don't—" Hank looked helplessly at Meg. "We don't drink."

"Champagne isn't drinking," Michael said jovially. "It's celebrating. Excuse me." He moved to the bar as if to freshen his drink and waited for Pandora to join him. "It's Hank."

"No." She added a splash of vermouth to her glass. "It's Carlson." Following the script, she glared at him. "You're an insufferable bore, Michael. Putting up with you isn't worth any amount of money."

"Intellectual snob." He toasted her. "I'm counting the days."

With a sweep of her skirts, Pandora walked over to Ginger. "I don't know how I manage to hold my temper with that man."

Ginger checked her face in a pretty silver compact. "I've always thought he was kind of cute."

"You haven't had to live with him. We were hardly together a week when he broke into my workshop and vandalized it. Then he tried to pass the whole thing off as the work of a vagrant."

Ginger frowned and touched a bit of powder to her nose. "It didn't seem like something he'd do to me. I told—" She caught herself and looked back at Pandora with a vague smile. "Those are pretty earrings."

Michael steeled himself to listen to Morgan's terse opinion on the stock market. The moment he found an opening, he broke in. "Once everything's settled, I'll have to come to you for advice. I've been thinking about getting more actively involved with one of Jolley's chemical firms. There's a lot of money in fertilizer—and pesticides." He watched Patience flutter her hands and subside at a glare from Morgan.

"Software," Morgan said briefly.

Michael only smiled. "I'll look into it."

Pandora tried unsuccessfully to pump Ginger. The five-minute conversation left her suspicious, confused and with the beginnings of a headache. She decided to try her luck on Biff.

"You're looking well." She smiled at him and nodded at his wife.

"You're looking a bit pale, cousin."

"The past six months haven't been a picnic." She cast a look at Michael. "Of course, you've always detested him."

"Of course," Biff said amiably.

"I've yet to discover why Uncle Jolley was fond of him. Besides being a bore, Michael has an affection for odd practical jokes. He got a tremendous kick out of locking me in the cellar."

Biff smiled into his glass. "He's never quite been in our class."

Pandora bit her tongue, then agreed. "Do you know, he even called me one night, disguising his voice. He tried to frighten me by saying someone was trying to kill me."

Biff's brows drew together as he stared into Pandora's eyes. "Odd."

"Well, things are almost settled. By the way, did you enjoy the champagne I sent you?"

Biff's fingers froze on his glass. "Champagne?"

"Right after Christmas."

"Oh yes." He lifted his glass again, studying her as he drank. "So it was you."

"I got the idea when someone sent Michael a bottle at Christmastime. He promises to finally open it tonight. Excuse me, I want to check on dinner."

Her eyes met Michael's briefly as she slipped from

the room. They'd set his scene, she thought. Now she had to move the action along. In the kitchen she found Sweeney finishing up the final preparation for the meal.

"If they're hungry," Sweeney began, "they'll just have to wait ten minutes."

"Sweeney, it's time to turn off the main power switch."

"I know, I know. I was just finishing this ham."

Sweeney had been instructed to, at Pandora's signal, go down to the cellar, turn off the power, then wait exactly one minute and turn it on again. She had been skeptical about the whole of Michael and Pandora's plan but had finally agreed to participate in it. Wiping her hands on her apron, the cook went to the cellar door. Pandora took a deep breath and walked back to the library.

Michael had positioned himself near the desk. He gave Pandora the slightest of nods when she entered. "Dinner in ten minutes," she announced brightly as she swept across the room.

"That gives us just enough time." Michael took the stage and couldn't resist starting with a tried and true line. He didn't have to see Pandora to know she was taking her position. "You all must be wondering why we brought you here tonight." He lifted his glass and looked from one face to the next. "One of you is a murderer."

On cue, the lights went out and pandemonium struck. Glasses shattered, women screamed, a table was overturned. When the lights blinked on, everyone froze. Lying half under the desk, facedown, was Pandora. Beside her was a letter opener with a curved, ornate hilt and blood on the blade. In an instant Michael was beside her, lifting her into his arms before anyone had a chance to react. Silently, he carried her from the room. Several minutes passed before he returned, alone. He gazed, hot and hard, at every face in the room.

"A murderer," he repeated. "She's dead."

"What do you mean she's dead?" Carlson pushed his way forward. "What kind of game is this? Let's have a look at her."

"No one's touching her." Michael effectively blocked his way. "No one's touching anything or leaving this room until the police get here."

"Police?" Pale and shaken, Carlson glanced around. "We don't want that. We'll have to handle this ourselves. She's just fainted."

"Her blood's all over this," Michael commented gesturing to the bloodstained letter opener.

"No!" Meg pushed forward until she'd broken through the crowd around the desk. "No one was supposed to be hurt. Only frightened. It wasn't supposed to be like this. Hank." She reached out, then buried her face against his chest.

"We were only going to play some tricks," he murmured.

"First-degree murder isn't a trick."

"We never—" He looked at Michael in shock. "Not murder," he managed, holding Meg as tightly as she was holding him.

"You didn't want to drink the champagne, either, did you, Hank?"

"That's when I wanted to stop." Still sobbing, Meg turned in her husband's arms. "I even called and tried to warn her. I thought it was wrong all along, just a mean trick, but we needed money. The gym's drained everything we have. We thought if we could make the two of you angry enough with each other, you'd break the terms of the will. But that's all. Hank and I stayed in the cabin and waited. Then he went into Pandora's shop and turned things upside down. If she thought you did it—"

"I never thought she would," Ginger piped up. Two tears rolled down her cheeks. "Really, it all seemed silly and—exciting."

Michael looked at his pretty, weeping cousin. "So you were part of it."

"Well, I didn't really do anything. But when Aunt Patience explained it to me…"

"Patience?" There were patterns and patterns. A new one emerged.

"Morgan deserved his share." The old woman wrung her hands and looked everywhere but at the blood-stained letter opener. She'd thought she'd done the right thing. It all sounded so simple. "We thought we could make one of you leave, then it would all be the way it should be."

"Message," Morgan said, puffing wide-eyed on his cigar. "Not murder." He turned to Carlson. "Your idea."

"It's preposterous." Carlson mopped his brow with a white silk handkerchief. "The lawyers were incompetent. They haven't been able to do a thing. I was merely protecting my rights."

"With murder."

"Don't be ridiculous." He nearly sounded staid and stuffy again. "The plan was to get you out of the house. I did nothing more than lock—her—in the cellar. When I heard about the champagne, I had a doubt or two, but after all, it wasn't fatal."

"Heard about the champagne." It was what Michael had waited for. "From whom?"

"It was Biff," Meg told him. "Biff set it all up, promised nothing would go wrong."

"Just an organizer." Biff gauged the odds, then shrugged. "All's fair, cousin. Everyone in this room had their hand in." He held his up, examining it. "There's no blood on mine. I'd vote for you." He gave Michael a cool smile. "After all, it's no secret you couldn't abide each other."

"You set it up." Michael took a step closer. "There's also a matter of tampering with my car."

Biff moved his shoulders again, but Michael saw the sweat bead above his lips. "Everyone in this room had a part in it. Any of you willing to turn yourselves in?" His breath came faster as he backed away. "One of them panicked and did this. You won't find my fingerprints on that letter opener."

"When someone's attempted murder once," Michael said calmly, "it's easier to prove he tried again."

"You won't prove anything. Any of us might have drained the brake lines in your car. You can't prove I did."

"I don't need to." In a quick move, Michael caught him cleanly on the jaw and sent him reeling. Before he could fall, Michael had him by the collar. "I never said anything about draining the lines."

Feeling the trap close, Biff struck out blindly. Fists swinging, they tumbled to the floor. A Tiffany lamp shattered in a pile of color. They rolled, locked together, into a Belker table that shook from the impact. Shocked and ineffective, the rest stepped back and gave them room.

"Michael, that's quite enough." Pandora entered the

room, her hair mussed and her clothes disheveled. "We have company."

Panting, he dragged Biff to his feet. His wrist sang a bit, but he considered it a pleasure. Charles, looking dignified in his best suit, opened the library doors. "Dinner is served."

Two hours later, Pandora and Michael shared a small feast in the library. "I never thought it would work," Pandora said over a mouthful of ham. "It shouldn't have."

"The more predictable the moves, the more predictable the end."

"Lieutenant Randall didn't seem too pleased."

"He wanted to do it his way." Michael moved his shoulders. "Since he'd already discovered Biff had been visiting other members of the family and making calls to them, he was bound to find out something eventually."

"The easy way." She rubbed the back of her neck. "Do you know how uncomfortable it is to play dead?"

"You were great." He leaned over to kiss her. "A star."

"The letter opener with the stage blood was a nice touch. Still, if they'd all stuck together…"

"We already knew someone was weakening because of the warning call. Turned out that Meg had had enough."

"I've been thinking about investing in their gym."

"It wouldn't hurt."

"What do you think's going to happen?"

"Oh, Carlson'll get off more or less along with the rest of them, excluding Biff. I don't think we have to worry about going to court over the will. As for our dear cousin—" Michael lifted a glass of champagne "—he's going to be facing tougher charges than malicious mischief or burglary. I may never get my television back, but he isn't going to be wearing any Brooks Brothers suits for a while. Only prison blues."

"You gave him another black eye," Pandora mused.

"Yeah." With a grin, Michael drank the wine. "Now you and I only have to cruise through the next two weeks."

"Then it's over."

"No." He took her hand before she could rise. "Then it begins." He slipped the glass from her other hand and pressed her back against the cushions. "How long?"

Pandora struggled to keep the tension from showing. "How long what?"

"Have you been in love with me?"

She jerked, then was frustrated when he held her back. "I'm not sitting here feeding your ego."

"All right, we'll start with me." He leaned back companionably and boxed her in. "I think I fell in love with you when you came back from the Canary Islands and walked into the parlor. You had legs all the way to your waist and you looked down your nose at me. I've never been the same."

"I've had enough games, Michael," she said stiffly.

"So've I." He traced a finger down her cheek. "You said you loved me, Pandora."

"Under duress."

"Then I'll just have to keep you under duress because I'm not giving you up now. Why don't we get married right here?"

She'd started to give him a hefty shove and stopped with her hands pressed against his chest. "What?"

"Right here in the library." He glanced around, ignoring the overturned tables and broken china. "It'd be a nice touch."

"I don't know what you're talking about."

"It's very simple. Here's the plot. You love me, I love you."

"That's not simple," she managed. "I've just been accessible. Once you get back to your blond dancers and busty starlets, you'll—"

"What blond dancers? I can't stand blond dancers."

"Michael, this isn't anything I can joke about."

"Just wait. You buy a nice white dress, maybe a veil. A veil would suit you. We get a minister, lots of flowers and have a very traditional marriage ceremony. After that, we settle into the Folley, each pursuing our respective careers. In a year, two at the most, we give Charles and Sweeney a baby to fuss over. See?" He kissed her ear.

"People's lives aren't screenplays," she began.

"I'm crazy about you, Pandora. Look at me." He took her chin and held it so that their faces were close. "As an artist, you're supposed to be able to see below the surface. That should be easy since you've always told me I'm shallow."

"I was wrong." She wanted to believe. Her heart already did. "Michael, if you're playing games with me, I'll kill you myself."

"Games are over. I love you, it's that simple."

"Simple," she murmured, surprised she could speak at all. "You want to get married?"

"Living together's too easy."

She was more surprised that she could laugh. "Easy?"

"That's right." He shifted her until she was lying flat

on the sofa, his body pressed into hers. When his mouth came down, it wasn't patient, wasn't gentle, and everything he thought, everything he felt, communicated itself through that one contact. As she did rarely, as he asked rarely, she went limp and pliant. Her arms went around him. Perhaps it was easy after all.

"I love you, Michael."

"We're getting married."

"It looks that way."

His eyes were intense when he lifted his head. "I'm going to make life tough on you, Pandora. That's just to pay you back for the fact that you'll be the most exasperating wife on record. Do we understand each other?"

Her smile bloomed slowly. "I suppose we always have."

Michael pressed a kiss to her forehead, to the tip of her nose, then to her lips. "He understood both of us."

She followed his gaze to Jolley's portrait. "Crazy old goat has us right where he wants us. I imagine he's having a good laugh." She rubbed her cheek against Michael's. "I just wish he could be here to see us married."

Michael lifted a brow. "Who says he won't be?" He pulled her up and picked up both glasses. "To Maximillian Jolley McVie."

"To Uncle Jolley." Pandora clinked her glass to Michael's. "To us."

* * * * *

LOCAL HERO

For Dan, with thanks for the idea
and the tons of research material.
And for Jason, for keeping me in tune
with the ten-year-old mind.

Chapter 1

Zark drew a painful breath, knowing it could be his last. The ship was nearly out of oxygen, and he was nearly out of time. A life span could pass in front of the eyes in a matter of seconds. He was grateful that he was alone so no one else could witness his joys and mistakes.

Leilah, it was always Leilah. With each ragged breath he could see her, the clear blue eyes and golden hair of his one and only beloved. As the warning siren inside the cockpit wailed, he could hear Leilah's laughter. Tender, sweet. Then mocking.

"By the red sun, how happy we were together!" The words shuddered out between gasps as he dragged himself over the floor toward the command console. "Lovers, partners, friends."

The pain in his lungs grew worse. It seared through

him like dozens of hot knives tipped with poison from the pits of Argenham. He couldn't waste air on useless words. But his thoughts...his thoughts even now were on Leilah.

That she, the only woman he had ever loved, should be the cause of his ultimate destruction! His destruction, and the world's as they knew it. What fiendish twist of fate had caused the freak accident that had turned her from a devoted scientist to a force of evil and hate?

She was his enemy now, the woman who had once been his wife. Who was still his wife, Zark told himself as he painfully pulled himself up to the console. If he lived, and stopped her latest scheme to obliterate civilization on Perth, he would have to go after her. He would have to destroy her. If he had the strength.

Commander Zark, Defender of the Universe, Leader of Perth, hero and husband, pressed a trembling finger to the button.

CONTINUED IN THE NEXT EXCITING ISSUE!

"Damn!" Radley Wallace mumbled the oath, then looked around quickly to be sure his mother hadn't heard. He'd started to swear, mostly in whispers, about six months ago, and wasn't anxious for her to find out. She'd get that look on her face.

But she was busy going through the first boxes the movers had delivered. He was supposed to be putting his books away, but had decided it was time to take a break. He liked breaks best when they included Universal Comics and Commander Zark. His mother liked him to read real books, but they didn't have many pictures. As far as Radley was concerned, Zark had it all over Long John Silver or Huck Finn.

Rolling over on his back, Radley stared at the freshly painted ceiling of his new room. The new apartment was okay. Mostly he liked the view of the park, and having an elevator was cool. But he wasn't looking forward to starting in a new school on Monday.

Mom had told him it would be fine, that he would make new friends and still be able to visit with some of the old ones. She was real good about it, stroking his hair and smiling in that way that made him feel everything was really okay. But she wouldn't be there when all the kids gave him the once-over. He wasn't going to wear that new sweater, either, even if Mom said the color matched his eyes. He wanted to wear one of his old sweatshirts so at least something would be familiar. He figured she'd understand, because Mom always did.

She still looked sad sometimes, though. Radley squirmed up to the pillow with the comic clutched in his hand. He wished she wouldn't feel bad because his father had gone away. It had been a long time now, and he had to think hard to bring a picture of his father to his mind. He never visited, and only phoned a couple of times a year. That was okay. Radley wished he could tell his mother it was okay, but he was afraid she'd get upset and start crying.

He didn't really need a dad when he had her. He'd told her that once, and she'd hugged him so hard he hadn't been able to breathe. Then he'd heard her crying in her room that night. So he hadn't told her that again.

Big people were funny, Radley thought with the wisdom of his almost ten years. But his mom was the best. She hardly ever yelled at him, and was always sorry when she did. And she was pretty. Radley smiled as he began to sleep. He guessed his mom was just about as pretty as Princess Leilah. Even though her hair was brown instead of golden and her eyes were gray instead of cobalt blue.

She'd promised they could have pizza for dinner, too, to celebrate their new apartment. He liked pizza best, next to Commander Zark.

He drifted off to sleep so he, with the help of Zark, could save the universe.

When Hester looked in a short time later, she saw her son, her universe, dreaming with an issue of Universal Comics in his hand. Most of his books, some of which he paged through from time to time, were still in the packing boxes. Another time she would have given him a mild lecture on responsibility when he woke, but she didn't have the heart for it now. He was taking the move so well. Another upheaval in his life.

"This one's going to be good for you, sweetie." Forgetting the mountain of her own unpacking, she sat on the edge of the bed to watch him.

He looked so much like his father. The dark blond hair, the dark eyes and sturdy chin. It was a rare thing now for her to look at her son and think of the man who had been her husband. But today was different. Today was another beginning for them, and beginnings made her think of endings.

Over six years now, she thought, a bit amazed at the passage of time. Radley had been just a toddler when Allan had walked out on them, tired of bills, tired of family, tired of her in particular. That pain had passed, though it had been a long, slow process. But she had never forgiven, and would never forgive, the man for leaving his son without a second glance.

Sometimes she worried that it seemed to mean so little to Radley. Selfishly she was relieved that he had never formed a strong, enduring bond with the man who would leave them behind, yet she often wondered, late at night when everything was quiet, if her little boy held something inside.

When she looked at him, it didn't seem possible. Hester stroked his hair now and turned to look at his view of Central Park. Radley was outgoing, happy and good-natured. She'd worked hard to help him be those things. She never spoke ill of his father, though there had been times, especially in the early years, when the bitterness and anger had simmered very close to the surface. She'd tried to be both mother and father, and most of the time thought she'd succeeded.

She'd read books on baseball so she would know how to coach him. She'd raced beside him, clinging to the back of the seat of his first two-wheeler. When it had been time to let go, she'd forced back the urge to hang on and had cheered as he'd made his wobbly way down the bike path.

She even knew about Commander Zark. With a smile, Hester eased the wrinkled comic book from his fist. Poor, heroic Zark and his misguided wife Leilah. Yes, Hester knew all about Perth's politics and tribulations. Trying to wean Radley from Zark to Dickens or Twain wasn't easy, but neither was raising a child on your own.

"There's time enough," she murmured as she stretched out beside her son. Time enough for real books and for real life. "Oh, Rad, I hope I've done the right thing." She closed her eyes, wishing, as she'd learned to wish rarely, that she had someone to talk to, someone who could advise her or make decisions, right or wrong.

Then, with her arm hooked around her son's waist, she, too, slept.

The room was dim with dusk when she awoke, groggy and disoriented. The first thing Hester realized was that Radley was no longer curled beside her. Grogginess disappeared in a quick flash of panic she knew was foolish. Radley could be trusted not to leave the apartment without permission. He wasn't a blindly obedient child, but her top ten rules were respected. Rising, she went to find him.

"Hi, Mom." He was in the kitchen, where her homing instinct had taken her first. He held a dripping peanut butter and jelly sandwich in his hands.

"I thought you wanted pizza," she said, noting the good-sized glop of jelly on the counter and the yet-to-be-resealed loaf of bread.

"I do." He took a healthy bite, then grinned. "But I needed something now."

"Don't talk with your mouth full, Rad," she said automatically, even as she bent to kiss him. "You could have woken me if you were hungry."

"That's okay, but I couldn't find the glasses."

She glanced around, seeing that he'd emptied two boxes in his quest. Hester reminded herself that she should have made the kitchen arrangements her first priority. "Well, we can take care of that."

"It was snowing when I woke up."

"Was it?" Hester pushed the hair out of her eyes and straightened to see for herself. "Still is."

"Maybe it'll snow ten feet and there won't be any

school on Monday." Radley climbed onto a stool to sit at the kitchen counter.

Along with no first day on the new job, Hester thought, indulging in some wishful thinking of her own for a moment. No new pressures, new responsibilities. "I don't think there's much chance of that." As she washed out glasses, she looked over her shoulder. "Are you really worried about it, Rad?"

"Sort of." He shrugged his shoulders. Monday was still a day away. A lot could happen. Earthquakes, blizzards, an attack from outer space. He concentrated on the last.

He, Captain Radley Wallace of Earth's Special Forces, would protect and shield, would fight to the death, would—

"I could go in with you if you'd like."

"Aw, Mom, the kids would make fun of me." He bit into his sandwich. Grape jelly oozed out the sides. "It won't be so bad. At least that dumb Angela Wiseberry won't be at this school."

She didn't have the heart to tell him there was a dumb Angela Wiseberry at every school. "Tell you what. We'll both go to our new jobs Monday, then convene back here at 1600 for a full report."

His face brightened instantly. There was nothing Radley liked better than a military operation. "Aye, aye, sir."

"Good. Now I'll order the pizza, and while we're waiting we'll put the rest of the dishes away."

"Let the prisoners do it."

"Escaped. All of them."

"Heads will roll," Radley mumbled as he stuffed the last of the sandwich into his mouth.

* * *

Mitchell Dempsey II sat at his drawing board without an idea in his head. He sipped cold coffee, hoping it would stimulate his imagination, but his mind remained as blank as the paper in front of him. Blocks happened, he knew, but they rarely happened to him. And not on deadline. Of course, he was going about it backward. Mitch cracked another peanut, then tossed the shell in the direction of the bowl. It hit the side and fell on the floor to join several others. Normally the story line would have come first, then the illustrations. Since he'd been having no luck that way, Mitch had switched in the hope that the change in routine would jog something loose.

It wasn't working, and neither was he.

Closing his eyes, Mitch tried for an out-of-body experience. The old Slim Whitman song on the radio cruised on, but he didn't hear it. He was traveling light-years away; a century was passing. The second millennium, he thought with a smile. He'd been born too soon. Though he didn't think he could blame his parents for having him a hundred years too early.

Nothing came. No solutions, no inspiration. Mitch opened his eyes again and stared at the blank white paper. With an editor like Rich Skinner, he couldn't afford to claim artistic temperament. Famine or plague would barely get you by. Disgusted, Mitch reached for another peanut.

What he needed was a change of scene, a distraction. His life was becoming too settled, too ordinary and, despite the temporary block, too easy. He needed challenge. Pitching the shells, he rose to pace.

He had a long, limber body made solid by the hours

he spent each week with weights. As a boy he'd been preposterously skinny, though he'd always eaten like a horse. He hadn't minded the teasing too much until he'd discovered girls. Then, with the quiet determination he'd been born with, Mitch had changed what could be changed. It had taken him a couple of years and a lot of sweat to build himself, but he had. He still didn't take his body for granted, and exercised it as regularly as he did his mind.

His office was littered with books, all read and reread. He was tempted to pull one out now and bury himself in it. But he was on deadline. The big brown mutt on the floor rolled over on his stomach and watched.

Mitch had named him Taz, after the Tasmanian Devil from the old Warner Brothers cartoons, but Taz was hardly a whirlwind of energy. He yawned now and rubbed his back lazily on the rug. He liked Mitch. Mitch never expected him to do anything that he didn't care to, and hardly ever complained about dog hair on the furniture or an occasional forage into the trash. Mitch had a nice voice, too, low and patient. Taz liked it best when Mitch sat on the floor with him and stroked his heavy brown fur, talking out one of his ideas. Taz could look up into the lean face as if he understood every word.

Taz liked Mitch's face, too. It was kind and strong, and the mouth rarely firmed into a disapproving line. His eyes were pale and dreamy. Mitch's wide, strong hands knew the right places to scratch. Taz was a very contented dog. He yawned and went back to sleep.

When the knock came to the door, the dog stirred enough to thump his tail and make a series of low noises in his throat.

"No, I'm not expecting anyone. You?" Mitch responded. "I'll go see." He stepped on peanut shells in his bare feet and swore, but didn't bother to stoop and pick them up. There was a pile of newspapers to be skirted around, and a bag of clothes that hadn't made it to the laundry. Taz had left one of his bones on the Aubusson. Mitch simply kicked it into a corner before he opened the door.

"Pizza delivery."

A scrawny kid of about eighteen was holding a box that smelled like heaven. Mitch took one long, avaricious sniff. "I didn't order any."

"This 406?"

"Yeah, but I didn't order any pizza." He sniffed again. "Wish I had."

"Wallace?"

"Dempsey."

"Shoot."

Wallace, Mitch thought as the kid shifted from foot to foot. Wallace was taking over the Henley apartment, 604. He rubbed a hand over his chin and considered. If Wallace was that leggy brunette he'd seen hauling in boxes that morning, it might be worth investigating.

"I know the Wallaces," he said, and pulled crumpled bills out of his pocket. "I'll take it on up to them."

"I don't know, I shouldn't—"

"Worry about a thing," Mitch finished, and added another bill. Pizza and the new neighbor might be just the distraction he needed.

The boy counted his tip. "Okay, thanks." For all he knew, the Wallaces wouldn't be half as generous.

With the box balanced in his hand, Mitch started out. Then he remembered his keys. He took a moment to search through his worn jeans before he remembered he'd tossed them at the gateleg table when he'd come in the night before. He found them under it, stuck them in one pocket, found the hole in it and stuck them in the other. He hoped the pizza had some pepperoni.

"That should be the pizza," Hester announced, but caught Radley before he could dash to the door. "Let me open it. Remember the rules?"

"Don't open the door unless you know who it is," Radley recited, rolling his eyes behind his mother's back.

Hester put a hand on the knob, but checked the peephole. She frowned a little at the face. She'd have sworn the man was looking straight back at her with amused and very clear blue eyes. His hair was dark and shaggy, as if it hadn't seen a barber or a comb in a little too long. But the face was fascinating, lean and bony and unshaven.

"Mom, are you going to open it?"

"What?" Hester stepped back when she realized she'd been staring at the delivery boy for a good deal longer than necessary.

"I'm starving," Radley reminded her.

"Sorry." Hester opened the door and discovered the fascinating face went with a long, athletic body. And bare feet.

"Did you order pizza?"

"Yes." But it was snowing outside. What was he doing barefoot?

"Good." Before Hester realized his intention, Mitch strolled inside.

"I'll take that," Hester said quickly. "Take this into the kitchen, Radley." She shielded her son with her body and wondered if she'd need a weapon.

"Nice place." Mitch looked casually around at crates and open boxes.

"I'll get your money."

"It's on the house." Mitch smiled at her. Hester wondered if the self-defense course she'd taken two years before would come back to her.

"Radley, take that into the kitchen while I pay the delivery man."

"Neighbor," Mitch corrected. "I'm in 406—you know, two floors down. The pizza got delivered to my place by mistake."

"I see." But for some reason it didn't make her any less nervous. "I'm sorry for the trouble." Hester reached for her purse.

"I took care of it." He wasn't sure whether she looked more likely to lunge or to flee, but he'd been right about her being worth investigating. She was a tall one, he thought, model height, with that same kind of understated body. Her rich, warm brown hair was pulled back from a diamond-shaped face dominated by big gray eyes and a mouth just one size too large.

"Why don't you consider the pizza my version of the welcoming committee?"

"That's really very kind, but I couldn't—"

"Refuse such a neighborly offer?"

Because she was a bit too cool and reserved for his taste, Mitch looked past her to the boy. "Hi, I'm Mitch." This time his smile was answered.

"I'm Rad. We just moved in."

"So I see. From out of town?"

"Uh-uh. We just changed apartments because Mom got a new job and the other was too small. I can see the park from my window."

"Me, too."

"Excuse me, Mr.—?"

"It's Mitch," he repeated with a glance at Hester.

"Yes, well, it's very kind of you to bring this up." As well as being very odd, she thought. "But I don't want to impose on your time."

"You can have a piece," Radley invited. "We never finish it all."

"Rad, I'm sure Mr.—Mitch has things to do."

"Not a thing." He knew his manners, had been taught them painstakingly. Another time, he might even have put them to use and bowed out, but something about the woman's reserve and the child's warmth made him obstinate. "Got a beer?"

"No, I'm sorry, I—"

"We've got soda," Radley piped up. "Mom lets me have one sometimes." There was nothing Radley liked more than company. He gave Mitch a totally ingenuous smile. "Want to see the kitchen?"

"Love to." With something close to a smirk for Hester, Mitch followed the boy.

She stood in the center of the room for a moment, hands on her hips, unsure whether to be exasperated or furious. The last thing she wanted after a day of lugging boxes was company. Especially a stranger's. The only thing to do now was to give him a piece of the damn pizza and blot out her obligation to him.

"We've got a garbage disposal. It makes great noises."

"I bet." Obligingly Mitch leaned over the sink while Radley flipped the switch.

"Rad, don't run that with nothing in it. As you can

see, we're a bit disorganized yet." Hester went to the freshly lined cupboard for plates.

"I've been here for five years, and I'm still disorganized."

"We're going to get a kitten." Radley climbed up on a stool, then reached for the napkins his mother had already put in one of her little wicker baskets. "The other place wouldn't allow pets, but we can have one here, can't we, Mom?"

"As soon as we're settled, Rad. Diet or regular?" she asked Mitch.

"Regular's fine. Looks like you've gotten a lot accomplished in one day." The kitchen was neat as a pin. A thriving asparagus fern hung in a macrame holder in the single window. She had less space than he did, which he thought was too bad. She would probably make better use of the kitchen than he. He took another glance around before settling at the counter. Stuck to the refrigerator was a large crayon drawing of a spaceship. "You do that?" Mitch asked Rad.

"Yeah." He picked up the pizza his mother had set on his plate and bit in eagerly—peanut butter and jelly long since forgotten.

"It's good."

"It's supposed to be the Second Millennium, that's Commander Zark's ship."

"I know." Mitch took a healthy bite of his own slice. "You did a good job."

As he plowed through his pizza, Radley took it for granted that Mitch would recognize Zark's name and mode of transportation. As far as he was concerned, everybody did. "I've been trying to do the Defiance,

Leilah's ship, but it's harder. Anyway, I think Commander Zark might blow it up in the next issue."

"Think so?" Mitch gave Hester an easy smile as she joined them at the counter.

"I don't know, he's in a pretty tough spot right now."

"He'll get out okay."

"Do you read comic books?" Hester asked. It wasn't until she sat down that she noticed how large his hands were. He might have been dressed with disregard, but his hands were clean and had the look of easy competence.

"All the time."

"I've got the biggest collection of all my friends. Mom got me the very first issue with Commander Zark in it for Christmas. It's ten years old. He was only a captain then. Want to see?"

The boy was a gem, Mitch thought, sweet, bright and unaffected. He'd have to reserve judgment on the mother. "Yeah, I'd like that."

Before Hester could tell him to finish his dinner, Radley was off and running. She sat in silence a moment, wondering what sort of man actually read comic books. Oh, she paged through them from time to time to keep a handle on what her son was consuming, but to actually read them? An adult?

"Terrific kid."

"Yes, he is. It's nice of you to…listen to him talk about his comics."

"Comics are my life," Mitch said, straight-faced.

Her reserve broke down long enough for her to stare at him. Clearing her throat, Hester went back to her meal. "I see."

Mitch put his tongue in his cheek. She was some

piece of work, all right, he decided. First meeting or not, he saw no reason to resist egging her on. "I take it you don't."

"Don't what?"

"Read comic books."

"No, I, ah, don't have a lot of time for light reading." She rolled her eyes, unaware that that was where Radley had picked up the habit. "Would you like another piece?"

"Yeah." He helped himself before she could serve him. "You ought to take some time, you know. Comics can be very educational. What's the new job?"

"Oh, I'm in banking. I'm the loan officer for National Trust."

Mitch gave an appreciative whistle. "Big job for someone your age."

Hester stiffened automatically. "I've been in banking since I was sixteen."

Touchy, too, he mused as he licked sauce from his thumb. "That was supposed to be a compliment. I have a feeling you don't take them well." Tough lady, he decided, then thought perhaps she'd had to be. There was no ring on her finger, not even the faintest white mark to show there had been one recently. "I've done some business with banks myself. You know, deposits, withdrawals, returned checks."

She shifted uncomfortably, wondering what was taking Radley so long. There was something unnerving about being alone with this man. Though she had always felt comfortable with eye contact, she was having a difficult time with Mitch. He never looked away for very long.

"I didn't mean to be abrupt."

"No, I don't suppose you did. If I wanted a loan at National Trust, who would I ask for?"

"Mrs. Wallace."

Definitely a tough one. "Mrs. is your first name?"

"Hester," she said, not understanding why she resented giving him that much.

"Hester, then." Mitch offered a hand. "Nice to meet you."

Her lips curved a bit. It was a cautious smile, Mitch thought, but better than none at all. "I'm sorry if I've been rude, but it's been a long day. A long week, really."

"I hate moving." He waited until she'd unbent enough to put her hand in his. Hers was cool and as slender as the rest of her. "Got anyone to help you?"

"No." She removed her hand, because his was as overwhelming as it looked. "We're doing fine."

"I can see that." *No Help Wanted.* The sign was up and posted in big letters. He'd known a few women like her, so fiercely independent, so suspicious of men in general that they had not only a defensive shield but an arsenal of poisonous darts behind it. A sensible man gave them a wide berth. Too bad, because she was a looker, and the kid was definitely a kick.

"I forgot where I'd packed it." Radley came back in, flushed with the effort. "It's a classic, the dealer even told Mom."

He'd also charged her an arm and a leg for it, Hester thought. But it had meant more to Radley than any of his other presents.

"Mint condition, too." Mitch turned the first page with the care of a jeweler cutting a diamond.

"I always make sure my hands are clean before I read it."

"Good idea." It was amazing that after all this time the pride would still be there. An enormous feeling it was, too, a huge burst of satisfaction.

It was there on the first page. Story and drawings by Mitch Dempsey. Commander Zark was his baby, and in ten years they'd become very close friends.

"It's a great story. It really explains why Commander Zark devoted his life to defending the universe against evil and corruption."

"Because his family had been wiped out by the evil Red Arrow in his search for power."

"Yeah." Radley's face lit up. "But he got even with Red Arrow."

"In issue 73."

Hester put her chin in her hand and stared at the two of them. The man was serious, she realized, not just humoring the child. He was as obsessed by comic books as her nine-year-old son.

Strange, he looked fairly normal; he even spoke well. In fact, sitting next to him had been uncomfortable largely because he was so blatantly masculine, with that tough body, angular face and large hands. Hester shook off her thoughts quickly. She certainly didn't want to lean in that direction toward a neighbor, particularly not one whose mental level seemed to have gotten stuck in adolescence.

Mitch turned a couple of pages. His drawing had improved over a decade. It helped to remind himself of that. But he'd managed to maintain the same purity, the same straightforward images that had come to him ten years ago when he'd been struggling unhappily in commercial art.

"Is he your favorite?" Mitch pointed a blunt fingertip toward a drawing of Zark.

"Oh, sure. I like Three Faces, and the Black Diamond's pretty neat, but Commander Zark's my favorite."

"Mine, too." Mitch ruffled the boy's hair. He hadn't realized when he'd delivered a pizza that he would find the inspiration he'd been struggling for all afternoon.

"You can read this sometime. I'd lend it to you, but—"

"I understand." He closed the book carefully and handed it back. "You can't lend out a collector's item."

"I'd better put it away."

"Before you know it, you and Rad will be trading issues." Hester stood up to clear the plates.

"That amuses the hell out of you, doesn't it?"

His tone had her glancing over quickly. There wasn't precisely an edge to it, and his eyes were still clear and mild, but…something warned her to take care.

"I didn't mean to insult you. I just find it unusual for a grown man to read comic books as a habit." She stacked the plates in the dishwasher. "I've always thought it was something boys grew out of at a certain age, but I suppose one could consider it, what, a hobby?"

His brow lifted. She was facing him again, that half smile on her lips. Obviously she was trying to make amends. He didn't think she should get off quite that easily. "Comic books are anything but a hobby with me, Mrs. Hester Wallace. I not only read them, I write them."

"Holy cow, really?" Radley stood staring at Mitch as though he'd just been crowned king. "Do you really? Honest? Oh, boy, are you Mitch Dempsey? The real Mitch Dempsey?"

"In the flesh." He tugged on Radley's ear while Hester looked at him as though he'd stepped in from another planet.

"Oh, boy, Mitch Dempsey right here! Mom, this is Commander Zark. None of the kids are going to believe it. Do you believe it, Mom, Commander Zark right here in our kitchen!"

"No," Hester murmured as she continued to stare. "I can't believe it."

Chapter 2

Hester wished she could afford to be a coward. It would be so easy to go back home, pull the covers over her head and hide out until Radley came home from school. No one who saw her would suspect that her stomach was in knots or that her palms were sweaty despite the frigid wind that whipped down the stairs as she emerged from the subway with a crowd of Manhattan's workforce.

If anyone had bothered to look, they would have seen a composed, slightly preoccupied woman in a long red wool coat and white scarf. Fortunately for Hester, the wind tunnel created by the skyscrapers whipped color into cheeks that would have been deadly pale. She had to concentrate on not chewing off her lipstick as she walked the half block to National Trust. And to her first day on the job.

It would only take her ten minutes to get back home, lock herself in and phone the office with some excuse. She was sick, there'd been a death in the family—preferably hers. She'd been robbed.

Hester clutched her briefcase tighter and kept walking. Big talk, she berated herself. She'd walked Radley to school that morning spouting off cheerful nonsense about how exciting new beginnings were, how much fun it was to start something new. Baloney, she thought, and hoped the little guy wasn't half as scared as she was.

She'd earned the position, Hester reminded herself. She was qualified and competent, with twelve years of experience under her belt. And she was scared right out of her shoes. Taking a deep breath, she walked into National Trust.

Laurence Rosen, the bank manager, checked his watch, gave a nod of approval and strode over to greet her. His dark blue suit was trim and conservative. A woman could have powdered her nose in the reflection from his shiny black shoes. "Right on time, Mrs. Wallace, an excellent beginning. I pride myself on having a staff that makes optimum use of time." He gestured toward the back of the bank, and her office.

"I'm looking forward to getting started, Mr. Rosen," she said, and felt a wave of relief that it was true. She'd always liked the feel of a bank before the doors opened to the public. The cathedral-like quiet, the pregame anticipation.

"Good, good, we'll do our best to keep you busy." He noted with a slight frown that two secretaries were not yet at their desks. In a habitual gesture, he passed a hand over his hair. "Your assistant will be in momentarily. Once you're settled, Mrs. Wallace, I'll expect you to keep close tabs on her comings and goings. Your efficiency depends largely on hers."

"Of course."

Her office was small and dull. She tried not to wish for something airier—or to notice that Rosen was as stuffy as they came. The increase this job would bring to her income would make things better for Radley. That, as always, was the bottom line. She'd make it work, Hester told herself as she took off her coat. She'd make it work well.

Rosen obviously approved of her trim black suit and understated jewelry. There was no room for flashy clothes or behavior in banking. "I trust you looked over the files I gave you."

"I familiarized myself with them over the weekend." She moved behind the desk, knowing it would establish her position. "I believe I understand National Trust's policy and procedure."

"Excellent, excellent. I'll leave you to get organized then. Your first appointment's at—" he turned pages over on her desk calendar "—9:15. If you have any problems, contact me. I'm always around somewhere."

She would have bet on it. "I'm sure everything will be fine, Mr. Rosen. Thank you."

With a final nod, Rosen strode out. The door closed behind him with a quiet click. Alone, Hester let herself slide bonelessly into her chair. She'd gotten past the first hurdle, she told herself. Rosen thought she was competent and suitable. Now all she had to do was be those things. She would be, because too much was riding on it. Not the least of those things was her pride. She hated making a fool of herself. She'd certainly done a good job of that the night before with the new neighbor.

Even hours later, remembering it, her cheeks warmed. She hadn't meant to insult the man's—even now she couldn't bring herself to call it a profession—his work, then, Hester decided. She certainly hadn't meant to make any personal observations. The problem had been that she hadn't been as much on her guard as usual. The man had thrown her off by inviting himself in and joining them for dinner and charming Radley, all in a matter of minutes. She wasn't used to people popping into her life. And she didn't like it.

Radley loved it. Hester picked up a sharpened pencil with the bank's logo on the side. He'd practically glowed with excitement, and hadn't been able to speak of anything else even after Mitch Dempsey had left.

She could be grateful for one thing. The visit had taken Radley's mind off the new school. Radley had always made friends easily, and if this Mitch was willing to give her son some pleasure, she shouldn't criticize. In any case, the man seemed harmless enough. Hester refused to admit to the uncomfortable thrill she'd experienced when his hand had closed over hers. What possible trouble could come from a man who wrote comic books for a living? She caught herself chewing at her lipstick at the question.

The knock on the door was brief and cheerful. Before she could call out, it was pushed open.

"Good morning, Mrs. Wallace. I'm Kay Lorimar, your assistant. Remember, we met for a few minutes a couple of weeks ago."

"Yes, good morning, Kay." Her assistant was everything Hester had always wanted to be herself: petite, well-rounded, blond, with small delicate features. She folded her hands on the fresh blotter and tried to look authoritative.

"Sorry I'm late." Kay smiled and didn't look the least bit sorry. "Everything takes longer than you think it does on Monday. Even if I pretend it's Tuesday it doesn't seem to help. I don't know why. Would you like some coffee?"

"No, thank you, I've an appointment in a few minutes."

"Just ring if you change your mind." Kay paused at the door. "This place could sure use some cheering up, it's dark as a dungeon. Mr. Blowfield, that's who you're replacing, he liked things dull—matched him, you know." Her smile was ingenuous, but Hester hesitated to answer it. It would hardly do for her to get a reputation as a gossip the first day on the job. "Anyway, if you decide to do any redecorating, let me know. My roommate's into interior design. He's a real artist."

"Thank you." How was she supposed to run an office with a pert little cheerleader in tow? Hester wondered. One day at a time. "Just send Mr. and Mrs. Browning in when they arrive, Kay."

"Yes, ma'am." She sure was more pleasant to look at than old Blowfield, Kay thought. But it looked as if she had the same soul. "Loan application forms are in the bottom left drawer of the desk, arranged according to type. Legal pads in the right. Bank stationery, top right. The list of current interest rates are in the middle drawer. The Brownings are looking for a loan to remodel their loft as they're expecting a child. He's in electronics, she works part-time at Bloomingdale's. They've been advised what papers to bring with them. I can make copies while they're here."

Hester lifted her brow. "Thank you, Kay," she said, not certain whether to be amused or impressed.

When the door closed again, Hester sat back and smiled. The office might be dull, but if the morning was any indication, nothing else at National Trust was going to be.

Mitch liked having a window that faced the front of the building. That way, whenever he took a break, he could watch the comings and goings. After five years, he figured he knew every tenant by sight and half of them by name. When things were slow or, better, when he was ahead of the game, he whiled away time by sketching the more interesting of them. If his time stretched further, he made a story line to go with the faces.

He considered it the best of practice because it amused him. Occasionally there was a face interesting enough to warrant special attention. Sometimes it was a cabdriver or a delivery boy. Mitch had learned to look close and quick, then sketch from lingering impressions. Years before, he had sketched faces for a living, if a pitiful one. Now he sketched them for entertainment and was a great deal more satisfied.

He spotted Hester and her son when they were still half a block away. The red coat she wore stood out like a beacon. It certainly made a statement, Mitch mused as he picked up his pencil. He wondered if the coolly distant Mrs. Wallace realized what signals she was sending out. He doubted it.

He didn't need to see her face to draw it. Already there were a half a dozen rough sketches of her tossed on the table in his workroom. Interesting features, he told himself as his pencil began to fly across the pad. Any artist would be compelled to capture them.

The boy was walking along beside her, his face all but obscured by a woolen scarf and hat. Even from this distance, Mitch could see the boy was chattering earnestly. His head was angled up toward his mother. Every now and again she would glance down as if to comment; then the boy would take over again. A few steps away from the building, she stopped. Mitch saw the wind catch at her hair as she tossed her head back and laughed. His fingers went limp on the pencil as he leaned closer to the window. He wanted to be nearer, near enough to hear the laugh, to see if her eyes lit up with it. He imagined they did, but how? Would that subtle, calm gray go silvery or smoky?

She continued to walk, and in seconds was in the building and out of sight.

Mitch stared down at his sketch pad. He had no more than a few lines and contours. He couldn't finish it, he thought as he set the pencil down. He could only see her laughing now, and to capture that on paper he'd need a closer look.

Picking up his keys, he jangled them in his hand. He'd given her the better part of a week. The aloof Mrs. Wallace might consider another neighborly visit out of line, but he didn't. Besides, he liked the kid. Mitch would have gone upstairs to see him before, but he'd been busy fleshing out his story. He owed the kid for that, too, Mitch considered. The little weekend visit had not only crumbled the block, but had given Mitch enough fuel for three issues. Yeah, he owed the kid.

He pushed the keys into his pocket and walked into his workroom. Taz was there, a bone clamped between his paws as he snoozed. "Don't get up," Mitch said mildly. "I'm going out for a while." As he spoke, he ruffled through papers. Taz opened his eyes to half-mast and grumbled. "I don't know how long I'll be." After wracking through his excuse for a filing system, Mitch found the sketch. Commander Zark in full military regalia, sober-faced, sad-eyed, his gleaming ship at his back. Beneath it was the caption: THE MISSION: Capture Princess Leilah—or DESTROY her!!

Mitch wished briefly that he had the time to ink and color it, but figured the kid would like it as is. With a careless stroke he signed it, then rolled it into a tube.

"Don't wait on dinner for me," he instructed Taz.

"I'll get it!" Radley danced to the door. It was Friday, and school was light-years away.

"Ask who it is."

Radley put his hand on the knob and shook his head. He'd been going to ask. Probably. "Who is it?"

"It's Mitch."

"It's Mitch!" Radley shouted, delighted. In the bedroom, Hester scowled and pulled the sweatshirt over her head.

"Hi." Breathless with excitement, Radley opened the door to his latest hero.

"Hi, Rad, how's it going?"

"Fine. I don't have any homework all weekend." He reached out a hand to draw Mitch inside. "I wanted to come down and see you, but Mom said no 'cause you'd be working or something."

"Or something," Mitch muttered. "Look, it's okay with me if you come over. Anytime."

"Really?"

"Really." The kid was irresistible, Mitch thought as he ruffled the boy's hair. Too bad his mother wasn't as friendly. "I thought you might like this." Mitch handed him the rolled sketch.

"Oh, wow." Awestruck, reverent, Radley stared at the drawing. "Jeez, Commander Zark and the Second Millennium. Can I have it, really? To keep?"

"Yeah."

"I gotta show Mom." Radley turned and dashed toward the bedroom as Hester came out. "Look what Mitch gave me. Isn't it great? He said I could keep it and everything."

"It's terrific." She put a hand on Radley's shoulder as she studied the sketch. The man was certainly talented, Hester decided. Even if he had chosen such an odd way to show it. Her hand remained on Radley's shoulder as she looked over at Mitch. "That was very nice of you."

He liked the way she looked in the pastel sweats, casual, approachable, if not completely relaxed. Her hair was down, too, with the ends just sweeping short of her shoulders. Parted softly on the side and unpinned, it gave her a completely different look.

"I wanted to thank Rad." Mitch forced himself to look away from her face, then smiled at the boy. "You helped me through a block last weekend."

"I did?" Radley's eyes widened. "Honest?"

"Honest. I was stuck, spinning wheels. After I talked to you that night, I went down and everything fell into place. I appreciate it."

"Wow, you're welcome. You could stay for dinner again. We're just having Chinese chicken, and maybe I could help you some more. It's okay, isn't it, Mom? Isn't it?"

Trapped again. And again she caught the gleam of amusement in Mitch's eyes. "Of course."

"Great. I want to go hang this up right away. Can I call Josh, too, and tell him about it? He won't believe it."

"Sure." She barely had time to run a hand over his hair before he was off and running.

"Thanks, Mitch." Radley paused at the turn of the hallway. "Thanks a lot."

Hester found the deep side pockets in her sweats and slipped her hands inside. There was absolutely no reason for the man to make her nervous. So why did he? "That was really very kind of you."

"Maybe, but I haven't done anything that's made me feel that good in a long time." He wasn't completely at ease himself, Mitch discovered, and he tucked his thumbs into the back pockets of his jeans. "You work fast," he commented as he glanced around the living room.

The boxes were gone. Bright, vivid prints hung on the walls and a vase of flowers, fresh as morning, sat near the window, where sheer curtains filtered the light. Pillows were plumped, furniture gleamed. The only signs of confusion were a miniature car wreck and a few plastic men scattered on the carpet. He was glad to see them. It meant she wasn't the type who expected the boy to play only in his room.

"Dali?" He walked over to a lithograph hung over the sofa.

She caught her bottom lip between her teeth as Mitch studied one of her rare extravagances. "I bought that in a little shop on Fifth that's always going out of business."

"Yeah, I know the one. It didn't take you long to put things together here."

"I wanted everything back to normal as soon as possible. The move wasn't easy for Radley."

"And you?" He turned then, catching her off guard with the sudden sharp look.

"Me? I—ah…"

"You know," he began as he crossed over to her, attracted by her simple bafflement. "You're a lot more articulate when you talk about Rad than you are when you talk about Hester."

She stepped back quickly, aware that he would have touched her and totally unsure what her reaction might have been. "I should start dinner."

"Want some help?"

"With what?"

This time she didn't move quickly enough. He cupped her chin in his hand and smiled. "With dinner."

It had been a long time since a man had touched her that way. He had a strong hand with gentle fingers. That had to be the reason her heart leaped up to her throat and pounded there. "Can you cook?"

What incredible eyes she had. So clear, so pale a gray they were almost translucent. For the first time in years he felt the urge to paint, just to see if he could bring those eyes to life on canvas. "I make a hell of a peanut butter sandwich."

She lifted a hand to his wrist, to move his away, she thought. But her fingers lay there lightly a moment, experimenting. "How are you at chopping vegetables?"

"I think I can handle it."

"All right, then." She backed up, amazed that she had allowed the contact to go for so long. "I still don't have any beer, but I do have some wine this time."

"Fine." What the hell were they talking about? Why

were they talking at all, when she had a mouth that was made to fit on a man's? A little baffled by his own train of thought, he followed her into the kitchen.

"It's really a simple meal," she began. "But when it's all mixed up, Radley hardly notices he's eating something nutritious. A Twinkie's the true way to his heart."

"My kind of kid."

She smiled a little, more relaxed now that she had her hands full. She set celery and mushrooms on the chopping block. "The trick's in moderation." Hester took the chicken out, then remembered the wine. "I'm willing to concede to Rad's sweet tooth in small doses. He's willing to accept broccoli on the same terms."

"Sounds like a wise arrangement." She opened the wine. Inexpensive, he thought with a glance at the label, but palatable. She filled two glasses, then handed him one. It was silly, but her hands were damp again. It had been some time since she'd shared a bottle of wine or fixed a simple dinner with a man. "To neighbors," he said, and thought she relaxed fractionally as he touched his glass to hers.

"Why don't you sit down while I bone the chicken? Then you can deal with the vegetables."

He didn't sit, but did lean back against the counter. He wasn't willing to give her the distance he was sure she wanted. Not when she smelled so good. She handled the knife like an expert, he noted as he sipped his wine. Impressive. Most of the career women he knew were more experienced in takeouts. "So, how's the new job?"

Hester moved her shoulders. "It's working out well. The manager's a stickler for efficiency, and that trickles down. Rad and I have been having conferences all week so we can compare notes."

Was that what they'd been talking about when they'd walked home today? he wondered. Was that why she'd laughed? "How's Radley taking the new school?"

"Amazingly well." Her lips softened and curved again. He was tempted to touch a fingertip to them to feel the movement. "Whatever happens in Rad's life, he rolls with. He's incredible."

There was a shadow there, a slight one, but he could see it in her eyes. "Divorce is tough," he said, and watched Hester freeze up.

"Yes." She put the boned and cubed chicken in a bowl. "You can chop this while I start the rice."

"Sure." No trespassing, he thought, and let it drop. For now. He'd gone with the law of averages when he'd mentioned divorce, and realized he'd been on the mark. But the mark was still raw. Unless he missed his guess, the divorce had been a lot tougher on her than on Radley. He was also sure that if he wanted to draw her out, it would have to be through the boy. "Rad mentioned that he wanted to come down and visit, but you'd put him off."

Hester handed Mitch an onion before she put a pan on the stove. "I didn't want him disturbing your work."

"We both know what you think of my work."

"I had no intention of offending you the other night," she said stiffly. "It was only that—"

"You can't conceive of a grown man making a living writing comic books."

Hester remained silent as she measured out water. "It's none of my business how you make your living."

"That's right." Mitch took a long sip of wine before he attacked the celery. "In any case, I want you to know that Rad can come see me whenever he likes."

"That's very nice of you, but—"

"No buts, Hester. I like him. And since I'm in the position of calling my own hours, he won't bother me. What do I do with the mushrooms?"

"Slice." She put the lid on the rice before crossing over to show him. "Not too thin. Just make sure…" Her words trailed off when he closed his hand over hers on the knife.

"Like this?" The move was easy. He didn't even have to think about it, but simply shifted until she was trapped between his arms, her back pressed against him. Giving in to the urge, he bent down so that his mouth was close to her ear.

"Yes, that's fine." She stared down at their joined hands and tried to keep her voice even. "It really doesn't matter."

"We aim to please."

"I have to put on the chicken." She turned and found herself in deeper water. It was a mistake to look up at him, to see that slight smile on his lips and that calm, confident look in his eyes. Instinctively she lifted a hand to his chest. Even that was a mistake. She could feel the slow, steady beat of his heart. She couldn't back up, because there was no place to go, and stepping forward was tempting, dangerously so. "Mitch, you're in my way."

He'd seen it. Though it had been free briefly and suppressed quickly, he'd seen the passion come into her eyes. So she could feel and want and wonder. Maybe it was best if they both wondered a little while longer. "I think you're going to find that happening a lot." But he shifted aside and let her pass. "You smell good, Hester, damn good."

That quiet statement did nothing to ease her pulse rate. Humoring Radley or not, she vowed this would be the last time she entertained Mitch Dempsey. Hester turned on the gas under the wok and added peanut oil. "I take it you do your work at home, then. No office?"

He'd let her have it her way for the time being. The minute she'd turned in his arms and looked up at him, he'd known he'd have it his way—have her his way—before too long. "I only have to go a couple of times a week. Some of the writers or artists prefer working in the office. I do better work at home. After I have the story and the sketches, I take them in for editing and inking."

"I see. So you don't do the inking yourself?" she asked, though she'd have been hard-pressed to define what inking was. She'd have to ask Radley.

"Not anymore. We have some real experts in that, and it gives me more time to work on the story. Believe it or not, we shoot for quality, the kind of vocabulary that challenges a kid and a story that entertains."

After adding chicken to the hot oil, Hester took a deep breath. "I really do apologize for anything I said that offended you. I'm sure your work's very important to you, and I know Radley certainly appreciates it."

"Well said, Mrs. Wallace." He slid the vegetable-laden chopping block toward her.

"Josh doesn't believe it." Radley bounced into the room, delighted with himself. "He wants to come over tomorrow and see. Can he? His mom says okay if it's okay with you? Okay, Mom?"

Hester turned from the chicken long enough to give Radley a hug. "Okay, Rad, but it has to be after noon. We have some shopping to do in the morning."

"Thanks. Just wait till he sees. He's gonna go crazy. I'll tell him."

"Dinner's nearly ready. Hurry up and wash your hands."

Radley rolled his eyes at Mitch as he raced from the room again.

"You're a big hit," Hester commented.

"He's nuts about you."

"The feeling's mutual."

"So I noticed." Mitch topped off his wine. "You know, I was curious. I always thought bankers kept bankers' hours. You and Rad don't get home until five or so." When she turned her head to look at him, he merely smiled. "Some of my windows face the front. I like to watch people going in and out."

It gave her an odd and not entirely comfortable feeling to know he'd watched her walk home. Hester dumped the vegetables in and stirred. "I get off at four, but then I have to pick Rad up from the sitter." She glanced over her shoulder again. "He hates it when I call her a sitter. Anyway, she's over by our old place, so it takes awhile. I have to start looking for someone closer."

"A lot of kids his age and younger come home on their own."

Her eyes did go smoky, he noted. All she needed was a touch of anger. Or passion. "Radley isn't going to be a latchkey child. He isn't coming home to an empty house because I have to work."

Mitch set her glass by her elbow. "Coming home to empty can be depressing," he murmured, remembering his own experiences. "He's lucky to have you."

"I'm luckier to have him." Her tone softened. "If you'd get out the plates, I'll dish this up."

Mitch remembered where she kept her plates, white ones with little violet sprigs along the edges. It was odd to realize they pleased him when he'd become so accustomed to disposable plastic. He took them out, then set them beside her. Most things were best done on impulse, he'd always thought. He went with the feeling now.

"I guess it would be a lot easier on Rad if he could come back here after school."

"Oh, yes. I hate having to drag him across town, though he's awfully good about it. It's just so hard to find someone you can trust, and who Radley really likes."

"How about me?"

Hester reached to turn off the gas, but stopped to stare at him. Vegetables and chicken popped in hot oil. "I'm sorry?"

"Rad could stay with me in the afternoons." Again Mitch put a hand over hers, this time to turn off the heat. "He'd only be a couple floors away from his own place."

"With you? No, I couldn't."

"Why not?" The more he thought of it, the more Mitch liked the idea. He and Taz could use the company in the afternoons, and as a bonus he'd be seeing a lot more of the very interesting Mrs. Wallace. "You want references? No criminal record, Hester. Well, there was the case of my motorcycle and the prize roses, but I was only eighteen."

"I didn't mean that—exactly." When he grinned, she began to fuss with the rice. "I mean I couldn't impose that way. I'm sure you're busy."

"Come on, you don't think I do anything all day but doodle. Let's be honest."

"We've already agreed it isn't any of my business," she began.

"Exactly. The point is I'm home in the afternoons, I'm available and I'm willing. Besides, I may even be able to use Rad as a consultant. He's good, you know." Mitch indicated the drawing on the refrigerator. "The kid could use some art lessons."

"I know. I was hoping I'd be able to swing it this summer, but I don't—"

"Want to look a gift horse in the mouth," Mitch finished. "Look, the kid likes me, I like him. And I'll swear to no more than one Twinkie an afternoon."

She laughed then, as he'd seen her laugh a few hours before from his window. It wasn't easy to hold himself back, but something told him if he made a move now, the door would slam in his face and the bolt would slide shut. "I don't know, Mitch. I do appreciate the offer, God knows it would make things easier, but I'm not sure you understand what you're asking for."

"I hasten to point out that I was once a small boy." He wanted to do it, he discovered. It was more than a gesture or impulse; he really wanted to have the kid around. "Look, why don't we put this to a vote and ask Rad?"

"Ask me what?" Radley had run some water over his hands after he'd finished talking to Josh, and figured his mother was too busy to give them a close look.

Mitch picked up his wine, then lifted a brow. My ball, Hester thought. She could have put the child off, but she'd always prided herself on being honest with him. "Mitch was just suggesting that you might like to stay with him after school in the afternoons instead of going over to Mrs. Cohen's."

"Really?" Astonishment and excitement warred until he was bouncing with both. "Really, can I?"

"Well, I wanted to think about it and talk to you before—"

"I'll behave." Radley rushed over to wrap his arms around his mother's waist. "I promise. Mitch is much better than Mrs. Cohen. Lots better. She smells like mothballs and pats me on the head."

"I rest my case," Mitch murmured.

Hester sent Mitch a smoldering look. She wasn't accustomed to being outnumbered or to making a decision without careful thought and consideration. "Now, Radley, you know Mrs. Cohen's very nice. You've been staying with her for over two years."

Radley squeezed harder and played his ace. "If I stayed with Mitch I could come right home. And I'd do my homework first." It was a rash promise, but it was a desperate situation. "You'd get home sooner, too, and everything. Please, Mom, say yes."

She hated to deny him anything, because there were too many things she'd already had to. He was looking up at her now with his cheeks rosy with pleasure. Bending, she kissed him. "All right, Rad, we'll try it and see how it works out."

"It's going to be great." He locked his arms around her neck before he turned to Mitch. "It's going to be just great."

Chapter 3

Mitch liked to sleep late on weekends—whenever he thought of them as weekends. Because he worked in his own home, at his own pace, he often forgot that to the vast majority there was a big difference between Monday mornings and Saturday mornings. This particular Saturday, however, he was spending in bed, largely dead to the world.

He'd been restless the evening before after he'd left Hester's apartment. Too restless to go back to his own alone. On the spur of the moment he'd gone out to the little lounge where the staff of Universal Comics often got together. He'd run into his inker, another artist and one of the staff writers for *The Great Beyond,* Universal's bid for the supernatural market. The music had been loud and none too good, which had been exactly what his mood had called for.

From there he'd been persuaded to attend an all-night horror film festival in Times Square. It had been past six when he'd come home, a little drunk and with only enough energy left to strip and tumble into bed—where he'd promised himself he'd stay for the next twenty-four hours. When the phone rang eight hours later, he answered it mostly because it annoyed him.

"Yeah?"

"Mitch?" Hester hesitated. It sounded as though he'd been asleep. Since it was after two in the afternoon, she dismissed the thought. "It's Hester Wallace. I'm sorry to bother you."

"What? No, it's all right." He rubbed a hand over his face, then pushed at the dog, who had shifted to the middle of the bed. "Damn it, Taz, shove over. You're breathing all over me."

Taz? Hester thought as both brows lifted. She hadn't thought that Mitch would have a roommate. She caught her bottom lip between her teeth. That was something she should have checked out. For Radley's sake.

"I really am sorry," she continued in a voice that had cooled dramatically. "Apparently I've caught you at a bad time."

"No." Give the stupid mutt an inch and he took a mile, Mitch thought as he hefted the phone and climbed to the other side of the bed. "What's up?"

"Are you?"

It was the mild disdain in her voice that had him bristling. That and the fact that it felt as though he'd eaten a sandbox. "Yeah, I'm up. I'm talking to you, aren't I?"

"I only called to give you all the numbers and information you need if you watch Radley next week."

"Oh." He pushed the hair out of his eyes and glanced

around, hoping he'd left a glass of watered-down soda or something close at hand. No luck. "Okay. You want to wait until I get a pencil?"

"Well, I..." He heard her put her hand over the receiver and speak to someone—Radley, he imagined from the quick intensity of the voice. "Actually, if it wouldn't put you out, Radley was hoping we could come by for a minute. He wants to introduce you to his friend. If you're busy, I can just drop the information by later."

Mitch started to tell her to do just that. Not only could he go back to sleep, but he might just be able to wrangle five minutes alone with her. Then he thought of Radley standing beside his mother, looking up at her with those big dark eyes. "Give me ten minutes," he muttered, and hung up before Hester could say a word.

Mitch pulled on jeans, then went into the bath to fill the sink with cold water. He took a deep breath and stuck his face in it. He came up swearing but awake. Five minutes later he was pulling on a sweatshirt and wondering if he'd remembered to wash any socks. All the clothes that had come back from the laundry neatly folded had been dumped on the chair in the corner of the bedroom. He briefly considered pushing his way through them, then let it go when he heard the knock. Taz's tail thumped on the mattress.

"Why don't you pick up this place?" Mitch asked him. "It's a pigsty."

Taz grinned, showing a set of big white teeth, then made a series of growls and groans.

"Excuses. Always excuses. And get out of bed. Don't you know it's after two?" Mitch rubbed a hand over his unshaven chin, then went to open the door.

She looked great, just plain great, with a hand on a

shoulder of each boy and a half smile on her face. Shy? he thought, a little surprised as he realized it. He had thought her cool and aloof, but now he believed she used that to hide an innate shyness, which he found amazingly sweet.

"Hiya, Rad."

"Hi, Mitch," Radley returned, almost bursting with importance. "This is my friend Josh Miller. He doesn't believe you're Commander Zark."

"Is that so?" Mitch looked down at the doubting Thomas, a skinny towhead about two inches taller than Rad. "Come on in."

"It's nice of you to put up with this," Hester began. "We weren't going to have any peace until Rad and Josh had it settled." The living room looked as though it had exploded. That was Hester's first thought as Mitch closed the door behind them. Papers and clothes and wrappers were everywhere. She imagined there was furniture, too, but she couldn't have described it.

"Tell Josh you're Commander Zark," Radley insisted.

"I guess you could say that." The notion pleased him. "I created him, anyway." He looked down again at Josh, whose pout had gone beyond doubt to true suspicion. "You two go to school together?"

"Used to." Josh stood close to Hester as he studied Mitch. "You don't look like Commander Zark."

Mitch rubbed a hand over his chin again. "Rough night."

"He is too Zark. Hey, look, Mom. Mitch has a DVR." Radley easily overlooked the clutter and homed in on the entertainment center. "I'm saving up my allowance to buy one. I've got seventeen dollars."

"It adds up," Mitch murmured, and flicked a finger

down his nose. "Why don't we go into the office? I'll show you what's cooking in the spring issue."

"Wow."

Taking this as an assent, Mitch led the way.

The office, Hester noted, was big and bright and every bit as chaotic as the living room. She was a creature of order, and it was beyond her how anyone could produce under these conditions. Yet there was a drawing board set up, and tacked to it were sketches and captions.

"You can see Zark's going to have his hands full when Leilah teams up with the Black Moth."

"The Black Moth. Holy cow." Faced with the facts, Josh was duly impressed. Then he remembered his comic book history, and suspicion reared again. "I thought he destroyed the Moth five issues ago."

"The Moth only went into hibernation after Zark bombarded the Zenith with experimental ZT-5. Leilah used her scientific genius to bring him out again."

"Wow." This came from Josh as he stared at the oversized words and drawings. "How come you make this so big? It can't fit in a comic book."

"It has to be reduced."

"I read all about that stuff." Radley gave Josh a superior glance. "I got this book out of the library that gave the history of comic books, all the way back to the 1930s."

"The Stone Age." Mitch smiled as the boys continued to admire his work. Hester was doing some admiring of her own. Beneath the clutter, she was certain there was a genuine, French rococo cupboard. And books. Hundreds of them. Mitch watched her wander the room.

And would have gone on watching if Josh hadn't tugged on his arm.

"Please, can I have your autograph?"

Mitch felt foolishly delighted as he stared down at the earnest face. "Sure." Shuffling through papers, he found a blank one and signed it. Then, with a flourish, he added a quick sketch of Zark.

"Neat." Josh folded the paper reverently and slipped it in his back pocket. "My brother's always bragging because he's got an autographed baseball, but this is better."

"Told ya." With a grin, Radley moved closer to Mitch. "And I'm going to be staying with Mitch after school until Mom gets home from work."

"No kidding?"

"All right, guys, we've taken up enough of Mr. Dempsey's time." Hester started to shoo the boys along when Taz strolled into the room.

"Gee whiz, he's really big." Radley started forward, hand out, when Hester caught him.

"Radley, you know better than to go up to a strange dog."

"Your mom's right," Mitch put in. "But in this case it's okay. Taz is harmless."

And enormous, Hester thought, keeping a firm grip on both boys.

Taz, who had a healthy respect for little people, sat in the doorway and eyed them both. Small boys had a tendency to want to play rough and pull ears, which Taz suffered heroically but could do without. Waiting to see which way the wind blew, he sat and thumped his tail.

"He's anything but an aggressive dog," Mitch reassured Hester. He stepped around her and put a hand on Taz's head. Without, Hester noted, having to bend over.

"Does he do tricks?" Radley wanted to know. It was one of his most secret wishes to own a dog. A big one. But he never asked, because he knew they couldn't keep one shut in an apartment all day alone.

"No, all Taz does is talk."

"Talk?" Josh went into a fit of laughter. "Dogs can't talk."

"He means bark," Hester said, relaxing a little.

"No, I mean talk." Mitch gave Taz a couple of friendly pats. "How's it going, Taz?"

In answer, the dog pushed his head hard against Mitch's leg and began to groan and grumble. Eyes wide and sincere, he looked up at his master and howled and hooted until both boys were nearly rolling with laughter.

"He *does* talk." Radley stepped forward, palm up. "He really does." Taz decided Radley didn't look like an ear puller and nuzzled his long snout in the boy's hand. "He likes me. Look, Mom." It was love at first sight as Radley threw his arms around the dog's neck. Automatically Hester started forward.

"He's as gentle as they come, I promise you." Mitch put a hand on Hester's arm. Even though the dog was already grumbling out his woes in Radley's ear and allowing Josh to pet him, Hester wasn't convinced.

"I don't imagine he's used to children."

"He fools around with kids in the park all the time." As if to prove it, Taz rolled over to expose his belly for stroking. "Added to that is the fact that he's bone lazy. He wouldn't work up the energy to bite anything that hadn't been put in a bowl for him. You aren't afraid of dogs, are you?"

"No, of course not." Not really, she added to herself. Because she hated to show a weakness, Hester crouched down to pet the huge head. Unknowingly she hit the perfect spot, and Taz recognized a patsy when he saw one. He shifted to lay a paw on her thigh and, with his dark, sad eyes on hers, began to moan. Laughing, Hester rubbed behind his ears. "You're just a big baby, aren't you?"

"An operator's more like it," Mitch murmured, wondering what sort of trick he'd have to do to get Hester to touch him with such feeling.

"I can play with him every day, can't I, Mitch?"

"Sure." Mitch smiled down at Radley. "Taz loves attention. You guys want to take him for a walk?"

The response was immediate and affirmative. Hester straightened up, looking doubtfully at Taz. "I don't know, Rad."

"Please, Mom, we'll be careful. You already said me and Josh could play in the park for a little while."

"Yes, I know, but Taz is awfully big. I wouldn't want him to get away from you."

"Taz is a firm believer in conserving energy. Why run if strolling gets you to the same place?" Mitch went back into his office, rooted around and came up with Taz's leash. "He doesn't chase cars, other dogs or park police. He will, however, stop at every tree."

With a giggle, Radley took the leash. "Okay, Mom?"

She hesitated, knowing there was a part of her that wanted to keep Radley with her, within arm's reach. And, for his sake, it was something she had to fight. "A half hour." The words were barely out when he and Josh let out a whoop. "You have to get your coats—and gloves."

"We will. Come on, Taz."

The dog gave a huge sigh before gathering himself up. Grumbling only a little, he stationed himself between the two boys as they headed out.

"Why is it every time I see that kid I feel good?"

"You're very kind to him. Well, I should go upstairs and make sure they bundle up."

"I think they can handle it. Why don't you sit down?" He took advantage of her brief hesitation by taking her arm. "Come over by the window. You can watch them go out."

She gave in because she knew how Radley hated to be hovered over. "Oh, I have my office number for you, and the name and number of his doctor and the school." Mitch took the paper and stuck it in his pocket. "If there's any trouble at all, call me. I can be home in ten minutes."

"Relax, Hester. We'll get along fine."

"I want to thank you again. It's the first time since he started school that Rad's looked forward to a Monday."

"I'm looking forward to it myself."

She looked down, waiting to see the familiar blue cap and coat. "We haven't discussed terms."

"What terms?"

"How much you want for watching him. Mrs. Cohen—"

"Good God, Hester, I don't want you to pay me."

"Don't be ridiculous. Of course I'll pay you."

He put a hand on her shoulder until she'd turned to face him. "I don't need the money, I don't want the money. I made the offer because Rad's a nice kid and I enjoy his company."

"That's very kind of you, but—"

His exasperated sigh cut her off. "Here come the buts again."

"I couldn't possibly let you do it for nothing."

Mitch studied her face. He'd thought her tough at their first meeting, and tough she was—at least on the outside. "Can't you accept a neighborly gesture?"

Her lips curved a bit, but her eyes remained solemn. "I guess not."

"Five bucks a day."

This time the smile reached her eyes. "Thank you."

He caught the ends of her hair between his thumb and forefinger. "You drive a hard bargain, lady."

"So I've been told." Cautiously she took a step away. "Here they come." He hadn't forgotten his gloves, she noted as she leaned closer to the window. Nor had he forgotten that he'd been taught to walk to the corner and cross at the light. "He's in heaven, you know. Rad's always wanted a dog." She touched a hand to the window and continued to watch. "He doesn't mention it because he knows we can't keep one in the apartment when no one's home all day. So he's settled for the promise of a kitten."

Mitch put a hand on her shoulder again, but gently this time. "He doesn't strike me as a deprived child, Hester. There's nothing for you to feel guilty about."

She looked at him then, her eyes wide and just a little sad. Mitch discovered he was just as drawn to that as he had been to her laughter. Without planning to, without knowing he'd needed to, he lifted a hand to her cheek. The pale gray of her irises deepened. Her skin warmed. Hester backed away quickly.

"I'd better go. I'm sure they'll want hot chocolate when they get back in."

"They have to bring Taz back here first," Mitch reminded her. "Take a break, Hester. Want some coffee?"

"Well, I—"

"Good. Sit down and I'll get it."

Hester stood in the center of the room a moment, a bit amazed at how smoothly he ran things—his way. She was much too used to setting her own rules to accept anyone else's. Still, she told herself it would be rude to leave, that her son would be back soon and that the least she could do after Mitch had been so good to the boy was bear his company for a little while.

She would have been lying if she'd denied that he interested her. In a casual way, of course. There was something about the way he looked at her, so deep and penetrating, while at the same time he appeared to take most of life as a joke. Yet there was nothing funny about the way he touched her.

Hester lifted fingertips to her cheek, where his had been. She would have to take care to avoid too much of that sort of contact. Perhaps, with effort, she could think of Mitch as a friend, as Radley did already. It might not sit well with her to be obliged to him, but she could swallow that. She'd swallowed worse.

He was kind. She let out a little breath as she tried to relax. Experience had given her a very sensitive antenna. She could recognize the kind of man who tried to ingratiate himself with the child to get to the mother. If she was sure of anything, it was that Mitch genuinely liked Radley. That, if nothing else, was a point in his favor.

But she wished he hadn't touched her that way, looked at her that way, made her feel that way.

"It's hot. Probably lousy, but hot." Mitch walked in with two mugs. "Don't you want to sit down?"

Hester smiled at him. "Where?"

Mitch set the mugs down on a stack of papers, then pushed magazines from the sofa. "Here."

"You know…" She stepped over a stack of old newspapers. "Radley's very good at tidying. He'd be glad to help you."

"I function best in controlled confusion."

Hester joined him on the sofa. "I can see the confusion, but not the controlled."

"It's here, believe me. I didn't ask if you wanted anything in the coffee, so I brought it black."

"Black's fine. This table—it's Queen Anne, isn't it?"

"Yeah." Mitch set his bare feet on it, then crossed them at the ankles. "You've got a good eye."

"One would have to under the circumstances." Because he laughed, she smiled as she took her first sip. "I've always loved antiques. I suppose it's the endurance. Not many things last."

"Sure they do. I once had a cold that lasted six weeks." He settled back as she laughed. "When you do that, you get a dimple at the corner of your mouth. Cute."

Hester was immediately self-conscious again. "You have a very natural way with children. Did you come from a large family?"

"No. Only child." He continued to study her, curious about her reaction to the most casual of compliments.

"Really? I wouldn't have guessed it."

"Don't tell me you're of the school who believes only a woman can relate to children?"

"No, not really," she hedged, because that had been

her experience thus far. "It's just that you're particularly
good with them. No children of your own?" The question
came out quickly, amazing and embarrassing her.

"No. I guess I've been too busy being a kid myself
to think about raising any."

"That hardly makes you unusual," she said coolly.

He tilted his head as he studied her. "Tossing me in
with Rad's father, Hester?"

Something flashed in her eyes. Mitch shook his head
as he sipped again. "Damn, Hester, what did the bastard do to you?" She froze instantly. Mitch was quicker.
Even as she started to rise, he put a restraining hand on
her arm. "Okay, hands off that one until you're ready. I
apologize if I hit a sore spot, but I'm curious. I've spent
a couple of evenings with Rad now, and he's never mentioned his father."

"I'd appreciate it if you wouldn't ask him any questions."

"Fine." Mitch was capable of being just as snotty. "I
didn't intend to grill the kid."

Hester was tempted to get up and excuse herself.
That would be the easiest way. But the fact was that she
was trusting her son to this man every afternoon. She
supposed it would be best if he had some background.

"Rad hasn't seen his father in almost seven years."

"At all?" He couldn't help his surprise. His own family had been undemonstrative and distant, but he never
went more than a year without seeing his parents. "Must
be rough on the kid."

"They were never close. I think Radley's adjusted
very well."

"Hold on. I wasn't criticizing you." He'd placed his
hand over hers again, too firmly to be shaken off. "I

know a happy, well-loved boy when I see one. You'd walk through fire for him. Maybe you don't think it shows, but it does."

"There's nothing that's more important to me than Radley." She wanted to relax again, but he was sitting too close, and his hand was still on hers. "I only told you this so that you wouldn't ask him questions that might upset him."

"Does that sort of thing happen often?"

"Sometimes." His fingers were linked with hers now. She couldn't quite figure out how he'd managed it. "A new friend, a new teacher. I really should go."

"How about you?" He touched her cheek gently and turned her face toward him. "How have you adjusted?"

"Just fine. I have Rad, and my work."

"And no relationships?"

She wasn't sure if it was embarrassment or anger, but the sensation was very strong. "That's none of your business."

"If people only talked about what was their business, they wouldn't get very far. You don't strike me as a man-hater, Hester."

She lifted a brow. When pushed, she could play the game by someone else's rules. And she could play it well. "I went through a period of time when I despised men on principle. Actually, it was a very rewarding time of my life. Then, gradually, I came to the opinion that some members of your species weren't lower forms of life."

"Sounds promising."

She smiled again, because he made it easy. "The point is, I don't blame all men for the faults of one."

"You're just cautious."

"If you like."

"The one thing I'm sure I like is your eyes. No, don't look away." Patiently, he turned her face back to his. "They're fabulous—take it from an artist's standpoint."

She had to stop being so jumpy, Hester ordered herself. With an effort, she remained still. "Does that mean they're going to appear in an upcoming issue?"

"They just might." He smiled, appreciating the thought and the fact that though tense, she was able to hold her own. "Poor old Zark deserves to meet someone who understands him. These eyes would."

"I'll take that as a compliment." And run. "The boys will be back in a minute."

"We've got some time yet. Hester, do you ever have fun?"

"What a stupid question. Of course I do."

"Not as Rad's mother, but as Hester." He ran a hand through her hair, captivated.

"I *am* Rad's mother." Though she managed to rise, he stood with her.

"You're also a woman. A gorgeous one." He saw the look in her eyes and ran his thumb along her jawline. "Take my word for it. I'm an honest man. You're one gorgeous bundle of nerves."

"That's silly. I don't have anything to be nervous about." Other than the fact that he was touching her, and his voice was quiet, and the apartment was empty.

"I'll take the shaft out of my heart later," he murmured. He bent to kiss her, then had to catch her when she nearly stumbled over the newspapers. "Take it easy. I'm not going to bite you. This time."

"I have to go." She was as close to panic as she ever allowed herself to come. "I have a dozen things to do."

"In a minute." He framed her face. She was trembling, he realized. It didn't surprise him. What did was that he wasn't steady himself. "What we have here, Mrs. Wallace, is called attraction, chemistry, lust. It doesn't really matter what label you put on it."

"Maybe not to you."

"Then we'll let you pick the label later." He stroked his thumbs over her cheekbones, gently, soothingly. "I already told you I'm not a maniac. I'll have to remember to get those references."

"Mitch, I told you I appreciate what you're doing for Rad, but I wish you'd—"

"Here and now doesn't concern Rad. This is you and me, Hester. When was the last time you let yourself be alone with a man who wanted you?" He casually brushed his thumb over her lips. Her eyes went to smoke. "When was the last time you let anyone do this?"

His mouth covered hers quickly, with a force that came as a shock. She hadn't been prepared for violence. His hands had been so gentle, his voice so soothing. She hadn't expected this edgy passion. But God, how she'd wanted it. With the same reckless need, she threw her arms around his neck and answered demand for demand.

"Too long," Mitch managed breathlessly when he tore his mouth from hers. "Thank God." Before she could utter more than a moan, he took her mouth again.

He hadn't been sure what he'd find in her—ice, anger, fear. The unrestrained heat came as much of a shock to his system as to hers. Her wide, generous mouth was warm and willing, with all traces of shyness swallowed by passion. She gave more than he would have asked for, and more than he'd been prepared to take.

His head spun, a fascinating and novel sensation he couldn't fully appreciate as he struggled to touch and taste. He dragged his hands through her hair, scattering the two thin silver pins she'd used to pull it back from her face. He wanted it free and wild in his hands, just as he wanted her free and wild in his bed. His plans to go slowly, to test the waters, evaporated in an overwhelming desire to dive in headfirst. Thinking only of this, he slipped his hands under her sweater. The skin there was tender and warm. The silky little concoction she wore was cool and soft. He slid his hands around her waist and up to cup her breasts.

She stiffened, then shuddered. She hadn't known how much she'd wanted to be touched like this. Needed like this. His taste was so dark, so tempting. She'd forgotten what it was like to hunger for such things. It was madness, the sweet release of madness. She heard him murmur her name as he moved his mouth down her throat and back again.

Madness. She understood it. She'd been there before, or thought she had. Though it seemed sweeter now, richer now, she knew she could never go there again.

"Mitch, please." It wasn't easy to resist what he was offering. It surprised Hester how difficult it was to draw away, to put the boundaries back. "We can't do this."

"We are," he pointed out, and drew the flavor from her lips again. "And very well."

"*I* can't." With the small sliver of willpower she had left, she struggled away. "I'm sorry. I should never have let this happen." Her cheeks were hot. Hester put her hands to them, then dragged them up through her hair.

His knees were weak. That was something to think about. But for the moment he concentrated on her. "You're taking a lot on yourself, Hester. It seems to be a habit of yours. I kissed you, and you just happened to kiss me back. Since we both enjoyed it, I don't see where apologies are necessary on either side."

"I should have made myself clear." She stepped back, hit the newspapers again, then skirted around them. "I do appreciate what you're doing for Rad—"

"Leave him out of this, for God's sake."

"I can't." Her voice rose, surprising her again. She knew better than to lose control. "I don't expect you to understand, but I can't leave him out of it." She took a deep breath, amazed that it did nothing to calm her pulse rate. "I'm not interested in casual sex. I have Rad to think about, and myself."

"Fair enough." He wanted to sit down until he'd recovered, but figured the situation called for an eye-to-eye discussion. "I wasn't feeling too casual about it myself."

That was what worried her. "Let's just drop it."

Anger was an amazing stimulant. Mitch stepped forward, and caught her chin in his hand. "Fat chance."

"I don't want to argue with you. I just think that—" The knock came as a blessed reprieve. "That's the boys."

"I know." But he didn't release her. "Whatever you're interested in, have time for, room for, might just have to be adjusted." He was angry, really angry, Mitch realized. It wasn't like him to lose his temper so quickly. "Life's full of adjustments, Hester." Letting her go, he opened the door.

"It was great." Rosy-cheeked and bright-eyed, Radley tumbled in ahead of Josh and the dog. "We even got Taz to run once, for a minute."

"Amazing." Mitch bent to unclip the leash. Grumbling with exhaustion, Taz walked to a spot by the window, then collapsed.

"You guys must be freezing." Hester kissed Radley's forehead. "It must be time for hot chocolate."

"Yeah!" Radley turned his beaming face to Mitch. "Want some? Mom makes real good hot chocolate."

It was tempting to put her on the spot. Perhaps it was a good thing for both of them that his temper was already fading. "Maybe next time." He pulled Radley's cap over his eyes. "I've got some things to do."

"Thanks a lot for letting us take Taz out. It was really neat, wasn't it, Josh?"

"Yeah. Thanks, Mr. Dempsey."

"Anytime. See you Monday, Rad."

"Okay." The boys fled, laughing and shoving. Mitch looked, but Hester was already gone.

Chapter 4

Mitchell Dempsey II had been born rich, privileged and, according to his parents, with an incorrigible imagination. Maybe that was why he'd taken to Radley so quickly. The boy was far from rich, not even privileged enough to have a set of parents, but his imagination was first-class.

Mitch had always liked crowds as much as one-on-one social situations. He was certainly no stranger to parties, given his mother's affection for entertaining and his own gregarious nature, and no one who knew him would ever have classed him as a loner. In his work, however, he had always preferred the solitary. He worked at home not because he didn't like distractions—he was really fond of them—but because he didn't care to have anyone looking over his shoulder or timing his progress. He'd never considered working any way other than alone. Until Radley.

They made a pact the first day. If Radley finished his homework, with or without Mitch's dubious help, he could then choose to either play with Taz or give his input into Mitch's latest story line. If Mitch had decided to call it quits for the day, they could entertain themselves with his extensive collection of videos or with Radley's growing army of plastic figures.

To Mitch, it was natural—to Radley, fantastic. For the first time in his young life he had a man who was part of his daily routine, one who talked to him and listened to him. He had someone who was not only as willing to spend time to set up a battle or wage a war as his mother was, but someone who understood his military strategy.

By the end of their first week, Mitch was not only a hero, creator of Zark and owner of Taz, but the most solid and dependable person in his life other than his mother. Radley loved, without guards or restrictions.

Mitch saw it, wondered at it and found himself just as captivated. He had told Hester no less than the truth when he'd said that he'd never thought about having children. He'd run his life on his own clock for so long that he'd never considered doing things differently. If he'd known what it was to love a small boy, to find pieces of himself in one, he might have done things differently.

Perhaps it was because of his discoveries that he thought of Radley's father. What kind of man could create something that special and then walk away from it? His own father had been stern and anything but understanding, but he'd been there. Mitch had never questioned the love.

A man didn't get to be thirty-five without knowing several contemporaries who'd been through divorces—many of them bitter. But he also was acquainted with several who'd managed to call a moratorium with their ex-wives in order to remain fathers. It was difficult enough to understand how Radley's father not only could have walked out, but could have walked away. After a week in Radley's company, it was all but impossible.

And what of Hester? What kind of man left a woman to struggle alone to raise a child they had brought into the world together? How much had she loved him? That was a thought that dug into his brain too often for comfort. The results of the experience were obvious. She was tense and overly cautious around men. Around him, certainly, Mitch thought with a grimace as he watched Radley sketch. So cautious that she'd stayed out of his path throughout the week.

Every day between 4:15 and 4:25, he received a polite call. Hester would ask him if everything had gone well, thank him for watching Radley, then ask him to send her son upstairs. That afternoon, Radley had handed him a neatly written check for twenty-five dollars drawn on the account of Hester Gentry Wallace. It was still crumpled in Mitch's pocket.

Did she really think he was going to quietly step aside after she'd knocked the wind out of him? He hadn't forgotten what she'd felt like pressed against him, inhibitions and caution stripped away for one brief, stunning moment. He intended to live that moment again, as well as the others his incorrigible imagination had conjured up.

If she did think he'd bow out gracefully, Mrs. Hester Wallace was in for a big surprise.

"I can't get the retro rockets right," Radley complained. "They never look right."

Mitch set aside his own work, which had stopped humming along the moment he'd started to think of Hester. "Let's have a look." He took the spare sketch pad he'd lent to Radley. "Hey, not bad." He grinned, foolishly pleased with Radley's attempt at the Defiance. It seemed the few pointers he'd given the kid had taken root. "You're a real natural, Rad."

The boy blushed with pleasure, then frowned again. "But see, the boosters and retros are all wrong. They look stupid."

"Only because you're trying to detail too soon. Look, light strokes, impressions first." He put a hand over the boy's to guide it. "Don't be afraid to make mistakes. That's why they make those big gum erasers."

"You don't make mistakes." Radley caught his tongue between his teeth as he struggled to make his hand move as expertly as Mitch's.

"Sure I do. This is my fifteenth eraser this year."

"You're the best artist in the whole world," Radley said, looking up, his heart in his eyes.

Moved and strangely humbled, Mitch ruffled the boy's hair. "Maybe one of the top twenty, but thanks." When the phone rang, Mitch felt a strange stab of disappointment. The weekend meant something different now—no Radley. For a man who had lived his entire adult life without responsibilities, it was a sobering thought to realize he would miss one. "That should be your mother."

"She said we could go out to the movies tonight 'cause it's Friday and all. You could come with us."

Giving a noncommittal grunt, Mitch answered the phone. "Hi, Hester."

"Mitch, I—everything okay?"

Something in her tone had his brows drawing together. "Just dandy."

"Did Radley give you the check?"

"Yeah. Sorry, I haven't had a chance to cash it yet."

If there was one thing she wasn't in the mood for at the moment, it was sarcasm. "Well, thanks. If you'd send Radley upstairs, I'd appreciate it."

"No problem." He hesitated. "Rough day, Hester?"

She pressed a hand to her throbbing temple. "A bit. Thank you, Mitch."

"Sure." He hung up, still frowning. Turning to Radley, he made the effort to smile. "Time to transfer your equipment, Corporal."

"Sir, yes, sir!" Radley gave a smart salute. The intergalactic army he'd left at Mitch's through the week was tossed into his backpack. After a brief search, both of his gloves were located and pushed in on top of the plastic figures. Radley stuffed his coat and hat in before kneeling down to hug Taz. "Bye, Taz. See ya." The dog rumbled a goodbye as he rubbed his snout into Radley's shoulder. "Bye, Mitch." He went to the door, then hesitated. "I guess I'll see you Monday."

"Sure. Hey, maybe I'll just walk up with you. Give your mom a full report."

"Okay!" Radley brightened instantly. "You left your keys in the kitchen. I'll get them." Mitch watched the tornado pass, then swirl back. "I got an A in spelling. When I tell Mom, she'll be in a real good mood. We'll probably get sodas."

"Sounds like a good deal to me," Mitch said, and let himself be dragged along.

Hester heard Radley's key in the lock and set down the ice pack. Leaning closer, she checked her face in the bathroom mirror, saw a bruise was already forming, and swore. She'd hoped to be able to tell Radley about the mishap, gloss over it and make it a joke before any battle scars showed. Hester downed two aspirin and prayed the headache would pass.

"Mom! Hey, Mom!"

"Right here, Radley." She winced at her own raised voice, then put on a smile as she walked out to greet him. The smile faded when she saw her son had brought company.

"Mitch came up to report," Radley began as he shrugged out of his backpack.

"What the hell happened to you?" Mitch crossed over to her in two strides. He had her face in his hands and fury in his eyes. "Are you all right?"

"Of course I am." She shot him a quick warning look, then turned to Radley. "I'm fine."

Radley stared up at her, his eyes widening, then his bottom lip trembling as he saw the black-and-blue mark under her eye. "Did you fall down?"

She wanted to lie and say yes, but she'd never lied to him. "Not exactly." She forced a smile, annoyed to have a witness to her explanation. "It seems that there was a man at the subway station who wanted my purse. I wanted it, too."

"You were mugged?" Mitch wasn't sure whether to swear at her or gather her close and check for injuries. Hester's long, withering look didn't give him the chance to do either.

"Sort of." She moved her shoulders to show Radley it was of little consequence. "It wasn't all that exciting, I'm afraid. The subway was crowded. Someone saw what was going on and called security, so the man changed his mind about my purse and ran away."

Radley looked closer. He'd seen a black eye before. Joey Phelps had had a really neat one once. But he'd never seen one on his mother. "Did he hit you?"

"Not really. That part was sort of an accident." An accident that hurt like the devil. "We were having this tug-of-war over my purse, and his elbow shot up. I didn't duck quick enough, that's all."

"Stupid," Mitch muttered loud enough to be heard.

"Did you hit him?"

"Of course not," Hester answered, and thought longingly of her ice pack. "Go put your things away now, Radley."

"But I want to know about—"

"Now," his mother interrupted in a tone she used rarely and to great effect.

"Yes, ma'am," Radley mumbled, and lugged the backpack off the couch.

Hester waited until he'd turned the corner into his room. "I want you to know I don't appreciate your interference."

"You haven't begun to see interference. What the hell's wrong with you? You know better than to fight with a mugger over a purse. What if he'd had a knife?"

Even the thought of it had his reliable imagination working overtime.

"He didn't have a knife." Hester felt her knees begin to tremble. The damnedest thing was that the reaction had chosen the most inopportune moment to set in. "And he doesn't have my purse, either."

"Or a black eye. For God's sake, Hester, you could have been seriously hurt, and I doubt there's anything in your purse that would warrant it. Credit cards can be canceled, a compact or a lipstick replaced."

"I suppose if someone had tried to lift your wallet you'd have given him your blessing."

"That's different."

"The hell it is."

He stopped pacing long enough to give her a long study. Her chin was thrust out, in the same way he'd seen Radley's go a few times. He'd expected the stubbornness, but he had to admit he hadn't expected the ready temper, or his admiration for it. But that was beside the point, he reminded himself as his gaze swept over her bruised cheekbone again.

"Let's just back up a minute. In the first place, you've got no business taking the subway alone."

She let out what might have been a laugh. "You've got to be kidding."

The funny thing was, he couldn't remember ever having said anything quite that stupid. It brought his own temper bubbling over. "Take a cab, damn it."

"I have no intention of taking a cab."

"Why?"

"In the first place it would be stupid, and in the second I can't afford it."

Mitch dragged the check out of his pocket and

pushed it into her hand. "Now you can afford it, along with a reasonable tip."

"I have no intention of taking this." She shoved the crumpled check back at him. "Or of taking a taxi when the subway is both inexpensive and convenient. And I have less intention of allowing you to take a small incident and blow it into a major calamity. I don't want Radley upset."

"Fine, then take a cab. For the kid's sake, if not your own. Think how it would have been for him if you'd really been hurt."

The bruise stood out darkly as her cheeks paled. "I don't need you or anyone to lecture me on the welfare of my son."

"No, you do just fine by him. It's when it comes to Hester that you've got a few loose screws." He jammed his hands into his pockets. "Okay, you won't take a cab. At least promise you won't play Sally Courageous the next time some lowlife decides he likes the color of your purse."

Hester brushed at the sleeve of her jacket. "Is that the name of one of your characters?"

"It might be." He told himself to calm down. He didn't have much of a temper as a rule, but when it started to perk, it could come to a boil in seconds. "Look, Hester, did you have your life savings in your bag?"

"Of course not."

"Family heirlooms?"

"No."

"Any microchips vital to national security?"

She let out an exasperated sigh and dropped onto the arm of a chair. "I left them at the office." She pouted as she looked up at him. "Don't give me that disgusting smile now."

"Sorry." He changed it to a grin.

"I just had such a rotten day." Without realizing it, she slipped off her shoe and began to massage her instep. "The first thing this morning, Mr. Rosen went on an efficiency campaign. Then there was the staff meeting, then the idiot settlement clerk, who made a pass at me."

"What idiot settlement clerk?"

"Never mind." Tired, she rubbed her temple. "Just take it that things went from bad to worse until I was ready to bite someone's head off. Then that jerk grabbed my purse, and I just exploded. At least I have the satisfaction of knowing he'll be walking with a limp for a few days."

"Got in a few licks, did you?"

Hester continued to pout as she gingerly touched her eye with her fingertips. "Yeah."

Mitch walked over, then bent down to her level. With a look more of curiosity than sympathy, he examined the damage. "You're going to have a hell of a shiner."

"Really?" Hester touched the bruise again. "I was hoping this was as bad as it would get."

"Not a chance. It's going to be a beaut."

She thought of the stares and the explanations that would be necessary the following week. "Terrific."

"Hurt?"

"Yes."

Mitch touched his lips to the bruise before she could evade him. "Try some ice."

"I've already thought of that."

"I put my things away." Radley stood in the hallway looking down at his shoes. "I had homework, but I already did it."

"That's good. Come here." Radley continued to look at his shoes as he walked to her. Hester put her arms around his neck and squeezed. "Sorry."

"'S okay. I didn't mean to make you mad."

"You didn't make me mad. Mr. Rosen made me mad. That man who wanted my purse made me mad, but not you, baby."

"I could get you a wet cloth the way you do when my head hurts."

"Thanks, but I think I need a hot bath and an ice pack." She gave him another squeeze, then remembered. "Oh, we had a date didn't we? Cheeseburgers and a movie."

"We can watch TV instead."

"Well, why don't we see how I feel in a little while?"

"I got an *A* on my spelling test."

"My hero," Hester said, laughing.

"You know, that hot bath's a good idea. Ice, too." Mitch was already making plans. "Why don't you get started on that while I borrow Rad for a little while."

"But he just got home."

"It'll only take a little while." Mitch took her arm and started to lead her toward the hall. "Put some bubbles in the tub. They're great for the morale. We'll be back in half an hour."

"But where are you going?"

"Just an errand I need to run. Rad can keep me company, can't you, Rad?"

"Sure."

The idea of a thirty-minute soak was too tempting. "No candy, it's too close to dinner."

"Okay, I won't eat any," Mitch promised, and scooted her into the bath. Putting a hand on Radley's shoulder, he marched back into the living room. "Ready to go out on a mission, Corporal?"

Radley's eyes twinkled as he saluted. "Ready and willing, sir."

The combination of ice pack, hot bath and aspirin proved successful. By the time the water had cooled in the tub, Hester's headache was down to dull and manageable. She supposed she owed Mitch for giving her a few minutes to herself, Hester admitted as she pulled on jeans. Along with most of the pain, the shakiness had drained away in the hot water. In fact, when she took the time to examine her bruised eye, she felt downright proud of herself. Mitch had been right, bubbles had been good for the morale.

She pulled a brush through her hair and wondered how disappointed Radley would be if they postponed their trip to the movies. Hot bath or no, the last thing she felt like doing at the moment was braving the cold to sit in a crowded theater. She thought a matinee the next day might satisfy him. It would mean adjusting her schedule a bit, but the idea of a quiet evening at home after the week she'd put in made doing the laundry after dinner a lot more acceptable.

And what a week, Hester thought as she pulled on slippers. Rosen was a tyrant and the settlement clerk was a pest. She'd spent almost as much time during the last five days placating one and discouraging the other as she had processing loans. She wasn't afraid of work, but she did resent having to account for every minute of her time. It was nothing personal; Hester had discovered that within the first eight-hour stretch. Rosen was equally overbearing and fussy with everyone on his staff.

And that fool Cummings. Hester pushed the thought of the overamorous clerk out of her mind and sat on the edge of the bed. She'd gotten through the first two weeks, hadn't she? She touched her cheekbone gingerly. With the scars to prove it. It would be easier now. She wouldn't have the strain of meeting all those new people. The biggest relief of all was that she didn't have to worry about Radley.

She'd never admit it to anyone, but she'd waited for Mitch to call every day that week to tell her Radley was too much trouble, he'd changed his mind, he was tired of spending his afternoons with a nine-year-old. But the fact was that every afternoon when Radley had come upstairs the boy had been full of stories about Mitch and Taz and what they'd done.

Mitch had showed him a series of sketches for the big anniversary issue. They'd taken Taz to the park. They'd watched the original, uncut, absolutely classic *King Kong*. Mitch had showed him his comic book collection, which included the first issues of *Superman* and *Tales From the Crypt*, which everyone knew, she'd been informed, were practically priceless. And did she know that Mitch had an original, honest-to-God *Captain Midnight* decoder ring? Wow.

Hester rolled her eyes, then winced when the movement reminded her of the bruise. The man might be odd, she decided, but he was certainly making Radley happy. Things would be fine as long as she continued to think of him as Radley's friend and forgot about that unexpected and unexplainable connection they'd made last weekend.

Hester preferred to think about it as a connection rather than any of the terms Mitch had used. Attraction, chemistry, lust. No, she didn't care for any of those words, or for her immediate and unrestrained reaction to him. She knew what she'd felt. Hester was too honest to deny that for one crazed moment she'd welcomed the sensation of being held and kissed and desired. It wasn't something to be ashamed of. A woman who'd been alone as long as she had was bound to feel certain stirrings around an attractive man.

Then why didn't she feel any of those stirrings around Cummings?

Don't answer that, she warned herself. Sometimes it was best not to dig too deeply when you really didn't want to know.

Think about dinner, she decided. Poor Radley was going to have to make do with soup and a sandwich instead of his beloved cheeseburger tonight. With a sigh, she rose as she heard the front door open.

"Mom! Mom, come see the surprise."

Hester made sure she was smiling, though she wasn't sure she could take any more surprises that day. "Rad, did you thank Mitch for...oh." He was back, Hester saw, automatically adjusting her sweater. The two of them stood just inside the doorway with identical grins on their faces. Radley carried two paper bags, and Mitch hefted what looked suspiciously like a DVR.

"What's all this?"

"Dinner and a double feature," Mitch informed her. "Rad said you like chocolate shakes."

"Yes, I do." The aroma finally carried to her. Sniffing, she eyed Radley's bags. "Cheeseburgers?"

"Yeah, and fries. Mitch said we could have double orders. We took Taz for a walk. He's eating his downstairs."

"He's got lousy table manners." Mitch carried the unit over to Hester's television.

"And I helped Mitch unhook the DVR. We got *Raiders of the Lost Ark*. Mitch has millions of movies."

"Rad said you like musical junk."

"Well, yes, I—"

"We got one of them, too." Rad set the bags down to go over and sit with Mitch on the floor. "Mitch said it's pretty funny, so I guess it'll be okay." He put a hand on Mitch's leg and leaned closer to watch the hookup.

"Singin' in the Rain." Handing Radley a cable, Mitch sat back to let him connect it.

"Really?"

He had to smile. There were times she sounded just like the kid. "Yeah. How's the eye?"

"Oh, it's better." Unable to resist, Hester walked over to watch. How odd it seemed to see her son's small hands working with those of a man.

"It's a tight squeeze, but the DVR just about fits under your television stand." Mitch gave Radley's shoulder a quick squeeze before he rose. "Colorful." With a finger under her chin, he turned Hester's face to the side to examine her eye. "Rad and I thought you looked a little beat, so we figured we'd bring the movie to you."

"I was." She touched her hand to his wrist a moment. "Thanks."

"Anytime." He wondered what her reaction, and Radley's, would be if he kissed her right now. Hester must have seen the question in his eyes, because she backed up quickly.

"Well, I guess I'd better get some plates so the food doesn't get cold."

"We've got plenty of napkins." He gestured toward the couch. "Sit down while my assistant and I finish up."

"I did it." Flushed with success, Radley scrambled back on all fours. "It's all hooked up."

Mitch bent to check the connections. "You're a regular mechanic, Corporal."

"We get to watch *Raiders* first, right?"

"That was the deal." Mitch handed him the movie. "You're in charge."

"It looks like I have to thank you again," Hester said when Mitch joined her on the couch.

"What for? I figured to wangle myself in on your date with Rad tonight." He pulled a burger out of the bag. "This is cheaper."

"Most men wouldn't choose to spend a Friday night with a small boy."

"Why not?" He took a healthy bite, and after swallowing continued, "I figure he won't eat half his fries, and I'll get the rest."

Radley took a running leap and plopped onto the couch between them. He gave a contented and very adult sigh as he snuggled down. "This is better than going out. Lots better."

He was right, Hester thought as she relaxed and let herself become caught up in Indiana Jones's adventures. There had been a time when she'd believed life could be that thrilling, romantic, heart-stopping. Circumstances had forced her to set those things aside, but she'd never lost her love of the fantasy of films. For a couple of hours it was possible to close off reality and the pressures that went with it and be innocent again.

Radley was bright-eyed and full of energy as he switched movies. Hester had no doubt his dreams that night would revolve around lost treasures and heroic deeds. Snuggling against her, he giggled at Donald O'Connor's mugging and pratfalls, but began to nod off soon after Gene Kelly's marvelous dance through the rain.

"Fabulous, isn't it?" Mitch murmured. Radley had shifted so that his head rested against Mitch's chest.

"Absolutely. I never get tired of this movie. When I was a little girl, we'd watch it whenever it came on TV. My father's a big movie buff. You can name almost any film, and he'll tell you who was in it. But his first love was always the musical."

Mitch fell silent again. It took very little to learn how one person felt about another—a mere inflection in their voice, a softening of their expression. Hester's family had been close, as he'd always regretted his hadn't been. His father had never shared Mitch's love of fantasy or film, as he had never shared his father's devotion to business. Though he would never have considered himself a lonely child—his imagination had been company enough—he'd always missed the warmth and affection he'd heard so clearly in Hester's voice when she'd spoken of her father.

When the credits rolled, he turned to her again. "Your parents live in the city?"

"Here? Oh, no." She had to laugh as she tried to picture either of her parents coping with life in New York. "No, I grew up in Rochester, but my parents moved to the Sunbelt almost ten years ago—Fort Worth. Dad's still in banking and my mother has a part-time job in a bookstore. We were all amazed when she went to work. I guess all of us thought she didn't know how to do anything but bake cookies and fold sheets."

"How many's we?"

Hester sighed a little as the screen went blank. She couldn't honestly remember when she'd enjoyed an evening more. "I have a brother and a sister. I'm the oldest. Luke's settled in Rochester with a wife and a new baby on the way, and Julia's in Atlanta. She's a disc jockey."

"No kidding?"

"Wake up, Atlanta, it's 6:00 a.m., time for three hits in a row." She laughed a little as she thought of her sister. "I'd give anything to take Rad down for a visit."

"Miss them?"

"It's just hard thinking how spread out we all are. I know how nice it would be for Rad to have more family close by."

"What about Hester?"

She looked over at him, a bit surprised to see how natural Radley looked dozing in the crook of his arm. "I have Rad."

"And that's enough?"

"More than." She smiled; then, uncurling her legs, she rose. "And speaking of Rad, I'd better take him in to bed."

Mitch picked the boy up and settled him over his shoulder. "I'll carry him."

"Oh, that's all right. I do it all the time."

"I've got him." Radley turned his face into Mitch's neck. What an amazing feeling, he thought, a little shaken by it. "Just show me where."

Telling herself it was silly to feel odd, Hester led him

into Radley's bedroom. The bed had been made à la Rad, which meant the *Star Wars* spread was pulled up over rumpled sheets. Mitch narrowly missed stepping on a pint-size robot and a worn rag dog. There was a night-light burning by the dresser, because for all Radley's bravado he was still a bit leery about what might or might not be in the closet.

Mitch laid him down on the bed, then began to help Hester take off the boy's sneakers. "You don't have to bother." Hester untangled a knot in the laces with the ease of experience.

"It's not a bother. Does he use pajamas?" Mitch was already tugging off Radley's jeans. In silence, Hester moved over to Radley's dresser and took out his favorites. Mitch studied the bold imprint of Commander Zark. "Good taste. It always ticked me off they didn't come in my size."

The laugh relaxed her again. Hester bundled the top over Radley's head while Mitch pulled the bottoms over his legs.

"Kid sleeps like a rock."

"I know. He always has. He rarely woke up during the night even as a baby." As a matter of habit, she picked up the rag dog and tucked it in beside him before kissing his cheek. "Don't mention Fido," she murmured. "Radley's a bit sensitive about still sleeping with him."

"I never saw a thing." Then, giving in to the need, he brushed a hand over Radley's hair. "Pretty special, isn't he?"

"Yes, he is."

"So are you." Mitch turned and touched her hair in turn. "Don't close up on me, Hester," he said as she shifted her gaze away from his. "The best way to accept a compliment is to say thank you. Give it a shot."

Embarrassed more by her reaction to him than by his words, she made herself look at him. "Thank you."

"That's a good start. Now let's try it again." He slipped his arms around her. "I've been thinking about kissing you again for almost a week."

"Mitch, I—"

"Did you forget your line?" She'd lifted her hands to his shoulders to hold him off. But her eyes... He much preferred the message he read in them. "That was another compliment. I don't make a habit of thinking about a woman who goes out of her way to avoid me."

"I haven't been. Exactly."

"That's okay, because I figured it was because you couldn't trust yourself around me."

That had her eyes locking on his again, strong and steady. "You have an amazing ego."

"Thanks. Let's try another angle, then." As he spoke, he moved his hand up and down her spine, lighting little fingers of heat. "Kiss me again, and if the bombs don't go off this time I'll figure I was wrong."

"No." But despite herself she couldn't dredge up the will to push him away. "Radley's—"

"Sleeping like a rock, remember?" He touched his lips, very gently, to the swelling under her eye. "And even if he woke up, I don't think the sight of me kissing his mother would give him nightmares."

She started to speak again, but the words were only a sigh as his mouth met hers. He was patient this time, even...tender. Yet the bombs went off. She would have sworn they shook the floor beneath her as she dug her fingers hard into his shoulders.

It was incredible. Impossible. But the need was there, instant, incendiary. It had never been so strong before, not for anyone. Once, when she'd been very young, she'd had a hint of what true, ripe passion could be. And then it had been over. She had come to believe that, like so many other things, such passions were only temporary. But this—this felt like forever.

He'd thought he knew all there was to know about women. Hester was proving him wrong. Even as he felt himself sliding down that warm, soft tunnel of desire, he warned himself not to move too quickly or take too much. There was a hurricane in her, one he had already realized had been channeled and repressed for a long, long time. The first time he'd held her he'd known he had to be the one to free it. But slowly. Carefully. Whether she knew it or not, she was as vulnerable as the child sleeping beside them.

Then her hands were in his hair, pulling him closer. For one mad moment, he dragged her hard against him and let them both taste of what might be.

"Bombs, Hester." She shuddered as he traced his tongue over her ear. "The city's in shambles."

She believed him. With his mouth hot on hers, she believed him. "I have to think."

"Yeah, maybe you do." But he kissed her again. "Maybe we both do." He ran his hands down her body in one long, possessive stroke. "But I have a feeling we're going to come up with the same answer."

Shaken, she backed away. And stumbled over the robot. The crash didn't penetrate Radley's dreams.

"You know, you run into things every time I kiss you." He was going to have to go now or not at all. "I'll pick up the DVR later."

There was a little breath of relief as she nodded. She'd been afraid he'd ask her to sleep with him, and she wasn't at all sure what her answer would have been. "Thank you for everything."

"Good, you're learning." He stroked a finger down her cheek. "Take care of the eye."

Cowardly or not, Hester stayed by Radley's bed until she heard the front door shut. Then, easing down, she put a hand on her sleeping son's shoulder. "Oh, Rad, what have I gotten into?"

Chapter 5

When the phone rang at 7:25, Mitch had his head buried under a pillow. He would have ignored it, but Taz rolled over, stuck his snout against Mitch's cheek and began to grumble in his ear. Mitch swore and shoved at the dog, then snatched up the receiver and dragged it under the pillow.

"What?"

On the other end of the line, Hester bit her lip. "Mitch, it's Hester."

"So?"

"I guess I woke you up."

"Right."

It was painfully obvious that Mitch Dempsey wasn't a morning person. "I'm sorry. I know it's early."

"Is that what you called to tell me?"

"No... I guess you haven't looked out the window yet."

"Honey, I haven't even looked past my eyelids yet."

"It's snowing. We've got about eight inches, and it's not expected to let up until around midday. They're calling for twelve to fifteen inches."

"Who are they?"

Hester switched the phone to her other hand. Her hair was still wet from the shower, and she'd only had a chance to gulp down one cup of coffee. "The National Weather Service."

"Well, thanks for the bulletin."

"Mitch! Don't hang up."

He let out a long sigh, then shifted away from Taz's wet nose. "Is there more news?"

"The schools are closed."

"Whoopee."

She was tempted, very tempted to hang up the phone in his ear. The trouble was, she needed him. "I hate to ask, but I'm not sure I can get Radley all the way over to Mrs. Cohen's. I'd take the day off, but I have back-to-back appointments most of the day. I'm going to try to shift things around and get off early, but—"

"Send him down."

There was the briefest of hesitations. "Are you sure?"

"Did you want me to say no?"

"I don't want to interfere with any plans you had."

"Got any hot coffee?"

"Well, yes, I—"

"Send that, too."

Hester stared at the phone after it clicked in her ear, and tried to remind herself to be grateful.

Radley couldn't have been more pleased. He took Taz for his morning walk, threw snowballs—which the dog, on principle, refused to chase—

blanket of snow until he was satis.

Since Mitch's supplies didn't run

Radley raided his mother's supply, the

of the morning happily involved with M.

books and his own sketches.

As for Mitch, he found the company appealing

than distracting. The boy lay sprawled on the floor

his office and, between his reading or sketching, ram

bled on about whatever struck his fancy. Because he

spoke to either Mitch or Taz, and seemed to be content

to be answered or not, it suited everyone nicely.

By noon the snow had thinned to occasional flurries,

dashing Radley's fantasy about another holiday. In tacit

agreement, Mitch pushed away from his drawing board.

"You like tacos?"

"Yeah." Radley turned away from the window. "You

know how to make them?"

"Nope. But I know how to buy them. Get your coat,

Corporal, we've got places to go."

Radley was struggling into his boots when Mitch

walked out with a trio of cardboard tubes. "I've got to

stop by the office and drop these off."

Radley's mouth dropped down to his toes. "You

mean the place where they make the comics?"

"Yeah." Mitch shrugged into his coat. "I guess I

could do it tomorrow if you don't want to bother."

"No, I want to." The boy was up and dragging

Mitch's sleeve. "Can we go today? I won't touch any-

thing, I promise. I'll be real quiet, too."

"How can you ask questions if you're quiet?" He

pulled the boy's collar up. "Get Taz, will you?"

It was always a bit of a trick, and usually an ex-

ve one, to find a cabdriver who didn't object to
ndred-and-fifty-pound dog as a passenger. Once
ide, however, Taz sat by the window and morosely
atched New York pass by.

"It's a mess out here, isn't it?" The cabbie shot a grin
in the rearview mirror, pleased with the tip Mitch had
given him in advance. "Don't like the snow myself,
but my kids do." He gave a tuneless whistle to accom-
pany the big-band music on his radio. "I guess your boy
there wasn't doing any complaining about not going to
school. No, sir," the driver continued, without any need
for an answer. "Nothing a kid likes better than a day
off from school, is there? Even going to the office with
your dad's better than school, isn't it, kid?" The cabbie let out a chuckle as he pulled to the curb. The snow
there had already turned gray. "Here you go. That's a
right nice dog you got there, boy." He gave Mitch his
change and continued to whistle as they got out. He had
another fare when he pulled away.

"He thought you were my dad," Radley murmured
as they walked down the sidewalk.

"Yeah." He started to put a hand on Radley's shoulder, then waited. "Does that bother you?"

The boy looked up, wide-eyed and, for the first time,
shy. "No. Does it bother you?"

Mitch bent down so they were at eye level. "Well,
maybe it wouldn't if you weren't so ugly."

Radley grinned. As they continued to walk, he
slipped his hand into Mitch's. He'd already begun to
fantasize about Mitch as his father. He'd done it once
before with his second grade teacher, but Mr. Stratham
hadn't been nearly as neat as Mitch.

"Is this it?" He stopped as Mitch walked toward a tall, scarred brownstone.

"This is it."

Radley struggled with disappointment. It looked so—ordinary. He'd thought they would at least have the flag of Perth or Ragamond flying. Understanding perfectly, Mitch led him inside.

There was a guard in the lobby who lifted a hand to Mitch and continued to eat his pastrami sandwich. Acknowledging the greeting, Mitch took Radley to an elevator and drew open the iron gate.

"This is pretty neat," Radley decided.

"It's neater when it works." Mitch pushed the button for the fifth floor, which housed the editorial department. "Let's hope for the best."

"Has it ever crashed?" The question was half wary, half hopeful.

"No, but it has been known to go on strike." The car shuddered to a stop on 5. Mitch swung the gate open again. He put a hand on Radley's head. "Welcome to bedlam."

It was precisely that. Radley forgot his disappointment with the exterior in his awe at the fifth floor. There was a reception area of sorts. In any case, there was a desk and a bank of phones manned by a harassed-looking black woman in a Princess Leilah sweatshirt. The walls around her were crammed with posters depicting Universal's most enduring characters: the Human Scorpion, the Velvet Saber, the deadly Black Moth and, of course, Commander Zark.

"How's it going, Lou?"

"Don't ask." She pushed a button on a phone. "I ask

you, is it my fault the deli won't deliver his corned beef?"

"If I put him in a good mood, will you dig up some samples for me?"

"Universal Comics, please hold." The receptionist pushed another button. "You put him in a good mood, you've got my firstborn."

"Just the samples, Lou. Put on your helmet, Corporal. This could be messy." He led Radley down a short hall into the big, brightly lit hub of activity. It was a series of cubicles with a high noise level and a look of chaos. Pinned to the corkboard walls were sketches, rude messages and an occasional photograph. In a corner was a pyramid made of empty soda cans. Someone was tossing wadded-up balls of paper at it.

"Scorpion's never been a joiner. What's his motivation for hooking up with Worldwide Law and Justice?"

A woman with pencils poking out of her wild red hair at dangerous angles shifted in her swivel chair. Her eyes, already huge, were accented by layers of liner and mascara. "Look, let's be real. He can't save the world's water supply on his own. He needs someone like Atlantis."

A man sat across from her, eating an enormous pickle. "They hate each other. Ever since they bumped heads over the Triangular Affair."

"That's the point, dummy. They'll have to put personal feelings aside for the sake of mankind. It's a moral." Glancing over, she caught sight of Mitch. "Hey, Dr. Deadly's poisoned the world's water supply. Scorpion's found an antidote. How's he going to distribute it?"

"Sounds like he'd better mend fences with Atlantis," Mitch replied. "What do you think, Radley?"

For a moment, Rad was so tongue-tied he could only stare. Then, taking a deep breath, he let the words blurt out. "I think they'd make a neat team, 'cause they'd always be fighting and trying to show each other up."

"I'm with you, kid." The redhead held out her hand. "I'm M. J. Jones."

"Wow, really?" He wasn't sure whether he was more impressed with meeting M. J. Jones or with discovering she was a woman. Mitch didn't see the point in mentioning that she was one of the few in the business.

"And this grouch over here is Rob Myers. You bring him as a shield, Mitch?" she asked without giving Rob time to swallow his pickle. They'd been married for six years, and she obviously enjoyed frustrating him.

"Do I need one?"

"If you don't have something terrific in those tubes, I'd advise you to slip back out again." She shoved aside a stack of preliminary sketches. "Maloney just quit, defected to Five Star."

"No kidding?"

"Skinner's been muttering about traitors all morning. And the snow didn't help his mood. So if I were you… Oops, too late." Respecting rats who deserted tyrannically captained ships, M.J. turned away and fell into deep discussion with her husband.

"Dempsey, you were supposed to be in two hours ago."

Mitch gave his editor an ingratiating smile. "My alarm didn't go off. This is Radley Wallace, a friend of mine. Rad, this is Rich Skinner."

Radley stared. Skinner looked exactly like Hank Wheeler, the tanklike and overbearing boss of Joe David, alias the Fly. Later, Mitch would tell him that the resemblance was no accident. Radley switched Taz's leash to his other hand.

"Hello, Mr. Skinner. I really like your comics. They're lots better than Five Star. I hardly ever buy Five Star, because the stories aren't as good."

"Right." Skinner dragged a hand through his thinning hair. "Right," he repeated with more conviction. "Don't waste your allowance on Five Star, kid."

"No, sir."

"Mitch, you know you're not supposed to bring that mutt in here."

"You know how Taz loves you." On cue, Taz lifted his head and howled.

Skinner started to swear, then remembered the boy. "You got something in those tubes, or did you just come by to brighten up my dull day?"

"Why don't you take a look for yourself?"

Grumbling, Skinner took the tubes and marched off. As Mitch started to follow, Radley grabbed at his hand. "Is he really mad?"

"Sure. He likes being mad best."

"Is he going to yell at you like Hank Wheeler yells at the Fly?"

"Maybe."

Radley swallowed and buried his hand in Mitch's. "Okay."

Amused, Mitch led Radley into Skinner's office, where the venetian blinds had been drawn to shut off any view of the snow. Skinner unrolled the contents of the first tube and spread them over his already cluttered desk. He didn't sit, but loomed over them while Taz plopped down on the linoleum and went to sleep.

"Not bad," Skinner announced after he had studied

the series of sketches and captions. "Not too bad. This new character, Mirium, you have plans to expand her?"

"I'd like to. I think Zark's ready to have his heart tugged from a different direction. Adds more emotional conflict. He loves his wife, but she's his biggest enemy. Now he runs into this empath and finds himself torn up all over again because he has feelings for her, as well."

"Zark never gets much of a break."

"I think he's the best," Radley piped in, forgetting himself.

Skinner lifted his bushy brows and studied Radley carefully. "You don't think he gets carried away with this honor and duty stuff?"

"Uh-uh." He wasn't sure if he was relieved or disappointed that Skinner wasn't going to yell. "You always know Zark's going to do the right thing. He doesn't have any super powers and stuff, but he's real smart."

Skinner nodded, accepting the opinion. "We'll give your Mirium a shot, Mitch, and see what the reader response is like." He let the papers roll into themselves again. "This is the first time I can remember you being this far ahead of deadline."

"That's because I have an assistant now." Mitch laid a hand on Radley's shoulder.

"Good work, kid. Why don't you take your assistant on a tour?"

It would take Radley weeks to stop talking about his hour at Universal Comics. When they left, he carried a shopping bag full of pencils with Universal's logo, a Mad Matilda mug that had been unearthed from someone's storage locker, a half dozen rejected sketches and a batch of comics fresh off the presses.

"This was the best day in my whole life," Radley

said, dancing down the snow-choked sidewalk. "Wait until I show Mom. She won't believe it."

Oddly enough, Mitch had been thinking of Hester himself. He lengthened his stride to keep up with Radley's skipping pace. "Why don't we go by and pay her a visit?"

"Okay." He slipped his hand into Mitch's again. "The bank's not nearly as neat as where you work, though. They don't let anyone play radios or yell at each other, but they have a vault where they keep lots of money— millions of dollars—and they have cameras everywhere so they can see anybody who tries to rob them. Mom's never been in a bank that's been robbed."

Since the statement came out as an apology, Mitch laughed. "We can't all be blessed." He ran a hand over his stomach. He hadn't put anything into it in at least two hours. "Let's grab that taco first."

Inside the staid and unthreatened walls of National Trust, Hester dealt with a stack of paperwork. She enjoyed this part of her job, the organized monotony of it. There was also the challenge of sorting through the facts and figures and translating them into real estate, automobiles, business equipment, stage sets or college funds. Nothing gave her greater pleasure than to be able to stamp a loan with her approval.

She'd had to teach herself not to be softhearted. There were times the facts and figures told you to say no, no matter how earnest the applicant might be. Part of her job was to dictate polite and impersonal letters of refusal. Hester might not have cared for it, but she accepted that responsibility, just as she accepted the occasional irate phone call from the recipient of a loan refusal.

At the moment she was stealing half an hour, with the muffin and coffee that would be her lunch, to put together three loan packages she wanted approved by the board when they met the following day. She had another appointment in fifteen minutes. And, with that and a lack of interruptions, she could just finish. She wasn't particularly pleased when her assistant buzzed through.

"Yes, Kay."

"There's a young man out here to see you, Mrs. Wallace."

"His appointment isn't for fifteen minutes. He'll have to wait."

"No, it isn't Mr. Greenburg. And I don't think he's here for a loan. Are you here for a loan, honey?"

Hester heard the familiar giggle and hurried to the door. "Rad? Is everything all right—oh."

He wasn't alone. Hester realized she'd been foolish to think Radley would have made the trip by himself. Mitch was with him, along with the huge, mild-eyed dog.

"We just ate tacos."

Hester eyed the faint smudge of salsa on Radley's chin. "So I see." She bent to hug him, then glanced up at Mitch. "Is everything okay?"

"Sure. We were just out taking care of a little business and decided to drop by." He took a good long look. She'd covered most of the colorful bruise with makeup. Only a hint of yellow and mauve showed through. "The eye looks better."

"I seem to have passed the crisis."

"That your office?" Without invitation, he strolled

over to stick his head inside. "God, how depressing. Maybe you can talk Radley into giving you one of his posters."

"You can have one," Radley agreed immediately. "I got a bunch of them when Mitch took me to Universal. Wow, Mom you should see it. I met M. J. Jones and Rich Skinner and I saw this room where they keep zillions of comics. See what I got." He held up his shopping bag. "For free. They said I could."

Her first feeling was one of discomfort. It seemed her obligation to Mitch grew with each day. Then she looked down at Radley's eager, glowing face. "Sounds like a pretty great morning."

"It was the best ever."

"Yellow alert," Kay murmured. "Rosen at three o'clock."

It didn't take words to show Mitch that Rosen was a force to be reckoned with. He saw Hester's face poker up instantly as she smoothed a hand over her hair to be sure it was in place.

"Good afternoon, Mrs. Wallace." He glanced meaningfully at the dog, who sniffed the toe of his shoe. "Perhaps you've forgotten that pets are not permitted inside the bank."

"No, sir. My son was just—"

"Your son?" Rosen gave Radley a brief nod. "How do you do, young man. Mrs. Wallace, I'm sure you remember that bank policy frowns on personal visits during working hours."

"Mrs. Wallace, I'll just put these papers on your desk for your signature—when your lunch break is over." Kay shuffled some forms importantly, then winked at Radley.

"Thank you, Kay."

Rosen harrumphed. He couldn't argue with a lunch break, but it was his duty to deal with other infractions of policy. "About this animal—"

Finding Rosen's tone upsetting, Taz pushed his nose against Radley's knee and moaned. "He's mine." Mitch stepped forward, his smile charming, his hand outstretched. Hester had time to think that with that look he could sell Florida swampland. "Mitchell Dempsey II. Hester and I are good friends, very good friends. She's told me so much about you and your bank." He gave Rosen's hand a hearty political shake. "My family has several holdings in New York. Hester's convinced me I should use my influence to have them transfer to National Trust. You might be familiar with some of the family companies. Trioptic, D and H Chemicals, Dempsey Paperworks?"

"Well, of course, of course." Rosen's limp grip on Mitch's hand tightened. "It's a pleasure to meet you, a real pleasure."

"Hester persuaded me to come by and see for myself how efficiently National Trust ticked." He definitely had the man's number, Mitch thought. Dollar signs were already flitting through the pudgy little brain. "I am impressed. Of course, I could have taken Hester's word for it." He gave her stiff shoulder an intimate little squeeze. "She's just a whiz at financial matters. I can tell you, my father would snatch her up as a corporate adviser in a minute. You're lucky to have her."

"Mrs. Wallace is one of our most valued employees."

"I'm glad to hear it. I'll have to bring up National Trust's advantages when I speak with my father."

"I'll be happy to take you on a tour personally. I'm sure you'd like to see the executive offices."

"Nothing I'd like better, but I am a bit pressed for time." If he'd had days stretching out before him, he wouldn't have spent a minute of them touring the stuffy corners of a bank. "Why don't you work up a package I can present at the next board meeting?"

"Delighted." Rosen's face beamed with pleasure. Bringing an account as large and diversified as Dempsey's to National Trust would be quite a coup for the stuffy bank manager.

"Just send it through Hester. You don't mind playing messenger, do you, darling?" Mitch said cheerfully.

"No," she managed.

"Excellent," Rosen said, the excitement evident in his voice. "I'm sure you'll find we can serve all your family's needs. We are the bank to grow with, after all." He patted Taz's head. "Lovely dog," he said and strode off with a new briskness in his step.

"What a fusty old snob," Mitch decided. "How do you stand it?"

"Would you come into my office a moment?" Hester's voice was as stiff as her shoulders. Recognizing the tone, Radley rolled his eyes at Mitch. "Kay, if Mr. Greenburg comes in, please have him wait."

"Yes, ma'am."

Hester led the way into her office, then closed the door and leaned against it. There was a part of her that wanted to laugh, to throw her arms around Mitch and howl with delight over the way he'd handled Rosen. There was another part, the part that needed a job, a regular salary and employee benefits, that cringed.

"How could you do that?"

"Do what?" Mitch took a look around the office. "The brown carpet has to go. And this paint. What do you call this?"

"Yuk," Radley ventured as he settled in a chair with Taz's head in his lap.

"Yeah, that's it. You know, your work area has a lot to do with your work production. Try that on Rosen."

"I won't be trying anything with Rosen once he finds out what you did. I'll be fired."

"Don't be silly. I never promised my family would move their interests to National Trust. Besides, if he puts together an intriguing enough package, they just might." He shrugged, indicating it made little difference to him. "If it'll make you happier, I can move my personal accounts here. A bank's a bank as far as I'm concerned."

"Damn it." It was very rare for her to swear out loud and with heat. Radley found the fur on Taz's neck of primary interest. "Rosen's got corporate dynasty on his mind, thanks to you. He's going to be furious with me when he finds out you made all that up."

Mitch tapped a hand on a tidy stack of papers. "You're obsessively neat, did you know that? And I didn't make anything up. I could have," he said thoughtfully. "I'm good at it, but there didn't seem to be any reason to."

"Would you stop?" Frustrated, she moved to him to slap his hands away from her work. "All that business about Trioptic and D and H Chemicals." Letting out a long sigh, she dropped down on the edge of the desk. "I know you did it to try to help me, and I appreciate the thought, but—"

"You do?" With a smile, he fingered the lapel of her suit jacket.

"You mean well, I suppose," Hester murmured.

"Sometimes." He leaned a little closer. "You smell much too good for this office."

"Mitch." She put a hand on his chest and glanced nervously at Radley. The boy had an arm hooked around Taz and was already deeply involved in one of his new comic books.

"Do you really think it would be a traumatic experience if the kid saw me kiss you?"

"No." At his slight movement, she pressed harder. "But that's beside the point."

"What *is* the point?" He took his hand from her jacket to fiddle with the gold triangle at her ear.

"The point is I'm going to have to see Rosen and explain to him that you were just…" What was the word she wanted? "Fantasizing."

"I've done a lot of that," he admitted as he moved his thumb down her jawline. "But I'm damned if I think it's any of his business. Want me to tell you the one about you and me in the life raft on the Indian Ocean?"

"No." This time she had to laugh, though the reaction in her stomach had more to do with heat than humor. Curiosity pricked at her so that she met his eyes, then looked quickly away again. "Why don't you and Rad go home? I have another appointment, then I'll go and explain things to Mr. Rosen."

"You're not mad anymore?"

She shook her head and gave in to the urge to touch his face. "You were just trying to help. It was sweet of you."

He imagined she'd have taken the same attitude with

Radley if he'd tried to wash the dishes and had smashed her violet-edged china on the floor. Telling himself it was a kind of test, he pressed his lips firmly to hers. He felt each layer of reaction—the shock, the tension, the need. When he drew back, he saw more than indulgence in her eyes. The fire flickered briefly, but with intensity.

"Come on, Rad, your mom has to get back to work. If we're not in the apartment when you get home, we're in the park."

"Fine." Unconsciously she pressed her lips together to seal in the warmth. "Thanks."

"Anytime."

"Bye, Rad, I'll be home soon."

"Okay." He lifted his arms to squeeze her neck. "You're not mad at Mitch anymore?"

"No," she answered in the same carrying whisper. "I'm not mad at anyone."

She was smiling when she straightened, but Mitch saw the worried look in her eye. He paused with his hand on the knob. "You're really going to go up to Rosen and tell him I made that business up?"

"I have to." Then, because she felt guilty about launching her earlier attack, she smiled. "Don't worry. I'm sure I can handle him."

"What if I told you I didn't make it up, that my family founded Trioptic forty-seven years ago?"

Hester lifted a brow. "I'd say don't forget your gloves. It's cold out there."

"Okay, but do yourself a favor before you bare your soul to Rosen. Look it up in *Who's Who.*"

With her hands in her pockets, Hester walked to her office door. From there she saw Radley reach up to put a gloved hand into Mitch's bare one.

"Your son's adorable," Kay said, offering Hester a file. The little skirmish with Rosen had completely changed her opinion of the reserved Mrs. Wallace.

"Thanks." When Hester smiled, Kay's new opinion was cemented. "And I do appreciate you covering for me that way."

"That's no big deal. I don't see what's wrong with your son dropping by for a minute."

"Bank policy," Hester murmured under her breath, and Kay let out a snort.

"Rosen policy, you mean. Beneath that gruff exterior is a gruff interior. But don't worry about him. I happen to know he considers your work production far superior to your predecessor's. As far as he's concerned, that's the bottom line."

Kay hesitated a moment as Hester nodded and flipped through the file. "It's tough raising a kid on your own. My sister has a little girl, she's just five. I know some nights Annie's just knocked out from wearing all the badges, you know."

"Yes, I do."

"My parents want her to move back home so Mom can watch Sarah while Annie works, but Annie's not sure it's the best thing."

"Sometimes it's hard to know if accepting help's right," Hester murmured, thinking of Mitch. "And sometimes we forget to be grateful that someone's there to offer it." She shook herself and tucked the file under her arm. "Is Mr. Greenburg here?"

"Just came in."

"Fine, send him in, Kay." She started for her office, then stopped. "Oh, and Kay, dig me up a copy of *Who's Who*."

Chapter 6

He was loaded.

Hester was still dazed when she let herself into her apartment. Her downstairs neighbor with the bare feet and the holes in his jeans was an heir to one of the biggest fortunes in the country.

Hester took off her coat and, out of habit, went to the closet to hang it up. The man who spent his days writing the further adventures of Commander Zark came from a family who owned polo ponies and summer houses. Yet he lived on the fourth floor of a very ordinary apartment building in Manhattan.

He was attracted to her. She'd have had to be blind and deaf not to be certain of that, and yet she'd known him for weeks and he hadn't once mentioned his family or his position in an effort to impress her.

Who was he? she wondered. She'd begun to think

she had a handle on him, but now he was a stranger all over again.

She had to call him, tell him she was home and to send Radley up. Hester looked at the phone with a feeling of acute embarrassment. She'd lectured him about spinning a tale to Mr. Rosen; then, in her soft-hearted and probably condescending way, she'd forgiven him. It all added up to her doing what she hated most. Making a fool of herself.

Swearing, Hester snatched up the phone. She would have felt much better if she could have rapped Mitchell Dempsey II over the head with it.

She'd dialed half the numbers when she heard Radley's howl of laughter and the sound of stomping feet in the hall outside. She opened the door just as Radley was digging his key out of his pocket.

Both of them were covered with snow. Some that was beginning to melt dripped from Radley's ski cap and boot tops. They looked unmistakably as if they'd been rolling in it.

"Hi, Mom. We've been in the park. We stopped by Mitch's to get my bag, then came on up because we thought you'd be home. Come on out with us."

"I don't think I'm dressed for snow wars."

She smiled and peeled off her son's snow-crusted cap but, Mitch noted, she didn't look up. "So change." He leaned against the doorjamb, ignoring the snow that fell at his feet.

"I built a fort. Please come out and see. I already started a snow warrior, but Mitch said we should check in so you wouldn't worry."

His consideration forced her to look up. "I appreciate that."

He was watching her thoughtfully—too thoughtfully, Hester decided. "Rad says you build a pretty good snow warrior yourself."

"Please, Mom. What if we got a freak heat wave and the snow was all gone tomorrow? It's like the greenhouse effect, you know. I read all about it."

She was trapped and knew it. "All right, I'll change. Why don't you fix Mitch some hot chocolate and warm up?"

"All right!" Radley dropped down on the floor just inside the door. "You have to take off your boots," he told Mitch. "She gets mad if you track up the carpet."

Mitch unbuttoned his coat as Hester walked away. "We wouldn't want to make her mad."

Within fifteen minutes, Hester had changed into corduroys, a bulky sweater and old boots. In place of her red coat was a blue parka that showed some wear. Mitch kept one hand on Taz's leash and the other in his pocket as they walked across to the park. He couldn't say why he enjoyed seeing her dressed casually with Radley's hand joined tight with hers. He couldn't say for certain why he'd wanted to spend this time with her, but it had been he who'd planted the idea of another outing in Radley's head, and he who'd suggested that they go up together to persuade her to come outside.

He liked the winter. Mitch took a deep gulp of cold air as they walked through the soft, deep snow of Central Park. Snow and stinging air had always appealed to him, particularly when the trees were draped in white and there were snow castles to be built.

When he'd been a boy, his family had often wintered in the Caribbean, away from what his mother had termed the "mess and inconvenience." He'd picked up an affection for scuba and white sand, but had never felt that a palm tree replaced a pine at Christmas.

The winters he'd liked best had been spent in his uncle's country home in New Hampshire, where there'd been woods to walk in and hills to sled. Oddly enough, he'd been thinking of going back there for a few weeks—until the Wallaces popped up two floors above, that is. He hadn't realized until today that he'd shuffled those plans to the back of his mind as soon as he'd seen Hester and her son.

Now she was embarrassed, annoyed and uncomfortable. Mitch turned to study her profile. Her cheeks were already rosy with cold, and she'd made certain that Radley walked between them. He wondered if she realized how obvious her strategies were. She didn't use the boy, not in the way some parents used their offspring for their own ambitions or purposes. He respected her for that more than he could have explained. But she had, by putting Radley in the center, relegated Mitch to the level of her son's friend.

And so he was, Mitch thought with a smile. But he'd be damned if he was going to let it stop there.

"There's the fort. See?" Radley tugged on Hester's hand, then let it go to run, too impatient to wait any longer.

"Pretty impressive, huh?" Before she could avoid it, Mitch draped a casual arm over her shoulder. "He's really got a knack."

Hester tried to ignore the warmth and pressure of his arm as she looked at her son's handiwork. The walls of the fort were about two feet high, smooth as stone, with one end sloping nearly a foot higher in the shape of a round tower. They'd made an arched doorway high enough for Radley to crawl through. When Hester reached the fort, she saw him pass through on his hands and knees and pop up inside, his arms held high.

"It's terrific, Rad. I imagine you had a great deal to do with it," she said quietly to Mitch.

"Here and there." Then he smiled, as though he was laughing at himself. "Rad's a better architect than I'll ever be."

"I'm going to finish my snow warrior." Belly down, Rad crawled through the opening again. "Build one, Mom, on the other side of the fort. They'll be the sentries." Rad began to pack and smooth snow on his already half-formed figure. "You help her, Mitch, 'cause I've got a head start."

"Fair's fair." Mitch scooped up a handful of snow. "Any objections to teamwork?"

"No, of course not." Still avoiding giving him a straight look, Hester knelt in the snow. Mitch dropped the handful of snow on her head.

"I figured that was the quickest way to get you to look at me." She glared, then began to push the snow into a mound. "Problem, Mrs. Wallace?"

Seconds ticked by as she pushed at the snow. "I got a copy of *Who's Who*."

"Oh?" Mitch knelt down beside her.

"You were telling the truth."

"I've been known to from time to time." He shoved some more snow on the mound she was forming. "So?"

Hester frowned and punched the snow into shape. "I feel like an idiot."

"I told the truth, and you feel like an idiot." Patiently Mitch smoothed over the base she was making. "Want to explain the correlation?"

"You let me lecture you."

"It's kinda hard to stop you when you get rolling."

Hester began to dig out snow with both hands to form the legs. "You let me think you were some poor, eccentric Good Samaritan. I was even going to offer to put patches on your jeans."

"No kidding." Incredibly touched, Mitch caught her chin in his snow-covered glove. "That's sweet."

There was no way she was going to let his charm brush away the discomfort of her embarrassment. "The fact is, you're a rich, eccentric Good Samaritan." She shoved his hand away and began to gather snow for the torso.

"Does this mean you won't patch my jeans?"

Hester's long-suffering breath came out in a white plume. "I don't want to talk about it."

"Yes, you do." Always helpful, Mitch packed on more snow and succeeded in burying her up to the elbows. "Money shouldn't bother you, Hester. You're a banker."

"Money doesn't bother me." She yanked her arms free and tossed two good-sized hunks of snow into his face. Because she had to fight back a giggle, she turned her back. "I just wish the situation had been made clear earlier, that's all."

Mitch wiped the snow from his face, then scooped up more, running his tongue along the inside of his lip. He'd had a lot of experience in forming what he considered the ultimate snowball. "What's the situation, Mrs. Wallace?"

"I wish you'd stop calling me that in that tone of voice." She turned, just in time to get the snowball right between the eyes.

"Sorry." Mitch smiled, then began to brush off her coat. "Must've slipped. About this situation…"

"There is no situation between us." Before she realized it, she'd shoved him hard enough to send him sprawling in the snow. "Excuse me." Her laughter came out in hitches that were difficult to swallow. "I didn't mean to do that. I don't know what it is about you that makes me do things like that." He sat up and continued to stare at her. "I *am* sorry," she repeated. "I think it's best if we just let this other business drop. Now, if I help you up, will you promise not to retaliate?"

"Sure." Mitch held out a gloved hand. The moment he closed it over hers, he yanked her forward. Hester went down, face first. "I don't *always* tell the truth, by the way." Before she could respond, he wrapped his arms around her and began to roll.

"Hey, you're supposed to be building another sentry."

"In a minute," Mitch called to Rad, while Hester tried to catch her breath. "I'm teaching your mom a new game. Like it?" he asked her as he rolled her underneath him again.

"Get off me. I've got snow down my sweater, down my jeans—"

"No use trying to seduce me here. I'm stronger than that."

"You're crazy." She tried to sit up, but he pinned her beneath him.

"Maybe." He licked a trace of snow from her cheek and felt her go utterly still. "But I'm not stupid." His voice had changed. It wasn't the easy, carefree voice of her neighbor now, but the slow, soft tones of a lover. "You feel something for me. You may not like it, but you feel it."

It wasn't the unexpected exercise that had stolen her breath, and she knew it. His eyes were so blue in the lowering sunlight, and his hair glistened with a dusting of snow. And his face was close, temptingly close. Yes, she felt something, she felt something almost from the first minute she saw him, but she wasn't stupid, either.

"If you let go of my arms I'll show you just how I feel."

"Why do I think I wouldn't like it? Never mind." He brushed his lips over hers before she could answer. "Hester, the situation is this. You have feelings for me that have nothing to do with my money, because you didn't know until a few hours ago that I had any to speak of. Some of those feelings don't have anything to do with the fact that I'm fond of your son. They're very personal, as in you and me."

He was right, absolutely and completely right. She could have murdered him for it. "Don't tell me how I feel."

"All right." After he spoke, he surprised her by rising and helping her to her feet. Then he took her in his arms again. "I'll tell you how *I* feel then. I care for you—more than I'd counted on."

She paled beneath her cold-tinted cheeks. There was more than a hint of desperation in her eyes as she shook her head and tried to back away. "Don't say that to me."

"Why not?" He struggled against impatience as he lowered his brow to hers. "You'll have to get used to it. I did."

"I don't want this. I don't want to feel this way."

He tipped her head back, and his eyes were very serious. "We'll have to talk about that."

"No. There's nothing to talk about. This is just getting out of hand."

"It's not out of hand yet." He tangled his fingers in the tips of her hair, but his eyes never left hers. "I'm almost certain it will be before long, but it isn't yet. You're too smart and too strong for that."

She'd be able to breathe easier in a moment. She was sure of it. She'd be able to breathe easier as soon as she was away from him. "No, I'm not afraid of you." Oddly, she discovered that much was true.

"Then kiss me." His voice was coaxing now, gentle. "It's nearly twilight. Kiss me, once, before the sun goes down."

She found herself leaning into him, lifting her lips up and letting her lashes fall without questioning why it should seem so right, so natural to do as he asked. There would be questions later, though she was certain the answers wouldn't come as easily. For now, she touched her lips to his and found them cool, cool and patient.

The world was all ice and snow, forts and fairylands, but his lips were real. They fit on hers firmly, warming her soft, sensitive skin while the racing of her heart heated her body. There was the rushing whoosh of traffic in the distance, but closer, more intimate, was the whisper of her coat sliding against his as they pressed tighter together.

He wanted to coax, to persuade, and just once to see her lips curve into a smile as he left them. He knew there were times when a man who preferred action and impulse had to go step by step. Especially when the prize at the top was precious.

He hadn't been prepared for her, but he knew he could accept what was happening between them with more ease than she. There were still secrets tucked inside her, hurts that had only partially healed. He knew better than to wish for the power to wipe all that aside. How she'd lived and what had happened to her were all part of the woman she was. The woman he was very, very close to falling in love with.

So he would take it step by step, Mitch told himself as he placed her away from him. And he would wait.

"That might have cleared up a few points, but I think we still have to talk." He took her hand to keep her close another moment. "Soon."

"I don't know." Had she ever been this confused before? She'd thought she'd left these feelings, these doubts behind her long ago.

"I'll come up or you can come down, but we'll talk."

He was jockeying her into a corner, one she knew she'd be backed into sooner or later. "Not tonight," she said, despising herself for being a coward. "Rad and I have a lot to do."

"Procrastination's not your style."

"It is this time," she murmured, and turned away quickly. "Radley, we have to go in."

"Look, Mom, I just finished, isn't it great?" He stood back to show off his warrior. "You hardly started yours."

"Maybe we'll finish it tomorrow." She walked to him quickly and took him by the hand. "We have to go in and fix dinner now."

"But can't we just—"

"No, it's nearly dark."

"Can Mitch come?"

"No, he can't." She shot a glance over her shoulder as they walked. He was hardly more than a shadow now, standing beside her son's fort. "Not tonight."

Mitch put a hand on his dog's head as Taz whined and started forward. "Nope. Not this time."

There didn't seem any way of avoiding him, Hester thought as she started down to Mitch's apartment at her son's request. She had to admit it had been foolish of her to try. On the surface, anyone would think that Mitch Dempsey was the solution to many of her problems. He was genuinely fond of Radley, and gave her son both a companion and a safe and convenient place to stay while she worked. His time was flexible, and he was very generous with it.

The truth was, he'd complicated her life. No matter how much she tried to look at him as Radley's friend or her slightly odd neighbor, he brought back feelings she hadn't experienced in almost ten years. Fluttery pulses and warm surges were things Hester had attributed to the very young or the very optimistic. She'd stopped being either when Radley's father had left them.

In all the years that had followed that moment, she'd devoted herself to her son—to making the best possible home for him, to make his life as normal and well balanced as possible. If Hester the woman had gotten lost somewhere in the shuffle, Radley's mother figured it was a fair exchange. Now Mitch Dempsey had come along and made her feel and, worse, had made her wish.

Taking a deep breath, Hester knocked on Mitch's door. Radley's friend's door, she told herself firmly. The only reason she was here was because Radley had been so excited about showing her something. She wasn't here to see Mitch; she wasn't hoping he would reach out and run his fingertips along her cheek as he sometimes did. Hester's skin warmed at the thought of it.

Hester linked her hands together and concentrated on Radley. She would see whatever it was he was so anxious for her to see, and then she would get them both back upstairs to their own apartment—and safety.

Mitch answered the door. He wore a sweatshirt sporting a decal of a rival superhero across the chest, and sweatpants with a gaping hole in one knee. There was a towel slung over his shoulders. He used one end of it to dry the sweat off his face.

"You haven't been out running in this weather?" she asked before she'd allowed herself to think, immediately regretting the question and the obvious concern in her voice.

"No." He took her hand to draw her inside. She smelled like the springtime that was still weeks and weeks away. Her dark blue suit gave her a look of uncreased professionalism he found ridiculously sexy. "Weights," he told her. The fact was, he'd been lifting weights a great deal since he'd met Hester Wallace. Mitch considered it the second best way to decrease tension and rid the body of excess energy.

"Oh." So that explained the strength she'd felt in his arms. "I didn't realize you went in for that sort of thing."

"The Mr. Macho routine?" he said, laughing. "No, I don't, actually. The thing is, if I don't work out regularly, my body turns into a toothpick. It's not a pretty sight." Because she looked nervous enough to jump out of her skin, Mitch couldn't resist. He leered and flexed his arm. "Want to feel my pecs?"

"I'll pass, thanks." Hester kept her hands by her sides. "Mr. Rosen sent this package." She slipped the fat bank portfolio out from where she'd held it at her side. "Just remember, you asked for it."

"So I did." Mitch accepted it, then tossed it on a pile of magazines on the coffee table. "Tell him I'll pass it along."

"And will you?"

He lifted a brow. "I usually keep my word."

She was certain of that. It reminded her that he'd said they would talk, and soon. "Radley called and said there was something he had to show me."

"He's in the office. Want some coffee?"

It was such a casual offer, so easy and friendly, that she nearly agreed. "Thanks, but we really can't stay. I had to bring some paperwork home with me."

"Fine. Just go on in. I need a drink."

"Mom!" The minute she stepped into the office, Radley jumped up and grabbed her hands. "Isn't it great? It's the neatest present I ever got in my life." With his hands still locked on hers, Radley dragged her over to a scaled-down drawing board.

It wasn't a toy. Hester could see immediately that it was top-of-the-line equipment, if child-sized. The small swivel stool was worn, but the seat was leather. Radley already had graph paper tacked to the board, and with compass and ruler had begun what appeared to be a set of blueprints.

"Is this Mitch's?"

"It was, but he said I could use it now, for as long as I wanted. See, I'm making the plans for a space station. This is the engine room. And over here and here are the living quarters. It's going to have a greenhouse, sort of like the one they had in this movie Mitch let me watch. Mitch showed me how to draw things to scale with these squares."

"I see." Pride in her son overshadowed any tension

as she crouched down for a better look. "You catch on fast, Rad. This is wonderful. I wonder if NASA has an opening."

He chuckled, facedown, as he did when he was both pleased and embarrassed. "Maybe I could be an engineer."

"You can be anything you want." She pressed a kiss to his temple. "If you keep drawing like this, I'm going to need an interpreter to know what you're doing. All these tools." She picked up a square. "I guess you know what they're for."

"Mitch told me. He uses them sometimes when he draws."

"Oh?" She turned the square over in her hand. It looked so—professional.

"Even comic art needs a certain discipline," Mitch said from the doorway. He held a large glass of orange juice, which was already half-gone. Hester rose. He looked—virile, she realized.

There was a faint vee of dampness down the center of his shirt. His hair had been combed through with no more than his fingers and, not for the first time, he hadn't bothered to shave off the night's growth of beard. Beside her, her son was happily remodeling his blueprint.

Virile, dangerous, nerve-wracking he might be, but a kinder man she'd never met. Concentrating on that, Hester stepped forward. "I don't know how to thank you."

"Rad already has."

She nodded, then laid a hand on Radley's shoulder. "You finish that up, Rad. I'll be in the other room with Mitch."

Hester walked into the living room. It was, as she'd

come to expect, cluttered and chaotic. Taz nosed around the carpet looking for cookie crumbs. "I thought I knew Rad inside and out," Hester began. "But I didn't know a drawing board would mean so much to him. I guess I would have thought him too young to appreciate it."

"I told you once he had a natural talent."

"I know." She gnawed on her lip. She wished she had accepted the offer of coffee so that she'd have something to do with her hands. "Rad told me that you were giving him some art lessons. You've done more for him than I ever could have expected. Certainly much more than you're obligated to."

He gave her a long, searching look. "It hasn't got anything to do with obligation. Why don't you sit down?"

"No." She linked her hands together, then pulled them apart again. "No, that's all right."

"Would you rather pace?"

It was the ease of his smile that had her unbending another notch. "Maybe later. I just wanted to tell you how grateful I am. Rad's never had…" A father. The words had nearly come out before Hester had swallowed them in a kind of horror. She hadn't meant that, she assured herself. "He's never had anyone to give him so much attention—besides me." She let out a little breath. That was what she'd meant to say. Of course it was. "The drawing board was very generous. Rad said it was yours."

"My father had it made for me when I was about Rad's age. He'd hoped I'd stop sketching monsters and start doing something productive." He said it without bitterness, but with a trace of amusement. Mitch had long since stopped resenting his parents' lack of understanding.

"It must mean a great deal to you for you to have kept it all this time. I know Rad loves it, but shouldn't you keep it for your own children?"

Mitch took a sip of juice and glanced around the apartment. "I don't seem to have any around at the moment."

"But still—"

"Hester, I wouldn't have given it to him if I hadn't wanted him to have it. It's been in storage for years, gathering dust. It gives me a kick to see Rad putting it to use." He finished off the juice, then set the glass down before he crossed to her. "The present's for Rad, with no strings attached to his mother."

"I know that, I didn't mean—"

"No, I don't think you did, exactly." He was watching her now, unsmiling, with that quiet intensity he drew out at unexpected moments. "I doubt if it was even in the front of your mind, but it was milling around in there somewhere."

"I don't think you're using Radley to get to me, if that's what you mean."

"Good." He did as she'd imagined he might, and ran a finger along her jawline. "Because the fact is, Mrs. Wallace, I'd like the kid without you, or you without the kid. It just so happens that in this case, you came as a set."

"That's just it. Radley and I are a unit. What affects him affects me."

Mitch tilted his head as a new thought began to dawn. "I think I'm getting a signal here. You don't think I'm playing pals and buddies with Rad to get Rad's mother between the sheets?"

"Of course not." She drew back sharply, looking toward the office. "If I had thought that, Radley wouldn't be within ten feet of you."

"But..." He laid his arms on her shoulders, linking his hands loosely behind her neck. "You're wondering if your feelings for me might be residual of Radley's feelings."

"I never said I had feelings for you."

"Yes, you did. And you say it again every time I manage to get this close. No, don't pull away, Hester." He tightened his hands. "Let's be upfront. I want to sleep with you. It has nothing to do with Rad, and less than I figured to do with the primal urge I felt the first time I saw your legs." Her eyes lifted warily to his, but held. "It has to do with the fact that I find you attractive in a lot of ways. You're smart, you're strong and you're stable. It might not sound very romantic, but the fact is, your stability is very alluring. I've never had a lot of it myself."

He brushed his linked hands up the back of her neck. "Now, maybe you're not ready to take a step like this at the moment. But I'd appreciate it if you'd take a straight look at what you want, at what you feel."

"I'm not sure I can. You only have yourself. I have Rad. Whatever I do, whatever decisions I make, ripple down to affect him. I promised myself years ago that he would never be hurt by another one of his parents. I'm going to keep that promise."

He wanted to demand that she tell him about Radley's father then and there, but the boy was just in the next room. "Let me tell you what I believe. You could never make a decision that could hurt Rad. But I do think you could make one that could hurt yourself. I want to be with you, Hester, and I don't think our being together is going to hurt Radley."

"It's all done." Radley streamed out of the office, the graph paper in both hands. Hester immediately started to move away. To prove a point to both of them, Mitch held her where she was. "I want to take it and show Josh tomorrow. Okay?"

Knowing a struggle would be worse than submission, Hester stayed still with Mitch's arms on her shoulders. "Sure you can."

Radley studied them a moment. He'd never seen a man with his arms around his mother, except his grandpa or his uncle. He wondered if this made Mitch like family. "I'm going over to Josh's tomorrow afternoon and I'm staying for a sleepover. We're going to stay up all night."

"Then I'll just have to look after your mom, won't I?"

"I guess." Radley began to roll the graph paper into a tube as Mitch had shown him.

"Radley knows I don't have to be looked after."

Ignoring her, Mitch continued to speak to Radley. "How about if I took your mom on a date?"

"You mean get dressed up and go to a restaurant and stuff?"

"Something like that."

"That'd be okay."

"Good. I'll pick her up at seven."

"I really don't think—"

"Seven's not good?" Mitch interrupted Hester. "All right, seven-thirty, but that's as late as it gets. If I don't eat by eight I get nasty." He gave Hester a quick kiss on the temple before releasing her. "Have a good time at Josh's."

"I will." Radley gathered up his coat and backpack. Then he walked to Mitch and hugged him. The words that had been on the tip of Hester's tongue dried up. "Thanks for the drawing board and everything. It's really neat."

"You're welcome. See you Monday." He waited until Hester was at the door. "Seven-thirty."

She nodded and closed the door quietly behind her.

Chapter 7

She could have made excuses, but the fact was, Hester didn't want to. She knew Mitch had hustled her into this dinner date, but as she crossed the wide leather belt at her waist and secured it, she discovered she didn't mind. In fact, she was relieved that he'd made the decision for her—almost.

The nerves were there. She stood in front of the bureau mirror and took a few long, deep breaths. Yes, there were nerves, but they weren't the stomach-roiling sort she experienced when she went on job interviews. Though she wasn't quite sure where her feelings lay when it came to Mitch Dempsey, she was glad to be certain she wasn't afraid.

Picking up her brush, she studied her reflection as she smoothed her hair. She didn't look nervous, Hester decided. That was another point in her favor. The black wool dress was flattering with its deep cowl neck and nipped-in waist. The red slash of belt accented the line before the skirt flared out. For some reason, red gave her confidence. She considered the bold color another kind of defense for a far-from-bold person.

She fixed oversized scarlet swirls at her ears. Like most of her wardrobe, the dress was practical. It could go to the office, to a PTA meeting or a business lunch. Tonight, she thought with a half smile, it was going on a date.

Hester tried not to dwell on how long it had been since she'd been on a date, but comforted herself with the fact that she knew Mitch well enough to keep up an easy conversation through an evening. An adult evening. As much as she adored Radley, she couldn't help but look forward to it.

When she heard the knock, she gave herself a last quick check, then went to answer. The moment she opened the door, her confidence vanished.

He didn't look like Mitch. Gone were the scruffy jeans and baggy sweatshirts. This man wore a dark suit with a pale blue shirt. And a tie. The top button of the shirt was open, and the tie of dark blue silk was knotted loose and low, but it was still a tie. He was clean-shaven, and though some might have thought he still needed a trim, his hair waved dark and glossy over his ears and the collar of his shirt.

Hester was suddenly and painfully shy.

She looked terrific. Mitch felt a moment's awkwardness himself as he looked at her. Her evening shoes put her to within an inch of his height so that they were eye to eye. It was the wariness in hers that had him relaxing with a smile.

"Looks like I picked the right color." He offered her an armful of red roses.

She knew it was foolish for a woman of her age to be flustered by something as simple as flowers. But her heart rushed up to her throat as she gathered them to her.

"Did you forget your line again?" he murmured.

"My line?"

"Thank you."

The scent of the roses flowed around her, soft and sweet. "Thank you."

He touched one of the petals. He already knew her skin felt much the same. "Now you're supposed to put them in water."

Feeling a great deal more than foolish, Hester stepped back. "Of course. Come in."

"The apartment feels different without Rad," he commented when Hester went to get a vase.

"I know. Whenever he goes to a sleepover, it takes me hours to get used to the quiet." He'd followed her into the kitchen. Hester busied herself with arranging the roses. I am a grown woman, she reminded herself, and just because I haven't been on a date since high school doesn't mean I don't remember how.

"What do you usually do when you have a free evening?"

"Oh, I read, watch a late movie." She turned with the vase and nearly collided with him. Water sloshed dangerously close to the top of the vase.

"The eye's barely noticeable now." He lifted a fingertip to where the bruise had faded to a shadow.

"It wasn't such a calamity." Her throat had tightened. Grown woman or not, she found herself enormously glad that the vase of roses was between them. "I'll get my coat."

After carrying the roses to the table beside the sofa, Hester went to the closet. She slipped one arm into the sleeve before Mitch came up behind her to help her finish. He made such an ordinary task sensual, she thought as she stared straight ahead. He brushed his hands over her shoulders, lingered, then trailed them down her arms before bringing them up again to gently release her hair from the coat collar.

Hester's hands were balled into fists as she turned her head. "Thank you."

"You're welcome." With his hands on her shoulders, Mitch turned her to face him. "Maybe you'll feel better if we get this out of the way now." He kept his hands where they were and touched his lips, firm and warm, to hers. Hester's rigid hands went lax. There was nothing demanding or passionate in the kiss. It moved her unbearably with its understanding.

"Feel better?" Mitch murmured.

"I'm not sure."

With a laugh, he touched his lips to hers again. "Well, I do." Linking his hand with hers, he walked to the door.

The restaurant was French, subdued and very exclusive. The pale flowered walls glowed in the quiet light and the flicker of candles. Diners murmured their private conversations over linen cloths and crystal stemware. The hustle and bustle of the streets were shut out by beveled glass doors.

"Ah, Monsieur Dempsey, we haven't seen you in some time." The maitre d' stepped forward to greet him.

"You know I always come back for your snails."

With a laugh, the maitre d' waved a waiter aside. "Good evening, *mademoiselle*. I'll take you to your table."

The little booth was candlelit and secluded, a place for hand-holding and intimate secrets. Hester's leg brushed Mitch's as they settled.

"The sommelier will be right with you. Enjoy your evening."

"No need to ask if you've been here before."

"From time to time I get tired of frozen pizza. Would you like champagne?"

"I'd love it."

He ordered a bottle, pleasing the wine steward with the vintage. Hester opened her menu and sighed over the elegant foods. "I'm going to remember this the next time I'm biting into half a tuna sandwich between appointments."

"You like your job?"

"Very much." She wondered if *soufflé de crabe* was what it sounded like. "Rosen can be a pain, but he does push you to be efficient."

"And you like being efficient."

"It's important to me."

"What else is, other than Rad?"

"Security." She looked over at him with a half smile. "I suppose that has to do with Rad. The truth is, anything that's been important to me over the last few years has to do with Rad."

She glanced up as the steward brought the wine and began his routine for Mitch's approval. Hester watched the wine rise in her fluted glass, pale gold and frothy. "To Rad, then," Mitch said as he lifted his glass to touch hers. "And his fascinating mother."

Hester sipped, a bit stunned that anything could taste so good. She'd had champagne before, but like everything that had to do with Mitch, it hadn't been quite like this. "I've never considered myself fascinating."

"A beautiful woman raising a boy on her own in one of the toughest cities in the world fascinates me." He sipped and grinned. "Added to that, you do have terrific legs, Hester."

She laughed, and even when he slipped his hand over hers, felt no embarrassment. "So you said before. They're long, anyway. I was taller than my brother until he was out of high school. It infuriated him, and I had to live down the name Stretch."

"Mine was String."

"String?"

"You know those pictures of the eighty-pound weakling? That was me."

Over the rim of her glass, Hester studied the way he filled out the suit jacket. "I don't believe it."

"One day, if I'm drunk enough, I'll show you pictures."

Mitch ordered in flawless French that had Hester staring. This was the comic-book writer, she thought, who built snow forts and talked to his dog. Catching the look, Mitch lifted a brow. "I spent a couple of summers in Paris during high school."

"Oh." It reminded her forcefully where he'd come from. "You said you didn't have any brothers or sisters. Do your parents live in New York?"

"No." He broke off a hunk of crusty French bread. "My mother zips in from time to time to shop or go to the theater, and my father might come in occasionally

on business, but New York isn't their style. They still
live most of the year in Newport, where I grew up."

"Oh, Newport. We drove through once when I was
a kid. We'd always take these rambling car vacations in
the summer." She tucked her hair behind her ear in an
unconscious gesture that gave him a tantalizing view of
her throat. "I remember the houses, the enormous man-
sions with the pillars and flowers and ornamental trees.
We even took pictures. It was hard to believe anyone
really lived there." Then she caught herself up abruptly
and glanced over at Mitch's amused face. "You did."

"It's funny. I spent some time with binoculars watching the tourists in the summer. I might have homed in
on your family."

"We were the ones in the station wagon with the
suitcases strapped to the roof."

"Sure, I remember you." He offered her a piece of
bread. "I envied you a great deal."

"Really?" She paused with her butter knife in mid-
air. "Why?"

"Because you were going on vacation and eating hot
dogs. You were staying in motels with soda machines
outside the door and playing car bingo between cities."

"Yes," she murmured. "I suppose that sums it up."

"I'm not pulling poor-little-rich boy," he added when
he saw the change in her eyes. "I'm just saying that having a big house isn't necessarily better than having a
station wagon." He added more wine to her glass. "In
any case, I finished my rebellious money-is-beneath-
me stage a long time ago."

"I don't know if I can believe that from someone who
lets dust collect on his Louis Quinze."

"That's not rebellion, that's laziness."

"Not to mention sinful," she put in. "It makes me itch for a polishing cloth and lemon oil."

"Any time you want to rub my mahogany, feel free."

She lifted a brow when he smiled at her. "So what did you do during your rebellious stage?"

Her fingertips grazed his. It was one of the few times she'd touched him without coaxing. Mitch lifted his gaze from their hands to her face. "You really want to know?"

"Yes."

"Then we'll make a deal. One slightly abridged life story for another."

It wasn't the wine that was making her reckless, Hester knew, but him. "All right. Yours first."

"We'll start off by saying my parents wanted me to be an architect. It was the only practical and acceptable profession they could see me using my drawing abilities for. The stories I made up didn't really appall them, they merely baffled them—so they were easily ignored. Straight out of high school, I decided to sacrifice my life to art."

Their appetizers were served. Mitch sighed approvingly over his escargots.

"So you came to New York?"

"No, New Orleans. At that time my money was still in trusts, though I doubt I would have used it, in any case. Since I refused to use my parents' financial backing, New Orleans was as close to Paris as I could afford to get. God, I loved it. I starved, but I loved the city. Those dripping, steamy afternoons, the smell of the river. It was my first great adventure. Want one of these? They're incredible."

"No, I—"

"Come on, you'll thank me." He lifted his fork to her lips. Reluctantly, Hester parted them and accepted.

"Oh." The flavor streamed, warm and exotic, over her tongue. "It's not what I expected."

"The best things usually aren't."

She lifted her glass and wondered what Radley's reaction would be when she told him she'd eaten a snail. "So what did you do in New Orleans?"

"I set up an easel in Jackson Square and made my living sketching tourists and selling watercolors. For three years I lived in one room where I baked in the summer and froze in the winter and considered myself one lucky guy."

"What happened?"

"There was a woman. I thought I was crazy about her and vice versa. She modeled for me when I was going through my Matisse period. You should have seen me then. My hair was about your length, and I wore it pulled back and fastened with a leather thong. I even had a gold earring in my left ear."

"You wore an earring?"

"Don't smirk, they're very fashionable now. I was ahead of my time." Appetizers were cleared away to make room for green salads. "Anyway, we were going to play house in my miserable little room. One night, when I'd had a little too much wine, I told her about my parents and how they'd never understood my artistic drive. She got absolutely furious."

"She was angry with your parents?"

"You are sweet," he said unexpectedly, and kissed her hand. "No, she was angry with me. I was rich and hadn't told her. I had piles of money and expected her to be satisfied with one filthy little room in the Quarter where she had to cook red beans and rice on a hot plate. The funny thing was she really cared for me when she'd thought I was poor, but when she found out I wasn't, and that I didn't intend to use what was available to me—and, by association, to her—she was infuriated. We had one hell of a fight, where she let me know what she really thought of me and my work."

Hester could picture him, young, idealistic and struggling. "People say things they don't mean when they're angry."

He lifted her hand and kissed her fingers. "Yes, very sweet." His hand remained on hers as he continued. "Anyway, she left and gave me the opportunity to take stock of myself. For three years I'd been living day to day, telling myself I was a great artist whose time was coming. The truth was I wasn't a great artist. I was a clever one, but I'd never be a great one. So I left New Orleans for New York and commercial art. I was good. I worked fast tucked in my little cubicle and generally made the client happy—and I was miserable. But my credentials there got me a spot at Universal, originally as an inker, then as an artist. And then—" he lifted his glass in salute "—there was Zark. The rest is history."

"You're happy." She turned her hand under his so their palms met. "It shows. Not everyone is as content with themselves as you are, as at ease with himself and what he does."

"It took me awhile."

"And your parents? Have you reconciled with them?"

"We came to the mutual understanding that we'd never understand each other. But we're family. I have my stock portfolio, so they can tell their friends the comic-book business is something that amuses me. Which is true enough."

Mitch ordered another bottle of champagne with the main course. "Now it's your turn."

She smiled and let the delicate soufflé melt on her tongue. "Oh, I don't have anything so exotic as an artist's garret in New Orleans. I had a very average childhood with a very average family. Board games on Saturday nights, pot roast on Sundays. Dad had a good job, Mom stayed home and kept the house. We loved each other very much, but didn't always get along. My sister was very outgoing, head cheerleader, that sort of thing. I was miserably shy."

"You're still shy," Mitch murmured as he wound his fingers around hers.

"I didn't think it showed."

"In a very appealing way. What about Rad's father?" He felt her hand stiffen in his. "I've wanted to ask, Hester, but we don't have to talk about it now if it upsets you."

She drew her hand from his to reach for her glass. The champagne was cold and crisp. "It was a long time ago. We met in high school. Radley looks a great deal like his father, so you can understand that he was very attractive. He was also just a little wild, and I found that magnetic."

She moved her shoulders a little, restlessly, but was determined to finish what she'd started. "I really was painfully shy and a bit withdrawn, so he seemed like something exciting to me, even a little larger than life. I fell desperately in love with him the first time he noticed me. It was as simple as that. In any case, we went together for two years and were married a few weeks after graduation. I wasn't quite eighteen and was absolutely sure that marriage was going to be one adventure after another."

"And it wasn't?" he asked when she paused.

"For a while it was. We were young, so it never seemed terribly important that Allan moved from one job to another, or quit altogether for weeks at a time. Once he sold the living room set that my parents had given us as a wedding present so that we could take a trip to Jamaica. It seemed impetuous and romantic, and at that time we didn't have any responsibilities except to ourselves. Then I got pregnant."

She paused again and, looking back, remembered her own excitement and wonder and fear at the idea of carrying a child. "I was thrilled. Allan got a tremendous kick out of it and started buying strollers and high chairs on credit. Money was tight, but we were optimistic, even when I had to cut down to part-time work toward the end of my pregnancy and then take maternity leave after Radley was born. He was beautiful." She laughed a little. "I know all mothers say that about their babies, but he was honestly the most beautiful, the most precious thing I'd ever seen. He changed my life. He didn't change Allan's."

She toyed with the stem of her glass and tried to work out in her mind what she hadn't allowed herself to think about for a very long time. "I couldn't understand it at the time, but Allan resented having the burden of responsibility. He hated it that we couldn't just stroll out of the apartment and go to the movies or go dancing whenever we chose. He was still unbelievably reckless with money, and because of Rad I had to compensate."

"In other words," Mitch said quietly, "you grew up."

"Yes." It surprised her that he saw that so quickly, and it relieved her that he seemed to understand. "Allan wanted to go back to the way things were, but we weren't children anymore. As I look back, I can see that he was jealous of Radley, but at the time I just wanted him to grow up, to be a father, to take charge. At twenty he was still the sixteen-year-old boy I'd known in high school, but I wasn't the same girl. I was a mother. I'd gone back to work because I'd thought the extra income would ease some of the strain. One day I'd come home after picking Radley up at the sitter's, and Allan was gone. He'd left a note saying he just couldn't handle being tied down any longer."

"Did you know he was leaving?"

"No, I honestly didn't. In all probability it was done on impulse, the way Allan did most things. It would never have occurred to him that it was desertion, to him it would've meant moving on. He thought he was being fair by taking only half the money, but he left all the bills. I had to get another part-time job in the evenings. I hated that, leaving Rad with a sitter and not seeing him. That six months was the worst time of my life."

Her eyes darkened a moment; then she shook her head and pushed it all back into the past. "After a while I'd straightened things out enough to quit the second job. About that time, Allan called. It was the first I'd heard from him since he'd left. He was very amiable, as if we'd been nothing more than passing acquaintances. He told me he was heading up to Alaska to work. After he hung up, I called a lawyer and got a very simple divorce."

"It must have been difficult for you." Difficult? he

thought—he couldn't even imagine what kind of hell it had been. "You could have gone home to your parents."

"No. I was angry for a long, long time. The anger made me determined to stay right here in New York and make it work for me and Radley. By the time the anger had died down, I was making it work."

"He's never come back to see Rad?"

"No, never."

"His loss." He cupped her chin, then leaned over to kiss her lightly. "His very great loss."

She found it easy to lift a hand to his cheek. "The same can be said about that woman in New Orleans."

"Thanks." He nibbled her lips again, enjoying the faint hint of champagne. "Dessert?"

"Hmmm?"

He felt a wild thrill of triumph at her soft, distracted sigh. "Let's skip it." Moving back only slightly, he signaled the waiter for the check, then handed Hester the last of the champagne. "I think we should walk awhile."

The air was biting, almost as exhilarating as the wine. Yet the wine warmed her, making her feel as though she could walk for miles without feeling the wind. She didn't object to Mitch's arm around her shoulders or to the fact that he set the direction. She didn't care where they walked as long as the feelings that stirred inside her didn't fade.

She knew what it was like to fall in love—to be in love. Time slowed down. Everything around you went quickly, but not in a blur. Colors were brighter, sounds sharper, and even in midwinter you could smell flowers. She had been there once before, had felt this intensely once before, but had thought she would never find that place again. Even as a part of her mind struggled to remind her that this couldn't be love—or certainly shouldn't be—she simply ignored it. Tonight she was just a woman.

There were skaters at Rockefeller Center, swirling around and around the ice as the music flowed. Hester watched them, tucked in the warmth of Mitch's arms. His cheek rested on her hair, and she could feel the strong, steady rhythm of his heart.

"Sometimes I bring Rad here on Sundays to skate or just to watch like this. It seems different tonight." She turned her head, and her lips were barely a whisper from his. "Everything seems different tonight."

If she looked at him like that again, Mitch knew he'd break his vow to give her enough time to clear her head and would bundle her into the nearest cab so that he could have her home and in bed before the look broke. Calling on willpower, he shifted her so he could brush his lips over her temple. "Things look different at night, especially after champagne." He relaxed again, her head against his shoulder. "It's a nice difference. Not necessarily steeped in reality, but nice. You can get enough reality from nine to five."

"Not you." Unaware of the tug-of-war she was causing inside him, she turned in his arms. "You make fantasies from nine to five, or whatever hours you choose."

"You should hear the one I'm making up now." He drew another deep breath. "Let's walk some more, and you can tell me about one of yours."

"A fantasy?" Her stride matched his easily. "Mine isn't nearly as earth-shaking as yours, I imagine. It's just a house."

"A house." He walked toward the Park, hoping they'd

both be a little steadier on their feet by the time they reached home. "What kind of house?"

"A country house, one of those big old farmhouses with shutters at the windows and porches all around. Lots of windows so you could look at the woods—there would have to be woods. Inside there would be high ceilings and big fireplaces. Outside would be a garden with wisteria climbing on a trellis." She felt the sting of winter on her cheeks, but could almost smell the summer.

"You'd be able to hear the bees hum in it all summer long. There'd be a big yard for Radley, and he could have a dog. I'd have a swing on the porch so I could sit outside in the evening and watch him catch lightning bugs in a jar." She laughed and let her head rest on his shoulder. "I told you it wasn't earth-shaking."

"I like it." He liked it so well he could picture it, white shuttered and hip roofed, with a barn off in the distance. "But you need a stream so Rad could fish."

She closed her eyes a moment, then shook her head. "As much as I love him, I don't think I could bait a hook. Build a tree house maybe, or throw a curveball, but no worms."

"You throw a curveball?"

She tilted her head and smiled. "Right in the strike zone. I helped coach Little League last year."

"The woman's full of surprises. You wear shorts in the dugout?"

"You're obsessed with my legs."

"For a start."

He steered her into their building and toward the elevators. "I haven't had an evening like this in a very long time."

"Neither have I."

She drew back far enough to study him as they began the ride to her floor. "I've wondered about that, about the fact that you don't seem to be involved with anyone."

He touched her chin with his fingertip. "Aren't I?"

She heard the warning signal, but wasn't quite sure what to do about it. "I mean, I haven't noticed you dating or spending any time with women."

Amused, he flicked the finger down her throat. "Do I look like a monk?"

"No." Embarrassed and more than a little unsettled, she looked away. "No, of course not."

"The fact is, Hester, after you've had your share of wild oats, you lose your taste for them. Spending time with a woman just because you don't want to be alone isn't very satisfying."

"From the stories I hear around the office from the single women, there are plenty of men who disagree with you."

He shrugged as they stepped off the elevator. "It's obvious you haven't played the singles scene." Her brows drew together as she dug for her key. "That was a compliment, but my point is it gets to be a strain or a bore—"

"And this is the age of the meaningful relationship."

"You say that like a cynic. Terribly uncharacteristic, Hester." He leaned against the jamb as she opened the door. "In any case, I'm not big on catchphrases. Are you going to ask me in?"

She hesitated. The walk had cleared her head enough for the doubts to seep through. But along with the doubts was the echo of the way she'd felt when they'd stood together in the cold. The echo was stronger. "All right. Would you like some coffee?"

"No." He shrugged out of his coat as he watched her.

"It's no trouble. It'll only take a minute."

He caught her hands. "I don't want coffee, Hester. I want you." He slipped her coat from her shoulders. "And I want you so bad it makes me jumpy."

She didn't back away, but stood, waiting. "I don't know what to say. I'm out of practice."

"I know." For the first time his own nerves were evident as he dragged a hand through his hair. "That's given me some bad moments. I don't want to seduce you." Then he laughed and walked a few paces away. "The hell I don't."

"I knew—I tried to tell myself I didn't, but I knew when I went out with you tonight that we'd come back here like this." She pressed a hand to her stomach, surprised that it was tied in knots. "I think I was hoping you'd just sort of sweep me away so I wouldn't have to make a decision."

He turned to her. "That's a cop-out, Hester."

"I know." She couldn't look at him then, wasn't certain she dared. "I've never been with anyone but Rad's father. The truth is, I've never wanted to be."

"And now?" He only wanted a word, one word.

She pressed her lips together. "It's been so long, Mitch. I'm frightened."

"Would it help if I told you I am, too?"

"I don't know."

"Hester." He crossed to her to lay his hands on her shoulders. "Look at me." When she did, her eyes were wide and achingly clear. "I want you to be sure, because I don't want regrets in the morning. Tell me what you want."

It seemed her life was a series of decisions. There was no one to tell her which was right or which was wrong. As always, she reminded herself that once the decision was made, she alone would deal with the consequences and accept the responsibility.

"Stay with me tonight," she whispered. "I want you."

Chapter 8

He cupped her face in his hands and felt her tremble. He touched his lips to hers and heard her sigh. It was a moment he knew he would always remember. Her acceptance, her desire, her vulnerability.

The apartment was silent. He would have given her music. The scent of the roses she'd put in a vase was pale next to the fragrance of the garden he imagined for her. The lamp burned brightly. He wouldn't have chosen the secrets of the dark, but rather the mystery of candlelight.

How could he explain to her that there was nothing ordinary, nothing casual in what they were about to give each other? How could he make her understand that he had been waiting all his life for a moment like this? He wasn't certain he could choose the right words, or that the words he did choose would reach her.

So he would show her.

With his lips still lingering on hers, he swept her up into his arms. Though he heard her quick intake of breath, she wrapped her arms around him.

"Mitch—"

"I'm not much of a white knight." He looked at her, half smiling, half questioning. "But for tonight we can pretend."

He looked heroic and strong and incredibly, impossibly sweet. Whatever doubts had remained slipped quietly away. "I don't need a white knight."

"Tonight I need to give you one." He kissed her once more before he carried her into the bedroom.

There was a part of him that needed, ached with that need, so much so that he wanted to lay her down on the bed and cover her with his body. There were times that love ran swiftly, even violently. He understood that and knew that she would, too. But he set her down on the floor beside the bed and touched only her hand.

He drew away just a little. "The light."

"But—"

"I want to see you, Hester."

It was foolish to be shy. It was wrong, she knew, to want to have this moment pass in the dark, anonymously. She reached for the bedside lamp and turned the switch.

The light bathed them, capturing them both standing hand in hand and eye to eye. The quick panic returned, pounding in her head and her heart. Then he touched her and quieted it. He drew off her earrings and set them on the bedside table so that the metal clicked quietly against the wood. She felt a rush of heat, as though with that one simple, intimate move he had already undressed her.

He reached for her belt, then paused when her hands fluttered nervously to his. "I won't hurt you."

"No." She believed him and let her hands drop away. He unhooked her belt to let it slide to the floor. When he lowered his lips to hers again, she slipped her arms around his waist and let the power guide her.

This was what she wanted. She couldn't lie to herself or make excuses. For tonight, she wanted to think only as a woman, to be thought of only as a woman. To be desired, enjoyed, wondered over. When their lips parted, their eyes met. And she smiled.

"I've been waiting for that." He touched a finger to her lips, overcome with a pleasure that was so purely emotional even he couldn't describe it.

"For what?"

"For you to smile at me when I kiss you." He brought his hand to her face. "Let's try it again."

This time the kiss went deeper, edging closer to those uncharted territories. She lifted her hands to his shoulders, then slid them around to encircle his neck. He felt her fingers touch the skin there, shyly at first, then with more confidence.

"Still afraid?"

"No." Then she smiled again. "Yes, a little. I'm not—" She looked away, and he once more brought her face back to his.

"What?"

"I'm not sure what to do. What you like."

He wasn't stunned by her words so much as humbled. He'd said he'd cared for her, and that was true. But now his heart, which had been teetering on the edge, fell over into love.

"Hester, you leave me speechless." He drew her against him, hard, and just held her there. "Tonight, just do what seems right. I think we'll be fine."

He began by kissing her hair, drawing in the scent that had so appealed to him. The mood was already set, seduction on either side unnecessary. He felt her heart begin to race against his; then she turned her head and found his lips with her own.

His hands weren't steady as he drew down the long zipper at her back. He knew it was an imperfect world, but needed badly to give her one perfect night. No one would ever have called him a selfish man, but it was a fact that he'd never before put someone else's needs so entirely before his own.

He drew the wool from her shoulders, down her arms. She wore a simple chemise beneath it, plain white without frills or lace. No fantasy of silk or satin could have excited him more.

"You're lovely." He pressed a kiss to one shoulder, then the other. "Absolutely lovely."

She wanted to be. It had been so long since she'd felt the need to be any more than presentable. When she saw his eyes, she felt lovely. Gathering her courage together, she began to undress him in turn.

He knew it wasn't easy for her. She drew his jacket off, then began to unknot his tie before she was able to lift her gaze to his again. He could feel her fingers tremble lightly against him as she unbuttoned his shirt.

"You're lovely, too," she murmured. The last, the only man she had ever touched this way had been little more than a boy. Mitch's muscles were subtle but hard, and though his chest was smooth, it was that of a man. Her movements were slow, from shyness rather than a knowledge of arousal. His stomach muscles quivered as she reached for the hook of his slacks.

"You're driving me crazy."

She drew her hands back automatically. "I'm sorry."

"No." He tried to laugh, but it sounded like a groan. "I like it."

Her fingers trembled all the more as she slid his slacks over his hips. Lean hips, with the muscles long and hard. She felt a surge that was both fascination and delight as she brought her hands to them. Then she was against him, and the shock of flesh against flesh vibrated through her.

He was fighting every instinct that pushed him to move quickly, to take quickly. Her shy hands and wondering eyes had taken him to the brink and he had to claw his way back. She sensed a war going on inside him, felt the rigidity of his muscles and heard the raggedness of his breathing.

"Mitch?"

"Just a minute." He buried his face in her hair. The battle for control was hard won. He felt weakened by it, weakened and stunned. When he found the soft, sensitive skin of her neck, he concentrated on that alone.

She strained against him, turning her head instinctively to give him freer access. It seemed as though a veil had floated down over her eyes so that the room, which had become so familiar to her, was hazy. She could feel her blood begin to pound where his lips rubbed and nibbled; then it was throbbing hot, close to the skin, softening it, sensitizing it. Her moan sounded primitive in her own ears. Then it was she who was drawing him down to the bed.

He'd wanted another minute before he let his body spread over hers. There were explosions bombarding his system, from head to heart to loins. He knew he had to calm them before they shattered his senses. But her hands were moving over him, her hips straining upward. With an effort, Mitch rolled so that they were side by side.

He brought his lips down on her, and for a moment all the needs, the fantasies, the darker desires centered there. Her mouth was moist and hot, pounding into his brain how she would be when he filled her. He was already dragging the thin barrier of her chemise aside so that she gasped when her breasts met him unencumbered. As his lips closed over the first firm point, he heard her cry out his name.

This was abandonment. She'd been sure she'd never wanted it, but now, as her body went fluid in her movements against his, she thought she might never want anything else. The feelings of flesh against flesh, growing hot and damp, were new and exhilarating. As were the avid seeking of mouths and the tastes they found and drew in. His murmurs to her were hot and incoherent, but she responded. The light played over his hands as he showed her how a touch could make the soul soar.

She was naked, but the shyness was gone. She wanted him to touch and taste and look his fill, just as she was driven to. His body was a fascination of muscle and taut skin. She hadn't known until now that to touch another, to please another, could bring on such wild waves of passion. He cupped a hand over her, and the passion contracted into a ball of flame in her center that abruptly, almost violently, burst. Gasping for breath, she reached for him.

He'd never had a woman respond so utterly. Watching her rise and peak had given him a delirious thrust of pleasure. He wanted badly to take her up and over again and again, until she was limp and mindless. But his control was slipping, and she was calling for him.

His body covered hers, and he filled her.

He couldn't have said how long they moved together—minutes, hours. But he would never forget how her eyes had opened and stared into his.

He was a little shaken as he lay with her on top of the crumpled spread with drops of freezing rain striking the windows. He turned his head toward the hiss and wondered idly how long it had been going on. As far as he could remember, he'd never been so involved with a woman that the outside world, and all its sights and sounds, had simply ceased to exist.

He turned away again and drew Hester against him. His body was cooling rapidly, but he had no desire to move. "You're quiet," he murmured.

Her eyes were closed. She wasn't ready to open them again. "I don't know what to say."

"How about 'Wow'?"

She was surprised she could laugh after such intensity. "Okay. Wow."

"Try for more enthusiasm. How about 'Fantastic, incredible, earth-shattering'?"

She opened her eyes now and looked into his. "How about beautiful?"

He caught her hand in his and kissed it. "Yeah, that'll do." When he propped himself up on his elbow to look down at her, she shifted. "Too late to be shy now," he told her. Then he ran a hand, light and possessively, down her body. "You know, I was right about your legs. I don't suppose I could talk you into putting on a pair of shorts and those little socks that stop at the ankles."

"I beg your pardon?"

Her tone had him gathering her to him and covering her face with kisses. "I have a thing about long legs in shorts and socks. I drive myself crazy watching women jog in the park in the summer. When they color-coordinate them, I'm finished."

"You're crazy."

"Come on, Hester, don't you have some secret turn-on? Men in muscle shirts, in tuxedos with black tie and studs undone?"

"Don't be silly."

"Why not?"

Why not, indeed, she thought, catching her bottom lip between her teeth. "Well, there is something about jeans riding low on the hips with the snap undone."

"I'll never snap my jeans again as long as I live."

She laughed again. "That doesn't mean I'm going to start wearing shorts and socks."

"That's okay. I get excited when I see you in a business suit."

"You do not."

"Oh, yes, I do." He rolled her on top of him and began to play with her hair. "Those slim lapels and high-collar blouses. And you always wear your hair up." With it caught in his hands, he lifted it on top of her head. It wasn't the same look at all, but one that still succeeded in making his mouth dry. "The efficient and dependable Mrs. Wallace. Every time I see you dressed that way I imagine how fascinating it would be to peel off those professional clothes and take out those tidy little pins." He let her hair slide down through his fingers.

Thoughtful, Hester rested her cheek against his cheek. "You're a strange man, Mitch."

"More than likely."

"You depend so much on your imagination, on what it might be, on fantasies and make-believe. With me it's facts and figures, profit and loss, what is or what isn't."

"Are you talking about our jobs or our personalities?"

"Isn't one really the same as the other?"

"No. I'm not Commander Zark, Hester."

She shifted, lulled by the rhythm of his heart. "I suppose what I mean is that the artist in you, the writer in you, thrives on imagination or possibilities. I guess the banker in me looks for checks and balances."

He was silent for a moment, stroking her hair. Didn't she realize how much more there was to her? This was the woman who fantasized about a home in the country, the one who threw a curveball, the one who had just taken a man of flesh and blood and turned him into a puddle of need.

"I don't want to get overly philosophical, but why do you think you chose to deal with loans? Do you get the same feeling when you turn down an application as you do when you approve one?"

"No, of course not."

"Of course not," he repeated. "Because when you approve one, you've had a hand in the possibilities. I have no doubt that you play by the book, that's part of your charm, but I'd wager you get a great deal of personal satisfaction by being able to say, 'Okay, buy your home, start your business, expand.'"

She lifted her head. "You seem to understand me very well." No one else had, she realized with a jolt. Ever.

"I've been giving you a great deal of thought." He drew her to him, wondering if she could feel how well their bodies fit. "A very great deal. In fact, I haven't thought about another woman since I delivered your pizza."

She smiled at that, and would have settled against him again, but he held her back. "Hester..." It was one of the few times in his life he'd ever felt self-conscious. She was looking at him expectantly, even patiently, while he struggled for the right words. "The thing is, I don't want to think about another woman, or be with another woman—this way." He struggled again, then swore. "Damn, I feel like I'm back in high school."

Her smile was cautious. "Are you going to ask me to go steady?"

It wasn't exactly what he'd had in mind, but he could see by the look in her eyes that he'd better go slowly. "I could probably find my class ring if you want."

She looked down at her hand, which was resting so naturally on his heart. Was it foolish to be so moved? If not, it was certainly dangerous. "Maybe we can just leave it that there's no one else I want to be with this way, either."

He started to speak, then stopped himself. She needed time to be sure that was true, didn't she? There had only been one other man in her life, and she'd been no more than a girl then. To be fair, he had to give her room to be certain. But he didn't want to be fair. No, Mitch Dempsey was no self-sacrificing Commander Zark.

"All right." He'd devised and won enough wars to

know how to plan strategy. He'd win Hester before she realized there'd been a battle.

Drawing her down to him, he closed his mouth over hers and began the first siege.

It was an odd and rather wonderful feeling to wake up in the morning beside a lover—even one who nudged you over to the edge of the mattress. Hester opened her eyes and, lying very still, savored it.

His face was buried against the back of her neck, and his arm was wrapped tightly around her waist—which was fortunate, as without it she would have rolled onto the floor. Hester shifted slightly and experienced the arousing sensation of having her sleep-warmed skin rub cozily against his.

She'd never had a lover. A husband, yes, but her wedding night, her first initiation into womanhood, had been nothing like the night she'd just shared with Mitch. Was it fair to compare them? she wondered. Would she be human if she didn't?

That first night so long ago had been frenzied, complicated by her nerves and her husband's hurry. Last night the passion had built layer by layer, as though there'd been all the time in the world to enjoy it. She'd never known that making love could be so liberating. In truth, she hadn't known a man could sincerely want to give pleasure as much as he desired to take it.

She snuggled into the pillow and watched the thin winter light come through the windows. Would things be different this morning? Would there be an awkwardness between them or, worse, a casualness that would diminish the depth of what they'd shared? The simple fact was she didn't know what it was like to have a lover—or to be one.

She was putting too much emphasis on one evening, she told herself, sighing. How could she not, when the evening had been so special?

Hester touched a hand to his, let it linger a moment, then shifted to rise. Mitch's arm clamped down.

"Going somewhere?"

She tried to turn over, but discovered his legs had pinned her. "It's almost nine."

"So?" His fingers spread out lazily to stroke.

"I have to get up. I need to pick Rad up in a couple of hours."

"Hmmm." He watched his little dream bubble of a morning in bed with her deflate, then reconstructed it to fit two hours. "You feel so good." He released his hold, but only so he could turn her around so they were face-to-face. "Look good, too," he decided as he studied her face through half-closed eyes. "And taste—" he touched his lips to hers, and there was nothing awkward, nothing casual "—wonderful. Imagine this." He ran a hand down her flank. "We're on an island—the South Seas, let's say. The ship was wrecked a week ago, and we're the only survivors." His eyes closed as he pressed a kiss to her forehead. "We've been living on fruit and the fish I cleverly catch with my pointed stick."

"Who cleans them?"

"This is a fantasy, you don't worry about details like that. Last night there was a storm—a big, busting tropical storm—and we had to huddle together for warmth and safety under the lean-to I built."

"You built?" Her lips curved against his. "Do I do anything useful?"

"You can do all you want in your own fantasy. Now shut up." He snuggled closer and could almost smell the salt air. "It's morning, and the storm washed everything clean. There are gulls swooping down near the surf. We're lying together on an old blanket."

"Which you heroically salvaged from the wreck."

"Now you're catching on. When we wake up, we discover we'd tangled together during the night, drawn together despite ourselves. The sun's hot—it's already warmed our half-naked bodies. Still dazed with sleep, already aroused, we come together. And then..." His lips hovered a breath away from hers. Hester let her eyes close as she found herself caught up in the picture he painted. "And then a wild boar attacks, and I have to wrestle him."

"Half-naked and unarmed?"

"That's right. I'm badly bitten, but I kill him with my bare hands."

Hester opened her eyes again to narrow slits. "And while you're doing that, I put the blanket over my head and whimper."

"Okay." Mitch kissed the tip of her nose. "But afterward you're very, very grateful that I saved your life."

"Poor, defenseless female that I am."

"That's the ticket. You're so grateful you tear the rags of your skirt to make bandages for my wounds, and then..." He paused for impact. "You make me coffee."

Hester drew back, not certain whether to be amazed or amused. "You went through that whole scenario so I'd offer to make you coffee?"

"Not just coffee, morning coffee, the first cup of coffee. Life's blood."

"I'd have made it even without the story."

"Yeah, but did you like the story?"

She combed the hair away from her face as she considered. "Next time I get to catch the fish."

"Deal."

She rose and, though she knew it was foolish, wished that she'd had her robe within arm's reach. Going to the closet, she slipped it on with her back still to him. "Do you want some breakfast?"

He was sitting up, rubbing his hands over his face when she turned. "Breakfast? You mean likes eggs or something? Hot food?" The only time he managed a hot breakfast was when he had the energy to drag himself to the corner diner. "Mrs. Wallace, for a hot breakfast you can have the crown jewels of Perth."

"All that for bacon and eggs?"

"Bacon, too? God, what a woman."

She laughed, sure he was joking. "Go ahead and get a shower if you want. It won't take long."

He hadn't been joking. Mitch watched her walk from the room and shook his head. He didn't expect a woman to offer to cook for him, or for one to offer as though he had a right to expect it. But this, he remembered, was the woman who would have sewed patches on his jeans because she'd thought he couldn't afford new ones.

Mitch climbed out of bed, then slowly, thoughtfully ran a hand through his hair. The aloof and professional Hester Wallace was a very warm and special woman, and he had no intention of letting her get away.

She was stirring eggs in a skillet when he came into the kitchen. Bacon was draining on a rack, and coffee was already hot. He stood in the doorway a moment, more than a little surprised that such a simple domestic scene would affect him so strongly. Her robe was flannel and covered her from neck to ankle, but to him Hester had never looked more alluring. He hadn't realized he'd been looking for this—the morning smells, the morning sounds of the Sunday news on the radio on the counter, the morning sights of the woman who'd shared his night moving competently in the kitchen.

As a child, Sunday mornings had been almost formal affairs—brunch at eleven, served by a uniformed member of the staff. Orange juice in Waterford, shirred eggs on Wedgwood. He'd been taught to spread the Irish linen on his lap and make polite conversation. In later years, Sunday mornings had meant a bleary-eyed search through the cupboards or a dash down to the nearest diner.

He felt foolish, but he wanted to tell Hester that the simple meal at her kitchen counter meant as much to him as the long night in her bed. Crossing to her, he wrapped his arms around her waist and pressed a kiss to her neck.

Strange how a touch could speed up the heart rate and warm the blood. Absorbing the sensation, she leaned back against him. "It's almost done. You didn't say how you liked your eggs, so you've got them scrambled with a little dill and cheese."

She could have offered him cardboard and told him to eat it with a plastic fork. Mitch turned her to face him and kissed her long and hard. "Thanks."

He'd flustered her again. Hester turned to the eggs in time to prevent them from burning. "Why don't you sit down?" She poured coffee into a mug and handed it to him. "With your life's blood."

He finished half the mug before he sat. "Hester, you know what I said about your legs?"

She glanced over as she heaped eggs on a plate. "Yes?"

"Your coffee's almost as good as they are. Tremendous qualities in a woman."

"Thanks." She set the plate in front of him before moving to the toaster.

"Aren't you eating any of this?"

"No, just toast."

Mitch looked down at the pile of golden eggs and crisp bacon. "Hester, I didn't expect you to fix me all this when you aren't eating."

"It's all right." She arranged a stack of toast on a plate. "I do it for Rad all the time."

He covered her hand with his as she sat beside him. "I appreciate it."

"It's only a couple of eggs," she said, embarrassed. "You should eat them before they get cold."

"The woman's a marvel," Mitch commented as he obliged her. "She raises an interesting and well-balanced son, holds down a demanding job, and cooks." Mitch bit into a piece of bacon. "Want to get married?"

She laughed and added more coffee to both mugs. "If it only takes scrambled eggs to get you to propose, I'm surprised you don't have three or four wives hidden in the closet."

He hadn't been joking. She would have seen it in his eyes if she'd looked at him, but she was busy spreading butter on toast. Mitch watched her competent, ringless hands a moment. It had been a stupid way to propose and a useless way to make her see he was serious. It was also too soon, he admitted as he scooped up another forkful of eggs.

The trick would be first to get her used to having him around, then to have her trust him enough to believe he would stay around. Then there was the big one, he mused as he lifted his cup. She had to need him. She wouldn't ever need him for the roof over her head or the food in her cupboards. She was much too self-sufficient for that, and he admired it. In time, she might come to need him for emotional support and companionship. It would be a start.

The courting of Hester would have to be both complex and subtle. He wasn't certain he knew exactly how to go about it, but he was more than ready to start. Today was as good a time as any.

"Got any plans for later?"

"I've got to pick up Rad around noon." She lingered over her toast, realizing it had been years since she had shared adult company over breakfast and that it had an appeal all its own. "Then I promised that I'd take him and Josh to a matinee. *The Moon of Andromeda*."

"Yeah? Terrific movie. The special effects are tremendous."

"You've seen it?" She felt a twinge of disappointment. She'd been wondering if he might be willing to come along.

"Twice. There's a scene between the mad scientist and the sane scientist that'll knock you out. And there's this mutant that looks like a carp. Fantastic."

"A carp." Hester sipped her coffee. "Sounds wonderful."

"A cinematic treat for the eyes. Can I tag along?"

"You just said you've seen it twice already."

"So? The only movies I see once are dogs. Besides, I'd like to see Rad's reaction to the laser battle in deep space."

"Is it gory?"

"Nothing Rad can't handle."

"I wasn't asking for him."

With a laugh, Mitch took her hand. "I'll be there to protect you. How about it? I'll spring for the popcorn." He brought her hand up to his lips. "Buttered."

"How could I pass up a deal like that?"

"Good. Look, I'll give you a hand with the dishes, then I've got to go down and take Taz out before his bladder causes us both embarrassment."

"Go on ahead. There isn't that much, and Taz is probably moaning at the door by this time."

"Okay." He stood with her. "But next time I cook."

Hester gathered up the plates. "Peanut butter and jelly?"

"I can do better than that if it impresses you."

She smiled and reached for his empty mug. "You don't have to impress me."

He caught her face in his hands while she stood with her hands full of dishes. "Yes, I do." He nibbled at her lips, then abruptly deepened the kiss until they were both breathless. She was forced to swallow when he released her.

"That's a good start."

He was smiling as he brushed his lips over her forehead. "I'll be up in an hour."

Hester stood where she was until she heard the door close, then quietly set the dishes down again. How in the world had it happened? she wondered. She'd fallen in love with the man. He'd be gone only an hour, yet she wanted him back already.

Taking a deep breath, she sat down again. She had to keep herself from overreacting, from taking this, as she took too many other things, too seriously. He was fun, he was kind, but he wasn't permanent. There was nothing permanent but her and Radley. She'd promised herself years ago that she would never forget that again. Now, more than ever, she had to remember it.

In her eyes, she wanted to stay in his arms all of her life.
"You can't hurt me," he told her.

"I don't know about that," she whispered against his neck.
She knew it wasn't true. She knew he was the kind of
man that could take a woman's heart and break it. Every
little thing about him made her want to lose herself
forever. He'd let her climb into his arms and keep her
close, until she couldn't feel the hurt anymore.

Chapter 9

"Rich, you know I hate business discussions before noon."

Mitch sat in Skinner's office with Taz snoozing at his feet. Though it was after ten and he'd been up working for a couple of hours, he hadn't been ready to venture out and talk shop. He'd had to leave his characters on the drawing board in a hell of a predicament, and Mitch imagined they resented being left dangling as much as he resented leaving them.

"If you're going to give me a raise, that's fine by me, but you could've waited until after lunch."

"You're not getting a raise." Skinner ignored the phone that rang on his desk. "You're already overpaid."

"Well, if I'm fired, you could definitely have waited a couple of hours."

"You're not fired." Skinner drew his brows together

until they met above his nose. "But if you keep bringing that hound in here, I could change my mind."

"I made Taz my agent. Anything you say to me you can say in front of him."

Skinner sat back in his chair and folded hands that were swollen at the knuckles from years of nervous cracking. "You know, Dempsey, someone who didn't know you so well would think you were joking. The problem is, I happen to know you're crazy."

"That's why we get along so well, right? Listen, Rich, I've got Mirium trapped in a roomful of wounded rebels from Zirial. Being an empath, she's not feeling too good herself. Why don't we wrap this up so I can get back and take her to the crisis point?"

"Rebels from Zirial," Skinner mused. "You aren't thinking of bringing back Nimrod the Sorceror?"

"It's crossed my mind, and I could get back and figure out what he's got up his invisible sleeve if you'd tell me why you dragged me in here."

"You work here," Skinner pointed out.

"That's no excuse."

Skinner puffed out his cheeks and let the subject drop. "You know Two Moon Pictures has been negotiating with Universal for the rights to product Zark as a full-length film?"

"Sure. That's been going on a year, a year and a half now." Since the wheeling and dealing didn't interest him, Mitch stretched out a leg and began to massage Taz's flank with his foot. "The last thing you told me was that the alfalfa sprouts from L.A. couldn't get out of their hot tubs long enough to close the deal." Mitch grinned. "You've got a real way with words, Rich."

"The deal closed yesterday," Rich said flatly. "Two Moon wants to go with Zark."

Mitch's grin faded. "You're serious?"

"I'm always serious," Rich said, studying Mitch's reaction. "I thought you'd be a little more enthusiastic. Your baby's going to be a movie star."

"To tell you the truth, I don't know how I feel." Pushing himself out of the chair, Mitch began to pace Rich's cramped office. As he passed the window, he pulled open the blinds to let in slants of hard winter light. "Zark's always been personal. I don't know how I feel about him going Hollywood."

"You got a kick out of when B.C. Toys made the dolls."

"Action figures," Mitch corrected automatically. "I guess that's because they stayed pretty true to the theme." It was silly, he knew. Zark didn't belong to him. He'd created him, true, but Zark belonged to Universal, just like all the other heroes and villains of the staff's fertile imaginations. If, like Maloney, Mitch decided to move on, Zark would stay behind, the responsibility of someone else's imagination. "Did we retain any creative leeway?"

"Afraid they're going to exploit your firstborn?"

"Maybe."

"Listen, Two Moon bought the rights to Zark because he has potential at the box office—the way he is. It wouldn't be smart businesswise to change him. Let's look at the bottom line—comics are big business. A hundred and thirty million a year isn't something to shrug off. The business is thriving now the way it hasn't since the forties, and even though it's bound to level off, it's going to stay hot. Those jokers on the coast might dress funny, but they know a winner when they see one. Still, if you're worried, you could take their offer."

"What offer?"

"They want you to write the screenplay."

Mitch stopped where he was. "Me? I don't write movies."

"You write Zark—apparently that's enough for the producers. Our publishers aren't stupid, either. Stingy," he added with a glance at his worn linoleum, "but not stupid. They wanted the script to come from in-house, and there's a clause in the contract that says we have a shot. Two Moon agreed to accept a treatment from you first. If it doesn't pan out, they still want you on the project as a creative consultant."

"Creative consultant." Mitch rolled the title around on his tongue.

"If I were you, Dempsey, I'd get myself a two-legged agent."

"I just might. Look, I'm going to have to think about it. How long are they giving me?"

"Nobody mentioned a time frame. I don't think the possibility of your saying no occurred to them. But then, they don't know you like I do."

"I need a couple of days. There's someone I have to talk to."

Skinner waited until he'd started out. "Mitch, opportunity doesn't often kick down your door this way."

"Just let me make sure I'm at home first. I'll be in touch."

When it rains it pours, Mitch thought as he and Taz walked. It had started off as a fairly normal, even ordinary new year. He'd planned to dig his heels in a bit and get ahead of schedule so that he could take three or four weeks off to ski, drink brandy and kick up some snow on his uncle's farm. He'd figured on meeting one or two attractive women on the slopes to make the evenings interesting. He'd thought to sketch a little, sleep a lot and cruise the lodges. Very simple.

Then, within weeks, everything had changed. In Hester he'd found everything he'd ever wanted in his personal life, but he'd only begun to convince her that he was everything she'd ever wanted in hers. Now he was being offered one of the biggest opportunities of his professional life, but he couldn't think of one without considering the other.

In truth, he'd never been able to draw a hard line of demarcation between his professional and personal lives. He was the same man whether he was having a couple of drinks with friends or burning the midnight oil with Zark. If he'd changed at all, it had been Hester and Radley who had caused it. Since he'd fallen for them, he wanted the strings he'd always avoided, the responsibilities he'd always blithely shrugged off.

So he went to her first.

Mitch strolled into the bank with his ears tingling from the cold. The long walk had given him time to think through everything Skinner had told him, and to feel the first twinges of excitement. Zark, in Technicolor, in stereophonic sound, in Panavision.

Mitch stopped at Kay's desk. "She had lunch yet?"

Kay rolled back from her terminal. "Nope."

"Anybody with her now?"

"Not a soul."

"Good. When's her next appointment?"

Kay ran her finger down the appointment book. "Two-fifteen."

"She'll be back. If Rosen stops by, tell him I took Mrs. Wallace to lunch to discuss some refinancing."

"Yes, sir."

She was working on a long column of figures when Mitch opened the door. She moved her fingers quickly over the adding machine, which clicked as it spewed out a stream of tape. "Kay, I'm going to need Lorimar's construction estimate. And would you mind ordering me a sandwich? Anything as long as it's quick. I'd like to have these figures upstairs by the end of the day. Oh, and I'll need the barter exchange transactions on the Duberry account. Look up the 1099."

Mitch shut the door at his back. "God, all this bank talk excites me."

"Mitch." Hester glanced up with the last of the figures still rolling through her head. "What are you doing here?"

"Breaking you out, and we have to move fast. Taz'll distract the guards." He was already taking her coat from the rack behind the door. "Let's go. Just keep your head down and look natural."

"Mitch, I've got—"

"To eat Chinese take-out and make love with me. In whatever order you like. Here, button up."

"I've only half-finished with these figures."

"They won't run away." He buttoned her coat, then closed his hands over her collar. "Hester, do you know how long it's been since we had an hour alone? Four days."

"I know. I'm sorry, things have been busy."

"Busy." He nodded toward her desk. "No one's going to argue with you there, but you've also been holding me off."

"No, I haven't." The truth was she'd been holding herself off, trying to prove to herself that she didn't need him as badly as it seemed. It hadn't been working as well as she'd hoped. There was tangible proof of that now as she stood facing him with her heart beating fast. "Mitch, I explained how I felt about...being with you with Radley in the apartment."

"And I'm not arguing that point, either." Though he would have liked to. "But Rad's in school and you have a constitutional right to a lunch hour. Come with me, Hester." He let his brow rest on hers. "I need you."

She couldn't resist or refuse or pretend she didn't want to be with him. Knowing she might regret it later, she turned her back on her work. "I'd settle for a peanut butter and jelly. I'm not very hungry."

"You got it."

Fifteen minutes later, they were walking into Mitch's apartment. As usual, his curtains were open wide so that the sun poured through. It was warm, Hester thought as she slipped out of her coat. She imagined he kept the thermostat up so that he could be comfortable in his bare feet and short-sleeved sweatshirts. Hester stood with her coat in her hands and wondered what to do next.

"Here, let me take that." Mitch tossed her coat carelessly over a chair. "Nice suit, Mrs. Wallace," he murmured, fingering the lapel of the dark blue pin-stripe.

She put a hand over his, once again afraid that things were moving too fast. "I feel..."

"Decadent?"

Once again, it was the humor in his eyes that relaxed her. "More like I've just climbed out my bedroom window at midnight."

"Did you ever?"

"No. I thought about it a lot, but I could never figure out what I was supposed to do once I climbed down."

"That's why I'm nuts about you." He kissed her cautious smile and felt her lips soften and give under his. "Climb out the bedroom window to me, Hester. I'll show you what to do." Then his hands were in her hair, and her control scattered as quickly as the pins.

She wanted him. Perhaps it had a great deal to do with madness, but oh, how she wanted him. In the long nights since they'd been together like this, she'd thought of him, of how he touched her, where he touched her, and now his hands were there, just as she remembered. This time she moved faster than he, pulling his sweater up over his head to feast on the warm, taut flesh beneath. Her teeth nipped into his lip, insisting, inciting, until he was dragging the jacket from her and fumbling with the buttons that ranged down the back of her blouse.

His touch wasn't as gentle when he found her, nor was he as patient. But she had long since thrown caution aside. Now, pressed hard against him, she gripped passion with both hands. Whether it was day or night no longer mattered. She was where she wanted to be, where, no matter how she struggled to pretend otherwise, she needed to be.

Madness, yes, it was madness. She wondered how she'd lived so long without it.

He unfastened her skirt so that it flowed over her hips and onto the floor. With a groan of satisfaction he pressed his mouth to her throat. Four days? Had it only been four days? It seemed like years since he had had her close and alone. She was as hot and as desperate against him as he'd dreamed she would be. He could savor the feel of her even as desire clamped inside his gut and swam in his head. He wanted to spend hours touching, being touched, but the intensity of the moment, the lack of time and her urgent murmurs made it impossible.

"The bedroom," she managed as he pulled the thin straps of her lingerie over her shoulders.

"No, here. Right here." He fastened his mouth on hers and pulled her to the floor.

He would have given her more. Even though his own system was straining toward the breaking point, he would have given her more, but she was wrapped around him. Before he could catch his breath, her hands were on his hips, guiding her to him. She dug her fingers into his flesh as she murmured his name, and whole galaxies seemed to explode inside his head.

When she could think again, Hester stared at the dust motes that danced in a beam of sunlight. She was lying on a priceless Aubusson with Mitch's head pillowed between her breasts. It was the middle of the day, she had a pile of paperwork on her desk, and she'd just spent the better part of her lunch making love on the floor. She couldn't remember ever being more content.

She hadn't known life could be like this—an adventure, a carnival. For years she hadn't believed there was room for the madness of love and lovemaking in a world that revolved around responsibilities. Now, just now, she was beginning to realize she could have both. For how long, she couldn't be sure. Perhaps one day would be enough. She combed her fingers through his hair.

"I'm glad you came to take me to lunch."

"If this is any indication, we're going to have to make it a habit. Still want that sandwich?"

"Uh-uh. I don't need anything." But you. Hester sighed, realizing she was going to have to accept that. "I'm going to have to get back."

"You don't have an appointment until after two. I checked. Your barter exchange transactions can wait a few more minutes, can't they?"

"I suppose."

"Come on." He was up and pulling her to her feet.

"Where?"

"We'll have a quick shower, then I need to talk to you."

Hester accepted his offer of a robe and tried not to worry about what he had to say. She understood Mitch well enough to know he was full of surprises. The trouble was, she wasn't certain she was ready for another. Shoulders tense, she sat beside him on the couch and waited.

"You look like you're waiting for the blindfold and your last cigarette."

Hester shook back her still damp hair and tried to smile. "No, it's just that you sounded so serious."

"I've told you before, I have my serious moments." He shoved magazines off the table with his foot. "I had some news today, and I haven't decided how I feel about it. I wanted to see what you thought."

"Your family?" she began, instantly concerned.

"No." He took her hand. "I guess I'm making it sound like bad news, and it's not. At least I don't think it is. A production company in Hollywood just cut a deal with Universal to make a movie out of Zark."

Hester stared at him a moment, then blinked. "A

movie. Well, that's wonderful. Isn't it? I mean, I know he's very popular in comics, but a movie would be even bigger. You should be thrilled, and very proud that your work can translate that way."

"I just don't know if they can pull it off, if they can bring him to the screen with the right tone, the right emotion. Don't look at me that way."

"Mitch, I know how you feel about Zark. At least I think I do. He's your creation, and he's important to you."

"He's real to me," Mitch corrected. "Up here," he said, tapping his temple. "And, as corny as it might sound, in here." He touched a hand to his heart. "He made a difference in my life, made a difference in how I looked at myself and my work. I don't want to see them screw him up and make him into some cardboard hero or, worse, into something infallible and perfect."

Hester was silent a moment. She began to understand that giving birth to an idea might be as life-altering as giving birth to a child. "Let me ask you something: why did you create him?"

"I wanted to make a hero—a very human one—with flaws and vulnerabilities, and I guess with high standards. Someone kids could relate to because he was just flesh and blood, but powerful enough inside to fight back. Kids don't have a hell of a lot of choices, you know. I remember when I was young I wanted to be able to say 'no, I don't want to, I don't like that.' When I read, I could see there were possibilities, ways out. That's what I wanted Zark to be."

"Do you think you succeeded?"

"Yeah. On a personal level, I succeeded when I came up with the first issue. Professionally, Zark has pushed

Universal to the top. He translates into millions of dollars a year for the business."

"Do you resent that?"

"No, why should I?"

"Then you shouldn't resent seeing him take the next step."

Mitch fell silent, thinking. He might have known Hester would see things more clearly and be able to cut through everything to the most practical level. Wasn't that just one more reason he needed her?

"They offered to let me do the screenplay."

"What?" She was sitting straight up now, eyes wide. "Oh, Mitch, that's wonderful. I'm so proud of you."

He continued to play with her fingers. "I haven't done it yet."

"Don't you think you can?"

"I'm not sure."

She started to speak, then caught herself. After a moment, she spoke carefully. "Strange, if anyone had asked, I would have said you were the most self-confident man I'd ever met. Added to that, I'd have said that you'd be much too selfish with Zark to let anyone else write him."

"There's a difference between writing a story line for a comic series and writing a screenplay for a major motion picture."

"So?"

He had to laugh. "Tossing my own words back at me, aren't you?"

"You can write, I'd be the first to say that you have a very fluid imagination, and you know your character better than anyone else. I don't see the problem."

"Screwing up is the problem. Anyway, if I don't do the script, they want me as creative consultant."

"I can't tell you what to do, Mitch."

"But?"

She leaned forward, putting her hands on his shoulders. "Write the script, Mitch. You'll hate yourself if you don't try. There aren't any guarantees, but if you don't take the risk, there's no reward either."

He lifted a hand to hers and held it firmly as he watched her. "Do you really feel that way?"

"Yes, I do. I also believe in you." She leaned closer and touched her mouth to his.

"Marry me, Hester."

With her lips still on his, she froze. Slowly, very slowly, she drew away. "What?"

"Marry me." He took her hands in his to hold them still. "I love you."

"Don't. Please don't do this."

"Don't what? Don't love you?" He tightened his grip as she struggled to pull away. "It's a great deal too late for that, and I think you know it. I'm not lying when I tell you that I've never felt about anyone the way I feel about you. I want to spend my life with you."

"I can't." Her voice was breathless. It seemed each word she pushed out seared the back of her throat. "I can't marry you. I don't want to marry anyone. You don't understand what you're asking."

"Just because I haven't been there doesn't mean I don't know." He'd expected surprise, even some resistance. But he could see now he'd totally miscalculated. There was out-and-out fear in her eyes and full panic in her voice. "Hester, I'm not Allan and we both know you're not the same woman you were when you were married to him."

"It doesn't matter. I'm not going through that again, and I won't put Radley through it." She pulled away and started to dress. "You're not being reasonable."

"*I'm* not?" Struggling for calm, he walked behind her and began to do up her buttons. Her back went rigid. "You're the one who's basing her feelings now on something that happened years ago."

"I don't want to talk about it."

"Maybe not, and maybe now's not the best time, but you're going to have to." Though she resisted, he turned her around. "We're going to have to."

She wanted to get away, far enough that she could bury everything that had been said. But for the moment she had to face it. "Mitch, we've known each other for a matter of weeks, and we've just begun to be able to accept what's happening between us."

"What *is* happening?" he demanded. "Aren't you the one who said at the beginning that you weren't interested in casual sex?"

She paled a bit, then turned away to pick up her suit jacket. "There wasn't anything casual about it."

"No, there wasn't, not for either of us. You understand that?"

"Yes, but—"

"Hester, I said I loved you. Now I want to know how you feel about me."

"I don't know." She let out a gasp when he grabbed her shoulders again. "I tell you I don't know. I think I love you. Today. You're asking me to risk everything I've done, the life I've built for myself and Rad, over an emotion I already know can change overnight."

"Love doesn't change overnight," he corrected. "It can be killed or it can be nurtured. That's up to the people involved. I want a commitment from you, a family, and I want to give those things back to you."

"Mitch, this is all happening too fast, much too fast for both of us."

"Damn it, Hester, I'm thirty-five years old, not some kid with hot pants and no brains. I don't want to marry you so I can have convenient sex and a hot breakfast, but because I know we could have something together, something real, something important."

"You don't know what marriage is like, you're only imagining."

"And you're only remembering a bad one. Hester, look at me. Look at me," he demanded again. "When the hell are you going to stop using Radley's father as a yardstick?"

"He's the only one I've got." She shook him off again and tried to catch her breath. "Mitch, I'm flattered that you want me."

"The hell with that."

"Please." She dragged a hand through her hair. "I do care about you, and the only thing I'm really sure of is that I don't want to lose you."

"Marriage isn't the end of a relationship, Hester."

"I can't think about marriage. I'm sorry." The panic flowed in and out of her voice until she was forced to stop and calm it. "If you don't want to see me anymore, I'll try to understand. But I'd rather... I hope we can just let things go on the way they are."

He dug his hands into his pockets. He had a habit of pushing too far too fast, and knew it. But he hated to waste the time he could already imagine them having together. "For how long, Hester?"

"For as long as it lasts." She closed her eyes. "That sounds hard. I don't mean it to. You mean a great deal to me, more than I thought anyone ever would again."

Mitch brushed a finger over her cheek and brought it away wet. "A low blow," he murmured, studying the tear.

"I'm sorry. I don't mean to do this. I had no idea that you were thinking along these lines."

"I can see that." He gave a self-deprecating laugh. "In three dimensions."

"I've hurt you. I can't tell you how much I regret that."

"Don't. I asked for it. The truth is, I hadn't planned on asking you to marry me for at least a week."

She started to touch his hand, then stopped. "Mitch, can we just forget all this, go on as we were?"

He reached out and straightened the collar of her jacket. "I'm afraid not. I've made up my mind, Hester. That's something I try to do only once or twice a year. Once I've done it, there's no turning back." His gaze came up to hers with that rush of intensity she felt to the bone. "I'm going to marry you, sooner or later. If it has to be later, that's fine. I'll just give you some time to get used to it."

"Mitch, I won't change my mind. It wouldn't be fair if I let you think I would. It isn't a matter of a whim, but of a promise I made to myself."

"Some promises are best broken."

She shook her head. "I don't know what else to say. I just wish—"

He pressed his finger to her lips. "We'll talk about it later. I'll take you back to work."

"No, don't bother. Really," she said when he started to argue. "I'd like some time to think, anyway. Being with you makes that difficult."

"That's a good start." He took her chin in his hand and studied her face. "You look fine, but next time don't cry when I ask you to marry me. It's hell on the ego." He kissed her before she could speak. "See you later, Mrs. Wallace. Thanks for lunch."

A little dazed, she walked out into the hall. "I'll call you later."

"Do that. I'll be around."

He closed the door, then turned to lean back against it. Hurt? He rubbed a spot just under his heart. Damn right it hurt. If anyone had told him that being in love could cause the heart to twist, he'd have continued to avoid it. He'd had a twinge when his long-ago love in New Orleans had deserted him. It hadn't prepared him for this sledgehammer blow. What could possibly have?

But he wasn't giving up. What he had to do was figure out a plan of attack—subtle, clever and irresistible. Mitch glanced down at Taz consideringly.

"Where do you think Hester would like to go on our honeymoon?"

The dog grumbled, then rolled over on his back.

"No," Mitch decided. "Bermuda's overdone. Never mind, I'll come up with something."

Chapter 10

"Radley, you and your friends have to tone down the volume on the war, please." Hester took the measuring tape from around her neck and stretched it out over the wall space. Perfect, she thought with a satisfied nod. Then she took the pencil from behind her ear to mark two *X*s where the nails would go.

The little glass shelves she would hang were a present to herself, one that was completely unnecessary and pleased her a great deal. She didn't consider the act of hanging them herself a show of competence or independence, but simply one more of the ordinary chores she'd been doing on her own for years. With a hammer in one hand, she lined up the first nail. She'd given it two good whacks when someone knocked on the door.

"Just a minute." She gave the nail a final smack. From Radley's bedroom came the sounds of antiaircraft and whistling missiles. Hester took the second nail out of her mouth and stuck it in her pocket. "Rad, we're going to be arrested for disturbing the peace." She opened the door to Mitch. "Hi."

The pleasure showed instantly, gratifying him. It had been two days since he'd seen her, since he'd told her he loved her and wanted to marry her. In two days he'd done a lot of hard thinking, and could only hope that, despite herself, Hester had done some thinking, too.

"Doing some remodeling?" he asked with a nod at the hammer.

"Just hanging a shelf." She wrapped both hands around the handle of the hammer, feeling like a teenager. "Come in."

He glanced toward Radley's room as she shut the door. It sounded as though a major air strike was in progress. "You didn't mention you were opening a playground."

"It's been a lifelong dream of mine. Rad, they've just signed a treaty—hold your fire!" With a cautious smile for Mitch, she waved him toward a chair. "Radley has Josh over today, and Ernie—Ernie lives upstairs and goes to school with Rad."

"Sure, the Bitterman kid. I know him. Nice," he commented as he looked at the shelves.

"They're a present for completing a successful month at National Trust." Hester ran a finger along a beveled edge. She really did want this more than a new outfit.

"You're on the reward program?"

"Self-reward."

"The best kind. Want me to finish that for you?"

"Oh?" She glanced down at the hammer. "Oh, no,

thanks. I can do it. Why don't you sit down? I'll get you some coffee."

"You hang the shelf, I'll get the coffee." He kissed the tip of her nose. "And relax, will you?"

"Mitch." He'd taken only two steps away when she reached for his arm. "I'm awfully glad to see you. I was afraid, well, that you were angry."

"Angry?" He gave her a baffled look. "About what?"

"About…" She trailed off as he continued to stare at her in a half interested, half curious way that made her wonder if she'd imagined everything he'd said. "Nothing." She dug the nail out of her pocket. "Help yourself to the coffee."

"Thanks." He grinned at the back of her head. He'd done exactly what he'd set out to do—confuse her. Now she'd be thinking about him, about what had been said between them. The more she thought about it, the closer she'd be to seeing reason.

Whistling between his teeth, he strolled into the kitchen while Hester banged in the second nail.

He *had* asked her to marry him. She remembered everything he'd said, everything she'd said in return. And she knew that he'd been angry and hurt. Hadn't she spent two days regretting that she'd had to cause that? Now he strolled in as though nothing had happened.

Hester set down the hammer, then lifted the shelves. Maybe he'd cooled off enough to be relieved that she'd said no. That could be it, she decided, wondering why the idea didn't ease her mind as much as it should have.

"You made cookies." Mitch came in carrying two mugs, with a plate of fresh cookies balanced on top of one.

"This morning." She smiled over her shoulder as she adjusted the shelves.

"You want to bring that up a little on the right." He sat on the arm of a chair, then set her mug down so his hands would be free for the chocolate-chip cookies. "Terrific," he decided after the first bite. "And, if I say so myself, I'm an expert."

"I'm glad they pass." With her mind on her shelves, Hester stepped back to admire them.

"It's important. I don't know if I could marry a woman who made lousy cookies." He picked up a second one and examined it. "Yeah, maybe I could," he said as Hester turned slowly to stare at him. "But it would be tough." He devoured the second one and smiled at her. "Luckily, it won't have to be an issue."

"Mitch." Before she could work out what to say, Radley came barreling in, his two friends behind him.

"Mitch!" Delighted with the company, Radley screeched to a halt beside him so that Mitch's arm went naturally around his shoulders. "We just had the neatest battle. We're the only survivors."

"Hungry work. Have a cookie."

Radley took one and shoved it into his mouth. "We've got to go up to Ernie's and get more weapons." He reached for another cookie, then caught his mother's eye. "You didn't bring Taz up."

"He stayed up late watching a movie. He's sleeping in today."

"Okay." Radley accepted this before turning to his mother. "Is it okay if we go up to Ernie's for a while?"

"Sure. Just don't go outside unless you let me know."

"We won't. You guys go ahead. I gotta get something."

He raced back to the bedroom while his friends trooped to the door.

"I'm glad he's making some new friends," Hester commented as she reached for her mug. "He was worried about it."

"Radley's not the kind of kid who has trouble making friends."

"No, he's not."

"He's also fortunate to have a mother who lets them come around and bakes cookies for them." He took another sip of coffee. His mother's cook had baked little cakes. He thought Hester would understand it wasn't quite the same thing. "Of course, once we're married we'll have to give him some brothers and sisters. What are you going to put on the shelf?"

"Useless things," she murmured, staring at him. "Mitch, I don't want to fight, but I think we should clear this up."

"Clear what up? Oh, I meant to tell you I started on the script. It's going pretty well."

"I'm glad." And confused. "Really, that's wonderful, but I think we should talk about this business first."

"Sure, what business was that?"

She opened her mouth, and was once more interrupted by her son. When Radley came in, Hester walked away to put a small china cat on the bottom shelf.

"I made something for you in school." Embarrassed, Radley held his hands behind his back.

"Yeah?" Mitch set his coffee down. "Do I get to see it?"

"It's Valentine's Day, you know." After a moment's hesitation, he handed Mitch a card fashioned out of construction paper and blue ribbon. "I made Mom this heart with lace stuff, but I thought the ribbon was better for guys." Radley shuffled his feet. "It opens."

Not certain he could trust his voice, Mitch opened the card. Radley had used his very best block printing.

"To my best friend, Mitch. I love you, Radley." He had to clear his throat, and hoped he wouldn't make a fool out of himself. "It's great. I, ah, nobody ever made me a card before."

"Really?" Embarrassment faded with surprise. "I make them for Mom all the time. She says she likes them better than the ones you buy."

"I like this one a lot better," Mitch told him. He wasn't sure boys that were nearly ten tolerated being kissed, but he ran a hand over Radley's hair and kissed him anyway. "Thanks."

"You're welcome. See ya."

"Yeah." Mitch heard the door slam as he stared down at the little folded piece of construction paper.

"I didn't know he'd made it," Hester said quietly. "I guess he wanted to keep it a secret."

"He did a nice job." At the moment, he didn't have the capacity to explain what the paper and ribbon meant to him. Rising, he walked to the window with the card in his hands. "I'm crazy about him."

"I know." She moistened her lips. She did know it. If she'd ever doubted the extent of Mitch's feelings for her son, she'd just seen full proof of it. It only made things more difficult. "In just a few weeks, you've done so much for him. I know neither one of us have the right to expect you to be there, but I want you to know it means a lot that you are."

He had to clamp down on a surge of fury. He didn't want her gratitude, but one hell of a lot more. Keep cool,

Dempsey, he warned himself. "The best advice I can give you is to get used to it, Hester."

"That's exactly what I can't do." Driven, she went to him. "Mitch, I do care for you, but I'm not going to depend on you. I can't afford to expect or anticipate or rely."

"So you've said." He set the card down carefully on the table. "I'm not arguing."

"What were you saying before—"

"What did I say?"

"About when we were married."

"Did I say that?" He smiled at her as he wound her hair around his finger. "I don't know what I could have been thinking of."

"Mitch, I have a feeling you're trying to throw me off guard."

"Is it working?"

Treat it lightly, she told herself. If he wanted to make a game of it, she'd oblige him. "Only to the point that it confirms what I've always thought about you. You're a very strange man."

"In what context?"

"Okay, to begin with, you talk to your dog."

"He talks back, so that doesn't count. Try again." With her hair still wound around his finger, he tugged her a bit closer. Whether she realized it or not, they were talking about their relationship, and she was relaxed.

"You write comic books for a living. And you read them."

"Being a woman with banking experience, you should understand the importance of a good investment. Do you know what the double issue of my *Defenders of Perth* is worth to a collector? Modesty prevents me from naming figures."

"I bet it does."

He acknowledged this with a slight nod. "And, Mrs. Wallace, I'd be happy to debate the value of literature in any form with you. Did I mention that I was captain of the debating team in high school?"

"No." She had her hands on his chest, once again drawn to the tough, disciplined body beneath the tattered sweater. "There's also the fact that you haven't thrown out a newspaper or magazine in five years."

"I'm saving up for the big paper drive of the second millennium. Conservation is my middle name."

"You also have an answer for everything."

"There's only one I want from you. Did I mention that I fell for your eyes right after I fell for your legs?"

"No, you didn't." Her lips curved just a little. "I never told you that the first time I saw you, through the peephole, I stared at you for a long time."

"I know." He grinned back at her. "If you look in those things right, you can see a shadow."

"Oh," she said, and could think of nothing else to say.

"You know, Mrs. Wallace, those kids could come running back in here anytime. Do you mind if we stop talking for a few minutes?"

"No." She slipped her arms around him. "I don't mind at all."

She didn't want to admit even to herself that she felt safe, protected, with his arms around her. But she did. She didn't want to accept that she'd been afraid of losing him, terrified of the hole he would have left in her life. But the fear had been very real. It faded now as she lifted her lips to his.

She couldn't think about tomorrow or the future Mitch sketched so easily with talk of marriage and family. She'd been taught that marriage was forever, but she'd learned that it was a promise easily made and easily broken. There would be no more broken promises in her life, no more broken vows.

Feelings might rush through her, bringing with them longings and silver-dusted dreams. Her heart might be lost to him, but her will was still her own. Even as her hands gripped him tighter, pulled him closer, Hester told herself it was that will that would save them both unhappiness later.

"I love you, Hester." He murmured the words against her mouth, knowing she might not want to hear them but that it was something he had to say. If he said it enough, she might begin to believe the words and, more, the meaning behind them.

He wanted forever from her—forever for her—not just a moment like this, stolen in the sunlight that poured through the window, or other moments, taken in the shadows. Only once before had he wanted anything with something close to this intensity. That had been something abstract, something nebulous called art. The time had eventually come when he'd been forced to admit that dream would never be within reach.

But Hester was here in his arms. He could hold her like this and taste the sweet, warm longings that stirred in her. She wasn't a dream, but a woman he loved and wanted and would have. If keeping her meant playing games until the layers of her resistance were washed away, then he'd play.

He lifted his hands to her face, twining his fingers into her hair. "I guess the kids will be coming back."

"Probably." Her lips sought his again. Had she ever felt this sense of urgency before? "I wish we had more time."

"Do you?"

Her eyes were half-closed as he drew away. "Yes."

"Let me come back tonight."

"Oh, Mitch." She stepped into his arms to rest her head on his shoulder. For the first time in a decade, she found the mother and the woman at war. "I want you. You know that, don't you?"

Her heart was still pumping hard and fast against his. "I think I figured it out."

"I wish we could be together tonight, but there's Rad."

"I know how you feel about me staying here with Rad in the next room. Hester…" He ran his hands up her arms to rest them on her shoulders. "Why not be honest with him, tell him we care about each other and want to be together?"

"Mitch, he's only a baby."

"No, he's not. No, wait," he continued before she could speak again. "I'm not saying we should make it seem casual or careless, but that we should let Radley know how we feel about each other, and when two grown people feel this strongly about each other they need to show it."

It seemed so simple when he said it, so logical, so natural. Gathering her thoughts, she stepped back. "Mitch, Rad loves you, and he loves with the innocence and lack of restriction of a child."

"I love him, too."

She looked into his eyes and nodded. "Yes, I think you do, and if it's true, I hope you'll understand. I'm afraid that if I bring Radley into this at this point he'll come to depend on you even more than he already does. He'd come to look at you as…"

"As a father," Mitch finished. "You don't want a father in his life, do you, Hester?"

"That's not fair." Her eyes, usually so calm and clear, turned to smoke.

"Maybe not, but if I were you I'd give it some hard thought."

"There's no reason to say cruel things because I won't have sex with you when my son's sleeping in the next room."

He caught her by the shirt so fast she could only stare. She'd seen him annoyed, pushed close to the edge, but never furious. "Damn you, do you think that's all I'm talking about? If all I wanted was sex, I could go downstairs and pick up the phone. Sex is easy, Hester. All it takes is two people and a little spare time."

"I'm sorry." She closed her eyes, knowing she'd never said or done anything in her life she'd been more ashamed of. "That was stupid, Mitch, I just keep feeling as though my back's against the wall. I need some time, please."

"So do I. But the time I need is with you." He dropped his hands and stuck them in his pockets. "I'm pressuring you. I know it and I'm not going to stop, because I believe in us."

"I wish I could, also, honestly I do, but there's too much at stake for me."

And for himself, Mitch thought, but was calm enough now to hold off. "We'll let it ride for a while. Are you and Rad up to hitting a few arcades at Times Square tonight?"

"Sure. He'd love it." She stepped toward him again. "So would I."

"You say that now, but you won't after I humiliate you with my superior skill."

"I love you."

He let out a long breath, fighting back the urge to grab her again and refuse to let go. "You going to let me know when you're comfortable with that?"

"You'll be the first."

He picked up the card Radley had made him. "Tell Rad I'll see him later."

"I will." He was halfway to the door when she started after him. "Mitch, why don't you come to dinner tomorrow? I'll fix a pot roast."

He tilted his head. "The kind with the little potatoes and carrots all around?"

"Sure."

"And biscuits?"

She smiled. "If you want."

"Sounds great, but I'm tied up."

"Oh." She struggled with the need to ask how, but reminded herself she didn't have the right.

Mitch smiled, selfishly pleased to see her disappointment. "Can I have a rain check?"

"Sure." She tried to answer the smile. "I guess Radley told you about his birthday next week," she said when Mitch reached the door.

"Only five or six times." He paused, his hand on the knob.

"He's having a party next Saturday afternoon. I know he'd like you to come if you can."

"I'll be there. Look, why don't we take off about seven? I'll bring the quarters."

"We'll be ready." He wasn't going to kiss her good-bye, she thought. "Mitch, I—"

"I almost forgot." Casually he reached in his back pocket and pulled out a small box.

"What is it?"

"It's Valentine's Day, isn't it?" He put it in her hand. "So this is a Valentine's Day present."

"A Valentine's Day present," she repeated dumbly.

"Yeah, tradition, remember? I thought about candy, but I figured you'd spend a whole lot of time making sure Radley didn't eat too much of it. But look, if you'd rather have candy, I'll just take this back and—"

"No." She pulled the box out of his reach, then laughed. "I don't even know what it is."

"You'd probably find out if you open the box."

Flipping the lid, she saw the thin gold chain that held a heart no bigger than her thumbnail. It glittered with the diamonds that formed it. "Oh, Mitch, it's gorgeous."

"Something told me it'd be a bigger hit with you than candy. Candy would have made you think about oral hygiene."

"I'm not that bad," she countered, then lifted the heart out of the box. "Mitch, it's really beautiful, I love it, but it's too—"

"Conventional, I know," he interrupted as he took it from her. "But I'm just that kind of guy."

"You are?"

"Just turn around and let me hook it for you."

She obeyed, lifting one hand up under her hair. "I do love it, but I don't expect you to buy me expensive presents."

"Um-hmm." His brows were drawn together as he worked the clasp. "I didn't expect bacon and eggs, but you seemed to get a kick out of fixing them." The clasp secured, he turned her around to face him. "I get a kick out of seeing you wear my heart around your neck."

"Thank you." She touched a finger to the heart. "I didn't buy you any candy, either, but maybe I can give you something else."

She was smiling when she kissed him, gently, teasingly, with a power that surprised them both. It took only an instant, an instant to be lost, to need, to imagine. His back was to the door as he moved his hands from her face to her hair to her shoulders, then to her hips to mold her even more truly against him. The fire burned, hot and fast, so that even when she drew away he felt singed by it. With his eyes on hers, Mitch let out a very long, very slow breath.

"I guess those kids will be coming back."

"Any minute."

"Uh-huh." He kissed her lightly on the brow before he turned and opened the door. "See you later."

He would go down to get Taz, Mitch thought as he started down the hall. Then he was going for a walk. A long one.

True to his word Mitch's pockets were filled with quarters. The arcades were packed with people and echoed with the pings and whistles and machine-gun sound effects of the games. Hester stood to the side as Mitch and Radley used their combined talents to save the world from intergalactic wars.

"Nice shooting, Corporal." Mitch slapped the boy's shoulder as a Phaser II rocket disintegrated in a flash of colored light.

"It's your turn." Radley relinquished the controls to his superior officer. "Watch out for the sensor missiles."

"Don't worry. I'm a veteran."

"We're going to beat the high score." Radley tore his eyes away from the screen long enough to look at his mother. "Then we can put our initials up. Isn't this a neat place? It's got everything."

Everything, Hester thought, including some seamy-looking characters in leather and tattoos. The machine behind her let out a high-pitched scream. "Just stay close, okay?"

"Okay, Corporal, we're only seven hundred points away from the high score. Keep your eyes peeled for nuclear satellites."

"Aye, aye, sir." Radley clenched his jaw and took the controls.

"Good reflexes," Mitch said to Hester as he watched Radley control his ship with one hand and fire surface-to-air missiles with the other.

"Josh has one of those home video games. Rad loves to go over and play things like this." She caught her bottom lip between her teeth as Radley's ship barely missed annihilation. "I can never figure out how he can tell what's going on. Oh, look, he's passed the high score."

They continued to watch in tense silence as Radley fought bravely to the last man. As a finale, the screen exploded in brilliant fireworks of sound and light.

"A new record." Mitch hoisted Radley in the air. "This calls for a field promotion. Sergeant, inscribe your initials."

"But you got more points than I did."

"Who's counting? Go ahead."

Face flushed with pride, Radley clicked the button

that ran through the alphabet. R.A.W. A for Allan, Mitch thought, and said nothing.

"My initials spell raw, and backward they spell war—pretty neat, huh?"

"Pretty neat," Mitch agreed. "Want to give it a shot, Hester?"

"No, thanks. I'll just watch."

"Mom doesn't like to play," Radley confided. "Her palms sweat."

"Your palms sweat?" Mitch repeated with a grin.

Hester sent a telling look in Radley's direction. "It's the pressure. I can't take being responsible for the fate of the world. I know it's a game," she said before Mitch could respond. "But I get, well, caught up."

"You're terrific, Mrs. Wallace." He kissed her as Radley looked on and considered.

It made him feel funny to see Mitch kiss his mother. He wasn't sure if it was a good funny or a bad funny. Then Mitch dropped a hand to his shoulder. It always made Radley feel nice when Mitch put his hand there.

"Okay, what'll it be next, the Amazon jungles, medieval times, a search for the killer shark?"

"I like the one with the ninja. I saw a ninja movie at Josh's once—well, almost did. Josh's mom turned it off because one of the women was taking her clothes off and stuff."

"Oh, yeah?" Mitch stifled a laugh as Hester's mouth dropped open. "What was the name?"

"Never mind." Hester gripped Radley's hand. "I'm sure Josh's parents just made a mistake."

"Josh's father thought it was about throwing stars and kung fu. Josh's mom got mad and made him take it back to the video place and get something else. But I still like ninjas."

"Let's see if we can find a free machine." Mitch fell into step beside Hester. "I don't think he was marked for life."

"I'd still like to know what 'and stuff' means."

"Me, too." He swung an arm around her shoulders to steer her through a clutch of teenagers. "Maybe we could rent it."

"I'll pass, thanks."

"You don't want to see *Naked Ninjas from Naga-saki*?" When she turned around to stare at him, Mitch held out both hands, palms up. "I made it up. I swear."

"Hmmm."

"Here's one. Can I play this one?"

Mitch continued to grin at Hester as he dug out quarters.

The time passed so that Hester almost stopped hearing the noise from both machines and people. To placate Radley she played a few of the less intense games, ones that didn't deal with world domination or universal destruction. But for the most part she watched him, pleased to see him enjoying what was for him a real night on the town.

They must look like a family, she thought as Radley and Mitch bent over the controls in a head-to-head duel. She wished she still believed in such things. But to her, families and lifetime commitments were as fanciful as the machines that spewed out color and light around them.

Day-to-day, Hester thought with a little sigh. That was all she could afford to believe in now. In a few hours she would tuck Radley in bed and go to her room alone. That was the only way to make sure they were both safe. She heard Mitch laugh and shout encouragement to Radley, and looked away. It was the only way, she told herself again. No matter how much she wanted or was tempted to believe again, she couldn't risk it.

"How about the pinball machines?" Mitch suggested.

"They're okay." Though they rang with wild colors and lights, Radley didn't find them terribly exciting. "Mom likes them though."

"Are you any good?"

Hester pushed aside her uneasy thoughts. "Not bad."

"Care to go one-on-one?" He jingled the quarters in his pockets.

Though she'd never considered herself highly competitive, she was swayed by his smug look. "All right."

She'd always had a touch for pinball, a light enough, quick enough touch to have beaten her brother nine times out of ten. Though these machines were electronic and more sophisticated than the ones she'd played in her youth, she didn't doubt she could make a good showing.

"I could give you a handicap," Mitch suggested as he pushed coins into the slot.

"Funny, I was just going to say the same thing to you." With a smile, Hester took the controls.

It had something to do with black magic and white knights. Hester tuned out the sounds and concentrated on keeping the ball in play. Her timing was sharp. Mitch stood behind her with his hands tucked in his back pockets and nodded as she sent the ball spinning.

He liked the way she leaned into the machine, her lips slightly parted, her eyes narrowed and alert. Now and then she would catch her tongue between her teeth and push her body forward as if to follow the ball on its quick, erratic course.

The little silver ball rammed into rubber, sending bells ringing and lights flashing. By the time her first ball dropped, she'd already racked up an impressive score.

"Not bad for an amateur," Mitch commented with a wink at Radley.

"I'm just warming up." With a smile, she stepped back.

Radley watched the progress of the ball as Mitch took control. But he had to stand on his toes to get the full effect. It was pretty neat when the ball got hung up in the top of the machine where the bumpers sent it vibrating back and forth in a blur. He glanced behind him at the rows of other machines and wished he'd thought to ask for another quarter before they'd started to play. But if he couldn't play, he could watch. He edged away to get a closer look at a nearby game.

"Looks like I'm ahead by a hundred," Mitch said as he stepped aside for Hester.

"I didn't want to blow you away with the first ball. It seemed rude." She pulled back the plunger and let the ball rip.

This time she had the feel and the rhythm down pat. She didn't let the ball rest as she set it right, then left, then up the middle where it streaked through a tunnel and crashed into a lighted dragon. It took her back to her childhood, when her wants had been simple and her dreams still gilt-edged. As the machine rocked with noise, she laughed and threw herself into the competition.

Her score flashed higher and higher with enough

fanfare to draw a small crowd. Before her second ball dropped, people were choosing up sides.

Mitch took position. Unlike Hester, he didn't block out the sounds and lights, but used them to pump the adrenaline. He nearly lost the ball, causing indrawn breaths behind him, but caught it on the tip of his flipper to shoot it hard into a corner. This time he finished fifty points behind her.

The third and final turn brought more people. Hester thought she heard someone placing bets before she tuned them out and put all her concentration on the ball and her timing. She was nearly exhausted before she backed away again.

"You're going to need a miracle, Mitch."

"Don't get cocky." He flicked his wrists like a concert pianist and earned a few hoots and cheers from the crowd.

Hester had to admit as she watched his technique that he played brilliantly. He took chances that could have cost him his last ball, but turned them into triumph. He stood spread-legged and relaxed, but she saw in his eyes that kind of deep concentration that she'd come to expect from him, but had yet to become used to. His hair fell over his forehead, as careless as he was. There was a slight smile on his face that struck her as both pleased and reckless.

She found herself watching him rather than the ball as she toyed with the little diamond heart she'd worn over a plain black turtleneck.

This was the kind of man women dreamed about and made heroes of. This was the kind of man a woman could come to lean upon if she wasn't careful. With a man like him, a woman could have years of laughter. The defenses around her heart weakened a bit with her sigh.

The ball was lost in the dragon's cave with a series of roars.

"She got you by ten points," someone in the crowd pointed out. "Ten points, buddy."

"Got yourself a free game," someone else said, giving Hester a friendly slap on the back.

Mitch shook his head as he wiped his hands on the thighs of his jeans. "About that handicap—" he began.

"Too late." Ridiculously pleased with herself, Hester hooked her thumbs in her belt loops and studied her score. "Superior reflexes. It's all in the wrist."

"How about a rematch?"

"I don't want to humiliate you again." She turned, intending to offer Radley the free game. "Rad, why don't you... Rad?" She nudged her way through the few lingering onlookers. "Radley?" A little splinter of panic shot straight up her spine. "He's not here."

"He was here a minute ago." Mitch put a hand on her arm and scanned what he could see of the room.

"I wasn't paying any attention." She brought a hand up to her throat, where the fear had already lodged, and began to walk quickly. "I know better than to take my eyes off him in a place like this."

"Stop." He kept his voice calm, but her fear had already transferred itself to him. He knew how easy it was to whisk one small boy away in a crowd. You couldn't pour your milk in the morning without being aware of it. "He's just wandering around the machines. We'll find him. I'll go around this way, you go down here."

She nodded and spun away without a word. They were six or seven deep at some of the machines. Hester stopped at each one, searching for a small blond boy in a blue sweater. She called for him over the noise and clatter of machines.

When she passed the big glass doors and looked outside to the lights and crowded sidewalks of Times Square, her heart turned over in her breast. He hadn't gone outside, she told herself. Radley would never do something so expressly forbidden. Unless someone had taken him, or...

Gripping her hands together tightly, she turned away. She wouldn't think like that. But the room was so big, filled with so many people, all strangers. And the noise, the noise was more deafening than she'd remembered. How could she have heard him if he'd called out for her?

She started down the next row, calling. Once she heard a young boy laugh and spun around. But it wasn't Radley. She'd covered half the room, and ten minutes was gone, when she thought she would have to call the police. She quickened her pace and tried to look everywhere at once she went from row to row.

There was so much noise, and the lights were so bright. Maybe she should double back—she might have missed him. Maybe he was waiting for her now by that damn pinball machine, wondering where she'd gone. He might be afraid. He could be calling for her. He could be...

Then she saw him, hoisted in Mitch's arms. Hester shoved two people aside as she ran for them. "Radley!" She threw her arms around both of them and buried her face in his hair.

"He'd gone over to watch someone play," Mitch began as he stroked a hand up and down her back. "He ran into someone he knew from school."

"It was Ricky Nesbit, Mom. He was with his big brother, and they lent me a quarter. We went to play a game. I didn't know it was so far away."

"Radley." She struggled with the tears and kept her voice firm. "You know the rules about staying with me. This is a big place with a lot of people. I have to be able to trust you not to wander away."

"I didn't mean to. It was just that Ricky said it would just take a minute. I was coming right back."

"Rules have reasons, Radley, and we've been through them."

"But, Mom—"

"Rad." Mitch shifted the boy in his arms. "You scared your mother and me."

"I'm sorry." His eyes clouded up. "I didn't mean to make you scared."

"Don't do it again." Her voice softened as she kissed his cheek. "Next time it's solitary confinement. You're all I've got, Rad." She hugged him again. Her eyes were closed so that she didn't see the change in Mitch's expression. "I can't let anything happen to you."

"I won't do it again."

All she had, Mitch thought as he set the boy down. Was she still so stubborn that she couldn't admit, even to herself, that she had someone else now, too? He jammed his hands into his pockets and tried to force back both anger and hurt. She was going to have to make room in her life soon, very soon, or he'd damn well make it for her.

Chapter 11

He wasn't sure if he was doing more harm than good by staying out of Hester's way for a few days, but Mitch needed time himself. It wasn't his style to dissect and analyze, but to feel and act. However, he'd never felt quite this strongly before or acted quite so rashly.

When possible, he buried himself in work and in the fantasies he could control. When it wasn't, he stayed alone in his rooms, with old movies flickering on the television or music blaring through the stereo. He continued to work on the screenplay he didn't know if he could write, in the hope that the challenge of it would stop him from marching two floors up and demanding that Hester Wallace came to her senses.

She wanted him, yet she didn't want him. She opened to him, yet kept the most precious part of her closed. She trusted him, yet didn't believe in him enough to share her life with him.

You're all I've got, Rad. And all she wanted? Mitch was forced to ask himself the question. How could such a bright, giving woman base the rest of her life on a mistake she'd made over ten years before?

The helplessness of it infuriated him. Even when he'd hit bottom in New Orleans, he hadn't been helpless. He'd faced his limitations, accepted them, and had channeled his talents differently. Had the time come for him to face and accept his limitations with Hester?

He spent hours thinking about it, considering compromises and then rejecting them. Could he do as she asked and leave things as they were? They would be lovers, with no promises between them and no talk of a future. They could have a relationship as long as there was no hint of permanency or bonds. No, he couldn't do as she asked. Now that he had found the only woman he wanted in his life, he couldn't accept her either part-time or partway.

It was something of a shock to discover he was such an advocate of marriage. He couldn't say that he'd seen very many that had been made in heaven. His parents had been well suited—the same tastes, the same class, the same outlook—but he couldn't remember ever witnessing any passion between them. Affection and loyalty, yes, and a united front against their son's ambitions, but they lacked the spark and simmer that added excitement.

He asked himself if it was only passion he felt for Hester, but knew the answer already. Even as he sat alone he could imagine them twenty years in the future, sitting on the porch swing she'd described. He could see them growing older together, filing away memories and traditions.

He wasn't going to lose that. However long it took, however many walls he had to scale, he wasn't going to lose that.

Mitch dragged a hand through his hair, then gathered up the boxes he needed to lug upstairs.

She was afraid he wasn't coming. There had been some subtle change in Mitch since the night they'd gone to Times Square. He'd been strangely distant on the phone, and though she'd invited him up more than once, he'd always made an excuse.

She was losing him. Hester poured punch into paper cups and reminded herself that she'd known it was only temporary. He had the right to live his own life, to go his own way. She could hardly expect him to tolerate the distance she felt she had to put between them or to understand the lack of time and attention she could give him because of Radley and her job. All she could hope was that he would remain a friend.

Oh, God, she missed him. She missed having him to talk to, to laugh with, even to lean on—though she could only allow herself to lean a little. Hester set the pitcher on the counter and took a deep breath. It couldn't matter, she couldn't *let* it matter now. There were ten excited and noisy boys in the other room. Her responsibility, she reminded herself. She couldn't stand here listing her regrets when she had obligations.

As she carried the tray of drinks into the living room, two boys shot by her. Three more were wrestling on the floor, while the others shouted to be heard over the record player. Hester had already noted that one of Radley's newest friends wore a silver earring and spoke knowledgeably about girls. She set the tray down and glanced quickly at the ceiling.

Give me a few more years of comic books and erector sets. Please, I'm just not ready for the rest of it yet.

"Drink break," she said out loud. "Michael, why don't you let Ernie out of that headlock now and have some punch? Rad, set down the kitten. They get cranky if they're handled too much."

With reluctance, Radley set the little bundle of black-and-white fur in a padded basket. "He's really neat. I like him the best." He snatched a drink off the tray as several other hands reached out. "I really like my watch, too." He held it out, pushing a button that sent it from time mode to the first in a series of miniature video games.

"Just make sure you don't play with it when you should be paying attention in school."

Several boys groaned and elbowed Radley. Hester had just about convinced them to settle down with one of Radley's board games when the knock sounded at the door.

"I'll get it!" Radley hopped up and raced for the door. He had one more birthday wish. When he opened the door, it came true. "Mitch! I knew you'd come. Mom said you'd probably gotten real busy, but I knew you'd come. I got a kitten. I named him Zark. Want to see?"

"As soon as I get rid of some of these boxes." Even arms as well tuned as his were beginning to feel the strain. Mitch set them on the sofa and turned, only to have Zark's namesake shoved into his hands. The kitten purred and arched under a stroking finger. "Cute. We'll have to take him down and introduce him to Taz."

"Won't Taz eat him?"

"You've got to be kidding." Mitch tucked the kitten under his arm and looked at Hester. "Hi."

"Hi." He needed a shave, his sweater had a hole in the seam, and he looked wonderful. "We were afraid you wouldn't make it."

"I said I'd be here." Lazily he scratched between the kitten's ears. "I keep my promises."

"I got this watch, too." Radley held up his wrist. "It tells the time and the date and stuff, then you can play Dive Bomb and Scrimmage."

"Oh, yeah, Dive Bomb?" Mitch sat on the arm of the couch and watched Radley send the little dots spinning. "Never have to be bored on a long subway ride again, right?"

"Or at the dentist's office. You want to play?"

"Later. I'm sorry I'm late. I got hung up in the store."

"That's okay. We didn't have the cake yet 'cause I wanted to wait. It's chocolate."

"Great. Aren't you going to ask for your present?"

"I'm not supposed to." He sneaked a look at his mother, who was busy keeping some of his friends from wrestling again. "Did you really get me something?"

"Nah." Laughing at Radley's expression, he ruffled his hair. "Sure I did. It's right there on the couch."

"Which one?"

"All of them."

Radley's eyes grew big as saucers. "All of them?"

"They all sort of go together. Why don't you open that one first?"

Because of the lack of time and materials, Mitch hadn't wrapped the boxes. He'd barely had enough forethought to put tape over the name brand and model, but buying presents for young boys was a new experience, and one he'd enjoyed immensely. Radley began to pry open the heavy cardboard with assistance from his more curious friends.

"Wow, a PC." Josh craned his head over Radley's shoulder. "Robert Sawyer's got one just like it. You can play all kinds of things on it."

"A computer." Radley stared in amazement at the open box, then turned to Mitch. "Is it for me, really? To keep?"

"Sure you can keep it—it's a present. I was hoping you'd let me play with it sometime."

"You can play with it anytime, anytime you want." He threw his arms around Mitch's neck, forgetting to be embarrassed because his friends were watching. "Thanks. Can we hook it up right now?"

"I thought you'd never ask."

"Rad, you'll have to clear off the desk in your room. Hold it," Hester added when a flood of young bodies started by. "That doesn't mean shoving everything on the floor, okay? You take care of it properly, and Mitch and I will bring this in."

They streaked away with war whoops that warned her she'd be finding surprises under Radley's bed and under the rug for some time. She'd worry about that later. Now she crossed the room to stand beside Mitch.

"That was a terribly generous thing to do."

"He's bright. A kid that bright deserves one of these."

"Yes." She looked at the boxes yet to be opened. There'd be a monitor, disk drives, software. "I've wanted to get him one, but haven't been able to swing it."

"I didn't mean that as a criticism, Hester."

"I know you didn't." She gnawed at her lip in a gesture that told him her nerves were working at her. "I also know this isn't the time to talk, and that we have to. But before we take this in to Rad, I want to tell you how glad I am that you're here."

"It's where I want to be." He ran a thumb along her jawline. "You're going to have to start believing that."

She took his hand and turned her lips into his palm. "You might not feel the same way after you spend the next hour or so with ten fifth-graders." She smiled as the first minor crash sounded from Radley's bedroom. "'Once more unto the breach'?"

The crash was followed by several young voices raised in passionate argument. "How about, 'Lay on, MacDuff'?"

"Whatever." Drawing a deep breath, Hester lifted the first box.

It was over. The last birthday guest had been dragged away by his parents. A strange and wonderful silence lay over the living room. Hester sat in a chair, her eyes half-closed, while Mitch lay sprawled on the couch with his closed completely. In the silence Hester could hear the occasional click of Radley's new computer, and the mewing of Zark, who sat in his lap. With a contented sigh, she surveyed the living room.

It was in shambles. Paper cups and plates were strewn everywhere. The remains of potato chips and pretzels were in bowls, with a good portion of them crushed into the carpet. Scraps of wrapping paper were scattered among the toys the boys had decided worthy of attention. She didn't want to dwell on what the kitchen looked like.

Mitch opened one eye and looked at her. "Did we win?"

"Absolutely." Reluctantly, Hester dragged herself up. "It was a brilliant victory. Want a pillow?"

"No." Taking her hand, he flipped her down on top of him.

"Mitch, Radley is—"

"Playing with his computer," he finished, then nuzzled her bottom lip. "I'm betting he breaks down and puts some of the educational software in before it's over."

"It was pretty clever of you to mix those in."

"I'm a pretty clever kind of guy." He shifted her until she fit into the curve of his shoulder. "Besides, I figured I'd win you over with the machine's practicality, and Rad and I could play the games."

"I'm surprised you don't have one of your own."

"Actually…it seemed like such a good idea when I went in for Rad's that I picked up two. To balance my household accounts," he said when Hester looked up at him. "And modernize my filing system."

"You don't have a filing system."

"See?" He settled his cheek on her hair. "Hester, do you know what one of the ten greatest boons to civilization is?"

"The microwave oven?"

"The afternoon nap. This is a great sofa you've got here."

"It needs reupholstering."

"You can't see that when you're lying on it." He tucked his arm around her waist. "Sleep with me awhile."

"I really have to clean up." But she found it easy to close her eyes.

"Why? Expecting company?"

"No. But don't you have to go down and take Taz out?"

"I slipped Ernie a couple of bucks to walk him."

Hester snuggled into his shoulder. "You are clever."

"That's what I've been trying to tell you."

"I haven't even thought about dinner," she murmured as her mind began to drift.

"Let 'em eat cake."

With a quiet laugh, she slipped into sleep beside him.

Radley wandered in a few moments later, the kitten curled in his arms. He'd wanted to tell them about his latest score. Standing at the foot of the sofa, he scratched the kitten's ears and studied his mom and Mitch thoughtfully. Sometimes when he had a bad dream or wasn't feeling very good, his mom would sleep with him. It always made him feel better. Maybe sleeping with Mitch made his mom feel better.

He wondered if Mitch loved his mom. It made his stomach feel funny to think about it. He wanted Mitch to stay and be his friend. If they got married, did that mean Mitch would go away? He would have to ask, Radley decided. His mom always told him the truth. Shifting the kitten to one arm, he lifted the bowl of chips and carried it into his room.

It was nearly dark when she awoke. Hester opened her eyes and looked directly into Mitch's. She blinked, trying to orient herself. Then he kissed her, and she remembered everything.

"We must have slept for an hour," she murmured.

"Closer to two. How do you feel?"

"Groggy. I always feel groggy if I sleep during the day." She stretched her shoulders and heard Radley giggling in his room. "He must still be at that computer. I don't think I've ever seen him happier."

"And you?"

"Yes." She traced his lips with her fingertip. "I'm happy."

"If you're groggy and happy, this might be the perfect time for me to ask you to marry me again."

"Mitch."

"No? Okay, I'll wait until I can get you drunk. Any more of that cake left?"

"A little. You're not angry?"

Mitch combed his fingers through his hair as he sat up. "About what?"

Hester put her hands on his shoulders, then rested her cheek on his. "I'm sorry I can't give you what you want."

He tightened his arms around her; then with an effort, he relaxed. "Good. That means you're close to changing your mind. I'd like a double-ring ceremony."

"Mitch!"

"What?"

She drew back and, because she didn't trust his smile, shook her head. "Nothing. I think it's best to say nothing. Go ahead and help yourself to the cake. I'm going to get started in here."

Mitch glanced around the room, which looked to be in pretty good shape by his standards. "You really want to clean this up tonight?"

"You don't expect me to leave this mess until the

morning," she began, then stopped herself. "Forget I said that. I forgot who I was talking to."

Mitch narrowed his eyes suspiciously. "Are you accusing me of being sloppy?"

"Not at all. I'm sure there's a lot to be said for living in a 'junkyard' decor with a touch of 'paper drive' thrown in. It's uniquely you." She began to gather up paper plates. "It probably comes from having maids as a child."

"Actually, it comes from never being able to mess up a room. My mother couldn't stand disorder." He'd always been fond of it, Mitch mused, but there was something to be said for watching Hester tidy up. "For my tenth birthday, she hired a magician. We sat in little folding chairs—the boys in suits, the girls in organdy dresses—and watched the performance. Then we were served a light lunch on the terrace. There were enough servants around so that when it was over there wasn't a crumb to be picked up. I guess I'm overcompensating."

"Maybe a little." She kissed both of his cheeks. What an odd man he was, she thought, so calm and easygoing on one hand, so driven by demons on the other. She strongly believed that childhood affected adulthood, even to old age. It was the strength of that belief that made her so fiercely determined to do the best she could by Radley. "You're entitled to your dust and clutter, Mitch. Don't let anyone take it away from you."

He kissed her cheek in return. "I guess you're entitled to your neat and tidy. Where's your vacuum?"

She drew back, brow lifted. "Do you know what one is?"

"Cute. Very cute." He pinched her, hard, just under

the ribs. Hester jumped back with a squeal. "Ah, ticklish, huh?"

"Cut it out," she warned, holding out the stack of paper plates like a shield. "I wouldn't want to hurt you."

"Come on." He crouched like a wrestler. "Two falls out of three."

"I'm warning you." Wary of the gleam in his eye, she backed up as he advanced. "I'll get violent."

"Promise?" He lunged, gripping her under the waist. In reflex, Hester lifted her arms. The plates, dripping with cake and ice cream, caught him full in the face. "Oh, God." Her own scream of laughter had her falling backward into a chair. She opened her mouth to speak, but only doubled up again.

Very slowly Mitch wiped a hand over his cheek, then studied the smear of chocolate. Watching, Hester let out another peal of laughter and held her sides helplessly.

"What's going on?" Radley came into the living room staring at his mother, who could do nothing but point. Shifting his gaze, Radley stared in turn at Mitch. "Jeez." Radley rolled his eyes and began to giggle. "Mike's little sister gets food all over her face like that. She's almost two."

The control Hester had been scratching for slipped out of her grip. Choking with laughter, she pulled Radley against her. "It was—it was an accident," she managed, then collapsed again.

"It was a deliberate sneak attack," Mitch corrected. "And it calls for immediate retribution."

"Oh, please." Hester held out a hand, knowing she was too weak to defend herself. "I'm sorry. I swear. It was a reflex, that's all."

"So's this." He came closer, and though she ducked

behind Radley, Mitch merely sandwiched the giggling boy between them. And he kissed her, her mouth, her nose, her cheeks, while she squirmed and laughed and struggled. When he was finished, he'd transferred a satisfactory amount of chocolate to her face. Radley took one look at his mother and slipped, cackling, to the floor.

"Maniac," she accused as she wiped chocolate from her chin with the back of her hand.

"You look beautiful in chocolate, Hester."

It took more than an hour to put everything to rights again. By popular vote, they ended up sharing a pizza as they once had before, then spending the rest of the evening trying out Radley's birthday treasures. When he began to nod over the keyboard, Hester nudged him into bed.

"Quite a day." Hester set the kitten in his basket at the foot of Radley's bed, then stepped out into the hall.

"I'd say it's a birthday he'll remember."

"So will I." She reached up to rub at a slight stiffness at the base of her neck. "Would you like some wine?"

"I'll get it." He turned her toward the living room. "Go sit down."

"Thanks." Hester sat on the couch, stretched out her legs and slipped off her shoes. It was definitely a day she would remember. Sometime during it, she'd come to realize that she could also have a night to remember.

"Here you go." Mitch handed her a glass of wine, then slipped onto the sofa beside her. Holding his own glass up, he shifted her so that she rested against him.

"This is nice." With a sigh, she brought the wine to her lips.

"Very nice." He bent to brush his lips over her neck. "I told you this was a great sofa."

"Sometimes I forget what it's like to relax like this. Everything's done, Radley's happy and tucked into bed, tomorrow's Sunday and there's nothing urgent to think about."

"No restless urge to go out dancing or carousing?"

"No." She stretched her shoulders. "You?"

"I'm happy right here."

"Then stay." She pressed her lips together a moment. "Stay tonight."

He was silent. His hand stopped its easy massage of her neck, then began again, slowly. "Are you sure that's what you want?"

"Yes." She drew a deep breath before she turned to look at him. "I've missed you. I wish I knew what was right and what was wrong, what was best for all of us, but I know I've missed you. Will you stay?"

"I'm not going anywhere."

She settled back against him, content. For a long time they sat just as they were, half dreaming, in silence, with lamplight glowing behind them.

"Are you still working on the script?" she asked at length.

"Mmm-hmm." He could get used to this, he thought, very used to having Hester snuggled beside him in the late evening with the lamplight dim and the scent of her hair teasing his senses. "You were right. I'd have hated myself if I hadn't tried to write it. I guess I had to get past the nerves."

"Nerves?" She smiled over her shoulder. "You?"

"I've been known to have them, when something's

either unfamiliar or important. They were stretched pretty thin the first time I made love with you."

Hearing it not only surprised her but made the memory of it all the sweeter. "They didn't show."

"Take my word for it." He stroked the outside of her thigh, lightly and with a casualness that was its own kind of seduction. "I was afraid that I'd make the wrong move and screw up something that was more important than anything else in my life."

"You didn't make any wrong moves, and you make me feel very special."

When she rose, it felt natural to hold out a hand to him, to have his close over hers. She switched off lights as they walked to the bedroom.

Mitch closed the door. Hester turned down the bed. He knew it could be like this every night, for all the years they had left. She was on the edge of believing it. He knew it, he could see it in her eyes when he crossed to her. Her eyes remained on his while she unbuttoned her blouse.

They undressed in silence, but the air had already started to hum. Though nerves had relaxed, anticipation was edgier than ever. Now they knew what they could bring to each other. They slipped into bed together and turned to each other.

It felt so right, just the way his arms slipped around her to bring her close. Just the way their bodies met, merging warmth to warmth. She knew the feel of him now, the firmness, the strength. She knew how easily hers fit against it. She tipped her head back and, with her eyes still on his, offered her mouth.

Kissing him was like sliding down a cool river toward churning white water.

The sound of pleasure came deep in his throat as she pressed against him. The shyness was still there, but without the reserve and hesitation. Now there was only sweetness and an offering.

It was like this each time they came together. Exhilarating, stunning and right. He cupped the back of her head in his hand as she leaned over him. The light zing of the wine hadn't completely faded from her tongue. He tasted it, and her, as she explored his mouth. He sensed a boldness growing in her that hadn't been there before, a new confidence that caused her to come to him with her own demands and needs.

Her heart was open, he thought as her lips raced over his throat. And Hester was free. He'd wanted this for her—for them. With something like a laugh, he rolled over her and began to drive her toward madness.

She couldn't get enough of him. She took her hands, her mouth, over him quickly, almost fiercely, but found it impossible to assuage the greed. How could she have known a man could feel so good, so exciting? How could she have known that the scent of his skin would make her head reel and her desires sharpen? Just her name murmured in his voice aroused her.

Locked together, they tumbled over the sheets, tangling in the blanket, shoving it aside because the need for its warmth was long past. He moved as quickly as she, discovering new secrets to delight and torment her. She heard him gasp out her name as she ranged kisses over his chest. She felt his body tense and arch as she moved her hands lower.

Perhaps the power had always been there inside her, but Hester was certain it had been born in her that night. The power to arouse a man past the civilized, and perhaps past the wise. Wise or not, she gloried in it when he trapped her beneath him and let desire rule.

His mouth was hot and hungry as it raced over her. Demands, promises, pleas swirled through her head, but she couldn't speak. Even her breath was trapped as he drove her up and up. She caught him close, as though he were a lifeline in a sea that raged.

Then they both went under.

Chapter 12

The sky was cloudy and threatening snow. Half dozing, Hester turned away from the window to reach for Mitch. The bed beside her was rumpled but empty.

Had he left her during the night? she wondered as she ran her hand over the sheets where he'd slept. Her first reaction was disappointment. It would have been so sweet to have had him there to turn to in the morning. Then she drew her hand back and cupped it under her cheek.

Perhaps it was best that he'd gone. She couldn't be sure how Radley would feel. If Mitch was there to reach out to, she knew it would only become more difficult to keep herself from doing so again and again. No one knew how hard and painfully she'd worked to stop herself from needing anyone. Now, after all the years of struggling, she'd just begun to see real progress. She'd made a good home for Radley in a good neighborhood and had a strong, well-paying job. Security, stability.

She couldn't risk those things again for the emotional morass that came with depending on someone else. But she was already beginning to depend on him, Hester thought as she pushed back the blankets. No matter how much her head told her it was best that he wasn't here, she was sorry he wasn't. She *was* sorry, sorrier than he could ever know, that she was strong enough to stand apart from him.

Hester slipped on her robe and went to see if Radley wanted breakfast.

She found them together, hunched over the keyboard of Radley's computer while graphics exploded on the screen. "This thing's defective," Mitch insisted. "That was a dead-on shot."

"You missed by a mile."

"I'm going to tell your mother you need glasses. Look, this is definite interference. How am I supposed to concentrate when this stupid cat's chewing on my toes?"

"Poor sportsmanship," Radley said soberly as Mitch's last man was obliterated.

"Poor sportsmanship! I'll show you poor sportsmanship." With that he snatched Radley up and held him upside down. "Now is this machine defective, or what?"

"No." Giggling, Radley braced his hands on the floor. "Maybe *you* need glasses."

"I'm going to have to drop you on your head. You really leave me no choice. Oh, hi, Hester." With his arm hooked around Radley's legs, he smiled at her.

"Hi, Mom!" Though his cheeks were turning pink,

Radley was delighted with his upside-down position. "I beat Mitch three times. But he's not really mad."

"Says who?" Mitch flipped the boy upright, then dropped him lightly on the bed. "I've been humiliated."

"I destroyed him," Radley said with satisfaction.

"I can't believe I slept through it." She offered them both a cautious smile. It didn't seem as though Radley was anything but delighted to find Mitch here. As for herself, she wasn't having an easy time keeping the pleasure down, either. "I suppose after three major battles you'd both like some breakfast."

"We already ate." Radley leaned over the bed to reach for the kitten. "I showed Mitch how to make French toast. He said it was real good."

"That was before you cheated."

"I did not." Radley rolled on his back and let the kitten creep up his stomach. "Mitch washed the pan, and I dried it. We were going to fix you some, but you just kept on sleeping."

The idea of the two men in her life fiddling in the kitchen while she slept left her flustered. "I guess I didn't expect anyone to be up so early."

"Hester." Mitch stepped closer to swing an arm over her shoulders. "I hate to break this to you, but it's after eleven."

"Eleven?"

"Yeah. How about lunch?"

"Well, I…"

"You think about it. I guess I should go down and take care of Taz."

"I'll do it." Radley was up and bouncing. "I can give him his food and take him for a walk and everything. I know how, you showed me."

"It's okay with me. Hester?"

She was having trouble just keeping up. "All right. But you'll have to bundle up."

"I will." He was already reaching for his coat. "Can I bring Taz back with me? He hasn't met Zark yet."

Hester glanced at the tiny ball of fur, thinking of Taz's big white teeth. "I don't know if Taz would care for Zark."

"He loves cats," Mitch assured her as he picked up Radley's ski cap off the floor. "In a purely noncannibalistic way." He reached in his pocket for his keys.

"Be careful," she called as Radley rushed by, jingling Mitch's keys. The front door slammed with a vengeance.

"Good morning," Mitch said, and turned her into his arms.

"Good morning. You could have woken me up."

"It was tempting." He ran his hands up the back of her robe. "Actually, I was going to make some coffee and bring you in a cup. Then Radley came in. Before I knew it, I was up to my wrists in egg batter."

"He, ah, didn't wonder what you were doing here?"

"No." Knowing exactly how her mind was working, he kissed the tip of her nose. Then, shifting her to his side, he began to walk with her to the kitchen. "He came in while I was boiling water and asked if I was fixing breakfast. After a brief consultation, we decided he was the better qualified of the two. There's some coffee left, but I think you'd be better off pouring it out and starting again."

"I'm sure it's fine."

"I love an optimist."

She almost managed a smile as she reached in the refrigerator for the milk. "I thought you'd gone."

"Would you rather I had?"

She shook her head but didn't look at him. "Mitch, it's so hard. It just keeps getting harder."

"What does?"

"Trying not to want you here like this all the time."

"Say the word and I'll move in, bag and dog."

"I wish I could. I really wish I could. Mitch, when I walked into Rad's bedroom this morning and saw the two of you together, something just clicked. I stood there thinking this is the way it could be for us."

"That's the way it *will* be for us, Hester."

"You're so sure." With a small laugh, she turned to lean her palms on the counter. "You're so absolutely sure, and have been almost from the beginning. Maybe that's one of the things that frightens me."

"A light went on for me when I saw you, Hester." He came closer to put his hands on her shoulders. "I haven't gone through my life knowing exactly what I wanted, and I can't claim that everything always goes the way I'd planned, but with you I'm sure." He pressed his lips to her hair. "Do you love me, Hester?"

"Yes." With a long sigh, she shut her eyes. "Yes, I love you."

"Then marry me." Gently he turned her around to face him. "I won't ask you to change anything but your name."

She wanted to believe him, to believe it was possible to start a new life just once more. Her heart was thudding hard against her ribs as she wrapped her arms around him. *Take the chance,* it seemed to be telling her. *Don't throw love away.* Her fingers tensed against him. "Mitch, I—" When the phone rang, Hester let out a pent-up breath. "I'm sorry."

"So am I," he muttered, but released her.

Her legs were still unsteady as she picked up the receiver to the wall phone. "Hello." The giddiness fled, and with it all the blossoming pleasure. "Allan."

Mitch looked around quickly. Her eyes were as flat as her voice. She'd already twisted the phone cord around her hand as if she wanted to anchor herself. "Fine," she said. "We're both fine. Florida? I thought you were in San Diego."

So he'd moved again, Hester thought as she listened to the familiar voice, restless as ever. She listened with the cold patience of experience as he told her how wonderful, how terrific, how incredibly he was doing.

"Rad isn't here at the moment," she told him, though Allan hadn't asked. "If you want to wish him a happy birthday, I can have him call you back." There was a pause, and Mitch saw her eyes change and the anger come. "Yesterday." She set her teeth, then took a long breath through them. "He's ten, Allan. Radley was ten yesterday. Yes, I'm sure it's difficult for you to imagine."

She fell silent again, listening. The dull anger lodged itself in her throat, and when she spoke again, her voice was hollow. "Congratulations. Hard feelings?" She didn't care for the sound of her own laugh. "No, Allan, there are no feelings whatsoever. All right, then, good luck. I'm sorry, that's as enthusiastic as it gets. I'll tell Radley you called."

She hung up, careful to bolt down the need to slam down the receiver. Slowly she unwound the cord which was biting into her hand.

"You okay?"

She nodded and walked to the stove to pour coffee

she didn't want. "He called to tell me he's getting married again. He thought I'd be interested."

"Does it matter?"

"No." She sipped it black and welcomed the bitterness. "What he does stopped mattering years ago. He didn't know it was Radley's birthday." The anger came bubbling to the surface no matter how hard she tried to keep it submerged. "He didn't even know how old he was." She slammed the cup down so that coffee sloshed over the sides. "Radley stopped being real for him the minute he walked out the door. All he had to do was shut it behind him."

"What difference does it make now?"

"He's Radley's father."

"No." His own anger sprang out. "That's something you've got to work out of your system, something you've got to start accepting. The only part he played in Rad's life was biological. There's no trick to that, and no automatic bond of loyalty comes with it."

"He has a responsibility."

"He doesn't want it, Hester." Struggling for patience, he took her hands. "He's cut himself off from Rad completely. No one's going to call that admirable, and it's obvious it wasn't done for the boy's sake. But would you rather have him strolling in and out of Radley's life at his own whim, leaving the kid confused and hurting?"

"No, but I—"

"You want him to care, and he doesn't care." Though her hands remained in his, he felt the change. "You're pulling back from me."

It was true. She could regret it, but she couldn't stop it. "I don't want to."

"But you are." This time, it was he who pulled away. "It only took a phone call."

"Mitch, please try to understand."

"I've been trying to understand." There was an edge to his voice now that she hadn't heard before. "The man left you, and it hurt, but it's been over a long time."

"It's not the hurt," she began, then dragged a hand through her hair. "Or maybe it is, partly. I don't want to go through that ever again, the fear, the emptiness. I loved him. You have to understand that maybe I was young, maybe I was stupid, but I loved him."

"I've always understood that," he said, though he didn't like to hear it. "A woman like you doesn't make promises lightly."

"No, when I make them I mean to keep them. I wanted to keep this one." She picked up the coffee again, wrapping both hands around the cup to keep them warm. "I can't tell you how badly I wanted to keep my marriage together, how hard I tried. I gave up part of myself when I married Allan. He told me we were going to move to New York, we were going to do things in a big way, and I went. Leaving my home, my family and friends was the most terrifying thing I'd ever done, but I went because he wanted it. Almost everything I did during our marriage I did because he wanted it. And because it was easier to go along than to refuse. I built my life around his. Then, at the age of twenty, I discovered I didn't have a life at all."

"So you made one, for yourself and for Radley. That's something to be proud of."

"I am. It's taken me eight years, eight years to feel I'm really on solid ground again. Now there's you."

"Now there's me," he said slowly, watching her. "And

you just can't get past the idea that I'll pull the rug out from under you again."

"I don't want to be that woman again." She said the words desperately, searching for the answers even as she struggled to give them to him. "A woman who focuses all her needs and goals around someone else. If I found myself alone this time, I'm not sure I could stand up again."

"Listen to yourself. You'd rather be alone now than risk the fact that things might not work out for the next fifty years? Take a good look at me, Hester, I'm not Allan Wallace. I'm not asking you to bury yourself to make me happy. It's the woman you are today who I love, the woman you are today who I want to spend my life with."

"People change, Mitch."

"And they can change together." He drew a deep breath. "Or they can change separately. Why don't you let me know when you make up your mind what you want to do?"

She opened her mouth, then closed it again when he walked away. She didn't have the right to call him back.

He shouldn't complain, Mitch thought as he sat at his new keyboard and toyed with the next scene in his script. The work was going better than he'd expected—and faster. It was becoming easy for him to bury himself in Zark's problems and let his own stew.

At this point, Zark was waiting by Leilah's bedside, praying that she would survive the freak accident that had left her beauty intact but her brain damaged. Of course, when she awoke she would be a stranger. His wife of two years would become his greatest enemy, her mind as brilliant as ever but warped and evil. All his plans and dreams would be shattered forever. Whole galaxies would be in peril.

"You think you've got problems?" Mitch muttered. "Things aren't exactly bouncing along for me, either."

Eyes narrowed, he studied the screen. The atmosphere was good, he thought as he tipped back. Mitch didn't have any problem imagining a twenty-third-century hospital room. He didn't have any trouble imagining Zark's distress or the madness brewing in Leilah's unconscious brain. What he did have trouble imagining was his life without Hester.

"Stupid." The dog at his feet yawned in agreement. "What I should do is go down to that damn bank and drag her out. She'd love that, wouldn't she?" he said with a laugh as he pushed away from the machine and stretched. "I could beg." Mitch rolled that around in his mind and found it uncomfortable. "I could, but we'd probably both be sorry. There's not much left after reasoning, and I've tried that. What would Zark do?"

Mitch rocked back on his heels and closed his eyes. Would Zark, hero and saint, back off? Would Zark, defender of right and justice, bow out gracefully? Nope, Mitch decided. When it came to love, Zark was a patsy. Leilah kept kicking astrodust in his face, but he was still determined to win her back.

At least Hester hadn't tried to poison him with nerve gas. Leilah had pulled that and more, but Zark was still nuts about her.

Mitch studied the poster of Zark he'd tacked to the wall for inspiration. We're in the same boat, buddy, but I'm not going to pull out the oars and start rowing, either. And Hester's going to find herself in some turbulent waters.

He glanced at the clock on his desk, but remembered it had stopped two days before. He was pretty sure he'd sent his watch to the laundry along with his socks. Because he wanted to see how much time he had before Hester was due home, he walked into the living room. There, on the table, was an old mantel clock that Mitch was fond enough of to remember to wind. Just as he glanced at it, he heard Radley at the door.

"Right on time," Mitch said when he swung the door open. "How cold is it?" He grazed his knuckles down Radley's cheek in a routine they'd developed. "Forty-three degrees."

"It's sunny," Radley said, dragging off his backpack.

"Shooting for the park, are you?" Mitch waited until Radley had folded his coat neatly over the arm of the sofa. "Maybe I can handle it after I fortify myself. Mrs. Jablanski next door made cookies. She feels sorry for me because no one's fixing me hot meals, so I copped a dozen."

"What kind?"

"Peanut butter."

"All right!" Radley was already streaking into the kitchen. He liked the ebony wood and smoked glass table Mitch had set by the wall. Mostly because Mitch didn't mind if the glass got smeared with fingerprints. He settled down, content with milk and cookies and Mitch's company. "We have to do a dumb state project," he said with his mouth full. "I got Rhode Island. It's the smallest state. I wanted Texas."

"Rhode Island." Mitch smiled and munched on a cookie. "Is that so bad?"

"Nobody cares about Rhode Island. I mean, they've got the Alamo and stuff in Texas."

"Well, maybe I can give you a hand with it. I was born there."

"In Rhode Island? Honest?" The tiny state took on a new interest.

"Yeah. How long do you have?"

"Six weeks," Radley said with a shrug as he reached for another cookie. "We've got to do illustrations, which is okay, but we've got to do junk like manufacturing and natural resources, too. How come you moved away?"

He started to make some easy remark, then decided to honor Hester's code of honesty. "I didn't get along with my parents very well. We're better friends now."

"Sometimes people go away and don't come back."

The boy spoke so matter-of-factly that Mitch found himself responding the same way. "I know."

"I used to worry that Mom would go away. She didn't."

"She loves you." Mitch ran a hand along the boy's hair.

"Are you going to marry her?"

Mitch paused in midstroke. "Well, I…" Just how did he handle this one? "I guess I've been thinking about it." Feeling ridiculously nervous, he rose to heat up his coffee. "Actually, I've been thinking about it a lot. How would you feel if I did?"

"Would you live with us all the time?"

"That's the idea." He poured the coffee, then sat down beside Radley again. "Would that bother you?"

Radley looked at him with dark and suddenly inscrutable eyes. "One of my friends' moms got married again. Kevin says since they did his stepfather isn't his friend anymore."

"Do you think if I married your mom I'd stop being your friend?" He caught Radley's chin in his hand. "I'm not your friend because of your mom, but because of you. I can promise that won't change when I'm your stepfather."

"You wouldn't be my stepfather. I don't want one of those." Radley's chin trembled in Mitch's hand. "I want a real one. Real ones don't go away."

Mitch slipped his hands under Radley's arms and lifted him onto his lap. "You're right. Real ones don't." Out of the mouth of babes, he thought, and nuzzled Radley against him. "You know, I haven't had much practice being a father. Are you going to get mad at me if I mess up once in a while?"

Radley shook his head and burrowed closer. "Can we tell Mom?"

Mitch managed a laugh. "Yeah, good idea. Get your coat, Sergeant, we're going on a very important mission."

Hester was up to her elbows in numbers. For some reason, she was having a great deal of trouble adding two and two. It didn't seem terribly important anymore. That, she knew, was a sure sign of trouble. She went through files, calculated and assessed, then closed them again with no feeling at all.

His fault, she told herself. It was Mitch's fault that she was only going through the motions, and thinking about going through the same motions day after day for the next twenty years. He'd made her question herself. He'd made her deal with the pain and anger she'd tried to bury. He'd made her want what she'd once sworn never to want again.

And now what? She propped her elbows on the stack of files and stared into space. She was in love, more deeply and more richly in love than she'd ever been before. The man she was in love with was exciting, kind and committed, and he was offering her a new beginning.

That was what she was afraid of, Hester admitted. That was what she kept heading away from. She hadn't fully understood before that she had blamed herself, not Allan, all these years. She had looked on the breakup of her marriage as a personal mistake, a private failure. Rather than risk another failure, she was turning away her first true hope.

She said it was because of Radley, but that was only partly true. Just as the divorce had been a private failure, making a full commitment to Mitch had been a private fear.

He'd been right, she told herself. He'd been right about so many things all along. She wasn't the same woman who had loved and married Allan Wallace. She wasn't even the same woman who had struggled for a handhold when she'd found herself alone with a small child.

When was she going to stop punishing herself? Now, Hester decided, picking up the phone. Right now. Her hand was steady as she dialed Mitch's number, but her heart wasn't. She caught her bottom lip between her teeth and listened to the phone ring—and ring.

"Oh, Mitch, won't we ever get the timing right?" She hung up the receiver and promised herself she wouldn't lose her courage. In an hour she would go home and tell him she was ready for that new beginning.

At Kay's buzz, Hester picked up the receiver again. "Yes, Kay."

"Mrs. Wallace, there's someone here to see you about a loan."

With a frown, Hester checked her calendar. "I don't have anything scheduled."

"I thought you could fit him in."

"All right, but buzz me in twenty minutes. I've got to clear some things up before I leave."

"Yes, ma'am."

Hester tidied her desk and was preparing to rise when Mitch walked in. "Mitch? I was just... What are you doing here? Rad?"

"He's waiting with Taz in the lobby."

"Kay said I had someone waiting to see me."

"That's me." He stepped up to the desk and set down a briefcase.

She started to reach for his hand, but his face seemed so set. "Mitch, you didn't have to say you'd come to apply for a loan."

"That's just what I'm doing."

She smiled and settled back. "Don't be silly."

"Mrs. Wallace, you *are* the loan officer at this bank?"

"Mitch, really, this isn't necessary."

"I'd hate to tell Rosen you sent me to a competitor." He flipped open the briefcase. "I've brought the financial information usual in these cases. I assume you have the necessary forms for a mortgage application?"

"Of course, but—"

"Then why don't you get one out?"

"All right, then." If he wanted to play games, she'd

oblige him. "So you're interested in securing a mortgage. Are you purchasing the property for investment purposes, for rental or for a business?"

"No, it's purely personal."

"I see. Do you have a contract of sale?"

"Right here." It pleased him to see her mouth drop open.

Taking the papers from him, Hester studied them. "This is real."

"Of course it's real. I put a bid on the place a couple of weeks ago." He scratched at his chin as if thinking back. "Let's see, that would have been the day I had to forgo pot roast. You haven't offered it again."

"You bought a house?" She scanned the papers again. "In Connecticut?"

"They accepted my offer. The papers just came through. I believe the bank will want to get its own appraisal. There is a fee for that, isn't there?"

"What? Oh, yes, I'll fill out the papers."

"Fine. In the meantime, I do have some snapshots and a blueprint." He slipped them out of the briefcase and placed them on her desk. "You might want to look them over."

"I don't understand."

"You might begin to if you look at the pictures."

She lifted them and stared at her fantasy house. It was big and sprawling, with porches all around and tall, wide windows. Snow mantled the evergreens beside the steps and lay stark and white on the roof.

"There are a couple of outbuildings you can't see. A barn, a henhouse—both unoccupied at the moment. The lot is about five acres, with woods and a stream. The real estate agent claims the fishing's good. The roof needs some work and the gutters have to be replaced, and inside it could use some paint or paper and a little help with the plumbing. But it's sound." He watched her as he spoke. She didn't look up at him, but continued to stare, mesmerized by the snapshots. "The house has been standing for a hundred and fifty years. I figure it'll hold up a while longer."

"It's lovely." Tears pricked the back of her eyes, but she blinked them away. "Really lovely."

"Is that from the bank's point of view?"

She shook her head. He wasn't going to make it easy. And he shouldn't, she admitted to herself. She'd already made it difficult enough for both of them. "I didn't know you were thinking of relocating. What about your work?"

"I can set up my drawing board in Connecticut just as easily as I can here. It's a reasonable commute, and I don't exactly spend a lot of time in the office."

"That's true." She picked up a pen, but rather than writing down the necessary information only ran it through her fingers.

"I'm told there's a bank in town. Nothing along the lines of National Trust, but a small independent bank. Seems to me someone with experience could get a good position there."

"I've always preferred small banks." There was a lump in her throat that had to be swallowed. "Small towns."

"They've got a couple of good schools. The elementary school is next to a farm. I'm told sometimes the cows get over the fence and into the playground."

"Looks like you've covered everything."

"I think so."

She stared down at the pictures, wondering how he could have found what she'd always wanted and how she could have been lucky enough that he would have cared. "Are you doing this for me?"

"No." He waited until she looked at him. "I'm doing it for us."

Her eyes filled again. "I don't deserve you."

"I know." Then he took both her hands and lifted her to her feet. "So you'd be pretty stupid to turn down such a good deal."

"I'd hate to think I was stupid." She drew her hands away to come around the desk to him. "I need to tell you something, but I'd like you to kiss me first."

"Is that the way you get loans around here?" Taking her by the lapels, he dragged her against him. "I'm going to have to report you, Mrs. Wallace. Later."

He closed his mouth over hers and felt the give, the strength and the acceptance. With a quiet sound of pleasure, he slipped his hands up to her face and felt the slow, lovely curve of her lips as she smiled.

"Does this mean I get the loan?"

"We'll talk business in a minute." She held on just a little longer, then drew away. "Before you came in, I'd been sitting here. Actually, I'd been sitting here for the last couple of days, not getting anything done because I was thinking of you."

"Go on, I think I'm going to like this story."

"When I wasn't thinking about you, I was thinking about myself and the last dozen years of my life I've put a lot of energy into *not* thinking about it, so it wasn't easy."

She kept his hand in hers, but took another step away. "I realize that what happened to me and Allan was destined to happen. If I'd been smarter, or stronger, I would have been able to admit a long time ago that what we had could only be temporary. Maybe if he hadn't left the way he did…" She trailed off, shaking her head. "It doesn't matter now. That's the point I had to come to, that it just doesn't matter. Mitch, I don't want to live the rest of my life wondering if you and I could have made it work. I'd rather spend the rest of my life *trying* to make it work. Before you came in today with all of this, I'd decided to ask you if you still wanted to marry me."

"The answer to that is yes, with a couple of stipulations."

She'd already started to move into his arms, but drew back. "Stipulations?"

"Yeah, you're a banker, you know about stipulations, right?"

"Yes, but I don't look at this as a transaction."

"You better hear me out, because it's a big one." He ran his hands up her arms, then dropped them to his side. "I want to be Rad's father."

"If we were married, you would be."

"I believe stepfather's the term used in that case. Rad and I agreed we didn't go for it."

"Agreed?" She spoke carefully, on guard again. "You discussed this with Rad?"

"Yeah, I discussed it with Rad. He brought it up, but I'd have wanted to talk to him, anyway. He asked me this afternoon if I was going to marry you. Did you want me to lie to him?"

"No." She paused a moment, then shook her head. "No, of course not. What did he say?"

"Basically he wanted to know if I'd still be his friend, because he'd heard sometimes stepfathers change a bit once their foot's in the door. Once we'd gotten past that hurdle, he told me he didn't want me as a stepfather."

"Oh, Mitch." She sank down on the edge of the desk.

"He wants a real father, Hester, because real fathers don't go away." Her eyes darkened very slowly before she closed them.

"I see."

"The way I look at it, you've got another decision to make. Are you going to let me adopt him?" Her eyes shot open again with quick surprise. "You've decided to share yourself. I want to know if you're going to share Rad, all the way. I don't see a problem with me being his father emotionally. I just want you to know that I want it legally. I don't think there'd be a problem with your ex-husband."

"No, I'm sure there wouldn't be."

"And I don't think there'd be a problem with Rad. So is there a problem with you?"

Hester rose from the desk to pace a few steps away. "I don't know what to say to you. I can't come up with the right words."

"Pick some."

She turned back with a deep breath. "I guess the best I can come up with is that Radley's going to have a terrific father, in every way. And I love you very, very much."

"Those'll do." He caught her to him with relief. "Those'll do just fine." Then he was kissing her again, fast and desperate. With her arms around him, she laughed. "Does this mean you're going to approve the loan?"

"I'm sorry, I have to turn you down."

"What?"

"I would, however, approve a joint application from you and your wife." She caught his face in her hands. "Our house, our commitment."

"Those are terms I can live with—" he touched her lips with his "—for the next hundred years or so." He swung her around in one quick circle. "Let's go tell Rad." With their hands linked, they started out. "Say, Hester, how do you feel about honeymooning in Disneyland?"

She laughed and walked through the door with him. "I'd love it. I'd absolutely love it."

* * * * *